STANDING
WITH RIGHTEOUS RAGE

The Showdown Trilogy, Book 2

The Last Brigade, Book 5

William Alan Webb

δ
Dingbat Publishing
Humble, Texas

STANDING WITH RIGHTEOUS RAGE
Copyright © 2020 by William Alan Webb
Print ISBN 9798643649885

Published by Dingbat Publishing
Humble, Texas

All rights reserved. No part of this book may be reproduced in any form or by any means without written consent, excepting brief quotes used in reviews.

This book is licensed to the original purchaser only. Duplication or distribution via any means is illegal and a violation of International Copyright Law, subject to criminal prosecution and upon conviction, fines and/or imprisonment. No part of this book can be reproduced or sold by any person or business without the express permission of the publisher.

Thank you for respecting the hard work of this author.

This is a work of fiction. Names, places, characters, and events are entirely the produce of the author's imagination or are used fictitiously, and any resemblance to persons living or dead, actual locations, events, or organizations is coincidental.

He is Mad, Bad and Dangerous to know.
Lady Caroline Lamb

The Dark Man came to me yet again,
Swathed in black with a dead man's grin;
"You fight on still but you cannot win,
"You cannot win what you cannot transcend,
"And you cannot transcend your mortal skin,
"So save your skin and save your kin,
"To save your kin, you must give in,
"And once you give in, it can all begin."
    From 'The Dark Man' by Sergio Velazquez

Author's Foreword

At the top of the list of things I never saw coming was writing a foreword to Book 5 of The Last Brigade series. Right below that on the list is *writing* The Last Brigade series.

I want to thank every one of my readers for helping me get here. Be assured that I never forget that this is a two-way street, that in return for the time you spend with me and my stories, it is my obligation to deliver the best books of which I am capable. There's a bond between a writer and his or her readers that I take very seriously and work very hard to strengthen.

Standing Before Hell's Gate drew interesting reactions from some of my most loyal readers, including some not necessarily complimentary reviews. The general consensus seems to be that Tom Steeple has already drawn one too many breaths, so let me say right now that I am thrilled you feel that way. Another person said not to bother buying it, because it had a cliffhanger ending. I guess they didn't like *The Empire Strikes Back, The Two Towers, Harry Potter and the Goblet of Fire, Back to the Future II,* and a host of others. But maybe they had a point; if you're one of my readers, I listen to and value your input. It's just that after 137,000 words, I thought that book needed to end before it started feeling like Bilbo Baggins after 60 years of owning the Ring of Power — in other words, stretched, like too little butter scraped thin on a slice of toast. Plus, I grew up when weekly serials were on TV, and they always had a cliffhanger ending. I didn't see anything wrong with it then, and still don't. But to each his own.

Despite all that, as of this writing it's the best-reviewed book in the series.

So why did I let Nick make such a stupid mistake as leaving Overtime Prime when both Fleming and Tompkins were away and Tom Steeple was still above ground? There were two reasons.

First, throughout history, hubris has led the greatest men and women to make egregious errors in judgment. Hannibal was a tactical genius, but as a strategist he failed entirely to realize that one army couldn't invade a whole country filled with millions of people, not and expect to win. He roamed Italy at will for more than a decade, yet Carthage still lost the war, because Hannibal's hubris caused him to bet everything on the Romans doing what he expected they would do. Except when the time came, the Romans did what was best for the Romans, not the Carthaginians

Hubris caused Caesar to make nearly fatal mistakes against Pompey at Dyrrhachium. Rommel's hubris got his division strung out at Arras and it was almost destroyed, while Boudica thought that her manpower advantage of at least ten to one, and perhaps as high as thirty to one, would destroy the Roman army in Britain. Hubris caused her to believe what she wanted to believe, and the list of miscalculations by otherwise brilliant people is virtually endless. Lee ordered Pickett's Charge at Gettysburg because he believed the Army of Northern Virginia could achieve miracles. Even so great a general as Robert E. Lee could fall victim to hubris.

Nick Angriff is no exception. Nick is a great character, but nobody is perfect. Hubris led him to see things the way he wanted to see them, not the way they were.

The second reason for his otherwise myopic action is that non-writers make the mistake of thinking I can control the narrative. I can't. Once upon a time, I tried to make the characters do things they didn't want to do, and the results were an unmitigated disaster. Having learned better, I now let the characters do what they do, whether it's good for them or not. I have to if I want to chronicle their stories in an interesting way. That may seem like making excuses for what some might have considered a mistake in the plot, but it's not. It's the story I was told by my imagination, and if I deviated, it would sound hollow and false. That's just how it works with me.

Nick Angriff is the embodiment of a lot of people I admire, but one of them is *not* Michael the Archangel. Michael, as the

Sword of God, can do no wrong and makes no mistakes. That ain't Nick. He's as flawed as he is brilliant, and it is completely in character for him to leave Overtime in the hands of a trusted subordinate while he goes out in the field. But this time he got sloppy. Operation Overtime is very much a reflection of the society from which it sprang, both for good and for bad, and the situation the 7th Cav awakens to is meant to represent the world as it is now, fragmented and chaotic, with morality existing only in the eye of the beholder. Moral codes that once were the glue of the American national character are now scoffed at and ridiculed. There are pitfalls and wicked influences everywhere, and just because you know about them doesn't make them any less dangerous. And so it is with the 7th Cavalry. Some of them went into Long Sleep in 2023 or 2024, the era of moral equivalency, while others had gone cold two decades before that. There's an inherent conflict in worldview between those generations.

Put another way, the story is the story; I can't write it any other way. For those who don't know, I'm what other writers call a *pantser*. That is, I write by the seat of my pants. I don't outline anything, except in my brain, and a lot of the time I don't know what's going to happen until my fingers clack the keys. If you read something that surprises you, chances are excellent that it surprised me, too. When I started *The Showdown Trilogy*, I had only the vaguest idea of where it would lead... I can guarantee you I didn't know that Nick would be wandering in the desert like Moses, hunted by his own troops. I *did* know that Tom Steeple needed a bayonet shoved down his throat, though; even I hate the guy.

Anyway, for anyone who thinks I had some grand design or betrayal in line for *Standing Before Hell's Gate*, I only wish that I did. Sometimes I'd like to know what's going to happen before it does.

Oh, and one last thing... when writing military fiction, the author treads a very fine line between absolute reality and the expectations of their readers. Sometimes, the author (me) must change things in the interest of the book, things that military veterans might catch, but general interest readers won't. With my books, I'm trying to create the verisimilitude that my characters are living, breathing members of a professional military organization, while simultaneously moving the story along in an (hopefully) interesting way.

This is especially true of radio traffic, call signs, etc. The non-military reader could easily get lost in all the jargon, so I consciously try to make these exchanges palatable for both types of reader. To the veterans who read my works, I ask for your indulgence when I vary from accepted practice. For the non-veterans among us, please understand the need for following radio procedure more than you might wish. I hope I got it right for all of us.

This book has a lot of information about the Fairchild Republic A-10 Thunderbolt II, known far and wide as the Warthog. Some may feel that I went overboard in trying to have the reader see things through the characters' eyes, others might think I got it just right, while still others prefer knowing about every nut and bolt in this or that machine or weapon. Whatever you feel after reading the book, I hope you can feel how hard I tried to get it just right.

Horses play a big part in this book, and once again I wanted to make sure I didn't exceed their physical capabilities. The general consensus is that an average horse can travel 20–30 miles in a day at a reasonable speed, taking about eight hours for this. Horses that are bred and trained to go longer, however, and are in top physical condition, can at least double that, assuming the rider can stay on that long. I have paid special attention to the distances involved compared to the horses' capabilities, and am lucky enough to have a publisher who is even more familiar with horses than I am (and I own three of them).

Until next book, stay well, my friends.
Bill
March 18, 2020

Acknowledgements

I would be remiss not to thank those whose technical expertise has lent these books whatever verisimilitude they might have in terms of our military. Most prefer to remain anonymous, and among their ranks are several retired generals from both the Army and the Air Force, plus a number of captains, majors, and colonels.

Lee McNeil has advised me throughout the series on all questions relating to helicopters. Lee was a US Navy dual-certified fixed wing and helicopter pilot.

The scenes of the A-10 being re-assembled and readied for action were heavily influenced by the real-life Shannon Ortberg, a veteran USAF ground crewman. A few paragraphs are more or less in her own words, which lends authenticity that elevates the whole book, and makes it apparent that she needs to finish her own first novel. Any errors are mine; she's an innocent bystander.

The amazing Kevin Ikenberry, Lieutenant Colonel, US Army (Retired), the prolific and impressive author of multiple SF novels and short stories, allowed me to paraphrase a line from his awesome novel *Peacemaker*, set in the Four Horsemen Universe. I am extremely grateful and humbled to have a writer of his stature grant me such permission.

I am constantly receiving input from some awesome fans of my work, some of whom have made their way into this story. I want to thank each of you personally, but since that's more or less impossible, I originally had a long list of friends and readers here, but realized that would inevitably lead to hurt feeling for those I forget, which is the last thing I intend. So my blanket gratitude will have to suffice, but remember, you folks are the best!

CAST OF CHARACTERS

The Angriff family
Nicholas Trajanus Angriff — General of the Army. Nick the A to those who fear him. Idolizes George Patton's tactical genius and persona, but not as fussy as Patton about personal appearance and decorum. Like another hero of his, Winston Churchill, Angriff is sometimes accused of courting danger. As a three-star general, he led tactical missions more suited to a captain or lieutenant, usually against direct orders not to do so. His career survived because of his popularity with his men and the public, and his record of success.
Janine Marie Jackson Angriff — Nick's wife, a victim in the Lake Tahoe 'incident.'
Lieutenant Morgan Mary Randall, née Angriff — Oldest of Nick's two daughters. Lieutenant in the U.S. Army, executive officer First Platoon, Alpha Company, 1st Tank Battalion. Call sign Bulldozer One One Two. Married to Captain Joe Randall. Nicknamed Tank Girl.
Cynthia June Angriff — Nick's youngest daughter, caught in the same attack as her mother.
Nicholas Trajanus Bauer (Angriff), Jr. — The real name of Green Ghost
Nicole 'Nikki' Teresa Bauer (Angriff) — Real name of Nipple.

The Americans
Lt. General Norman Vincent Fleming — Executive officer of the 7th Cavalry, also the brigade S-3, Operations.

Norm is Nick Angriff's best friend, dating back to their days in OCS. Both men enlisted and worked their way through the ranks, an almost impossible feat. Fleming is the man Angriff trusts above all others.

Major General Dennis Tompkins — Survivor of The Collapse who did not go cold, but instead lived fifty years in post-Collapse America, leading his team of five survivors.

Captain Joseph Daniel Randall — The best helicopter pilot in the brigade. Married to Morgan Randall. Call sign Ripsaw Real.

Lieutenant George 'Bunny' Carlos — Joe Randall's best friend and co-pilot.

Lieutenant Alisa Plotz — Pilot of AH-72 *Hell's Hammer*.

Sergeant Andy Arnold — Co-pilot of *Hell's Hammer*.

Sergeant Lara Snowtiger — Marine sniper, a full-blooded Choctaw. Snowtiger embraced her heritage and is versed in Choctaw lore. She is considered as good as any sniper in the 7th Cavalry, including Zo Piccaldi.

Sergeant Major of the Army John Charles Schiller — Trusted subordinate who runs the day-to-day routine for Angriff's headquarters. Angriff often asks Schiller for advice.

Colonel William Emerson Schiller — Brother of Sergeant J.C. Schiller, he is the brigade's S-4, Supply Officer, and is considered a savant at supply chain organization and utilization.

Lt. Colonel Roger 'Rip' Kordibowski — Battalion S-2, Intelligence Officer.

Colonel Fitzhugh Howarth Claringdon — Former executive officer of the tank battalion. Imprisoned for the assassination attempt on General Angriff.

Lt. Colonel Astrid Naidoo — Temporary S-9, Civil-Military Cooperation.

Colonel Khin 'Chain Saw' Saw — Brigade S-1, Personnel.

Sergeant Howard Wilson Dupree — Communications specialist and computer whiz.

Sergeant Frances 'Frame' Rossi — Crew chief for *Tank Girl*.

Major Alexis Iskold — Deputy S-3 and Norm Fleming's right hand.

Major Edward Wincommer — C.O. of the 7th Cavalry Regiment, 7th Cavalry Brigade.

Major Samuel Ball — C.O. of the 1st Airborne Battalion.

Colonel Robert Young — C.O. of 1st Mechanized Infantry Regiment.

Major Dieter Strootman — Executive officer of 1st Mechanized Infantry Regiment.

Lieutenant Maria Ruiz — Staff officer 1st Mechanized Infantry Regiment.

Captain Martin Sully — C.O. of Dog Company, 1st Marine Recon Battalion, First Marines

Lieutenant Onni Hakala — Sully's E.O. and C.O. of 1st Platoon, Dog Company.

Captain April Jones — Commander of Echo Company, 1st Marine Recon Battalion, First Marines.

Lieutenant Shannon Hartmann, USAF — Technical specialist at Operation Comeback, currently assembling Warthogs.

Staff Sergeant Joe 'Toy' Ootoi — Gunner for Morgan Randall's M1A3 Abrams, named *Joe's Junk*, and boyfriend of Nikki Bauer.

Task Force Zombie, a/k/a 'The Nameless'

Green Ghost — Nick Angriff's only son. Longtime subordinate of Angriff's and currently his S-5, Security.

Vapor — Original member of TF Zombie. Wise-cracking member of the team. He and Green Ghost have known each other since childhood.

One Eye — Original member of TF Zombie. Nickname refers to his personality.

Wingnut — Original member of TF Zombie. Taciturn, a specialist at explosives and chemicals.

Glide — Replacement addition to TF Zombie, Glide is an ultra-dangerous computer specialist. She is gorgeous, and an 8th degree Krav Maga.

Nipple — Green Ghost's twin sister. Most think she is psychotic, but like her brother, her reflexes are off the chart.

Razor — Replacement addition, the newest member of the team.

Frosty — A veteran member who started out in Third Squad and transferred to First Squad after the Congo Operation.

Zeus — Original member of TF Zombie.

Claw — Former commander of Second Squad, Task Force Zombie, and an original member.

Other Americans
General Thomas Francis Steeple — Disgraced and imprisoned founder and driving force behind Operations Overtime and Comeback.

Colonel Amunet Mwangi — Norm Fleming's first cousin and formerly second in command of Operation Comeback. Tom Steeple's closest advisor and confidant.

Creech Air Force Base
General Jamal Kando — Base commander.

The Scrapers
Junker Jane — Jane scrapes Northern California, Nevada, Utah, and into the Pacific Northwest.

Kodiak Kate — Kate scrapes north into Canada and Alaska.

Shangri-La
Johnny Rainwater — Elected leader of Shangri-La.

Abigail Deak — Leader of the Jemez Pueblos and Johnny Rainwater's de facto deputy leader.

Mohammad Qadim — Muslim member of Shangri-La who refuses to follow the New Prophet.

Billy Two Trees — Young scout from Shangri-La.

Operation Evolution
Györgi Rosos — Billionaire who used his money to undermine capitalist republics around the world, in addition to financing part of Operations Overtime and Comeback, and his own independent operation. He believes in communist totalitarianism and greatly admires the North Korean Kim family dynasty.

Györgi Rosos, Jr. — Sometimes derisively called *ketto* (an Americanized version of the Hungarian word *kettő,* meaning *two*) by the rank and file at Evolution, the eldest son and namesake of Rosos Sr. is a naturally affable man who is constantly vying with his younger brother for their father's affection.

Károly Rosos — Only their father matches the younger Rosos' ruthlessness and ambition.

Adder — Former member of Task Force Zombie. As dangerous as Green Ghost but ruthless and cares only for himself.

The Sevens
Nabi Husam Allah — The Caliph of the Caliphate of the Seven Prayers of the New Prophet, self-proclaimed prophet of Allah. In truth, he is Larry Armstrong, a criminal conman. His adherents are fanatically loyal.

Abdul-Qudoos Fadil el Mofty — Emir of New Khorasan. His original name is Richard Lee Armstrong, brother of the Caliph, Larry Armstrong. He bears the title of Superior Imam, second only to the Caliph himself, who is the Supreme Imam. These titles were created by the Armstrong brothers to elevate them above all imams in Islam. He is also second in command of The Sword of the New Prophet, the military arm of the Caliphate.

Sati Bashara — Senior Aga and oldest nephew of Emir Abdul-Qudoos Fadil el Mofty, appointed head of the province of New Khorasan, a region of the larger Caliphate of the Seven Prayers of the New Prophet, encompassing parts of Arizona, New Mexico, and old Mexico. He is the second most powerful lieutenant in New Khorasan.

General Ahmednur Hussein Muhdin — Primary military commander of the Caliphate's Sword of the Prophet.

General Tracy Gollins — General of the Sword of the Prophet, and secret daughter of Richard Lee Armstrong.

The Apaches
Govind — Chief of the Western Apache.

Ma Kelly's
Dave Weiner — Proprietor of the trading post known as Ma Kelly's.

The Chinese
Generalissimo Zhang Wei — Commander of all Chinese forces in California.

Captain Chen Yi — Chinese liaison officer to 1st Mechanized Infantry Regiment.

Colonel Zhang Zongchang — Chinese liaison officer inside Overtime Prime.

Captain Tian Tao — Chinese liaison officer to 1st Mechanized Infantry Regiment's artillery.

Others
Lester Earl Hull, aka General Patton — Former ruler of the Republic of Arizona.

"The Civil War defined us as what we are and it opened us to being what we became, good and bad things... It was the crossroads of our being, and it was a hell of a crossroads."
Shelby Foote

PART 1

PIECES ON THE BOARD

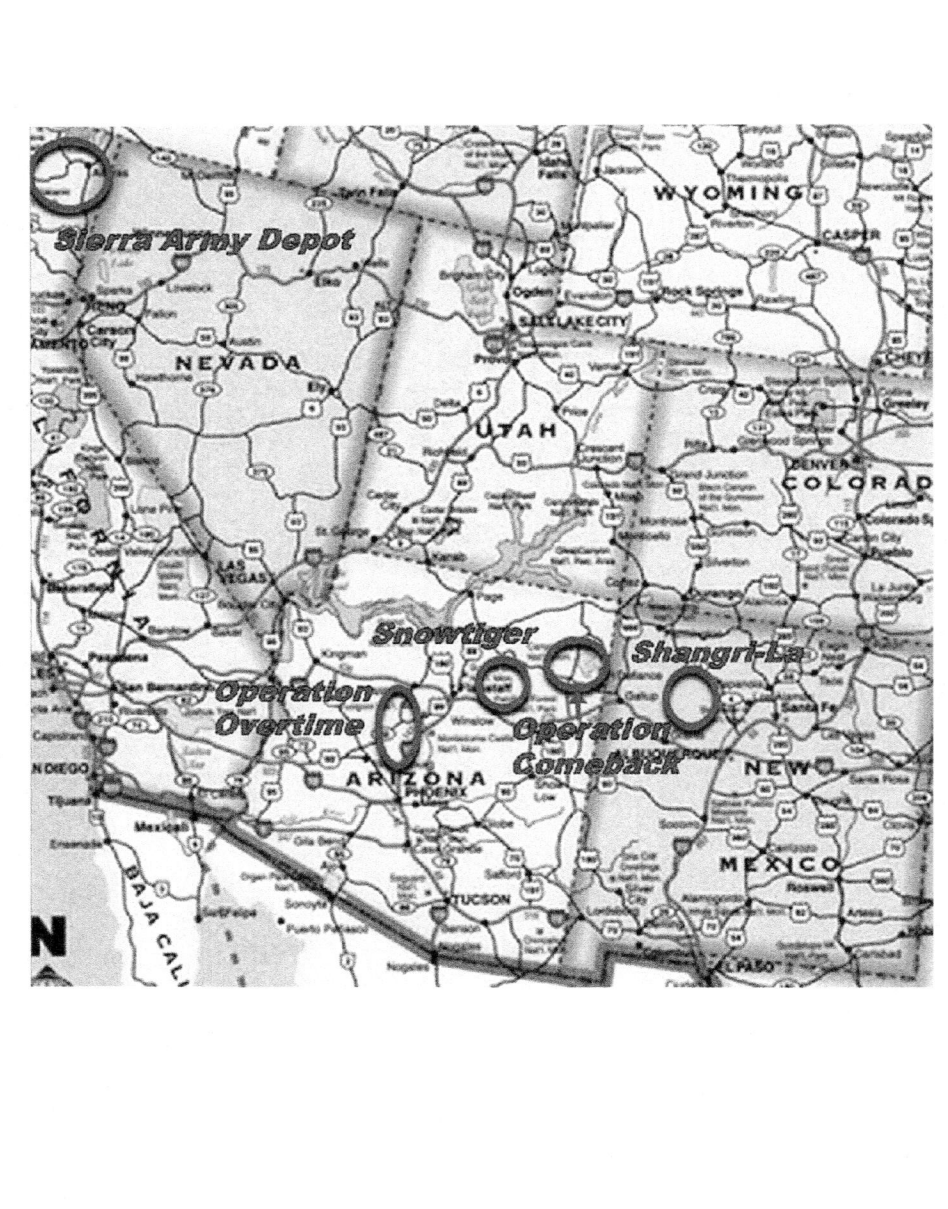

CHAPTER 1

It is better to have less thunder in the mouth and more lightning in the hand.
Apache proverb

Overtime Prime
April 30, 2120 hours

Janine Angriff lay in bed coughing when the base communications system came to life with a hiss and electric *pop*. At that time of night, well past nine, it could only be something important.

"Stand by for the commanding general," said a female voice.

Janine's heart quickened; was Nick back? Had that horrible Tom Steeple been put back where he belonged?

"Cynthia, are you here?" she called into the darkness, after she drank some water and managed to quit coughing. "Cynthia?" But her youngest daughter must have gone out without her hearing.

"All members of Operations Overtime and Comeback, this is General Steeple. I come to you tonight with the grim news that we have all suffered a grievous loss. It has been confirmed that earlier this afternoon, General Angriff was killed when a Humvee he was driving went off the side of a ravine and plunged one hundred feet to the bottom. Bad weather conditions have so far hampered recovery operations at the crash site.

"On a personal level, I want to send his family, friends, and subordinates my deepest condolences. He was a great husband and father, and one of America's greatest leaders. As we all seek to understand this tragedy, I find comfort in knowing that while I might not always understand why God allows terrible things to happen, ultimately I know that everything happens according to His divine plan. Nick Angriff will be sorely missed by us all."

Staring up at the large speaker outside of the southeast entrance, Cynthia Angriff covered her mouth, pulled herself out of the arms of Sergeant Howard Wilson Dupree, and ran toward the open doors that led back into Motor Bay D. Within ten steps she bent over, wracked by heaving sobs and fits of coughing, but straightened up and kept going despite her anguish. Hot tears ran diagonally down her cheeks like rain against a speeding windshield. She had to reach her mother. It was the only thought in her mind, that her mother needed her. Even when the burning in her lungs moved into her side, she kept moving.

Once inside the tunnel leading into the motor bay, she stumbled and would have fallen if Dupree hadn't sprinted and caught up with her. By then deep sobs intermingled with hoarse coughs left her gasping for air, so Dupree slipped his arm around her and half carried her to the elevators. Once inside, she collapsed into his shoulder.

"Oh, no," Nikki Bauer said as she bolted upright to a sitting position. The covers fell away and revealed her nakedness. Prior to meeting him, she had never been with a man, and had never wanted to. The thought of being nude with anyone else would have made her physically ill, but now it wasn't something she even thought about. "No, no, no, *no!*"

Joe Ootoi sat up, too, and hugged her as she cried. Before meeting him, she hadn't wept for decades. Now it seemed like she cried all the time. Except *now* she had a good reason.

"Drove into a ravine, my ass," she said. "This is Steeple's work."

"You think so?" Ootoi said.

"I *know* so."

To her surprise, although anger filled her for the first time in weeks, her voice trembled and tears flooded her eyes. This wasn't like the volcanic rage that fueled Nipple; this was something different. This felt... normal. The thought crossed her mind that she should fight her way into Steeple's office and rip his throat out, but that was all it was, a thought. Nipple would have acted on the impulse to kill. Nikki didn't. Instead she buried her head in Toy's shoulder and cried. Then she pulled on some clothes and went to find Janine.

0242 hours, May 1

Despite the late hour, the Clam Shell buzzed as the headquarters staff digested the shocking news of General Angriff's death. Colonel Amunet Mwangi had already made the rounds, assuring officers unable to attend the emergency staff meeting the next morning because of duties, or speaking with them via radio while they were still in the field, that no staff changes were anticipated at the time, even if they'd been appointed by General Angriff. Of course, in some cases those were bald-faced lies, but her believability was part of what made her so valuable to Tom Steeple. Some of the people she'd reassured would shortly be in the stockade.

Mwangi was surprised to find that the Chinese guard had been doubled at both the main entrance and at the top of the ramp leading to the Crystal Palace. She hadn't ordered it, which meant it must have been either Claringdon or Adder, but there was no mistaking the universal animosity toward the Chinese in the looks they got from the rank and file Americans. Venomous sidelong glances followed them wherever they went, even if it was only a few paces. Mwangi despised them, too, although her smile as she passed through the sliding main doors appeared genuine, and while she would never voice it, the alliance with the Chinese made her skin crawl. Necessary or not in their present situation, throughout her career she had always thought that a future war would come against the People's Republic, with no one ever suggesting they might become America's ally.

When she reached the top of the ramp, she was surprised to see Sergeant Schiller seated there at his desk.

Before she could pass, however, one of the two Chinese guards stepped into her way. "General Steeple must authorize your access." His tone left no doubt of the contempt he felt toward her.

Mwangi was barely five feet tall, and though the Chinese soldier wasn't tall either, she barely came to his chest. Nevertheless, she carried *gravitas* most officers never achieved and could project a palpable authority, and she knew it.

"Like hell he does. *I* run this headquarters now, Xiàshì." *Lance corporal.* The other guard, a private, took a half step backward when she used the Chinese term for the corporal's rank. "You do what *I* tell you, do you understand me? And *I* do what General Steeple tells me. Now if you don't understand that, or if your army doesn't teach its soldiers to obey the superior officers of any ally to whom they are attached, then perhaps that is something I should take up with your shàngjiàng?" *General.* "Should I get him on the radio so you can speak with him?"

Before the corporal could answer, the private nudged his elbow. "Bì zuǐ bèndàn." *Shut up, dumbass!*

Mwangi tried not to laugh. Even though the corporal outranked him, the two guards had to be friends. With eyes closed into hate-filled slits, the corporal took a step back and let her pass.

But instead of going directly to Tom Steeple's office, she made it a point to speak with the Americans on duty, and that included Sergeant Major Schiller. She already knew how close he'd been to the dead general, which was why she'd been surprised to see him back at work.

"Good morning, ma'am," he said. She couldn't help noticing the red and black circles around his eyes; he'd been crying. He began to rise.

But she waved a hand, knowing his recent wound still bothered him. "I know this news must have hurt, Sergeant. I'm very sorry for your loss."

"He was a fine commander, Colonel."

She made her tone as empathetic as she knew how. "Maybe a friend?"

"I don't think a general and a sergeant can be friends, ma'am, at least not when they're serving. Maybe after they retire... but I have a new commander now and he deserves my undivided loyalty."

Mwangi touched his shoulder. "It's all right to grieve."

"No offense, ma'am, but not on duty it's not."

She already knew the time but checked her wristwatch anyway. "It's almost oh-three-hundred, Sergeant. Why are you here?"

"If the general is here, I need to be here."

"The general? You mean General Steeple? He's still here?"

"Yes, ma'am, he's outside on the Eagle's Nest. That's what General Angriff called the outside ledge."

"I see. Well, I'm here now, Sergeant Major, and if the general needs anything I can see to it. Go get some sleep."

"I'm okay, ma'am."

"That's an order. Go."

Tom Steeple heard the inner airlock door close with a muffled *clang* one second before the outer door opened onto the covered platform. He stood at the far end and leaned on the handrail, at the level of his belt, pressing his nose against the chest-high wire lattice that prevented a fall into the desert far below. Without turning, he prayed the newcomer wasn't Károly Rosos.

"Tom?"

Relieved, he closed his eyes and let out his breath. "You should be in bed, Amy. We have a lot of work ahead of us."

"The same applies to you."

"I couldn't sleep. I'll be fine."

Mwangi moved close enough that Steeple could smell her sourness. She was even more fastidious than he was when it came to hygiene, and normally he liked the way she smelled, more clean than perfumed. But not in that moment. He didn't show it, though. He'd spent most of his adult life training his face and body not to betray his true feelings and he didn't then, either.

"You did the right thing, calling off the air strike on those Marines," she said.

"I suppose so."

"What's bothering you?" she said.

Rather than face her, he turned back to the desert. Something flitted past the setting moon and he followed its path until he lost it against the darkness. Was it a hawk? A prairie falcon? Somewhere in the far distance, a coyote howled.

Neither of them spoke for several minutes. Eventually Mwangi moved beside him and joined in watching the moonlit desert.

"This is not how I planned it," he said after a while. "It's not what I wanted." When he didn't continue, she knew him well enough to know that he wanted to explain that remark, but needed prodding.

"I don't follow, Tom. What isn't how you planned it?"

"Any of this... Chinese guards in my headquarters, Károly Rosos showing up unexpected and uninvited, my troops scattered all over southwest America, and Nick Angriff dead. Everything has gone to hell and now I have to make the best of it, but this is not what I wanted, nor how I planned it."

"I know. I've been there with you all along. I've watched how hard you've worked for this."

"I did things good men should never do, Amy, but I did them for the right reasons. I wanted Angriff to run the military side of things and for me to oversee the logistics and rebuilding. We could have made one hell of a great country together..." Again he lapsed into silence, letting his mind clear before going on. "But somebody derailed it, and they did it on purpose."

"You lost me again."

"You know that Act of Congress I told you about, the one elevating Angriff to five-star rank and superior to all other American officers?"

"That proclamation is framed, right outside the main entrance to the Clam—...to your headquarters." Steeple hated the nickname *Clam Shell* and, even worse, *the Crystal Palace*.

If Steeple noticed the near-slip, he ignored it. "Consider this. How did this so-called American Congress and president, none of whom are in our databases, know that he was the commander of Operation Overtime? For that matter, how did they know about Overtime at all, or Comeback? And even if there's a logical explanation for all of that, I sealed both operations when I went under, less than seven weeks after the Collapse, so how did that piece of paper get inside?"

"I... I don't know."

"Neither do I, and that's what bothers me. Something is going on of which I know nothing. Now Angriff is dead, and what if I'm next?"

#

CHAPTER 2

Strategy without tactics is the slowest route to victory. Tactics without strategy is the noise before defeat.
Sun Tzu

Operation Overtime
May 1, 0726 hours

Standing at the entrance of the short hallway that led to the conference room, Tom Steeple stifled a yawn. His body felt heavy and sluggish, a reminder that he wasn't forty any more, or even fifty, and nights with two hours of sleep could not be overcome strictly by will power, not any more. For a man who prided himself on keeping control at all times, of outthinking his opponents when he couldn't out-maneuver them, it was a depressing realization.

"Are you sure you want to do this now?" Amunet Mwangi asked. "You can put it off until this afternoon, or tomorrow, or the day after that. You're the commanding officer; you can do whatever you want."

He took a sip from the morning's first cup of coffee, and glanced down at the dark liquid like it was poison. The day before, that first cup had tasted so good, but now it was thick and bitter, with a burnt taste.

"I gave Sergeant Major Schiller the morning off," she said in response to his grimace. "Sorry."

"That's terrible," he said, handing it to Mwangi. "No, I don't want to put it off, so let's get on with it."

The instant she opened the conference room door and he saw everyone's attention settle on him, the fatigue vanished. This was *his* moment, the best chance he had to win over any lingering doubts about his ability to command Overtime. Even though the whole operation had been his baby from the start, the ten months under Nick Angriff had been extremely successful and productive. Now he needed to prove he could keep it rolling.

Everyone in the room stood to attention, and he let them. He'd been told that Angriff allowed his staff to remain seated when he entered the room, but to Steeple's mind it never hurt to remind your subordinates of who was in charge.

Once he'd sat in his chair at the head of the table, he waved them to sit. "Good morning," he said, keeping his tone businesslike. Anyone who had ever sat through one of his meetings knew he wasted no time on pleasantries, although in private it was usually just the opposite. "In the wake of last night's tragic news concerning General Angriff, it will be necessary for me to make some fundamental changes to the command structure of not only the Seventh Cavalry, but to all aspects of Operations Overtime and Comeback.

"From the outset, I want to be very clear about what has happened so far, and how it relates to my original vision for both operations. General Angriff was always supposed to be the Commander of Operations, stationed here at Overtime, and would have served as my deputy. Anything dealing with combat operations was to be under his purview. I would have overseen the total affairs of all projects, thereby coordinating combat needs with those of the other branches, such as maintenance, salvage, the restoration of order in populated areas, and so on. Obviously, that can no longer happen.

"I also wish to make this very clear... I held General Angriff in the highest esteem. It broke my heart when we fell out, especially when I learned that it was because of a forged document. You see, the so-called Act of Congress appointing him as commander of all United States Armed Forces could not possibly have been authentic. The last legitimately elected government had long since vanished, so whoever the people were who signed the document in question did not possess the authority to issue such an order.

"Because his actions stemmed from the fruit of a poisoned tree, General Angriff did not have the legal authority to perform any of the actions he undertook, not to issue the orders that he did, nor to hand out promotions. Therefore, any orders or promotions made or issued under his authority are invalid. At my sole discretion they may be reinstated, but only at my discretion."

That brought Colonel Khin Saw upright in his chair. "Sir, we have forces actively engaged with the enemy, based on orders issued by General Angriff. How does this affect them?"

"Are you referring to the Marines in New Mexico?"

"Yes, but not just them. There is the airborne battalion at Sierra Depot and our screening forces on the Mexican border. Not to mention the cavalry regiment under Major Wincommer, who are on patrol to the west and frequently encounter hostile forces. We also have FOBs in various positions, some quite far out from Prime."

Steeple nodded. That was the crux of it, the potential tripping point where he could lose support. Troops under fire who weren't supported by their superiors tended not to forget it.

"I appreciate your concerns, Khin. They are legitimate and of immediate import. Let me first go over decisions that have already been made. Those units must be withdrawn so that no further fighting takes place and I'm looking to you, as our new combat commander and my deputy, to see this happens, Brigadier General Saw."

Even as those sitting near him slapped his back and shook his hand, Saw's dark face narrowed in a scowl. Steeple grinned at him, winked, and started talking again before Saw could respond further.

"Our situation has fundamentally changed for the better. We now have allies instead of enemies. You have seen Chinese troops here inside our headquarters, and you may have noticed our esteemed liaison from the People's Liberation Army, Colonel Zhang Zongchang."

Steeple smiled and bowed his head at the stocky officer, all the while thinking that Zhang looked like an elephant, with the brain of a pig and the temperament of a cobra. The man had a perpetually turned-up nose, as if the stench of the Americans offended him. He didn't return Steeple's greeting, but sat immobile, watching.

"This is an indicator of our new relationship with the People's Republic of California, one which I hope to be a model moving forward. Likewise, the riders that I am told we have so colloquially labeled *rednecks* are representatives from the organization of Mister György Rosos..."

That brought several frowns, including a look of absolute disgust from Brigadier General Saw. A few others squirmed. Nor did he blame them. The Rosos money had been a necessary evil when constructing both Comeback and Overtime, and it was at Rosos' personal request that he'd allowed the Secretary of State to sell the Stingers used in the attack at Benghazi to an arms dealer, with the proviso that part of the proceeds went to Overtime. But he still loathed the man, even if he pretended otherwise.

Steeple had expected Saw's reaction, and no matter how much he privately agreed with the negative feelings, it had to be dealt with right now. First, however, he raised his eyebrows at Károly Rosos, who sat nearest on his right, in a gesture that meant 'See? I told you.'

"One thing needs to be made very clear. Without the Rosos family's money, there would be no Operation Overtime, much less Operation Comeback. Over a period of two decades, they gave more than ten billion dollars to help build this facility. *Ten... billion.* Think about that. And they continued their support even after the pandemic in 2020."

Khin Saw muttered under his breath, "That's ten billion they couldn't give to *Antikap*."

Steeple eyed him, but continued. "As the one scraping together every dollar from every source I could find, I can tell you that not only did that money help pay the costs of construction, but also convinced other wealthy people to give money as well."

Most of the hostile faces became more benign, all except Saw. He stared at Károly Rosos with open contempt.

"Now," Steeple said, "let's make some decisions on exactly what to do next."

The conference was more lecture than conference. It wasn't the way Steeple liked things to run, but he no longer had the power of the federal government lending him gravitas to command respect. It was a strange position for one used to getting his own way through a mixture of coercion, manipulation, and compromise, and he realized he was coming across as an autocrat, but it couldn't be helped. Steeple's energy began to wane as he listed the actions he wanted them to rubber-stamp. It took nearly an hour to get through it all.

"Colonel Mwangi, would you please read the list of things we've all agreed on, just to ensure everyone is on the same page."

With paper a precious commodity, Mwangi had covered both sides of the sheet in front of her with notes from the meeting. "Brigadier General Saw will inform Major Wincommer of the decision to withdraw his force at the trading post called..." She turned the paper over, looking for something. "...called... *Ma Kelly's.* Further, Major Wincommer will seek out riders affiliated with the Rosos family and inform them of the new state of affairs vis-à-vis their relationship with the 7th Cavalry Brigade.

"General Saw will also inform forces currently at Hoover Dam, in Las Vegas, at Creech Air Force Base, and on the periphery of Yuma that they are to remain in place until further notice. They are not to initiate combat of any sort. If attacked, they will inform higher headquarters and await instructions before responding.

"General Steeple will once again make contact with Marine forces in New Mexico, who, in violation of a direct order, have engaged in combat with forces of the Caliphate of the New Prophet. He will order them to withdraw west without engaging in further combat. Furthermore, mobile artillery and-or rocket batteries yet to be determined will prepare to move east with all necessary support material and personnel. They will move out as soon as they are ready. In conjunction with this, all efforts will be made to open a constructive dialogue with the leadership of the Caliphate's army.

"The man known as General Patton will be vetted as to his capacity for the command of the Prescott area, as an official part of this brigade's table of organization. If he is judged unfit, said judgment to be made by General Steeple, a suitable replacement will be found and given command of all forces in the Prescott area.

"Civilian assets will begin making plans for construction of a road between Operations Overtime and Comeback, as their first priority. It is also considered..." She squinted at something she had messed up. "...essential... yes, it's also considered essential to begin putting any and all oil production facilities back into operation, with a longer-term goal of repairing existing railroads.

"Lastly, efforts to recover the remains of General Angriff will be accorded high priority, so that he may be given the funeral and burial commensurate with his contributions to his country and to this brigade."

"Are there any questions?" Steeple said.

"What about Comeback?" Khin Saw said.

"Leave Colonel Schiller to me. He's a reasonable man and I personally recruited him for Overtime, so I don't anticipate any problems there. Are there any more questions?"

When no hands went up, he dismissed them.

#

CHAPTER 3

Never do an enemy a small slight.
Machiavelli

Sierra Army Depot, Herlong, CA
0728 hours, May 1

Fleming's headquarters, at the center of the row of metal warehouses, smelled of sweaty soldiers, but every man and woman in the building had long since grown used to that. They'd put the latrine on the southeastern corner, the direction from which the wind almost never blew. The heat and dust made his head wound ache like giant hands were trying to squeeze it until it popped.

"General, Third Platoon Echo reports vehicle incoming from the south. It's a Humvee, sir."

Fleming stepped away from the window facing west and turned to the radioman. "Any markings?"

"Three P-Echo, can you tell if they're good guys?"

"Negative, SAD." *Sierra Army Depot.* "Identity is obscured by dust. Stand by until the range closes."

Fleming crossed his arms, taking care not to pull any sutures loose. He took a slow deep breath, glad that his sternum no longer hurt when he moved slowly.

Another thirty seconds passed before the handheld radio came back to life. "SAD, be advised the Humvee bears 7th Cavalry markings. She's one of ours."

Cheers rang out from those within earshot. Fleming waved his arm to stop them. Everybody knew the relief column had arrived the previous afternoon, but after being turned away at the roadblock and with no further outreach, the tension among the paratroopers had ramped up overnight. The cheers had been nothing more than a release of tension, but Fleming couldn't let rumors outrun reality. Why hadn't Nick come to the roadblock in person yesterday afternoon? Or at least gotten Fleming on the radio? Something was wrong; he could feel it.

At his direction, the radioman asked how long before the column would arrive at Sierra. There was another pause before the reply came.

"SAD, be advised, there's a lieutenant on board who says she has a message for General Fleming's eyes only."

"Three-P, did she give a timeline on when we can expect relief?"

"Negative. She says the message to General Fleming will explain the situation. Should I send her your way?"

Several people glanced at Fleming, who rubbed his chin with his left thumb. This was damned strange. Nick was supposed to be with the relief column, but he would never send out a liaison vehicle. He'd parade into the base like Patton taking Messina ahead of Montgomery.

Instead of detailing the message to the radioman, Fleming took the mike and spoke himself. "Three-P, this is General Fleming. Blindfold the lieutenant and detail three men to drive her to headquarters. Detain her driver at your location. And be aware of the minefield."

"Blindfold her, sir? Did I hear that right?"

"You did. Blindfold her."

"Yes, sir!"

Standing up again, Fleming re-crossed his arms.

"What are you thinking, sir?" He hadn't noticed Major Ball, C.O. of the Airborne Battalion, come in.

"I don't know, Sam. It's very odd. First, Major Strootman not producing a counter-order from General Angriff yesterday and no radio contact with him at all. That's not like him. Have you seen Green Ghost?"

"He was in the infirmary ten minutes ago visiting his buddies."

"Have one of your men bring him here, please."

Green Ghost arrived before the liaison lieutenant did.

"Thank you for coming, Colonel," Fleming said. The only sign of Green Ghost's discomfort at hearing his rank was a slight narrowing of the eyes. Nevertheless, Fleming knew him well enough to notice, but also knew he wouldn't object in front of others. "We haven't had this discussion yet, so let me formally make it clear that you are second in command of this base and everyone on it, and Major Ball, you are third."

Green Ghost opened his mouth to speak but Fleming's look stopped him from protesting.

"Aye, sir. What's our situation?"

Outside, a Humvee squealed to a stop on the pavement.

"I think we're about to find out."

A blindfolded woman wearing dusty ACUs stumbled several times as a sergeant from Echo Company's Third Platoon held her elbow and led her into the headquarters. He saluted and Fleming nodded for him to remove the lieutenant's blindfold.

She was stocky, with black hair cut short, and blinked to clear her vision once she could see again. When she regained focus enough to recognize Fleming, she straightened to attention. "Lieutenant Maria Ruiz, with a message for General Fleming."

"At ease, Lieutenant. What's the message?"

Fleming noted Ruiz's gaze roaming his injuries with the same look Nick Angriff got from young officers, one of respect mixed with fear and something else... reverence? He'd never been the recipient of such an expression before and a spike of endorphins left him feeling like he'd just conquered the world. For the first time, he understood why Angriff reveled in the hero worship others so often gave him.

"The message?" Green Ghost said when Ruiz failed to speak.

"My apologies, sir." The young officer bit her bottom lip. "The message is from General Steeple—"

Major Ball jumped forward to interrupt but Fleming stopped him with a hand. "Go on, Ruiz," Fleming said.

"Yes, sir. Three days ago General Steeple took command of Operation Overtime and ordered General Angriff's detention, until the chain of command could be reorganized. General

Steeple now orders you to turn over Sierra Army Depot to my C.O., Colonel Young, and to return immediately to Overtime Prime by the fastest means possible. We have fuel trucks with us to refuel any serviceable aircraft."

Both Fleming and Green Ghost stood unmoving, watching Ruiz for non-verbal cues as to her feelings about her message. Major Ball mouthed curses but didn't speak out loud.

"Why didn't Major Strootman address this yesterday?"

"He was under orders to only deliver the message to you personally, General. When he was stopped at the roadblock, Colonel Young called him back for further discussion."

"Is General Angriff being held prisoner?" Green Ghost asked. Although he wore no insignia, by that time everybody in the brigade knew that not only was he the S-5, he was also one of the legendary Nameless from Task Force Zombie.

"Colonel Young ordered him taken into custody immediately," she said. "I don't think he wanted to."

"You didn't answer the colonel's question," Fleming said, this time in a sterner voice. "Is General Angriff being held prisoner?"

Ruiz began to sway back and forth, not much, but enough to show her discomfort.

"I don't shoot messengers, Lieutenant. Just tell me the truth as you know it and I promise that I won't hold it against you. Relax and tell me in your own words, like you would if we were in the O Club."

"Yes, General. So, General Angriff *was* taken into custody, although like I said, I don't think Colonel Young wanted to do it. I'm HHC Exec—" *Headquarters and Headquarters Company Executive Officer* "—and I saw his face when he issued the order to arrest General Angriff. I could tell that it made him sick. But he did it..."

"Go on."

"Colonel Young was ordered to leave a force at Creech capable of defending the base, and to proceed here with the rest of the regiment, as planned. However..." She swallowed and ran her tongue over her front teeth. "Colonel Young was told that if you refused to cooperate, we are to consider you and your command mutinous and are to contain you here until reinforcements arrive."

"Was the nature of these reinforcements revealed?"

"Yes, sir. At least one battery of artillery will join us here, while from the west... from the west, the Chinese will send a regiment of infantry and whatever armor and artillery they have left."

"Chinese?" Green Ghost said, leaning forward. He crossed his arms and stared at the younger officer.

Ruiz nodded. "Chinese. They are now our allies. Apparently General Steeple brought them in to guard critical positions inside Prime."

"There are Chinese inside Prime?" Fleming asked. The slightest narrowing of his eyes betrayed his outrage.

Ruiz looked down. "Yes, sir. I overheard a conversation Colonel Young had with the new S-5 about it."

Fleming and Green Ghost exchanged glances. "There's a new S-5? Did you hear who this person is?"

"I did, sir. Somebody named Adder. No rank or other name—" She cut her eyes to Green Ghost. "—just Adder."

For one of the few times since Fleming had known him, Green Ghost's face flushed. Usually he kept rigid control of his outward emotions, as did Fleming, but not this time. "You said Adder... are you absolutely positive the name was Adder?"

"I am."

"Not Addie, or Andy?"

"No, it was Adder. I'm sure of it."

"Lieutenant, I want to thank you for sharing all of this information with us," Fleming said. "Is there anything else we should know?"

"There is, sir. Ummm... General Steeple had issued strict orders that General Angriff be treated with all the courtesy due to a man with his rank. So when General Angriff said he needed to use the latrine, Colonel Young allowed him to do so with just one officer for an escort."

"That's curious," Fleming said. "Just one officer? No sentries?"

Ruiz couldn't help an upturn at one corner of her mouth. "Yes sir, just one. Major Strootman."

Fleming smiled at last; now he understood Ruiz's unspoken message. Young had strictly complied with orders, without complying with the spirit of the orders. He had a good idea what was coming next. "Go on."

"General Angriff never came back, sir. He overwhelmed the officer and stole the Humvee and drove into the desert. Colonel Young dispatched pursuit, but nobody could find him until... I..."

"I understand exactly what you're telling me, Lieutenant."

"I don't know that you do, sir. I... I don't know how to tell you this..."

Fleming's smile faded. Something was wrong. "General Angriff likes to say the easiest way to say something is to say it."

"Sir... General Angriff is dead."

Nobody spoke for a few seconds. Fleming pressed his lips together and studied Ruiz's face for signs of deception, but saw none. Green Ghost went rigid and Fleming saw him trembling.

"Why do you say that?"

"Yesterday afternoon, a search helicopter spotted him off in the distance, but before they could get close, he tried jumping over a deep ravine in the Humvee. It didn't make it. The only thing they saw below was the burning wreckage. A recovery team will look for the body, so the general can receive a proper military burial."

"Anything else?"

"No, sir."

"Thank you, Ruiz. I appreciate your candor."

"Please don't tell Colonel Young, sir, but I exceeded my orders for how much information to give you. I was only supposed to tell you that General Angriff was dead, not the circumstances that led to his death."

"There will be no repercussions, Lieutenant, at least not from me. I'm afraid we'll have to blindfold you again. I'm most sorry about that. Please give Colonel Young my regards."

"What should I tell him about your willingness to take orders from General Steeple?"

In the face of danger, Fleming didn't typically grin. In fact, he wasn't sure he had ever done so before, but this time he did. "Please tell General Steeple that it will be a cold day in Hell before I take orders from him."

The instant Ruiz stepped out of the warehouse, Fleming began giving orders. "Major, you heard the lieutenant — we can expect Chinese armor to our west in the near future. I want your men to scour the area for any salvageable weapons, ammunition, medical supplies, anything we might need to defend this base. Check the destroyed vehicles, too; there might still be some gas in their tanks that didn't burn up. I also want to see what's here that we can use. Maybe there's a few thousand mines in one of those bunkers."

"The original defenders said they laid them all before we got here," Ball said.

"I know, Sam, but let's be certain. Also, we know there are more Gustavs out there somewhere, so go find them. Give me a report on what you've found by twenty-one hundred hours. Green Ghost, let's you and me have a talk about—" He turned, but Green Ghost was gone.

"He went out the back door and turned left, General."

"What for?"

The major shrugged. "I couldn't say."

Fleming pivoted on one heel and immediately regretted doing so. Pain shot down the side of his head into his neck. He gulped air and then his chest ached.

"I hate getting shot," he said to no one in particular.

#

CHAPTER 4

Good iron does not make nails, good men do not make soldiers.
Chinese proverb

Sierra Army Depot, Herlong, CA
0742 hours, May 1

Fleming found him in the area they'd turned into a makeshift stable, talking with the woman named Junker Jane. She sat on a stool. Her right foot had layers of torn fabric wound around it. When Green Ghost saw Fleming, he went back to checking out a large brown and white horse.

"Why the sudden interest in horses?"

"Saint's out there. I'm going after him."

Fleming knew better than to argue or forbid him. Green Ghost *might* obey a direct order to stay, maybe, but the truth was he wanted to go look for Angriff, too. "You don't think he's dead?"

"Do you?"

"I'd like to think not, but one of these times it might actually be true. This could be that time."

"I don't believe that for even a second."

"But what if it *is* true?"

Green Ghost took a step toward him, fists clenched. "It's not!"

Fleming extended his hands in a placating gesture. "All right, I get it. But where do you intend to look? That's a big desert out there, son, as desolate as desolate gets. How will you know where to start looking?"

"I'll just know."

"That's not very good planning."

"You're not gonna talk me out of it, Socrates."

"I'm not trying to. I'd go with you if I could. I'm just trying to help you think it through. It's going to take a long time to get back to anywhere on horseback."

"I don't intend to do that. I'm gonna borrow a vehicle from our friends to the south."

Fleming nodded several small nods. "That could work. From anybody else I'd say it was insane, but from you the impossible only takes longer. Make sure you steal enough gas."

"Yeah."

"I wish I could give you a GPS heading."

"Me, too. Those days are gone."

"I think my dad told me about that. What is it?" It was the first thing Junker Jane had said.

Both men looked at her as if she'd materialized, like a ghost. Neither had realized she was even still in the stable.

"GPS? It means Global Positioning System," Fleming said. "Back in the days before the Collapse, we could see a jackrabbit on a rock from satellites orbiting high above the Earth, or pinpoint a man's location using a series of reference numbers."

"None of that makes sense to me. It's just words."

"Now that's all it is anyway, words."

"Who is this man you're going searching for?" she said, looking at Green Ghost. "Have I met this Saint?"

For a moment he didn't speak, so she turned to Fleming, but he only shook his head. "You asked him, not me. It's his question to answer."

Green Ghost bent down to examine the last of the horse's hooves, the rear right one. After running his finger across its surface to ensure there were no splits, he stood and met Jane's eyes. "Saint's his code name. You know him as General Nick Angriff. He's my father."

"Oh... damn, yeah, that I understand. Damn... but General Fleming has a good point. That's a big desert out there. If..." She stopped herself, remembering what happened when Fleming had said the same thing she was about to say. "Your father could be almost anywhere by the time we start tracking him."

"We? Why would you come with me? And why would I let you?"

"The first reason would be that's my horse you plan on riding, without asking me, and the second would be, do you have the first clue how to get all the way to wherever you're going? Much less what else is out there waiting for you? I grew up riding all over that desert. I know every coyote by name. I've scraped from Las Vegas all the way into old Mexico and South California."

"I don't—"

"The third reason is, you can't stop me unless you tie me up. I'm a lot more comfortable on horseback than sitting around here."

"What about your foot?"

"You think this is the first time I've been hurt?"

"You lost a lot of blood."

"And your doctors gave me a lot of... what's the word?"

"Transfusion."

"Yeah, transfusion. You'd be surprised what kind of medical stuff I know. You ever nursed a Hairy Man who's been shot?"

"A what?"

"Hairy Man. Tse-nahaha, as the Mountain People down where I live call 'em."

The two men hesitated. Fleming finally said, "Do you mean a Bigfoot?"

"I've heard 'em called that, yeah. A couple of years ago I helped one that'd been shot, dug the bullet out, and he's fine now."

"A Bigfoot? Seriously?"

"A Hairy Man. His name is Nepotia... so what, why are you worried about that? If I say I can ride with my foot, I can."

"Sorry, I'm still not convinced of that... in fact, right this minute I'm not sure you're sane."

"See, that's the fourth reason I'm going. 'Cause you're telling me I can't. And as for not getting anywhere... my horses could do upwards of seventy miles a day if I pushed them. I don't, but I could if I had to."

"I don't know horses like you do, but I always heard fifty miles was the top limit."

She shrugged. "They can't do that much for more than a day or two, but scrapers cover a lot of territory and my horses are bred for it. Our only limit will be if you can stay in the saddle that long."

"How long are you thinking?" Green Ghost said, with the slightest bit of concern in his tone.

"If we ever stop talking long enough to leave, we'll be going at least twelve hours today."

He lifted his chin. "If you can do it, so can I."

She laughed. "Sure you can."

"Are you taking NVG?" Fleming said. He patted the flank of the brown and white horse as Green Ghost tested its saddle straps.

"Packed away. I hope we grab a vehicle and are gone before I need them. If we could wait for darkness, it might give us cover, but we can't."

"You could. It is unlikely that Colonel Young's sentries will burn up their batteries using NVGs just for standing watch."

A bright morning sun in a cloudless sky washed out the spray of stars from the night before. The desert had a glow that was only seen in spring, before summer heat baked the landscape. Junker Jane had already mounted her horse, testing how her lightly bandaged foot felt inside her boot and stirrup, and trotted off a few strides.

Fleming laid one hand on the younger man's shoulder, something he'd never done before. "I'm praying you find your father, Nick, you know that." He had never used Green Ghost's real name before, either. "But if he's gone, I mean really gone this time, you've got to promise me you'll come back alive and won't do anything stupid."

"If Saint Nick is dead... if *my father* is dead, somebody is going to pay with their blood. You understand that; I know you do."

"You misunderstand me." Fleming grinned, but it wasn't from mirth. "I'm not saying don't go after Tom Steeple. I'm saying come get me so I can go with you."

"So you're definitely staying here?"

"We're not going anywhere... where would we go?"

"Don't die here, Socrates. Not in this shithole. It isn't worth it."

"Oh, I don't know. It's kind of growing on me." He reached down and scooped up a handful of powdery topsoil. "See? Moon dust, just like Afghanistan, the Garden Spot of the World."

3 miles east–southeast of Sierra Army Depot
0839 hours, May 1

"How far south do we need to go?" Jane asked.

"Five miles should do it. We'll get back behind that ridge and turn south, go three or four miles, and then turn west. That should do it."

"So we grab a vehicle and then what?"

Despite being night, it was bright enough to see him shrug. "We drive. Or *I* drive. I think you'd be better off heading for home. Didn't you tell me you live in the mountains west of Carson City?"

"Close enough."

"You should go home. That'll also solve the problem of what to do with the horses. I know you don't want to give up these saddles and all of this tack."

"True."

"So it's settled?"

"If you're hell-bent on being an idiot, then yeah, sure, it's settled."

That made him turn in his saddle. "Do you have a better idea?"

"Walking the whole way would be better than what you've got planned."

"Then please, tell me what's better. I don't want to be an idiot if I can help it."

She smiled at how his voice cracked as he grew angry. Most people probably wouldn't have noticed in the darkness, but she did. "You should fly."

"Fly?"

"Yes, fly."

"And how do I do that? Unless you mean for me to flap my arms and jump off a cliff?"

"Maybe you should try that. Find a really high cliff to jump from, with a lot of rocks below. But if it was me, I'd go talk to my friend Allen Pohl."

"Who the f—... who is Allen Pohl?"

She laughed. "I've heard that word before. Allen owns an air force."

"An air force? You mean, like an *air force* air force? Drones, fighters, zoomies... I mean pilots, all that sort of thing?"

"I don't know about all of that. Apparently back before the Collapse, Allen's dad was... what did you call it when somebody had a lot of money?"

"Rich?"

She nodded. "That's it, rich. He collected old airplanes and restored them so they'd fly again. It was like his... I can't think of that word, either."

"Hobby?"

"You're reading my mind tonight."

"It's a good thing you're not reading mine."

"I don't have to... men only think about one thing."

"Touché."

"What does that mean?"

"It's French. It means you're right."

"I knew that already. So Allen's father had all these airplanes and built a runway and had everything he needed to keep them flying. Allen was ten when the Collapse came and after that his father taught him everything he needed to know about the airplanes and the ranch. I met his father once... even in his old age he had a powerful spirit."

"His name sounds familiar."

"I can't help you with that."

"And you want me to follow you because this guy might be able to fly us south instead of us having to drive?"

"Time's not our friend, is it?"

"No."

"I think you answered your own question, then. Can I ask you something?"

"If I said no, would that stop you?"

"No."

"Like I said..."

"How did you get the name Green Ghost? You're not green and I don't think you're a ghost."

"Would you know a ghost if you saw one?"

She cocked her head as if trying to understand the question. "Yes. Wouldn't you?"

He realized she wasn't kidding, and after the earlier Bigfoot remark, decided not to pursue the existence of ghosts. "It happened the night before my mom died. Me, my sister, and some friends drove out to this place in Memphis called Voodoo Village—"

"You lost me."

"What part?"

"Okay, Memphis was a city, right?"

"Yeah, like Reno, or Las Vegas. Only far away, on the banks of the Mississippi River."

"That doesn't mean anything to me. But go on, I get it, Memphis was a city on a river a long way from here. You said you drove... I guess everybody drove cars?"

"Pretty much."

She shook her head. "There was that much fuel?"

"Oh, yeah, you could buy all you wanted."

"What was that other thing you said. Voo-something?"

"Voodoo Village. Voodoo was like this religion based in, I guess you'd call it magic, but that's not exactly right. I don't know that much about it, but priests called on spirits and stuff to help them out."

"Like a shaman for my friends the Miwoks, and the other people you call Indians. The Utes, the Apaches, the Navajo..." It wasn't a question.

"Uh, sure. Anyway, late one night we went to Voodoo Village, it was a place where all these voodoo people lived—"

"Why?"

"Why did they live there?"

"No, why did you go?"

Moonlight reflected from the sweat that ran down her cheeks, making streaks in the dust caked on her skin. The night's silver light turned her hair a faded shade of white. But despite the strange feelings he had every time he looked at her, he was also getting annoyed at being interrupted.

"Uhh... it was something we did back then. Kids, I mean. Growing up, I heard all these stories about this scary place where all these monsters practiced voodoo and did weird things."

Surprisingly, she seemed to understand. "Like sneaking into a bear's cave during their winter sleep. Nado did that when she was young."

Green Ghost thought of her daughter's tight, muscular body and wondered what she meant by *young*. Nado couldn't be more than twenty. "Why would she do that?"

"Because I did, and made the mistake of telling her about it. Go on with your story. You went to this voodoo place and thought it was a good idea to poke them and see what happened?"

"Dammit, we were seventeen, okay? It was stupid but we did it. Can I finish the story?"

"I wish you would."

She smirked, just a little. He felt his face flush with anger, although he didn't know why.

"In the middle of the night, we crept into this little compound and lying there was this dead twelve-year-old boy. Right there in the middle of the driveway. We were about to take off when all these really angry men surrounded us, saying *we* killed him. Then the boy's father showed up and wanted to kill us on the spot. I thought we were dead, until this old, old man hobbled out. He was all shrunk, you know? Bent over and walked with a cane. But his eyes, they shined in the dark. I remember that to this day, the way his eyes seemed like they had flashlights in them. This old voodoo priest looked into each of our faces and told the other men to put down their guns; we didn't kill the boy. He said I had some kind of spirit inside me, that I was the avenger, and that someday I'd kill his grandson's killer. He called the thing inside me the Green Ghost, so when it came time for me to pick a code name, that's what I picked."

"That's something else I don't understand. Why do you need these code names? Vapor, Claw, Green Ghost? None of it makes any sense."

"Didn't you name your daughter Tornado?"

At that she laughed. "What was it you said earlier, touchey?"

"Touché."

"Do you have another name, a real one?"

He hesitated. "Yeah."

"What is it?"

Saying it out loud felt like some sort of betrayal, like he was breaking an oath. They had all sworn to never reveal their birth names, but that vow had been made to a country that no longer existed, and for a reason that no longer existed. "Nick," he finally said. "My real name's Nick."

"Nick... I like that name. It sounds strong. So did you kill the killer?"

"Yeah, I did."

"Wanna tell me about it?"

"It's a long story."

"It's a long ride."

"I'll give you the short version. I was in Kenya... that's in Africa... getting ready for an op. Training, gathering intel... that's information about your enemy... making plans and in general getting ready. Claw and Vapor were there too, by the way. One day I got a call from my sister. I hadn't heard from her in two years so I knew it was important."

"A call on one of those radios?"

"A cell phone, but yeah, close enough. She told she'd kind of screwed up and shot too many people, and could I come home, back to Memphis that is, and help, because a lot of people were looking for her. So I did. I killed him in the course of what followed. As it turns out, I had a personal score to settle with him, too."

"How many people have you killed?"

He looked west, where the moon seemed impossibly close to Earth. "I don't know. A lot. Too many."

"Didn't they need killing?"

Her matter-of-fact tone brought a raised eyebrow. Was she really that hard?

"Most of them," he said, after a long pause. "But there's at least two more left to kill. One is General Steeple, and the other is the man named Adder."

#

Chapter 5

The rabbit runs faster than the fox, because the fox is running for its dinner, while the rabbit is running for its life.
Richard Dawkins

Somewhere in the Mojave Desert, Nevada
0903 hours, May 1

Nick Angriff knew that an overnight rainstorm in the Mojave Desert was so rare it might be taken as a sign of the Apocalypse, except that had already happened. Peeking out of the cave, he watched flash floods at the bottom of the ravine wash over the wreckage of his Humvee. It was perfect for his deception, as if divine intervention wanted to deceive anybody who came to recover his body. Regardless of how hot the fire had burned, something would have been left of him, maybe his bones, but now they couldn't be sure that all of him hadn't been washed away.

While they'd thought he was asleep, Angriff had heard them whispering about asking him what had happened. That brought a smile, but no answer; if they wanted to know, let them ask. It did give him time to consider his answer, though. Why *was* he hiding from his own troops?

Finally, Bunny Carlos asked the question they both wanted answered, but Randall was too afraid to ask. "If you don't mind my asking, General... what happened? Why are you here, in a cave in the middle of nowhere?"

Angriff peeked around them and watched the last of the storm moving off to the east. Framed high against the dark sky was a prairie falcon riding the winds. He drew on the cigar, exhaled, and got a faraway look in his eyes. "We've been here all night and you're just now asking?"

"Begging your pardon, General, but you can be a little intimidating."

"Only a little? I'm slipping. So, the short answer, boys, is that I tried to be somebody I'm not."

Both men wrinkled their eyebrows and cut their eyes toward each other. Randall shrugged slightly, but Angriff caught it all and knew what it meant.

"Gentlemen, after you went missing, I decided to leave Prime for an inspection tour up to and including the Sierra depot." A sudden thought made him pause. "By the way, do you two know how that turned out?"

"No, sir, we don't," Randall said.

"It was a close thing but we won. The paratroops got there at literally the last second. It was costly, but we saved the depot. You can hear the rest of the details later. So as I was saying, I felt it was high time to get my ass out in the field and see what we had liberated. I moved out with 2nd Mechanized Infantry, the whole regiment, never anticipating that I was leaving the foxes in charge of the henhouse."

"I don't follow, sir."

"Mindy Porter." He didn't say anything else right away and could see them wanting to ask what that meant, but for a few seconds his mind wandered to a different place and time. The pause lasted so long that Randall started to say something, when Angriff continued. "A long time ago, I was asked to do an interview with a reporter from a little town just west of Syracuse. I was there making a speech and figured what the hell, why not? This was about the time ISIS came on the scene. So this reporter, Mindy Porter, I'll never forget her name, she listens to the growing threat we faced in the Levant and then makes the stupidest comment I've ever heard from anyone. Not just journalists, *anybody*.

"I'd told her as much as I could about the personalities involved, maybe even a little more than I should have, because I really wanted her to understand the danger we and our allies faced from ISIS. Then, when I was done, she got this confused scowl and said that it sounded like we were fighting smirking, mustache-twirling villains, like you used to see on kids' cartoons, or in silent movies. She even inferred they were cardboard caricatures set up to fool the American public into going to war."

"*ISIS?*" Randall said. "She said that about ISIS?"

"Damn right she did. It goes to show how dismissive some people can be about your life's work, even if that work is to keep them alive."

"Yes sir, but that level of stupidity is..."

"Staggering?"

"Yes, sir, staggering."

"Maybe... but the Mindy Porters of the world don't matter any more; they're all dust now. As for what that has to do with Overtime, I pulled a Mindy Porter. I saw our enemies as caricatures. I'd beaten them and assumed any that were left would stay beaten. I scattered our leaders and forgot that most of the officers of Overtime were specifically chosen by Tom Steeple. Hell, most of the enlisted personnel were picked by him, too. They didn't sign on to serve under me; they signed on because he convinced them to. I assumed their loyalty automatically transferred to me when I took command... in other words, I got cocky and careless.

"As soon as I'd left, unknown elements released Steeple and took control of Prime. See, I tried to be a political general, like the ones I used to despise so much. Where Steeple was concerned, I tried to take the least controversial path that I could, which is why I didn't just court-martial him right away. I wanted to kill him for what he'd done to my family, but I let political considerations stop me. That won't ever happen again.

"I don't know exactly what happened or how that bastard took control, but this much I *can* tell you: my days of being conciliatory are over. It didn't work for Caesar and it didn't work for me, and I've learned my lesson. That will never happen again."

"No, sir," Randall said. "I mean, yes, sir."

But Angriff wasn't listening to anyone except his own inner voice, and that was who he responded to. "No, that won't happen again. This time when I kick their ass, it's gonna stay kicked."

While they'd been waiting for the weather to clear, Carlos and Randall had taken turns filling Angriff in on everything they'd seen and experienced at Area 51.

"I thought they called it something else," he'd said.

Carlos answered first. "Yes, sir, the Nevada Test and Training range, I think."

"Or Groom Lake?" Randall added.

"Oh, hell, just call it Area 51," Angriff said. "That's easier. But this is excellent news. Even the remnants of another Air Force base can add orders of magnitude to our capabilities. And if they've got flying F-22s, that's a game changer."

"They could have been F-35s," Carlos said, and then rolled his eyes at saying that in front of a general.

But Angriff smiled. "Only the Air Force could have dreamed that up."

Once the storm had finally passed, it took with it the dry smell of the parched desert, replacing it with something moist and vaguely floral. Angriff smoked the cigar down much further than usual, since he only had a handful left, and tossed the butt into the ravine. As the ember swirled into the darkness below, it brought back the memory of throwing away another cigar butt, off the parapet of the Hohensalzburg a lifetime ago. Moments after that had been when the entire course of his life changed, when he was summoned to meet Tom Steeple in that black airplane on a secret airfield.

"So what now, General?" Randall asked. "How can we help?"

"Just tell me who you want me to shoot," Carlos added.

Angriff grabbed Carlos' shoulder and allowed himself a second, amused smile. "I don't want my best gunship pilots lugging a rifle, Lieutenant." He paused as a vagrant memory flashed into his mind. "What is it they call you? Your nickname?"

"Uhh..."

"Bunny," Randall said.

"Bunny?"

Carlos' expression promised later retribution to Randall. "Yes, sir. That's the name of my favorite drummer."

"Or the size of your ears," Randall added.

Angriff couldn't help smiling. "I see. Well, Bunny, I have better plans for you two, plans that involve getting your Comanche back so it's not stalking me any more."

Randall jumped in, without apology. "Wait, sir... what?"

"It was your AH-72 that almost found me and forced me to run the Humvee off that cliff. I recognized my daughter's image on its side."

"*Tank Girl?*"

"*Tank Girl.*"

Both Carlos and Randall snarled at the same instant. "Wang!"

Despite the fact that they stood in a cave on the side of a deep crevice, in the middle of the Nevada desert, with no transport and people actively hunting them, Angriff couldn't help laughing at their exchange of expressions.

"Friend of yours?" he said.

They left the cave at first light the next morning. The two hovercraft had enough juice to lift them to the surface on the western side of the ravine, where they hid one in a pile of rock. Angriff took the other one, along with both batteries, to cross the ravine and fly southeast until the power gave out.

"You sure you don't want us to come with you, sir?" Randall said.

"Thanks, Joe, but I can get farther using both batteries alone. You two need to get *Tank Girl* back. But don't come after me; don't tell anybody I'm still alive. If Steeple finds out, he'll turn out the entire brigade to find me."

"I wouldn't blame him, General," Carlos said, instantly regretting it.

Instead of being angry though, Angriff grinned. "Me either."

After a quick salute, followed by handshakes, Randall and Carlos headed south toward Creech. For his part, Angriff mounted the hovercraft and took off without hesitation, as if he'd been doing it for years.

"How do you become that guy?" Carlos said once Angriff was gone.

"I don't know, Bunny... even when he's being nice, he scares the shit out of me."

"Yeah, and he *likes* you."

Prescott, Arizona

Colonel Todd Berger churned his knees as high as they would go, digging into the hard surface of the Prescott High School running track around the old football field. The Marines of the newly renamed 2nd Raider Battalion cheered as he raced the clock, exactly as they'd all had to do. Berger had promised that if they all passed, running three miles in under 18 minutes, then he'd do it, too. They'd offered to let him tack on the extra minute for Marines over the age of 45, but he had refused. Now he wished he could kick himself.

As he passed the start line, the entire battalion yelled, "Nine!" Berger made a fist and wore a triumphant expression when he really wanted to collapse and suck down air. Each breath burned his lungs, each step sent shockwaves of pain up through his calves, and there was the very real possibility of his muscles locking up on him.

One foot in front of the other, one foot in front of the other... He hung his head and focused on going just one more step. If he let himself think about two more laps after the one he was on, Berger knew his mind would convince him to quit. Then fate stepped in.

A Marine started jogging beside him. "Colonel, General Steeple wants you right away, sir," the PFC said.

"Well, damn!" Berger swore, stopping. With hands on hips, he bent over and gasped for air.

A few seconds later, the same PFC held out a radio handset.

"Colonel Berger here," he said, still heaving.

"Major, this is General Steeple. Are you okay?"

"Yes, sir," Berger said, not correcting Steeple about his rank. He'd heard that all promotions made by General Angriff had been rolled back, but didn't want to make an issue of it in front of the battalion. "Some PT with my men, sir."

"Team building. Well done, Major."

"Thank you, General." Somebody handed him a large squeezer of water and he drained it as Steeple spoke.

"Major, let me get right to the point. As you know, two companies from your battalion disregarded my direct order yesterday to avoid engaging the Army of the Caliphate over in New Mexico. I have no idea whether they even still exist or not..."

"They do, General, but those companies are in Lieutenant Colonel Strickland's battalion."

There was a long pause. "They gave you a situation report?"

"Lieutenant Colonel Strickland did, yes, General, as I'm his commanding officer, he duly reported their status to me."

"And you didn't relay that message to me?" Steeple's voice grew loud enough for those nearby to hear.

Berger knew that he should move out of earshot, but didn't. The moment had come to decide whether he would take orders from Steeple, and deciding on the answer was easier than he'd ever thought it would be. "You're not in my chain of command, sir."

"I'm not in your chain of command... well, Major, if I'm not, then who is?"

"First of all, *General*, my rank is full colonel, not major, and with the death of General Angriff, my commanding officer is General Fleming. Moreover, not only am I not bound by my oath to obey illegal orders, I am specifically prohibited from doing so by the UCMJ. Now, can I help you with anything else, sir?"

"You're going to regret this, Berger..." Another pause told Berger that Steeple was getting himself under control, so he waited. "Your Marines in New Mexico have two hours to withdraw to the west and break off their engagement with the Army of the Caliphate. If they do not, I am ordering air and artillery assets to make them regret that decision. If, within those same two hours, you do not inform me that you are willing to abide by my orders, then you will leave me no choice but to also consider you and your Marines as hostile forces. That includes the militia that you have mistakenly given the notion that they are United States Marines."

Berger raised his voice, to make certain that each Marine could hear him. "General Steeple, you couldn't wash the jockstrap of a real Marine, and you don't have to wait two hours for my answer. If you expect Marines to stand by while innocent American civilians are massacred by a foreign army, well, General... you are out of your fucking mind!"

Berger handed the handset back to the PFC. The entire battalion stood in silence, unsure how to respond to something none of them had ever expected to see, or hear. For that matter, Berger had never envisioned such a scenario, either.

"Where is Colonel Cranston?" he said.

Seconds later, Cranston pushed his way through the crowd, looking much trimmer than he had ten months earlier during the Battle of Prescott. "Here, Colonel."

"I need your battalion geared up and ready to deploy in thirty minutes, Colonel Cranston. Draw full ammunition and food for three days. Then I want you to scout to the north and northwest for likely medium and heavy artillery sites. Once you've identified them, draw up plans to ambush any batteries that may set up there. I'll be at the regimental CP with Mayor Parfist at the Courthouse, if you need me." He turned to the waiting men and women. "Are you Marines ready to fight like Marines?"

"Urrah!" they shouted as one.

"I can't hear you!"

They shouted again, louder. At the end, a smart ass in the rear yelled out, "Did you hear *that*, Colonel?"

"Lima Charlie, killer!"

Operation Overtime, The Crystal Palace
0927 hours

"He really said you were out of your... your mind?" Amunet Mwangi said. Sitting on the couch in Tom Steeple's office, she leaned forward to hear his reply.

"My *fucking* mind, Amy, and yes, he really said that."

She shook her head. "Marines."

"This whole situation is deteriorating, and between you and me, and *nobody* else, I do not blame Berger for refusing to obey the order. For denying my authority to issue the order, yes, that's on him, but not for the other part. Damn!"

"So what are you going to do?"

Steeple drummed his fingers on the desktop. "How many Chinese troops are here at Overtime?"

"Adder's the one with that number. I'm thinking between one hundred fifty and two hundred. I know Károly has ferried three groups from California; that's about seventy. And the V-22s came back full both times, so that's another hundred or so. There were already about twenty here that came in on the first flight, and probably some more I don't know about."

"Not enough. See, this is where Nick Angriff excelled, coming up with out-of-the-box tactical solutions. He could see things where others couldn't, me included."

"What are you thinking about doing?"

"I need to set an example of what happens when you disobey my orders, but it's becoming obvious that not all of our assets are willing to fire on other members of the brigade. So we will use indirect fire, such as at a city like Prescott, or that place in New Mexico."

"Shangri-La?"

"Yes. What an idiotic name. Here's what I want to do. Deploy two batteries of M109s to Prescott, with as many Chinese as we can scrape together as a defense force. Leave fifty here to guard vital areas and send the rest."

"We got the entire 2nd Mechanized Regiment for escort, if you want them."

"No, if they refuse to use direct fire against the Marines, this whole thing caves in. If the Marines overrun the Chinese and take the Paladins, at least they can't use those against us in here, and eventually General Wei will get here with the rest of the PLA."

"You don't want to just wait the Marines out? We're their sole source for food and fuel."

"That sets a bad precedent, and anyway would take too long. The longer this goes on before I can consolidate power, the worse our chances are of making it stick. This isn't going to be as easy as I'd hoped, all because Angriff had to go and die." He thought of something and pointed at Mwangi. "Let's send that General Patton to Prescott with the Chinese. Wasn't that new battalion of Marines recruited from his army? Maybe there's some residual loyalty there, and if not, and they kill him, it's one less mouth to feed."

"Air support at Prescott?"

"No, same reason we can't use American group troops. If they mutinied, we would lose everything. Let's wait until we can give them a better target than their friends."

"Do you want to deploy that third battery of M109s?"

"I do. Send them to New Mexico, with a strong escort from 2nd Mechanized Regiment. And have our longest-range helicopter stand by to take a direct message to the commander of the Caliphate Army. I'm going to propose a truce and the opening of negotiations."

"Anything else?"

"Not that I can think of."

"I'll pass this on to Colonel Claringdon right away."

"I want you to do the planning on this."

"Me, Tom? Claringdon's the brigade commander."

"Claringdon's value is in following orders and keeping his mouth shut. He's personally brave, he's proven that, but the man is not a combat leader or planner. I know you're the latter."

"What about the former?"

"You would probably do very well leading troops in combat, but you are much too valuable to me to allow that to happen. That's why I didn't give you the brigade, instead of him. I need you right where you are now, doing what you're doing right this minute."

"I appreciate the compliment, Tom. I think."

"Let's get to work. Tell Schiller to patch me through to that company commander over in New Mexico."

#

Chapter 6

*So much loss and so much pain,
Why must we endure it, time and again?*
Sergio Velazquez, from "A World Afire"

*Shangri-La, AKA Jemez Springs, New Mexico
1022 hours, May 1*

Marine Captain Martin Sully sat on a dusty boulder, scratching the stubble on his face while staring at a scruffy pinyon pine tree. Since he was tossing pebbles into the dust, he didn't hear his executive officer, Lieutenant Onni Hakala, stroll up behind him.

"You okay, Marty?" Hakala said, sitting beside his friend.

Sully didn't answer for a moment. "No, not really."

"It doesn't look like the Sevens are in the mood to come at us again."

"We hurt 'em pretty bad. No doubt they're reorganizing."

"So what's bothering you?"

"You weren't here this morning when we got the word. General Angriff is dead."

"Oh, fuck!"

"Yeah."

"Nick the A is dead? Fuck me."

"Fuck us all."

Despite his shock, Hakala turned in surprise, and Sully knew why. He'd never heard his usually stoic commander say *fuck* before. Ever. Sully disliked such language, but sometimes nothing else fit the situation.

After a minute or so of silence, Hakala said, "Well, we've already disobeyed a direct order just being here. I guess Steeple's gonna fry our asses either way."

"Maybe. We knew the other day that General Steeple had taken over, but in the back of my mind I always thought Nick would somehow return to power. You know, kick ass and take names. But now that's not gonna happen, and we don't have a home any more, not unless we pull out right now."

"We can't just leave. Where would we go?"

"We've been ordered to abandon these people to their fate. If we do that, General Steeple promised no repercussions for disobeying his order not to get involved here."

"And Steeple is the new brigade CO?"

"Of everything, yes. But Colonel Saw got a promotion to brigadier, and he's now in charge of the brigade, as Steeple's second-in-command."

"Chain Saw's supposed to be righteous. Did you protest the order to withdraw?"

"C'mon, Onni, you know me. I did everything I could short of telling him to shove it up his ass." Another expression that was very much unlike Sully, but once again he felt it was appropriate.

"Don't they know what'll happen?" Hakala said. "The Sevens will overrun this place, rape everything that can be raped, kill the ones too old to work and enslave the rest. That's what they've done everywhere they go. Prime's gotta know that!"

Sully nodded and tossed another rock. "They do."

"Then what gives?"

"They want the Sevens as allies, not enemies. Our orders are to take no action that might lead to a continuance of hostilities."

"Aw, shit. Allies with those assholes? Are they serious?"

"Not just them. The Chinese and the Rednecks, too."

"Wait a minute, now we're allies with the fucking PLA? Are you serious? I didn't sign up to be butt buddies with a fuckin' Chicom."

"Nope, neither did I."

"I don't mind killin' the bastards, or cutting their dicks off, but I'll be goat-fucked before I'll hold it while they piss. So what are we gonna do?"

"I'm going to do what I have to."

"And what's that?"

"I'm a Marine. I swore to protect the Constitution from all enemies, foreign and domestic, and to follow the orders of my legally appointed superiors."

"So we're withdrawing? You can't be serious!"

For the first time that morning, Sully cracked a little smile. "General Steeple wasn't legally appointed, Onni, but General Angriff was, by the Congress and the President of the United States. You saw the document hanging in the hallway near the Clam Shell, right? We all did. And with General Angriff dead, the chain of command goes through General Fleming, to General Tompkins, and then to Colonel Saw, or General Saw. General Steeple was under arrest for treason and had no place in the chain of command. He has no authority over this brigade, this company, or me."

"So we're staying? We're going to fight?"

"*I* am. I'm following the last legitimate orders I was given. But I can't order the rest of you to follow me into what is likely going to be hell."

"You can't order us to leave, either."

"I could."

"Didn't your last legitimate orders apply to the whole company?"

Now Sully grinned and gripped Hakala's shoulder. "You're not as dumb as you look."

"Thanks a lot."

"I do want to explain this to the men. All of it, including my reasoning."

"They've grown to respect you as their commander, Marty. You say we're heading for hell, I say they'll follow you there. I know I will."

"You might not be so happy when the Sevens are coming down that road."

Outside of Albuquerque, New Mexico
1315 hours

The Emir of New Khorasan, Superior Imam Abdul-Qudoos Fadil el Mofty, once known as Richard Lee Armstrong, criminal and con artist, rolled the muscles between his shoulder blades as a petite brunette named Mina rubbed her thumbs up his spine. Mina's grandmother had been a masseuse in

Texas Armstrong had shacked up with for a while. Before he'd had her killed, he'd made sure the woman taught her daughter, Mina's mother, everything she knew about giving a massage. In turn, she'd taught *her* daughter.

Mina fought a knot near his right shoulder blade and used her elbow to press on it. He grimaced as it burned, but when she released her elbow, the relief was palpable.

"You're a mess of knots today," she said, working the same one more gently with her fingers.

Lifting his head, he changed from lying on his left cheek to lying on his right. Eyes still closed, he drew a deep, satisfying breath. "The Prophet gives me a lot of work."

She leaned over and kissed the back of his neck. He smiled.

"He shouldn't overwork you like that."

"I'm just a simple man of Allah who obeys his prophet."

Lunch had already made him sleepy, and as he relaxed he felt himself drifting off... until a loud knock at the bedroom door startled both him and Mina.

Damn, he thought, but said, "Who is it?"

"It is Irfan, my lord. Captain Nouri sent me to fetch you. An American helicopter dropped something outside."

Despite being naked, el Mofty rolled off the table and grabbed his pants. "What do you mean, they dropped something? A bomb?"

"No, my lord, a message."

"What sort of message?"

"A paper, wrapped around a brick."

The house he'd made his headquarters was small, but had the distinct advantage of a roof that hadn't yet caved in or even leaked badly. Slipping a freshly washed white robe over his head, el Mofty opened the door and took the brick from Irfan. Written on the outside of an envelope, tied to the brick with string, were the words *to the leader of Sword of the New Prophet*.

After untying the envelope, el Mofty handed the brick and string back to Irfan. His lips moved as he read the message. *Too much blood has been spilt on both sides. I offer an immediate ceasefire, and with your permission will send an emissary to align our goals and movements. We should not be enemies, but rather allies. Sincerely, Thomas F. Steeple, General Commanding, United States Armed Forces.*

Tom Steeple, alive? And now in charge of the American forces fighting against him? He couldn't have been more dumbfounded if he'd learned that his brother really *was* a new prophet of Allah.

"Summon Generals Muhdin, Bashara, and Gollins. Tell them to suspend all attacks immediately and to meet me here tonight at seven pm. Also summon my council of advisors. See to that, Irfan."

"And the old one, my lord?"

El Mofty smiled at a memory. "Definitely the old one. Bid him be here early. Find extra prayer rugs, and tell the cook to prepare dinner for all of us."

Bowing his head, Irfan backed away three steps before turning and walking quickly out of the hallway.

"Qadil?"

He turned at Mina's beckoning voice.

"Are you coming back, my lord?"

Calculating what he had to do before the meeting, el Mofty nodded. "I think there's time to finish."

Albuquerque, New Mexico
1549 hours

"Irfan, why is it so dark in here?" El Mofty started across the den's tile floor to open the drapes on the western wall, but stopped when he saw the form huddled into a chair in the far corner.

"I told Irfan to close the curtains," said the old man. "I'm surprised they aren't in shreds; they're rotten as hell."

"You're here early."

"What else have I got to do?"

"Eat? Sleep? Screw?"

The old man blew his lips. "Food doesn't taste as good as it used to, I can't sleep more than an hour without getting up to pee, and as for screwing... that plumbing hasn't worked for a decade."

"Life is hell."

"Life is *pain*."

"What?"

"You said that last year in New Khorasan, remember? Right before you sent the Sword off to conquer Western Arizona?"

El Mofty leaned against a table and used the thumb and forefinger on his left hand to smooth his mustache. "Have you grown so tired of living that you insult me to my face?"

"Tired of living? No... just tired, my lord. I feel every day of every year in my joints, but suicide by insulting the Emir isn't my chosen method of leaving this world."

"Then if you're not here to ruin my afternoon, why *are* you here three hours early?"

"I heard a helicopter earlier, and saw it drop something that looked like a rock. Then I overheard some chatter about a note being tied to the rock, and I thought I'd see if you might want my insight or advice."

"You were only thinking of me?"

"It's the only reason for my continued existence on this mortal coil."

"You used to be a better liar, too."

The old man shrugged. "I diminish with age."

"Your continued existence is because you haven't pissed me off enough to kill you... yet. And over the years, you've given me some good advice, now and then. But don't push it."

"May a thousand sorrows be thrust upon me for upsetting your lordship. Would you care to share the contents of the note?"

"I never said there was a note."

"Fair enough, my lord. Then what was affixed to the rock?"

El Mofty squinted. "It wasn't a rock. It was a brick. And it had a note tied to it."

"A note... imagine that."

The Emir overlooked the sarcasm, because while he often wanted to cut the old man's throat, his counsel was *almost* never wrong. Instead, he took the note out of his pocket and read it aloud.

When he finished, the old man leaned forward, elbows on knees. "Steeple's alive?"

"Looks like it."

"That changes everything."

"Does it? I never actually met the guy. I only know what you've told me."

Straining, the old man stood up and began to pace, slowly, and with a limp, but pacing nonetheless. "Yes, it changes absolutely everything. If Tom Steeple is in charge of the American forces, nothing is impossible. His morals are malleable—"

"Speak English."

"He has no moral code. He does whatever it takes to maintain power."

"I've known a lot of men like that. You cannot trust them, they'll betray you faster than a striking rattlesnake, but you can surely do business with them."

"I agree that a man is reliable who always looks after his own interests first. That makes him predictable."

"So you think this offer is legitimate?"

"Oh, it's legitimate, all right. I don't know what Steeple's angle is, but you can bet he's got one. I can't see a downside to agreeing to a ceasefire long enough to hear what he's got to say."

El Mofty kept stroking his beard, thinking. The old man's advice had almost always been right... *almost* always. "The last time you advised me on a military matter, it turned out to be a disaster."

"Are you talking about Arizona? If I hadn't told you to send the whole army, nobody would have come back. As it is, two out of three men returned to fight again."

There was something in the old man that el Mofty didn't trust, something that had been there for years, just under the surface, but the Emir could never quite put his finger on what it was. His advice had been crucial to building and maintaining the Caliphate, and el Mofty valued his guidance above all other counselors, yet the doubt remained.

"I disagree with that, but I'm still leaning toward taking your advice. But I hope you're not wrong again. I wouldn't like that at all."

"Understood. Can I ask you one thing?"

"You may ask."

"Do you ever get tired of it?"

"Tired of what?"

"Being the emir. Do you ever wish you could just crack open a cold beer and watch a football game on TV?"

Before saying anything, el Mofty glanced around to make certain no one had entered without him noticing. He didn't have to answer the question, but the old man was the closest he had to a friend, and was one of the few who'd been with him for all of the past half century. Something compelled him to *want* to answer.

"All the time. Just once, I wish I could watch the Cowboys again. *Just once.*"

Operation Overtime, the Crystal Palace
1602 hours, May 2

Regulations, chains of command, and an inventory of every person and every piece of equipment in the 7th Cavalry, including status and location, was right up Tom Steeple's alley, so he stared at charts on the flat-screen monitor on the right side of his desk with rapt attention. To him, it was better than reading a classic book, and he was so deep in it that the knocking at his office door startled him.

"Come," he said, swallowing his annoyance.

Sergeant Major Schiller entered and Steeple immediately knew it was grim news.

"Go ahead, Sergeant, let me have it."

"I'm sorry to bother you, sir, but the recovery party just got out of the gorge where General Angriff died, and they didn't find a body. The fire was obviously so hot that very little would have been left, maybe a few bones, and scavengers had ransacked the wreckage. They also said parts of the Humvee were found more than a half mile away, probably because of several thunderstorms that were in the area after the crash."

"That's a shame," Steeple said, and meant it. Burying Angriff would have given him a chance to pay homage to the man, and maybe win over his supporters. It would have been the perfect opportunity to be seen as Angriff's colleague instead of his rival. "Thank you, Schiller. Was there anything else?"

"The prisoner you requested is being held outside."

Steeple glanced at his watch. "Is it fifteen hundred hours already? Let me shut this down, then you may show General Patton in."

1549 hours

Sergeant Major Schiller knocked twice, as instructed, before opening the office door. "Colonel Mwangi, sir."

"You wanted to see me, General?" Amunet Mwangi said as she walked past Schiller into the Crystal Palace.

"Thank you, Colonel." He waited until the door had closed, and then pushed the button to electrify the glass. It turned opaque within two seconds. "Sit down, Amy, please. What are you hearing out in the halls?"

It was the same question he used to ask her when she'd served under him at the Pentagon, and she understood exactly what he wanted.

"There's a lot of anger out there, and it's directed at you."

"The Chinese?"

She nodded. "And the Sevens. Nobody has said about the Rednecks. By and large, the lower ranks are a lot madder than the higher ranking officers."

"I know a couple of highly agitated colonels."

"I would not think anybody is happy, if I were you, Tom. Aside from Claringdon and a few others—"

"Adder."

"That's a very strange man."

"A very dangerous man. Between you and me, he may outlive his usefulness quickly. But not before my position is secure. Have you heard mention of any plans to... shall we say, change the command arrangement?"

"Grumbling, but as of now there's no one to base resistance around, no catalyst."

His voice dropped, as it always did when something troubled him. "Searchers got to the bottom of the ravine today. The one where Angriff crashed."

"Did they recover the body?"

He shook his head. "There are two theories — that most of it was consumed in the fire and scavengers made off with whatever was left, mostly bones, or the remains washed away in a thunderstorm. There was one, a pretty violent storm, within minutes of the crash."

"Wouldn't that have doused the fire?"

"Not necessarily."

"So what's bothering you, Tom? Are you afraid he didn't die?"

"What? No, not at all, there is no evidence whatsoever that he survived, or that it was some sort of ruse. What is disturbing is that without a body, or even the ashes of a body, there can be no burial. I intended to use the occasion to eulogize Angriff and explain that I never meant for this to happen."

"It's a lost opportunity."

"Yes."

"We can stage a memorial."

"And we will, but the effect will not be the same." He took a deep breath and rubbed his eyes.

"You need some sleep, Tom."

"After tomorrow, I can sleep."

Mwangi knew Steeple well enough to know that was true, but would never understand how he could compartmentalize his feelings the way he did. If she had to order American artillery to fire on other Americans, she might never sleep again. "What do you want to do about Comeback?"

"I have not decided yet. Are they still using thermite to try and get through the blast doors?"

"They are, but those doors are three feet thick. I'm not sure there's enough thermite in the world to melt that much titanium. We could try blasting through the walls."

"No, no, we are not doing that. The risk of a cave-in is too great. We need that airfield and those aircraft more than any other asset in that base."

"Then for now, we'll let them keep doing what they're doing?"

"Yes."

"Are you sending that Hull person to Prescott?"

"I have not decided yet. First we need to interview him."

"What's wrong with now?"

"Nothing." He smiled. "Nothing at all."

"Please sit down," Tom Steeple said in his coldest, sternest voice. Despite being physically unintimidating, he had long since mastered the manipulative art of threatening via the power of his position.

Lester Earl Hull shuffled forward a few steps and then stopped. Both his wrists and ankles were shackled. "It'd be a lot easier without the chains."

Amunet Mwangi sat on the office couch but said nothing.

"I am completely unconcerned with your ease or comfort, Lieutenant Hull. If you wish to sit, sit. If you wish to stand, then stand. But whatever you do, do it quickly. I'm very busy."

Along with having lost a lot of weight over the previous ten months, Hull's hair had gone from salt and pepper to snowy white, including a newly grown beard. He walked with a stoop now. Taking small steps, he fell into the nearest chair to face Steeple's desk. "So what d'ya want?"

"How would you like to get out of that cell?"

"Who do I have to kill?"

Mwangi bounced her left leg over her right knee. "So you're sending him to Prescott?"

"I am, but we need to make certain we only refer to him as General Patton. The man is a clown, it's true, but he is *our* clown. Besides, we only need him for a short while, just until he cleans out whatever seeds of independence have grown in the last year. Once that is done, he has served his purpose."

"Do you want me to cut some orders giving him command authority?"

"Over the Chinese, yes, but no American forces other than any militia in Prescott. Refer to him as the governor general of Prescott."

"I'm on it." She got up to leave.

But he stopped her. "I want you to move your office into the little conference room up here, the one beside this partition." He turned and knocked on the wall behind his desk. "Tell Schiller to do whatever it takes to make that happen. You are the one and only person in this whole base that I trust. Now that I think about it, you're the only person in the entire world that I trust."

"That's a hell of a thing, Tom, but it's true for both of us. You're the only one I know who won't stab *me* in the back."

"There is one more thing..."

Mwangi recognized that tone, and knew at once that Steeple was about to reveal the *real* reason he'd summoned her. She sat down again. "Am I going to like this?"

"You tell me. It's a combat command."

"I'll take it."

"You do not yet know its nature, but for the record, I was not offering you a choice. I *need* you to perform this service for me, Amy. As we just discussed, you are the only person I trust."

"I've already said I'll do it."

"I know, but I wanted to impress upon you its importance. I want you to fly to New Mexico and lead the negotiations for a truce with the Caliphate. Ultimately, I would like an alliance, and I am conferring upon you plenipotentiary powers to negotiate such an agreement based on a series of objectives I will provide you."

"You want a woman to do this? You do realize their opinion of women, right?"

"I do, but you will have eight M270s and half a battalion of mechanized infantry to convince them to listen, plus all the on-call air cover you might need."

She whistled. "That's a lot of firepower."

"Yes, it is. And you will also have tactical control of the two Marine companies, should the Caliphate need a demonstration of that power. But — and I cannot emphasize this enough — the use of force is absolutely the very last resort. I want an alliance with those people, not a war."

"How can we trust them to keep their word?"

"I'm privy to information that I'm not allowed to share, even with you. But based on what I know of the Caliphate's leadership, they will agree. Trust me when I say that, Amy, they *will* agree."

#

Chapter 7

"If you want to bully me, it's cool, go ahead. I want to kill you, so when you're finished it's my turn."
Nipple

Overtime Prime, lower level mess hall
1406 hours, May 1

"Mind if I join you?"

Nikki Bauer didn't bother glancing up. She recognized the voice — Adder. "It's a free country... well, not any more, but maybe you'll choke to death and I'll get to watch. That'd be cool."

"There's my girl!"

This time she did look up, and gave him the best death stare she could muster. But from the expression on his face, Nikki could tell it didn't have the desired effect.

"Are you lit?" Adder said, screwing up his face. "Did you find some crack layin' around?"

"Just high on life, asshole, something you'd never understand."

"Uh-huh." Adder had a strong jawline, which he rubbed with two fingers when thinking about something. "You really have changed, haven't you? I heard it, but didn't believe it. I think I liked the old Nipple better."

"You're breakin' my heart, butthead."

"You sound like Nipple, but the heat's gone. You used to sound like somebody doing twenty to life. Now you sound like somebody *pretending* to be doing twenty to life." Then he jabbed at her with his right index finger. "It's that guy, that's what it is. Toy something, right? He the one getting your panties wet?"

"What happened to you?" she said, tilting her head. "Did somebody molest you when you were a kid? How does somebody get so fucked up?"

"Yeah, you were way hotter the other way. *That* chick I could fuck 'til my dick fell off, but this one... jeez, I wouldn't fuck you with your brother's dick." He paused a minute. "I wonder what would happen if that other guy went away..."

Nikki leaned forward over the table. "Let's be clear about something, shit-for-brains: you do one thing to harm Joe Ootoi, or anybody else I care about, and I'll shove a knife so far up your ass, you'll shit through your belly button."

That brought a grin. He leaned back and folded his arms. "You're lookin' better."

"I'm not kidding, Adder. I told my brother you were a psycho, but he didn't listen. He told me about y'all's first op, the thing in Egypt, and said you executed some woman in cold blood—"

That changed his demeanor completely. The rage she'd seen so often before twisted his face, so that his eyes narrowed to slits. "Those were our *orders*! They were given to us by that dead fraud, Saint Nick—"

People at nearby tables picked up their trays and moved.

She drew in a loud breath. "I haven't hurt anybody in a while now, but—"

He went on as if she hadn't spoken. "—your brother could never have carried out that murder, so I did what had to be done. And that's what it was, too — it was murder. It was a kill mission. *I* should have been the lead guy for the Zombies, *I* proved it over and over again, but Saint Nick must have been butt-fucking your brother to keep me out of my rightful command."

Somewhere inside, Nikki could feel Nipple waking up. It was like having an alternate personality living within, one that Joe Ootoi had calmed but not driven out. The blinding anger that had marked most of her adult life wanted to take over again, and it was only by a strong effort of will that she controlled it. "I'm warning you again," she said. "You do anything to hurt Joe or my family, and I will cut your heart out."

That brought his grin back. "There's my girl. She's still in there somewhere!"

#

Chapter 8

One useless man is a shame, two is a law firm, and three is a Congress.
John Adams

Operation Overtime, the Crystal Palace
1600 hours, May 1

It had been a short night and a long day for everybody, so when Tom Steeple rose from behind his desk as Khin Saw entered the Crystal Palace, it immediately put the colonel on guard. Lines of fatigue etched into Steeple's face reflected the reality of the past 24 hours. That was not what set him on alert, but that Tom Steeple was known for being a stickler for protocol and rank consciousness, and superior officers didn't stand for subordinates except in rare circumstances. For him to do so now meant that he wanted something.

Already seated was Colonel Mwangi. In the background stood Károly Rosos, arms crossed, and the Chinese liaison officer. Colonel Claringdon sat on the couch.

"Sit down, Khin," Steeple said, using a hand to indicate the empty chair. Steeple's easy smile no longer reassured him; it now had the opposite effect. "I need to fill you in on a decision I've made. This was the hardest decision I've ever had to make, bar none. I want you to know that."

Steeple looked away and began to wring his hands. His breathing quickened, but Saw squinted, because the whole thing was an act. Somehow, Saw just knew it was rehearsed, and wondered how often Steeple had done this before. "Yes, sir."

"Not just hard, Khin, the hardest thing I've ever done."

Mwangi shifted in her chair. "I can verify that. It kept him up all night."

"All right," Saw said, drawing out the word while his gaze flicked from one to the other.

"As you know, General Fleming has refused to follow a direct order by allowing our Chinese allies into Sierra Army Depot. Shots have been fired and casualties inflicted. It's only by the greatest effort that we've restrained General Zhang Wei from avenging his fallen soldiers by launching a full-scale attack."

"He hasn't attacked because the air-cav would litter the field with dead Chicoms," Saw said, staring at the Chinese officer as he spoke. His voice had a natural gravelly tone that grew more pronounced when he got angry. Saw knew it, and used it. Now he sounded like he was gargling rocks.

The Chinese officer took a step forward. Claringdon's face widened in shock, while Károly Rosos grinned.

"Enough of that!" Steeple said, slamming his palm on the desk. "I will not allow you to insult our allies, General Saw. Do I make myself clear?"

Saw crossed his arms and stared at Steeple. "You do... sir."

Steeple turned to the Chinese officer, who had now advanced three steps, fists clenched at his sides. "That applies to you as well, Colonel Zongchang."

The Chinese officer sneered, staring at Saw as if his eyes could shoot death rays.

Steeple turned his attention back to Saw. "If at any time you feel that you cannot carry out my orders as commanding officer of the Seventh Cavalry, General Saw, I will accept your resignation."

"I understand, General Steeple." He sounded like a man about to have a tooth yanked out without Novocain.

"See that you do. I *need* you, Khin... we *all* need you. But if you can't get on board with my plan to move forward, then at least don't stand in the way. Now, as I was saying, General Fleming has chosen the unfortunate path of defying my orders. I am continuing my efforts to make him see reason, but in the meantime, I have ordered preparations made to transport four M119s, their crews, and ammunition to support Colonel Young and the First Mechanized Regiment in seizing the depot. This will have to be done in shifts, using the fuel trucks currently at Creech Air Force Base. They will then proceed to the area north of Reno, where Colonel Young will supply towing vehicles to get them into the combat zone. I hope and pray this causes General Fleming to see reason."

"And if it doesn't?"

"I would think that's obvious."

"I need to hear it."

"Anyone who does not follow my orders is mutinous. There is only one way to deal with mutineers."

"You will order them physically attacked."

Steeple nodded. "As a last resort, yes. But not before giving the individual soldiers the chance to do the right thing."

"The right thing..." Saw said, rubbing his lower lip and staring out the huge picture window on his left. Through two layers of glass, he spotted a speck in the sky that might have been a hawk, or maybe a prairie falcon.

"Yes, the right thing."

"What about the Marines over in New Mexico?"

"It's the same situation. As you heard in the meeting, I personally gave orders for them to withdraw or face the consequences. To that end, I ordered a battery of M270s to deploy there over the road, escorted by two companies from Second Mechanized Infantry Regiment."

"You sent an entire battery, eight machines?"

"Yes."

"So you don't want to just kill the Marines. You don't want to leave enough to bury."

"I don't *want* to do anything of the sort."

"If I'm the commanding officer of this brigade, why wasn't I consulted about this?"

"Would you have signed such orders?"

"No."

"Then you have your answer. This way, you have clean hands moving forward."

"Clean hands..." Saw paused. His eyes roamed across the floor as he formed the right words. "I was fortunate enough to know my great-grandfather. He was from India. Did you know that, General Steeple?"

"I did not."

Saw nodded. "Yes, he was. He was born during the days of the Raj, and lived a long, happy life, dying at ninety-seven—"

"Khin, where are we going with this?"

General Saw held up a hand for patience. "As I said, he was, by nature, a happy man. I never heard him say anything bad about anybody, with one exception… the British. He hated the British with more passion than Van Gogh had for his paintings, and he used a term that I think applies here."

Steeple's false smile faded some. "Is that right?"

"Yes… perfidious Albion. Are you familiar with the term, *sir*?"

Now the smile became outright anger. "I am."

"Then you know my answer to your perfidious Albion, General Steeple. I'll be in my quarters if you want me, but I have to warn you that I'm not giving up my sidearm, which is fully loaded."

Saw rose, turned, and walked out the door. The Chinese guards at the top of the ramp blocked enough of it that he would have to walk around them, but instead he stopped. Both towered over him. The taller of the two brought his rifle to port arms, legs braced apart, in a blatant sign of disrespect. Saw stepped close enough that neither man could use his rifle, drew his Sig Sauer M17, and stuck it under the man's chin.

"Are you going to move, or do I blow off the top of your head?"

Steeple's nostrils flared and his teeth hurt from clenching them so tight. Rarely had anyone spoken to him the way Saw had, and never, ever, in the presence of so many others. He pretended to wipe at the corner of his eye, only to realize his hand shook.

"Fitz," he said. His voice cracked with anger, so he cleared his throat and tried again. "Fitz, I am elevating you to acting commander of the brigade. This may or may not be permanent. If I make it permanent, you will get the rank to go with it. For the time being, Colonel Mwangi will act as your S-3."

Nobody in the room was more surprised than Claringdon. "Thank you, General Steeple."

"Do you have any qualms about the orders I have issued about dispatching artillery to support our allies?"

"No, sir, none."

"Good. Colonel Mwangi? Please draw up the appropriate order and have it distributed to all units."

"Yes, sir!"

"Colonel Claringdon, as your first official act, I order you to arrest Colonel Saw. The chain of command probably means you should order Adder to do it. He's touchy about things like that."

"What are your orders if General Saw resists?"

"*Colonel* Saw... as of this moment, he's no longer a general. And if he gives you any trouble, shoot him."

Claringdon's first act as brigade commander was to turn Khin Saw's arrest over to four Chinese guards who were off duty. As General Steeple had said, technically it should have been Adder's responsibility, but he found no reason to let that grotesque man share in General Steeple's goodwill. This had to be done for his fallen comrades in the RSVS.

With Khin Saw out of the way, his position was unassailable. The brigade only had so many senior officers, and most were now either dead or discredited. He'd never been to the secondary command center, nicknamed The Deuce, but he knew where it was, and while clearing out Fleming's people would take time, compared to his situation a week ago, he had no complaints.

#

Chapter 9

"Flying without feathers is not easy; my wings have no feathers."
Plautus

Operation Comeback, Air Force Annex
1918 hours, May 1

The underground runway stretched for nearly a full mile, every inch of it with high-rez, multi-colored LEDs embedded in the concrete floor and overhead lighting that could be switched on or off in sections. The main runway was 200 feet wide, with taxiways from revetments and workshop areas spaced every one hundred yards. Warehouses, machine shops, barracks, mess halls, latrines, and entertainment rooms all emptied into the main runway space. The entire structure had been designed with survivability in mind, against everything from earthquakes to nuclear weapons. Only a direct hit from a medium-sized nuke would penetrate the overhead protection.

With Operation Comeback now divided into opposing forces, Major General William Schiller didn't need to affect a stoic outward demeanor; it was his natural state. He rarely smiled or frowned, although he tended to scowl. He despised disorganization almost as much as he did displays of emotion, both of which made him an excellent logistician. The image he projected was of a no-nonsense, unemotional officer who valued only excellence in the performance of one's duty. But the one thing he couldn't control was the tips of his ears, which turned bright red whenever he was angry, excited, or embarrassed. It had earned him the code name *Red Ears* from his two Zombies, Glide and Frosty, both of whom rode in the emvee's third-row seats. Beside him in the middle row was Major Astrid Naidoo.

"Up here is where we're assembling the Warthogs," said the driver, 2nd Lieutenant Shannon Hartmann. Although small — she stood no taller than five feet — Hartmann handled the aircraft technicians like a circus ringmaster.

"Where do we stand with that?" asked Naidoo, beating General Schiller to the punch.

"Since the general told us to do them one at a time, a lot better. With all the techs awake and acclimated, we'll have the first one ready for testing in twenty-four to forty-eight hours. Whoever stored these for long-term preservation did a masterful job."

"I doubt we'll ever know who did it," Naidoo said.

"We do know, ma'am. It was me."

Naidoo laughed. Schiller kept his poker face, but once again his ears turned crimson. "Excellent work, Lieutenant," he said.

"Thank you, sir, but until we get pilots, it doesn't matter much."

"We were ordered to get them ready, Lieutenant, not to fly them."

"Yes, sir," Hartmann said. From her tone, he could tell that she wanted to say more.

"What else, Lieutenant? You won't anger me. I want to hear it."

"Sir, word has gotten around that since we have allied with the Chinese and the Sevens, and I guess the Rednecks, too, not all of our troops have gone along with these changes. I mean, that *is* why we've sealed off our part of Comeback, isn't it?"

The general nodded. "It is, Lieutenant. General Steeple is not the legal commander of the brigade."

"Yes, sir, that's what I thought you'd say. What they're worried about, my technicians, I mean, is that we'll put these A-10s back into service and they'll wind up being used against our own people."

Schiller thought about that. Hartmann made a good point, and he had to agree it was a valid concern. Unless something changed, if those A-10s got into the air on a strike mission, it didn't matter who they hit, they'd be attacking fellow Americans. *He* would never allow such a thing, but there was no guarantee he'd remain in command of them, and two squadrons of fully loaded A-10 Thunderbolt IIs represented an enormous amount of killing power. And while the base was sealed and supposedly impregnable, Schiller had read too much history about impregnable fortresses that somehow fell to the enemy anyway to be certain they could hold out.

"Lieutenant, I share your concern. Once those aircraft are in flyable condition, do we have access to explosives to rig demolition charges to prevent that from happening?"

"There could be some C-4 in storage."

Schiller shook his head. There wasn't, not at Comeback.

"It's not necessary anyway, General," Hartmann said. "We'll just whip up some Molotov cocktails."

"Very well, Lieutenant, please do so."

2049 hours

Major General Schiller put his left ear against the huge titanium blast door. A whirring sound was faint, but clearly audible. It could only mean one thing.

"When did this start?" he said, looking at his security chief, the Zombie named Glide.

"Frosty alerted me," Glide said, indicating her team member.

"It started maybe half an hour ago. I don't think I'd worry too much about it just yet; those doors are three feet thick."

"They have access to industrial mining drills and almost unlimited explosives, including C-4, dynamite, and thermite."

"Thermite?" Glide said. "In such a case, we are screwed."

"She's right, General," Frosty said. "Thermite can melt the shit out of titanium. If they've got enough to get through that door, that is, which would be a lot if we're talking about grenades. But it's still gonna take 'em a while. First they've gotta drill the holes and that'll take forever right there. I guess they could come through the walls..."

Schiller put his head down, thinking. "No, they can't do that," he said. "The walls are part of the mountain itself. If they go drilling into the living rock, they might cause a collapse."

"That doesn't mean they won't do it."

"Whatever they may be, I do not believe them to be stupid. All they need to do is continue what they're already doing. It will take time, but eventually they'll breach the door."

"Then what, we shoot 'em as they come through?"

Schiller grimaced. "Dear God, I hope it doesn't come to that."

"We could electrify the door," Glide said. "There are certainly portable electric generators here, yes?"

"If they were enemies, that would be an excellent suggestion," Schiller said. "But they're not, they're fellow Americans, and that much amperage could kill them."

Frosty shrugged. "So? It's them or us, right?"

"Perhaps so, but a man can only be responsible for what *he* does, not what others do."

They stood, listening, for a few more minutes, until Lieutenant Hartmann pulled up in an emvee. "Call for you, sir. It's General Steeple."

As he slid into the middle row, Schiller had no doubt what the call meant. Steeple needed Operation Comeback under his control again, and in particular, he needed the air assets that Schiller currently controlled. The problem was that eventually he would get them, regardless of what Schiller did next, and he expected Steeple to make precisely that argument. The disgraced Steeple would say anything to get Schiller to open up and let his supporters in without a fight, so in that regard it made for an easy decision. But how many of Lieutenant Hartmann's people would get hurt by his holding out? And what good would a few days make in the long run? Nobody made it to bird colonel without first commanding troops, but Schiller had never yet had to make decisions that could mean injury or death to most of his command.

Because the Air Force had lagged so far in time behind the Army in preparing their version of Operation Overtime, the most sophisticated and state-of-the-art equipment filled every inch of the communications center, the latest generation equipment from before the Collapse. The design of the aboveground antenna farm allowed for instantaneous global communications, so contact with Operation Overtime presented no problems at all.

Schiller sat in an office chair and one of the airmen handed him a headset with flip-down microphone. "Major General Schiller speaking," he said.

"Bill? Tom Steeple here. I wanted to inform you personally that I'm sending Colonel Claringdon over to Comeback to replace you. You and I need to have a face to face conversation concerning how you can best serve the brigade moving forward. I asked you to join Operation Overtime because I recognize your talent, and I can honestly say that I and your country will desperately need those talents in the future. I give my word there will be no repercussions for your... emotional outburst yesterday. It's entirely understandable. Colonel Claringdon should be there in the morning, arriving by helicopter. Please see to an orderly transition."

"It will be orderly, because there will be no transition, not until and unless General Angriff gives the order."

After a slight pause, Steeple continued. "Did you not hear what happened to General Angriff?"

"I heard your announcement, if that is what you mean."

"Then you know that he is dead."

"I know that you *stated* he is dead."

"I do not understand, Bill."

"I think you do. Stating that he is dead, and him being dead, are not the same thing."

"Are you calling me a liar?"

"I am stating a fact."

"I told my staff that you were reasonable. It would appear that I was wrong."

"Is there anything else?"

"No."

"Then I have work to do."

#

Chapter 10

"Death is the dropping of the flower that the fruit may swell."
Henry Ward Beecher

Operation Overtime, Angriff quarters
2225 hours, May 1

Despite the nausea and nagging cough she couldn't seem to shake, and the morning's horrific news about Nick's death, Janine Angriff gave Morgan a smile and hug after hearing that her daughter was pregnant. It lifted, if only for a moment, the pall of tragedy hanging over the family. Coupled with the uncertainly of Joe Randall's fate, it seemed to be more than she could bear, but now... soon she would have a grandchild, something new to live for.

"I am so happy for you, sweetheart," she said.

The small living room had never before held so many people, with both Joe Ootoi and Howard Dupree being visibly uncomfortable standing in a general's private quarters. Both had protested attending what amounted to a wake, not because they didn't want to support their girlfriends, but because it seemed like such an intrusion on the family's grief. With their patriarch dead, and Morgan's husband missing, neither man knew any words of comfort that would help. But Janine Angriff could read their body language like reading a book, and the moment they'd sat down, she'd patted both of them on the knee and thanked them for coming.

Attempts at conversation all died. Even Janine found it hard to put a good face on things. Her skin seemed to have shrunk into her body, and it had a blotchy pattern that she'd never seen before. Combined with all her other symptoms, she had thought there might be something dire going on with her and Cynthia, who felt as bad as she did. But now, even the news of a grandbaby seemed to render all of that irrelevant. If Nick was dead, how could she go on?

"Mom, are you okay?" Cynthia said.

Janine shook her head, coming out of the reverie. "I'm sorry. Yes, baby, I'm fine."

Instead of spurring conversation, the brief exchange was nothing more than an interlude in the silence.

Finally, Nikki spoke up. "I'm not trying to blow smoke, but... never mind."

Morgan smiled through tears that dripped off her cheeks. "It's okay, you're one of the family now. Say what you want to say."

"I've been around Saint Nick a lot. I mean, it's so weird to say it out loud, I've been around *Dad* a lot and... look, I'm not trying to give anybody false hope or anything, but I'm not buying it."

"Buying what?" Cynthia said.

"I don't think Dad's really dead."

#

Part Two

Pieces in Motion

Chapter 11

"When Jupiter calls me to wake, I shall wake."
Engraving discovered on a Roman memorial on the Capitoline Hill, Rome

CHILSS Chamber, Operation Comeback
0632 hours, May 2

When asked afterward the moment at which self-awareness returned, no one who came out of Long Sleep could ever pinpoint it to more than a vague realization of returning consciousness. It wasn't like flipping a switch, but more like slowly turning a dial. One moment everything seemed like a half-remembered dream, and then it crystallized into something more. Certainly Captain J. Babb, USAF, could not later be more specific.

The first thing he felt was a strange tightness in his chest when he drew a breath, almost as if gears were turning that hadn't been used in a while. It didn't hurt exactly; it was more like a weight had been lifted off his chest. His eyes felt heavy, like they did after the optometrist numbed them for a glaucoma test.

"Sir?" a voice said. "Captain Babb? You're awake again, sir. Can you hear me?"

Forcing open his eyes, he saw the round face of a man with black skin, but a bright light made him blink. He closed them again and turned his head away.

"That's good, Captain, you're regaining motor function. I'm Sergeant Hardaway, you're in a CHILSS inside Operation Comeback, and you're now waking up from Long Sleep. Can you tell me your name?"

Babb tried to moisten his lips, but his mouth was too dry. Hardaway held a squeezer of water with a straw-like neck close enough for him to sip. The first swallow hurt a little because the long unused throat muscles had to stretch, but the liquid felt wonderful going down, and the second mouthful went down much easier.

"Where... did..." he said in a hoarse whisper.

"You're at Operation Comeback, Captain Babb. Operation Comeback... But, sir, let's save the questions and work on getting your body used to moving again, okay? The sooner we get your blood pressure up to normal, the sooner you regain your mental acuity."

The USAF pilots had been brought to Overtime before the Air Force belatedly started their own cryogenics program. The initial priority had been to first build the underground complex attached to Operation Comeback, and then to relocate all Air Force personnel in Long Sleep to the new facility. In the meantime, they were to continue being housed at Overtime, since it was already set up to receive them. But the Air Force never got the chance to catch up, or the Navy either, before the Collapse began. Once that happened, there had been no time to plan for the future, only a mad scramble to save whatever could be saved. Only a few of the A-10 pilots had been transferred to the USAF facility at Comeback.

Babb was the most senior A-10 pilot among those in Long Sleep at Comeback, and by far had the most combat hours in the the flying dump truck affectionately called the Warthog. He was also the first person brought out of Long Sleep in more than six months. Most of those still in their CHILSS at the Air Force attachment were his fellow A-10 pilots, while those at Overtime had mostly logged their flight time in F-15s, F-16s, a few in F-22s, and the rest in F-35s.

After he woke up enough to hold a conversation, Sergeant Hardaway finally answered the questions Babb had been asking for nearly an hour — why was he being awakened now, and, more to the point, when *was* now?

Hardaway checked his chart before answering. "Let me answer the second question first, Captain. Now is sixty-four years after you went into Long Sleep."

"But that... that would make this 2076."

"Yes, sir, that's correct. As to why you were brought back now, you'll have to ask General Schiller that. He wants to meet with you as soon as you're medically cleared."

"Who is General Schiller?"

"Again, sir, it's a little complicated... actually, it's very complicated. I'm not even sure that *I* know exactly what's going on."

"I see," Babb said in his courtly Southern accent. "Then just one more thing, Sergeant... The country, how are things going with the country?"

"You mean America?"

"Yes."

Hardaway looked down and rolled his tongue over his teeth, obviously thinking. "Better than they were, Captain, better than they were."

0731 hours, May 2
Jemez Springs, NM, AKA Shangri-La

Abigail Deak could barely keep her eyes open. She'd been shoveling all night, along with a dozen other survivors of the fight three days ago, to bury the bodies of her friends and family who hadn't survived. She was so tired that her sense of smell was deadened to the stench of decaying flesh, and moisture from exhaling had soaked the rag tied around her nose and mouth.

In the beginning, it had been emotionally draining. Even now she worked through tears and heaving sobs. Streaks ran down her grimy cheeks as she gazed into the twisted faces of people she'd known her entire life. One young mother had part of her skull blown off, and flies crawled on the brain matter within the remaining cavity. A boy of ten, who had showed a talent for carving wood, had no legs below the thigh.

They'd put the cemetery near the walled enclosure generally referred to as The True. Inside was the amphitheater that gave the complex its name, which was a bastardization of the Greek word *théatro*, or theater. The True was the center of the greater Shangri-La community, acting as not only a meeting place, but also a market and repository for shared assets.

There was no time to bury the dead individually, so they dug until they couldn't dig any more and then filled the hole with bodies until it was full. If it was too shallow, they piled rocks on top. Shifts changed every twelve hours or so, because the biggest threat now was disease spread from the rotting corpses by flies, rats, and mosquitoes. Riflemen had to stand by in case scavenging coyotes came to investigate. Deak only took short breaks. As chief of the Jemez Pueblos, she felt it was her duty to outwork all others.

With the coming of dawn, Johnny Rainwater found her covered in dirt and slump-shouldered with exhaustion. He handed her a fired ceramic plate heaped with corn tortillas slathered with butter and honey, with three thick slabs of bacon. Raking hair out of her eyes, she first grabbed the water pitcher and drank half. Then, taking the plate, she plopped down right on the edge of the newest grave pit and pulled down the rag. Stench or no stench, she meant to eat before the flies could get it.

"I'm so hungry," she said between bites.

"After you finish eating, I want you to go get some sleep. I'll take over here."

"Why are they doing this, Johnny? We're no threat to anybody."

"I don't know, Abigail. I'm not even sure they know."

"It all makes no sense. They are dying for... what? What motivates people to die attacking other people who have done them no harm?"

"Mohammad Qadim says it's their religion, that they believe if they're killed fighting us, then their souls will go to Heaven."

"I don't understand."

"Neither do I. Eat your breakfast and then go sleep. I've got to meet with Captain Sully to discuss some adjustment of our defenses, and then I'll come back and help dig."

She nodded and chewed. It was a race to finish before she fell asleep sitting up.

Operation Overtime
0745 hours, May 2

Adder found Károly Rosos in the hangar beside the Bell UH-1Y Venom, flanked by four Chinese soldiers acting as his personal bodyguard. Rosos ordered the American ground personnel around like he was their commanding officer, cursing at them for delaying takeoff to finalize some pre-flight check, and while Adder wore a slight smile, given half a chance he would have thrown the asshole off the mountain, head first. He'd long ago sold his soul, it was true, but that didn't mean he liked civilians bitching at service members. Still, there was nothing he could do about it right now, so he lied with his face.

"You weren't gonna say goodbye?" he said when he'd gotten close enough to be heard over the various air and power tools. "Where you headed?"

"There you are," Rosos said, as if Adder was somehow hard to find. "These dolts are taking me to my jet down at Prescott, if they can ever figure out how to fly this thing."

The ground crew shot them both vicious looks, but with four armed Chinese standing by, they said nothing.

Taking Adder's arm, Rosos pulled him away from the Americans. The Chinese started to follow, but Rosos shook his head. Adder looked down at the sallow man's fingers wrapped around his forearm like they were wet seaweed.

Once satisfied they couldn't be overheard, Rosos continued. "Angriff's death changes everything, so I'm going home to consult with Gyorgi and Dad."

Dad? Adder hadn't seen Old Man Rosos for several months, and assumed he'd either died or gone into a coma. That he was still alive and directing his affairs came as news. "How did Saint Nick dying change anything?"

"C'mon, Adder, GOFO—"

Adder reacted without thinking. His face reddened. "What did you say?"

Although nearly six feet tall, Rosos was thin to the point of emaciation, with pale skin and fine hair. Adder only stood a few inches taller, but even two decades after he'd joined the Army, his body remained hard muscle. His suddenly rigid stance and balled fists caused Rosos to take a step back, until the former Zombie got control of himself.

"I'm sorry, Károly," he said.

Instead of being conciliatory, however, Rosos acted like Adder had peed on his shoes. "Don't ever speak to me that way again." He waited for Adder to acknowledge the rebuke, but when ten seconds stretched into twenty, he went on. "We had leverage on Angriff, don't you remember?"

"Oh, yeah, the Kraut and his magic juice."

"Make light of it if you will, but Angriff would given anything to have that bottle of *magic juice,* as you put it. Now that he's dead, that whole initiative was for nothing."

Adder shrugged. What were a few more dead people? After one hundred, he'd lost count. "You're worried about Steeple telling you to get fucked, is that it?"

"He could, and if he does, we have to have a plan already in place to deal with it."

"We've gotten the Chinese into Overtime. Shouldn't that keep Steeple in line?"

"No, that's worse! We needed them to suppress any residual internal loyalty to Angriff, but if he's gone, then Steeple doesn't need that support. Now we're left with an ally who expects to be paid off with American weapons and technology... *our* weapons and technology, which they could then potentially use against us. It's a worst-case scenario, and we've got to discuss how to proceed from here. In the meantime, you can take care of any opposition that might arise."

Once again Adder's fist clenched. For a spoiled brat like Károly Rosos, who wouldn't know a hard day's work if it bit him on the ass, to issue orders like he was an officer or something, absolutely infuriated him. He could feel his heart racing and, at that moment, wanted to beat the little shit to death with his bare fists. Guys like Saint Nick, or Green Ghost, might be pricks, but at least they weren't afraid to get their hands dirty.

"I'm on it," he finally said, through a forced smile.

Rosos didn't notice his renewed agitation. "I'll be back soon."

"I can't wait."

#

Chapter 12

One for all and all for one...
Thomas-Alexandre Dumas

"...and every man for himself."
Curly Howard

Operation Overtime, the Crystal Palace
0804 hours, May 2

Tom Steeple looked up at the knock on his office doorjamb. "Come."

Sergeant Major Schiller brought in four mugs of coffee and was careful to serve Steeple first, then Colonel Claringdon, Colonel Saw, and finally Colonel Mwangi. Adder only wanted water.

"Will there be anything else, General?"

"No, Schiller, thank you." Once they were alone again, Steeple folded his hands on the desk and smiled. "I trust you all slept well?"

Adder didn't even shift in place. "I never have trouble sleeping."

"It is not typically an affliction which troubles me," chimed in Claringdon.

"Amy?" Steeple was well aware that using her nickname implied a level of intimacy that he didn't share with Claringdon, which was his point in doing it. It was a reminder to Claringdon that, while he was higher in the chain of command than Mwangi, he shouldn't get too comfortable.

"Not bad."

"Khin?"

"Sorry, General, I don't sleep well with armed Chinese standing outside my door."

Adder shrugged and answered, as if Saw had spoken to him and not Steeple. "They're no better or worse than any other soldiers. You can trust 'em to do whatever is best for them."

"They're the enemy," Saw said.

"They're not *my* enemy, but right now they're yours," Adder said.

Rather than let the conversation deteriorate, which it could easily have done, Steeple cut them both off. "Khin, this is the new reality. It is not how I wanted it, but what is done is done. We all have to live with it. I asked you back here because I understand this is harder for some people, and I truly want your support."

"General Steeple, I will carry out any lawful order you give me. I don't have to agree with a policy to carry it out, but since it's obvious that I'm an outlier in this discussion, may I be excused to return to my quarters?"

Tom Steeple considered himself every bit the warrior that Khin Saw was, or Nick Angriff, for that matter. The difference was their chosen battlefields and weapons. Whereas Saw and Angriff used guns and tanks to defeat America's enemies, Steeple used guile and compromise to give them the tools they needed to do their jobs. He had perfected one of his most effective gestures during countless meetings over the decades, which he considered his battles, with everyone from recalcitrant lieutenants to presidents of the United States. He sucked in a noisy breath and exhaled in a grunt-like sigh that was just loud enough to be heard. It voiced his displeasure without the need for saying anything.

"Go, Colonel Saw, you may return to confinement. But know that I hope and pray for your early acceptance of the new reality."

Saw started to say something, then stopped himself and wasted no time in leaving. Steeple watched him pass the Chinese guards and noted the mutual hatred reflected in their faces. He shook his head, but ignored the confrontation to keep the meeting on track. Nor did he respond to Adder's smirk. "He may yet come around."

"You're dreaming, sir," Adder said. "He's a hardass just like Angriff was. Waving the flag is all they've got."

That's why I want him, you idiot, Steeple thought but didn't say. Nor did his face betray his true feelings. "Amy, have you finished your initial personnel review?"

"All except logistics and intelligence. I can't finish those until I know what's going to happen with Colonels Schiller and Kordibowski. If they're removed, it sets off a chain reaction in their sections."

"Schiller has burned his bridges, but do not let his brother know it. From what I can tell, Sergeant Major Schiller is doing an excellent job running this headquarters company, and doing that for *my* headquarters is not an easy thing to do. Now, with Kordibowski, there may still be hope. Keep him confined to quarters and treated correctly and then we'll see if a week alone changes his mind about serving under my leadership. By all accounts he is an excellent officer and an Academy man too, so we cannot simply flush such irreplaceable training and experience down the drain without first doing everything we can to bring him around."

Mwangi wrote on her legal pad before asking her next question. "What did you decide about... Hull, Lieutenant Lester Earl Hull?"

"He is a defeated, deflated old man who even in his prime was probably a second-rate officer, but I gave him command of the Chinese forces moving on Prescott as an escort for the artillery anyway. He has a history there."

Neither Mwangi nor Claringdon spoke up, so Adder did. "You gave him command of PLA forces? What the hell—" Adder stopped and took a moment to gather himself. "Sorry, General, but the man is a joke. He calls himself George Patton."

Steeple pursed his lips and nodded. "True. I have no faith in his leadership abilities beyond brutally suppressing whatever opposition he meets, which is why I sent Colonel Zongchang with him."

"Thereby getting him out of our hair," Claringdon said. "Very smart move, General."

"Didn't I hear there was a Marine battalion in Prescott?" Adder said. "The Chinese don't have more than a couple of rifle companies."

"They are Marines in name only," Steeple said. "Most are former members of a paramilitary organization run by Lieutenant Hull in his Patton persona, which is the main reason I sent him there. They are also commanded by a man named... what was his name, Amy?"

"Ummm... Cranston, Norbert Cranston."

"Yes, Cranston. He was Hull's senior officer."

Claringdon smirked, obviously glad to contribute to the discussion. "I think there is something of which you are not aware, General. Hull, or rather his people, had gotten six old M1s back into combat condition and they engaged elements of my tank battalion during the fighting in Prescott. Sadly, one of the M1s was a total write-off. It was destroyed by none other than General Angriff's oldest daughter, Lieutenant Randall."

"Morgan Randall," Mwangi said.

"I remember her and her husband," Steeple said. "Both very good at their jobs. I had to sign off on a waiver so they could both join. I'm not surprised she knocked out an enemy tank. What happened to the rest of them?"

"They were brought back up to factory specifications and stationed in Prescott as a ready reaction force, General," Claringdon said. "And so they're available to the so-called Marine battalion stationed there."

"That changes things," Adder said.

Steeple shook his head "I don't think that it does. Follow me on this. If those tanks fire on American vehicles or artillery, then they will be guilty of firing on friendly forces. It puts the onus on them, and not on us."

Claringdon snapped his fingers. "And we could then use air strikes against them!"

"Why couldn't we do that anyway?" said Mwangi.

"Psychologically, it makes a big difference, Amy," Steeple said. "If the pilots are asked to destroy tanks with American markings, then they're killing their countrymen, their fellow soldiers. However, if the tanks fire on other Americans first, then they are the ones killing their countrymen. The gunships could then go into action to protect American lives."

"Genius," she said. "I've worked for you a long time, General Steeple, and yet sometimes I still underestimate you."

"Thank you, Amy." Steeple noticed Adder's face darken and his eyes roll. That was a man he would have to watch very carefully. For now, he ignored the response. "Where do we stand with the artillery moving to New Mexico, Colonel Claringdon?"

"A full battery of M270s leaves this morning at eleven hundred hours, escorted by two companies from 3rd Mechanized Infantry Battalion, with their armor and one half of the battalion's logistics train. There will also be a company of engineers with bridging equipment and fuel trucks. The plan calls for a forward fuel and ammunition dump to be set up just over the New Mexico border. We estimate two days' travel time, plus another twenty-four hours to advance to contact and site the tubes. They should be ready for action no later than three days from now at twelve hundred hours."

"Excellent. Good work, Fitz."

Claringdon nodded in thanks, obviously pleased at being called by his nickname.

"What is the status of the battery we're sending to Sierra?"

"Colonel Coughlan is overseeing preparations and transport. He will have four guns in place in two days, along with sufficient ammunition supply and logistics support. He is personally deploying to the area."

Steeple rubbed his hands together and leaned back in the swivel chair, as he did when thinking. The next order of business was the stickiest: what to do about Comeback? "Thoughts?" he said, after asking for opinions on the subject.

All three of the other officers glanced at Adder.

"What are the points of ingress?" Adder said.

"There is only one that we know of," Steeple replied. "A blast door designed to withstand a medium-yield nuclear weapon. It connects the Air Force annex to the rest of Comeback. Our people inside Comeback are currently using drills, explosives, and thermite to try and get through the door, but as you might imagine, that is a slow process."

"May I suggest that we simply starve them out?" Claringdon said. "Their supplies cannot last forever."

"What about that, Amy?" Steeple said. "As I think you both know, Colonel Mwangi was my operations officer at Comeback. Do we have a good idea of their food supply?"

"Unfortunately, we do. If they're careful, they can hole in there for years."

Adder didn't bother hiding his disgust. "There's only *one* way in, and that's nuke-proof? What the hell were you thinking... sir?"

Steeple recognized that dealing with Adder meant letting rebukes like that one slide. "We did not build it, nor were we supplied with blueprints by the Air Force. Apparently they did not trust us with that information. There may be another point of ingress, but if there is, we are not aware of it."

"If it's able to survive a nuke, that means we can't go in from above."

Steeple spread his hands in a sort of mini-shrug. "Based on what we know, I would say that is correct."

"All right, let me think for a second." Easing forward, Adder leaned on his knees. "What's the reason for us needing to get in there? The assets?"

"Precisely. Two squadrons of A-10s could be an invaluable asset, but as we've seen already, the Air Force personnel are a wild card. In the hands of our enemies, those jets could be a potent weapon against us."

"And," Mwangi said, "they have a lot of Stingers. That puts our air component at risk, if they join with our enemies."

Adder said, "Just to clarify, by 'our enemies' you mean Americans who defy your authority, right?"

"Yes," Steeple said. "Now that we know where we stand, can anyone think of an action plan to get us in there?"

They all glanced at each other, making it obvious that nobody could think of a way into a bunker complex meant to survive anything short of a direct hit from a high-yield nuclear device. Silence held for half a minute.

Until Adder broke it. "How do they launch their planes?"

"They can do it in two ways," Mwangi said. "First, there's an above-ground runway, with two elevators for lifting aircraft. There's nothing special about the runway itself, but it's matched by an underground one of nearly the same length. At each end, there's an angled ramp that allows for takeoffs from directly underground."

"That's your answer, General," Adder said.

"Please elaborate."

"It's simple. I'm betting you know the location of this runway, right? So you post a fast-reaction force there. The second they start lowering a ramp or elevator, you use that to gain access to the underground base."

"It could be months or years before that happens," Claringdon said.

"Yeah, maybe, but it negates them using those Warthogs against us."

Steeple's face brightened. "I like it, Adder. I like it a lot. It is not an elegant solution, but sometimes brute force is all the elegance you need. Fitz, put together a company-sized unit for long-term deployment in the vicinity of the runway. Make sure they are equipped with Stingers. On my authorization, they are to nullify any aircraft that attempts to take off without my permission."

After the meeting ended, Mwangi held back as Claringdon and Adder left.

Steeple said nothing until they were alone. "Things are going well. So what's on your mind, Amy?"

"I want to make sure you haven't changed your mind about letting me accompany the task force to New Mexico."

Steeple opened his mouth to respond, closed it again, and leaned back. He finished his coffee, which was ice cold by that point. *Damn her.* She knew him too well.

"You *had* changed your mind, hadn't you?" she said.

"Convince me it's a good idea. Why would you want to do such a thing?"

"It's hard to explain, exactly. As you know, I've never had a combat command, yet I now find myself the S-3 for a combat general—"

"Khin Saw? I revoked his promotion and unless he accepts my authority, he will not lead this brigade."

"Not him, Tom, *you.*"

"Me? If Khin is not in charge of combat operations, then Claringdon is."

"You can deny it all you want, Tom, but you are the brigade commander. Khin would be *your* S-3."

"That's *your* position."

"No, it's not. You've effectively created a new position for whichever commander you settle on, and if something happens to you, then that man takes over. If it's Khin, then given his opposition to your initiatives, he could undo everything you're trying to accomplish."

"Do I have a choice? Khin has actually been in combat, Amy. Hell, from what I understand, he was under fire last year at Prescott. But since he is openly defying me, I'm boxed in. Claringdon is the only other realistic choice, and he also has combat experience."

"You cannot trust Khin, even if he crawls back on his hands and knees. And while I'm not doubting Claringdon's courage, I'm doubting his ability to lead the most complex military unit in the history of the U.S. Army. And as I said, if something happens to you, he's in charge. How do you think that would go? Honestly, not what you think I should hear, tell me what you really think."

"We have already had this conversation."

"And nothing was decided, Tom. I'm not trying to be a bitch here, okay? But if I can't tell you the truth, who can? Do you really think Claringdon can lead these people?"

"He's a fanatic."

"He's a damned Stalinist!"

Steeple slowed his words down to give them a thoughtful tone. "That is not necessarily a bad thing, Amy. The only difference between a murderous dictator and a benevolent one is who writes the history. Besides, do I have another choice?"

"Send me to New Mexico, and maybe you will."

"Are you saying that you want to be the combat commander?"

"I'm saying that I'm the only one you can count on to bring your vision for the new United States into being, because I'm the only one who knows what that means. I'm also the only one you know that you can one hundred percent trust. If I prove myself in combat, that might give you an option that you can count on no matter what."

They had known each other so long that Steeple recognized the sub-currents in their conversations, as he did now. "You're thinking about the Congressional order."

"Yes. Somebody entered Overtime after it was sealed, and until you know who, you can't trust anyone except me. But without combat experience, I can't expect veteran troops to follow me."

Steeple scratched his neck, rose, and walked over to the edge of the office and stared out the big picture window at the desert. Hands in his pockets, he stayed silent for nearly two minutes, and Mwangi knew better than to break his reverie. He finally responded without turning around.

"Okay, Amy, you win. Permission granted. But please be careful. As you have just so eloquently made clear, I cannot afford to lose you."

#

Chapter 13

For the strength of the pack is the wolf, and the strength of the wolf is the pack.
Rudyard Kipling

Sierra Army Depot, Herlong, CA
1129 hours, May 2

"Could you use some reinforcements, Socrates?"

Norm Fleming glanced up from the disassembled M4 on the work table, trying to keep the surprise out of his expression. The truth was, he'd never expected either man to be fit for combat again so soon, and where Claw was concerned, he hadn't been sure he could *ever* return to combat. Vapor had only been hit in the calf, so Fleming had assumed he'd be ready to fight again eventually. Yet here were both men holding rifles, wearing sidearms and helmets.

"If I didn't know better, I'd say you two were soldiers."

"That's just an ugly rumor," Claw said. Fleming noted that his breathing appeared shallow.

"Didn't you have broken ribs and a cracked sternum?"

"Something like that, but I heal fast."

"Uh-huh. And what about you, Vapor, didn't that bullet take a chunk out of your calf muscle?"

"No worries, boss. I've got more muscles than I know what to do with."

"Uh-huh. So what do you two cripples think you can do to help around here? I'd let you sweep the floor, but we don't have a broom."

"That truly hurts, sir," Vapor said.

Claw cut Vapor off to stop him from dragging it out. "Socrates, we figure you need scouts out to the west. I think you know that's kind of what we do, so with your permission we'd like to do it."

Fleming put down the rag he'd been using to clean his weapon, folded his arms, and leaned against the edge of the bench. There was only natural lighting inside the old metal warehouse he used as a headquarters, with daylight coming in through the wide, sliding double doors, the glassless windows, and a few score bullet holes left over from the battle nearly two weeks before. It made for a gloomy interior. Battle lamps used after dark gave only a third as much light.

"I can't spare any radios, boys, so how do you propose getting me reports?"

Both men looked around, telling Fleming all he needed to know; they hadn't thought that far ahead.

"Look, you've both done your part. Go back to the BAS and take it easy. Heal up. If the Chinese break through in the meantime, you've got your weapons and can defend those who can't defend themselves."

"Come on, boss—"

Fleming held up a hand. "I'll tell you what. Give yourselves three more days to get better, and then I'll send you out with a radio. Fair enough?"

Both men nodded.

"Good, get back to bed."

"One thing, Socrates."

"What's that?"

"The nurses, most of 'em have beards and smell bad."

#

Chapter 14

Then Allah sent among them a New Prophet, to bring them warnings of ruin should they continue to allow infidels to infest his Earth, and bade them now to pray seven times each day to show their repentance.
From The Revelations of Nabi Husem Allah, Chapter 1, Verse 3

Albuquerque, New Mexico
1619 hours, May 2

Mosquitoes had followed the three field generals of the Sword of the Prophet into the house, as el Mofty discovered when he smacked one feeding on the back of his left hand. The presence of General Muhdin surprised him. Four men carried him on a makeshift litter, a wooden door with a chair nailed down near one end. Muhdin wore his uniform coat and shirt. A blanket covered his lower half. The pallor of his skin told el Mofty all he needed about that general's condition. Sati Bashara and Tracy Gollins, the other two generals, also swatted at mosquitoes.

With them was Counselor Ibrahim Yaseen, his brother the Prophet's not-so-secret spy in his headquarters. A tray of meat and bread awaited them, along with a pitcher of water and a set of mismatched glasses. What weren't present were chairs. While the others stood, the litter bearers set Muhdin on the floor gently and then left without making eye contact with anyone, especially not with the only woman in the room.

Yaseen and the emir's nephew, Sati Bashara, stood beside Muhdin's litter, so the three males were all in the far corner of what had once been the house's den, while General Tracy Gollins stood in the center of the room, near el Mofty. The blatant animosity toward her irritated him, but it was his and his brother's own fault. The book that his brother, the New Prophet, allegedly wrote rigidly placed women as being subservient to men in all things, including the command of troops in the field, and at the moment that was a giant pain in the ass.

Sitting against his chair back, Muhdin spoke in a low voice. "My lord—"

El Mofty held up his hand. "The doctors tell me your wound is mortal, General Muhdin. I pray to Allah that they are wrong."

"Thank you, Blessed One. They told me not an hour ago that I may yet survive, if I can avoid infection."

"Then you must do exactly as they say. Do not tax your strength with us here. You may go."

"No, please, Blessed One, let me stay. If I die in service to our beloved New Prophet, then surely Allah cannot deny me a place in Heaven, not if you pray on my behalf."

El Mofty stroked his beard and smiled with his eyes, in the way he'd learned to do very early in life when he'd conned women into believing he was in love with them. Such deceptions had become second nature to him after so long. He held up his right hand, palm out, and muttered a benefaction for his wounded general, but losing Muhdin wouldn't be a terrible blow. Although quite good at turning a horde of ill-disciplined thugs into something resembling an army, Muhdin had proven to be a poor tactician. The biggest decision if he died would be whether to split up his command, or name a successor, and if he chose that option, who? None of Muhdin's officers showed much potential for higher command.

"How are your regiments, generals?" he said.

"Ready to renew the battle, Blessed One," Muhdin said, his chin held high. "They wish only to destroy the enemies of the New Prophet."

"How many men did you lose in the fighting?"

"I... my officers have not yet completed counting our losses."

"Approximately, then."

"One hundred dead, perhaps twice that number wounded." Muhdin grimaced, reached up to take something off the tray on the table, and pretended to eat a slice of goat. It didn't fool el Mofty, though, as Muhdin couldn't hide the agony ripping through his groin. "The infidel devils... put rattlesnakes in traps... at least five of my men were bitten."

"I heard, and that was a terrible thing to do. By definition, infidels are uncivilized, but your losses were reasonable, General Muhdin, considering the unexpected arrival of the American Marines once again. You and your men fought well."

Muhdin tried not to gasp as he spoke, but couldn't suppress it. "They were the same Marines as in Arizona, Blessed One."

"Do you mean, the exact same *men*?"

"I do. According to some of my men who fought last year, the markings on their vehicles match. Specifically, the bumper numbers are the same... could someone hand me a glass of water, please?" Closing his eyes, he lay against the chair back, panting. Bashara poured him some water and Muhdin drank it all.

"What about you, Sati? You had a terrible fight for Los Alamos, correct?"

"Yes, Uncle, the enemy were not many, but they fought well beyond their numbers. I lost seventy-seven men killed and eighty-two wounded. A terrible price."

"Yet less than it might have been. General Gollins, how did your regiments fare?"

"The infidels chopped down a lot of trees to block the road. We had to attack them in turn, one after the other. I stayed right up front to make sure we kept going. We lost somewhere around a hundred men dead, and maybe that many more wounded."

El Mofty shook his head and closed his eyes, as if in prayer. The truth was that the knot near his shoulder blade had begun to burn again. "Three hundred of our best men dead. That is a price I did not expect to pay for such a place. And yet now that we are engaged here, we cannot turn away. We must conquer this blasphemous citadel that is an affront to Allah, or die in the effort."

"Let us attack again at dawn, Uncle. I *know* that victory will be ours."

Counselor Yaseen hadn't spoken yet, so el Mofty decided it was time to make him commit to a course of action. Only after he'd set the stage properly would he reveal the contact made by the Americans. "Yaseen, you are a wise man. What is your counsel?"

"These are military matters, my lord. My talents lie elsewhere."

"Nonsense, wisdom is wisdom. It costs us nothing to share opinions here, among friends, and I would like to hear your thoughts on this matter. Should we attack again at first light, or not?"

But Yaseen had lived with the New Prophet and his ruthless brother for decades, which in the hierarchy of the Caliphate was no mean feat. He was not so easily trapped. "Before deciding, O Blessed One, I would need to know everything that you know. Perhaps there is a reason to wait of which I am unaware?"

El Mofty and his unloved counselor smiled at each other, with the firm knowledge there was nothing friendly about their exchange.

"Perhaps there is." That brought Gollins and Bashara to rigid attention, and even Muhdin sat up straighter. "Early today, I received a message from the American commander, General Steeple—"

"That is not who was in charge last year!" Bashara said. "It was General Angriff."

"Yes, my nephew, you are correct. Something has changed. I cannot say *why*, but the Americans claim to want a partnership of some sort."

"Such as an alliance?" said Yaseen. "That would change everything. We would have no enemies who could stand before us."

"What did this message say, Uncle?"

"General Steeple wants to align our interests as allies."

"Who is this General Steeple? Do we know?" said Yaseen. "For all we know, no such person exists."

El Mofty wanted to tell them how he *knew* that Steeple was real, but he couldn't. Even in the Caliphate, the Armstrong brothers had enemies, men hungry for power who would stop at nothing to replace them. To admit that he knew all about Tom Steeple risked alerting those potential rivals as to how he had come by such knowledge. In turn, that could lead places that could unravel five decades' worth of work. Fortunately, he didn't need to reveal what he knew.

"He exists." The raspy voice was that of El Mofty's mysterious advisor, known only as the old man. None except the Emir had even realized he was in the room until he spoke.

Bashara and Yaseen looked to el Mofty for guidance. Only rarely had they interacted with the old man, and not for quite some while. Muhdin hadn't heard the comment. He lay against the chair back, eyes closed, his teeth clenched, as if he were in great pain.

"How do you know this?" el Mofty asked, knowing damned well how he knew it.

"I don't actually *know* it, so perhaps I should say that he did exist in the pre-Collapse world. General Steeple was the most powerful man in the old United States Army, and had a reputation for ruthless cunning that was second to none."

"Would not the age of such a man, at such a time, have been at least fifty years?"

The old man nodded. "At least."

"So you are saying that he is more than one hundred years old?"

"I'm not saying anything of the sort, esteemed counselor. My information is that a General Steeple once lived, that he was very important, and that if it were possible for a man to still be alive after so much time has passed, he would be such a man."

"Thank you," el Mofty said, indicating that the old man's input was no longer wanted. "So, this is why I have called you all here tonight, to listen to your advice and decide how best to proceed from this point forward."

"If this is true," Yaseen said, "it is truly a blessing from Allah."

"*If* we can trust them," said Bashara. "But the timing of this is suspicious to me. Americans reinforced the infidels at Shangri-La, but they are not numerous enough to guarantee victory. So other Americans say they are coming to help us fight against the very people their comrades have just died to protect? It makes no sense to me. We should renew our attack before dawn tomorrow."

"The boy is right, Blessed One," Muhdin said, his voice weak but steady. "Our men will grow restless if we long delay. They are not professional soldiers, and do not have the discipline to stay inactive in the field for long."

El Mofty sat in a chair and stared into the distance, stroking his beard, as if all alone in the darkening room. He said nothing for nearly a minute. Then, "Your words make sense to me, Sati. They contain wisdom, it is true, and you have matured much in the past year as a commander. I am very proud of you. And yet the impulses of youth still haunt your judgments. As for you, Ahmednur, I fear that you are right. If we do not fight, then we must find something for the men to do, something productive that will keep their fighting spirit high."

Bashara pressed his lips together. "So you will not authorize a renewal of the attack?"

"No. This is the last army we can put in the field, and we have already lost more men than we can afford. If we attack again, we are going to suffer terrible losses again, losses we cannot replace."

"But if the Americans are lying—"

Once again el Mofty held up his hand for silence. "I know what you are going to say, Sati, that if the note is a deception, then the Americans may destroy us all. But let us say that I allow you to attack in the morning, and you capture this Shangri-La and kill the Americans there, while suffering the same casualties as you did yesterday. I have then lost hundreds more irreplaceable men, and my army is reduced by one in four of those I brought north.

"And let us then say the American General Steeple arrives and discovers that we have *not* waited for him, and instead have killed his men. If he seeks vengeance, we will be unable to withdraw, and must fight. Whether we win or we lose such a battle is of no consequence, because either way our army will be destroyed."

Again the room fell silent. There was really no argument that could be made without seeming insubordinate, and el Mofty knew it. He'd spent the entire afternoon going over his choices, and would brook no further argument on the subject, but he also had to throw his generals a bone.

"However, you are absolutely correct that we must find work for the men, and perhaps some entertainment, too. Sport, perhaps."

"We could stone some of the infidels we brought to use as shields," said Yaseen.

"Or crucify them," added Muhdin.

Even Bashara liked that idea. "The men do like blood sport."

For some reason their suggestions irritated el Mofty, although he wasn't sure exactly why. Was he getting sick of all the killing? With surprise, he realized that he might be. "Think of something else," he said,

"But Uncle, that is what must inevitably happen to infidels anyway. *The unrepentant must die.* The Revelations of Nabi Husem Allah, chapter 22, verse 3. We brought them north with us to act as human shields, but many remain alive to eat our food and drink our water. Let them serve Allah by dying, as infidels must."

Once again el Mofty slammed his fist onto the table, only this time he felt himself losing control of his temper. Even as he raged, he wasn't sure why. "I said think of something else!" He yelled so loud that an armed guard rushed into the room. "Get out, you fool!" The man blanched, wheeled, and left.

But it wasn't one of the men who spoke next, it was Gollins.

"Here's something that might work," she said.

Yaseen and Bashara turned away as if she carried leprosy, while Muhdin turned his head. El Mofty noted their disgust, and it poured gasoline onto the rage he was already fighting to control. It was his temper that had first landed him in jail all those decades ago, and he had worked hard to control it over the past fifty years. Even so, his tantrums were legendary in the Caliphate, and now the sheer idiocy of his generals pissed off the conman that still lived at his core. Stupidity among his fellow criminals was what had landed him in prison to begin with, and there it was, happening all over again a lifetime later.

None of them knew that Gollins was his daughter, and in the past he had said whatever they wanted to hear to get them to accept her in the short run. But he'd be damned if he put all of his manpower into the hands of men who could turn against him, even if one of them was his own nephew, Sati Bashara.

"I've had enough of your disrespect for one of my officers!" he screamed, slamming his fist so hard on the table that he upended the water pitcher. "*I* appointed General Gollins to command the Mecca Regiment, and when you turn your backs on her, you turn your backs on *me*! Is that your intent?"

All three men turned back around, even if they all kept scowling. And then, like the passing of a summer storm, he felt his anger subsiding. The heat in his cheeks cooled. Taking a cloth out of his robe, he wiped sweat from his face and then continued in a calmer voice. "We know not how long it will take before the Americans arrive to support our attack, while every day that passes sees us consuming more of our limited food stores, and the men grow restless. Yet when I asked you for advice, your best suggestions were more crucifixions!" He rose and stalked across the room to a picture window that had a big crack down one side. The floor felt mushy underfoot, and sagged in places.

"I am sorry, Uncle," Bashara said.

El Mofty waited for Yaleen and Muhdin to also apologize, but they didn't. Still facing the window, he turned his head and saw them both wearing defiant looks. In the shadows near the floor, Muhdin's expression might have been pain, but he didn't think so.

So it's like that, he thought. *At least now I know who I can count on, and who I can't.*

"Tell us your idea, General Gollins."

"We know the Americans are weak—"

"Weak? That's ridiculous!" Yaseen said, apparently unable to control his contempt for the woman. "Do not our dead testify to their strength?"

"Silence!" el Mofty said. "Let... her... *speak*!"

"The American are physically strong, yes, it's true, and our sacred dead are the proof. But morally they are corrupt, and that is their downfall. They value this life more than the one yet to come, and mistake compassion for strength."

"What are you suggesting, General?" asked el Mofty.

"We set the men to digging access trenches to within easy visual range of some point in the infidels' defenses. Then we dig another large trench, where we gather all of the infidels we brought with us, and the prisoners we have captured so far. If they are too many, we start with the women and children. We offer an equal trade with the infidels inside this so-called Shangri-La, one Marine for one hostage. For one of their fighting vehicles, twenty hostages. For all of the Marines and all of their weapons... all of the hostages."

"They will never accept such terms!" Yaseen said.

Muhdin nodded. "I agree. These Marines may be infidels, but they are warriors."

"But that works in our favor, too," Gollins said. "You see, we tell the people inside of Shangri-La that unless they agree to our terms, we will execute the hostages while they watch. If we assume the Marines won't surrender, then we will drive the hostages out of our trench, one by one, starting with the youngest. And once the Americans can see them clearly, we will set them afire. Then we release their mothers, and do the same to them. We let them run where they will until the flames consume them. If we do that a few times, the infidels will drive the Marines out for us."

"And if they don't?"

Gollins shrugged. "Watching infidels burn is more entertaining than watching them die on a cross."

"Yes," el Mofty said, holding up his index finger. "When the people at Shangri-La watch the blackened flesh of women and children peeling away in the flames, they will turn on the Marines. Even if they cannot drive them out, it will destroy their will to resist. This is brilliant, General Gollins, absolutely brilliant."

He grinned broadly. Minutes before, he'd been sick of all the killing, sick of death, because it reminded him of the age he felt in every joint and muscle, and of his own mortality. The grin was what his generals expected of him, just another facet of the fifty-year con. But as he visualized the deaths of which he spoke, el Mofty realized that he enjoyed them now. He had been a hardened criminal once, but not a cruel one. Sometime during the past fifty years that had changed.

Tracy Gollins bowed her head. "Thank you, my lord."

"If only the *men* leading my army were as imaginative," he said.

East of Reno, Nevada
0027 hours, May 3

The scraping sound of someone crawling toward her awakened Junker Jane, and she opened her left eye just enough to see who, or what, approached. All she could see was a moving black shadow, outlined against the embers of their fire. In the fog of sleep, she'd forgotten that Green Ghost had the first watch, so her hand inched toward the rifle which was never out of her reach. Whenever she made camp, it always had a round in the chamber.

"Jane." She barely heard the whisper, even from two feet away. Still half asleep, Jane's only thought was *It's about time.* But before she could roll over on her side, he whispered something more. "Predator."

A sudden infusion of adrenaline brought her instantly awake. In one slow but fluid motion, and without making the least sound, she brought the rifle to her right shoulder. The fire had burned down to orange coals, but it was enough. Twenty feet outside the small circle cast by the fire, a pair of round eyes glowed in the light.

"Cougar," she said in a low voice.

Green Ghost already had his rifle at the ready. "I don't have a shot."

"Don't shoot."

"What?"

Their voices grew louder as the conversation progressed.

"I said wait."

The cougar sank lower to the ground, and she knew it was in a crouch and ready to leap. She didn't have a shot, and its behavior made clear its aggressive intent, but there was one thing she had to do before they could fire.

"Toon, stop! It's Jane!" she yelled.

"What are you doing?"

Another loud growl brought the rifle to her shoulder. "That's not Toon."

The cougar sprang toward them. Green Ghost fired, but the animal's leap went higher and further than he'd anticipated. Jane knew better than to shoot when it was in the air. She would only get one shot and it had to count. The mountain lion was nothing more than a gray flash in the darkness, and it did something they didn't usually do; it leapt a second time. Both of their shots missed and she could see the huge paws and their deadly claws, the mouth filled with long, pointed teeth... and then something even bigger slammed into the cat's side and knocked it sideways in midair. It was another cougar. The two animals rolled away in a screaming heap.

Green Ghost kept the rifle trained on the sounds of the fight, which he could only dimly see. He set the M16 to automatic. "I can't make 'em out," he said.

"Don't shoot! You might hit Toon!"

"Who the fuck is Toon?"

"I'll explain later, just don't shoot!."

"Lady, if something runs toward me that's got big teeth and claws, it's getting shot!"

Green Ghost chanced throwing a couple of sticks onto the fire while the animals battled to the death. Anybody who had ever heard cats fight would have recognized the screeches and growls that came from the throats of the two cougars. The only difference was the lung power behind their screams. They saw shapes in the darkness and heard scuffling among the snarls, and then... nothing.

But Jane's nostrils dilated with a familiar scent. "Blood. One of them's dead. Be ready, but don't shoot unless I tell you."

"Look—"

She turned her head enough to give him a savage scowl. "No, you look! If you shoot my friend, the next thing you'd better be doing is running."

With new wood to consume, the flames cast a wider circle of firelight. In its flickering glare, the low-slung figure of a cougar approached their camp. The night quiet had returned and they clearly heard the big cat squawk.

"It *is* Toon," Jane said. Pointing her rifle at the ground, she grabbed a burning branch and walked into the darkness. When she got close enough, the cougar lay down on its stomach and watched her. Jane squatted down beside the big cat, using the small flame to examine it.

"Jane, what the fuck are you doing?"

"Look in my food bag. There's a jar of honey in there. Bring me that, and some water."

"Bring you?"

"Yes, bring them to me. Hurry up, she's hurt."

Three gashes along Toon's left jaw could only have come from the front claws of another cougar. Laying her rifle aside, Jane ran her hands over the cat's body, checking for more wounds. There were a few other claw scrapes, and at least one puncture wound, but nothing serious. Toon growled low in her throat as footsteps approached.

"Fuck me," Green Ghost said. He laid the bag and water bottle down beside Jane. "Is that thing your pet?"

"No, she's my friend." Rummaging in the bag, she found the honey and then noticed Toon staring up at the man with the rifle. "Go on back to camp. You're making her nervous."

"*I'm* making *her* nervous?"

"Yes."

After pouring water on the cat's face to clean away dirt, she smeared honey on it to prevent infection. Toon flicked her ears and swished her tail, but never moved until Jane had finished. Leaning close, she whispered "Thank you" in the cougar's ear, got up, and returned to her blanket.

"You want me to finish your watch?" she said, as if nothing had happened.

"I want you to explain what just happened."

"I raised Toon from a kitten, and we're friends. I protect her and she protects me. I don't know why she's here, because her territory is in the mountains around my homestead, but whyever she's here, I'm glad of it. We both missed that big male when he came for us."

Green Ghost sat with knees drawn close to his chest, arms wrapped around them. He looked as if somebody had just sucker-punched him. "This is all a dream, isn't it?"

She had to laugh at that. "Yes, it's all just a dream. And since you don't want me to start my watch, I'm going back to sleep."

"Go ahead," he said. "I might never sleep again."

#

Chapter 15

"Stupid people do stupid things. Why? Because they're stupid."
Green Ghost

Northwestern Nevada
0740 hours, May 3

At the first gray of approaching dawn, Green Ghost had gone to see if he really had dreamt the whole cougar thing, hoping that he had. But the half-eaten carcass of a dead mountain lion, covered with ants, killed that hope. They saddled up and rode off with him still unsure of what was real and what wasn't.

When sunrise once again lit the landscape, Green Ghost and Jane left Nevada State Highway 50 half a mile west of Silver Springs, right after passing the dilapidated Silver Springs Airport. Ruined houses and commercial buildings flanked them as they cut cross-country toward Alternate Highway 95. Green Ghost didn't say anything. He rode with the M16 in the crook of his right arm, on high alert for any signs of danger.

"I was through here last year," Jane said. "I didn't see anybody then. I doubt there's anybody now."

He didn't respond, or even look at her. Green Ghost hadn't survived countless firefights and missions in hostile territory by being careless, and it paid off now.

In his peripheral vision, he spotted a glint in the third floor window of a warehouse to his left. Battle-honed reflexes made him spin in the saddle, while simultaneously bringing the rifle up to his eye, before his brain even registered the danger. No decision had to be made about what the glint could have been, because he'd seen it many times in the past — it was sunlight, reflecting off a rifle barrel.

He followed a three-round burst with a second one. Jagged shards remaining attached to the window frame exploded. The unknown rifleman fired once but missed.

The horses reared and whinnied at the sudden gunfire. Jane controlled hers but Green Ghost's bolted and ran. By the time he got the animal under control again, the warehouse was blocked by the upper story of an old auto repair place with no roof. Jane wasn't beside him any more.

Damn!

He jerked the horse's head around and kicked it in the ribs. It leapt forward as he leaned over its neck, gripping its sweaty body tight with his legs. Muscles flexed and stretched under his fingers. Rounding the house's corner, he kicked the horse to greater speed and aimed it straight for the warehouse. On the side nearest him, Jane's horse grazed on clumps of greenery. Its saddle was empty because she'd beat him into the barn.

Reining in the horse proved harder than he'd imagined, and before he could dismount shots rang out in the warehouse, three at first, then two more. After running toward the nearest doorway, he stopped with his back to the wall, listening. The door hung at an angle from one rusted hinge, partially blocking the entrance.

His heart beat much faster than it should have, and Green Ghost couldn't understand why. As it pounded against his rib cage, it felt like the description of a heart attack that he'd heard, and he knew that such a powerful thumping could affect his aim. Closing his eyes, he went through the mental exercises every team guy knew, to slow his pulse and breathing.

Someone inside the warehouse yelled, a voice echoing in the empty space. "Why don't you make this easy, Jane? Your boyfriend took off like a scared rabbit; now you're alone. Come out... we don't wanna hurt you, come on out."

It was difficult to pinpoint the speaker's location inside without some sort of reference. He needed Jane to say something, *anything*, to help him triangulate her position relative to the speaker. And there had to be a second shooter, too, since the speaker had said *we*.

Then, as if on cue, another voice spoke up, this one female. "Dogface is tellin' the truth, girl, we ain't gonna hurt you." The woman's voice had an odd, raspy sound. "Step out, Jane, and let's talk about it afore somebody gets hurt."

Green Ghost could picture the interior in his mind. If he was standing in the doorway, the first speaker, the man, would be somewhere off to the left, with the woman to the right. Presumably that meant Jane was in the middle. A battle plan came to mind immediately. He'd already fired off six rounds from a 60-round magazine, leaving 54. Plenty for what he had in mind.

He would enter the warehouse at a dead run and head left, firing from the hip to pin down the man until he could either get behind cover or overrun his position. The female would be unlikely to hit such a fast-moving target. He took two deep breaths to oxygenate his body, sucked in a third, and was about to move when a single shot echoed in the warehouse.

What had happened? Listening closely, he heard an indistinct sound most people wouldn't recognize, but he did. It was a body slumping to the ground.

"Nick, are you out there?"

Jane! "I'm here. You good?"

"A lot better than this piece of shit."

"Where's the woman?"

"She's behind a table near the far end."

"Is there an exit down there?"

"Yes, but it's closed. If she opens it, there's nothing on the other side but open fields leading to the airport. We can run her to ground."

"No need," he said, catching on to her ploy. "I don't miss if it's less than five hundred yards. I'll blow her head off."

They paused to give the woman a chance to think about it.

"What about it, Tina? Matthew's dead, but that doesn't mean you have to die, too."

"If I come out, you're gonna kill me dead."

"I didn't kill you last time, and I won't now. I didn't want to kill Matthew, but you didn't give me much of a choice."

"You swear you won't kill me?"

"I swear on my daughter's life. Throw out your gun and come out real slow."

Something clattered on the floor, and again Green Ghost knew what it was just from the noise it made — a gun, hitting concrete. A few seconds later, Jane yelled for him to come in.

He went through the doorway with rifle sighted and ready to shoot.

Twenty feet to his left, he spotted Jane standing behind a pile of smashed wooden crates, her rifle trained on something to his right. He turned and acquired the target, a thick-bodied woman with long, tangled black hair, streaked with gray. Tears rolled down drooping cheeks that melted into a double chin. The woman walked forward, hands halfway up. Jane waved him inside and they both approached within ten feet, guns at hips but still trained on her.

"Nick, meet Tina Holmbo. Tina and her dead boyfriend over there, Matthew Kurtz, have been following me for years. A while back they set up an ambush, but I found out and could have shot them both. I didn't, because I don't like killing anybody unless I have to. I made them swear they wouldn't do it again, but apparently they don't take their own promises seriously."

"What do they want with you?"

"You wanna tell him, Tina?" The dumpy woman said nothing, her round face compressing into a glare. Jane shrugged. "Matthew liked hurting women, and Tina here liked watching him do it. Isn't that right, Tina?"

"They're all lies," Tina said. "Matthew never hurt nobody."

"That's not quite right, is it?" She looked up at Green Ghost. "A few years back, I came across one of their victims. She was a young Pauite girl, not much older than my Tornado was at the time. Bruises covered her whole body and what they did to her was obvious. Once they were done with the poor girl, they stabbed her in the stomach and left her there. She was barely alive when I found her... she could only whisper, but described her attackers perfectly. It was her and Kurtz. Tina and Matthew are quite a pair."

"*Were* quite a pair... of scumbags," Green Ghost said. He knew Jane was prepping the woman to give information, even if they hadn't discussed it. He'd seen it countless times before. "They're lucky you found them last time. I don't leave enemies alive to come after me later. I'd have killed them both and not thought twice about it."

"So what about that, Tina? Should I put a bullet in your head, or give you the chance to tell me why you broke your promise?"

"Go ahead and shoot me," Tina said. "You killed Matthew. Life ain't worth livin' now."

Jane nodded. "Okay." She lifted the rifle and fired. The round struck Tina's left ankle, smashed it, and exited the other side, where it ricocheted into the shadows. Tina screamed and fell. Rolling on the hard floor, she held her ankle and cried in pain.

Green Ghost raised his eyebrows in surprise, but Jane didn't see him. She squatted next to Tina, the rifle across her knees. "So what do you think now that you *know* I'll shoot you? Willing to tell me why you set up another ambush and shot at my friend here?"

Between heaves and sobs, Tina explained that they'd intended to find out the exact location of Jane's homestead. They knew she was a scraper and figured she must have a big storage area. When Tina finished, both women were quiet for a moment. Jane seemed lost in thought.

"And once you found it, then what?" Green Ghost said, not wanting to lose the momentum of the moment. "What happens to Jane?"

Closing her eyes against the pain in her foot, Tina answered through clenched teeth. "Then nothing... we didn't talk about that."

He shook his head, even if Tina wasn't looking. Another thing he'd learned along the way was that your attitude came across in your tone. "Bullshit. What would you have done to Jane?"

"And anybody else you found at my place," Jane added, her face turning red with anger. Up until that point she had treated it as just another thing to deal with, but now Green Ghost saw true rage welling inside her. "Right? You would have killed my daughter if she was there, and my caretaker, and his son and family, right? Tell me!"

"We didn't talk about it!"

Green Ghost shook his head. "If she's gonna keep lying, we might need to ruin her other foot." He picked up his right foot and let the boot hover over Tina's good ankle. "No need to waste ammo. I'll just step on it."

"No!" Tina screamed. A bird flapped away somewhere in the scaffolding overhead. "All right! Matthew wanted to kill anybody we found. I told him no, I didn't do that sort of thing. It was him, all him!"

"How did you know we were coming this way?" Green Ghost said. The bleeding from Tina's ankle had slowed, but the leaking blood had already formed a small puddle, which quickly turned black with flies. By the contortions of her face he could tell that the pain had gotten worse.

"We didn't... saw you coming... decided to take you. We lived here through... the winter."

He looked up. "She's telling the truth. We were targets of opportunity."

"Good, that makes me feel better. Thank you, Tina." Reaching into the small of her back, Jane withdrew a revolver and aimed at Tina's head.

"No!" Tina screamed.

Jane pulled the trigger. When she looked at Green Ghost, there were tears in her eyes. "Coming after me is one thing, but nobody threatens my friends."

"Remind me never to make you mad," Green Ghost said as they remounted the horses. They'd collected Matthew and Tina's weapons, a well-worn Winchester lever-action Model 1873 carbine, chambered in the original .44-40 caliber, and a cheap pump shotgun, along with boxes of ammo for both. The couple's camp had been inside the warehouse, but the rest of their belongings were grimy and worn out, except for a cast iron skillet, which Jane took.

"I've never shot somebody who couldn't shoot back before," she said, clearly troubled by killing Tina.

"You didn't have much choice. If you left her alive, sooner of later she'd come after you, or your family."

"I know you're right, but that doesn't make it any easier."

"No, it doesn't."

"Have you ever killed somebody like that?"

"Sort of. The first mission I led my team on was to kill this Austrian arms dealer who sold weapons to our enemies. I was ordered not to leave him, or his girlfriend, alive. I didn't actually kill either one of them, other members of my team did, but I would have. The woman was shot right in front of me."

"Would you do it again?"

He had to think about that. "It would depend on the target, but to save the lives of my team, or innocent people? Yeah... yeah, I'd do it again."

By tacit agreement neither of them spoke about Tina again that day. They rode southeast from the town, crossing Alternate Highway 95, and then rode through a flat desert area with a grid of paved streets marking a subdivision that was never finished. White PVC pipes stuck up here and there to connect future homes to the town's sewer and water systems.

The horses were spent by that point, but half a mile east was the Lahontan Reservoir, where morning sunlight glinted off the calm water like a mirror. They skirted three long fingers of the lake to enter a peninsula that pointed northeast. At the end of that land was a narrow channel separating the western shoreline from the east. Jane directed her horse into the lake without hesitation, and the water came up just past its belly. Green Ghost followed and minutes later they were both on the eastern bank.

"I wish I had a fishing rod," Green Ghost said, trying to lighten the mood. "I'll bet this lake has bass or catfish. Either would taste good about now."

If Jane heard him, she didn't react.

He tried again. "If it's much further, we really need to rest the horses."

She rode on without responding.

Revetment E-9, Operation Comeback
0844 hours, May 3

A rectangle made from heavy-gauge steel struts acted as a work bench for large pieces of an aircraft, such as the left wing of the first A-10 that Lieutenant Hartmann was putting back into service. An overhead crane hoisted the 27-foot wing into place following Hartmann's hand signals. With a maximum lifting capacity of 50 tons, the enormous crane ran the entire length of the runway complex and served all fifty revetments on the eastern side of the facility. An identical system served the western side, each side with ten cranes that could be used separately or in combination.

Lieutenant Colonel Astrid Naidoo watched from a far corner, careful to stay out of the way. She wasn't there to help, precisely, because she had no idea what the technicians working under Lieutenant Hartmann were doing. To her it all just looked like a bunch of parts, tools, lubricants, and arcane alchemy. Naidoo was a staff officer through and through, with a specialty in civilian affairs and a talent for organization, and was only there to see if Hartmann needed help in any way.

Once the wing was safely down, Hartmann stepped away and gave the crew a 15-minute break.

"I'm amazed at your technical expertise, Lieutenant," Naidoo said to Hartmann. "And please don't take this the wrong way, especially coming from a fellow woman, but you do not look like someone who would service jets."

Hartmann laughed and drained half a squeezer of water. "It's not the first time I've heard it, ma'am. I tell people I'm five feet tall, but really I'm about four-eleven, so I don't exactly look like a crew dog. I started out as a load toad, which was an even weirder fit for someone my size. IYAASAS."

"Beg pardon?"

"Sorry, ma'am, it's kind of the motto for the munitions crews. 'If you ain't ammo, you ain't... spit.'"

Naidoo laughed. "Somehow I doubt the real word is 'spit.' What's a booger hooker? I overheard one of the communications techs say that."

"Did you really, ma'am? Could you tell me which one said that?"

"I take it that's not a compliment?"

"Not exactly, no, ma'am."

Naidoo laughed again. "Forget I said anything. So what got you into this line of duty?"

"There's something about the odor of JP-8 that smells like kicking ass."

Naidoo gave her a look that meant *c'mon, I'm serious.*

"Okay, ma'am," Hartmann said. "I'm not really sure. Even as a little kid, I preferred building model airplanes to playing with dolls. I like knowing how things work, and jets fascinate me."

"What's the hardest part about getting one of these back in the air?" Naidoo said, pointing to the A-10.

"It's hard to pick out one thing... when an engine has been in storage for a long time, there's a process you have to go through to put them back in service. The blades have to be turned, but you can't do that without first applying auxiliary power, without the main power and fuel lines being connected. You also have to pull the circuit breakers.

"Then, the first time you light the fire, start the engine, you get this thick smoke because of the oil used to mothball the fuel lines. That's one of the reasons you turn the blades using auxiliary power, to burn off some of that lubricant. The first time you fire up the engines, it burns off the rest of the oil. It's hella scary if you don't know it's coming; the aircraft looks like it's on fire. Doesn't hurt anything, just looks bad."

"Oh, my."

"Funny thing is, the engines are the easy part. It's all the other sh—...stuff... that's tricky."

Naidoo decided against interrupting her again for a translation of that one.

Hartmann didn't seem to notice her confusion and rambled on. "When you've got creepy-crawlies nearby, you try not to do that stuff in the dark. It's like lighting a bonfire and saying, 'Hey, bad guys, over here!' Might as well put up a giant target."

"Sure, that makes sense. I'm guessing you were in Iraqi Freedom?"

"Five deployments, all the way to Syria, yes, ma'am."

"General Schiller would like a rough estimate of when this aircraft might be ready for combat. We already have the pilot awake and acclimating."

"Hard to say for certain, Colonel. First thing, I've got to do an NDI on the wing and the root — that's a non-destructive inspection. It uses X-ray imaging to check the metal for weaknesses. Usually we find such defects in the wing root, if they exist, and that's a simple fix. We just add a beef-up plate. Once that's finished, we attach the wing using four bolts."

"That's it? Only four bolts?"

"Well, they're really big bolts, Colonel. You'll see when we bring 'em out. The bolts are the size of my arm. The torque wrench is as tall as I am and about six inches in diameter. The sockets are the size of my fist, or maybe as big as your fist. I have small hands — my fist fits *inside* the socket. On bigger aircraft, such as a C130 and big heavies like that, they use eight bolts to hold the wing on. Once the plane is ready, we really need a test flight so we can torque the wings afterward."

"There might not be time for that."

Hartmann shrugged. "We'll make it work."

"Yeah, I'm guessing wing failure wouldn't be a good thing."

"Well, it *is* an A-10, ma'am... wings are optional."

#

Chapter 16

*So it was in the dreaming past,
And life is a shifting maze,
Summer on summer fading fast,
In a mist of yesterdays.*
Robert E. Howard, from "The Hills Were Ancient Then"

Southwest of Silver Springs, Nevada
1004 hours, May 3

East of the reservoir, a line of mountains rose from the harsh desert. With the sun fully in their faces, Jane spoke for the first time since shortly after shooting Tina, announcing that they were entering the Dead Camel Mountains. Green Ghost wondered out loud about how mountains in Nevada got named after animals that lived half a world away, but Jane only shrugged. A tight frown indicated how much shooting Tina in cold blood still bothered her, so Green Ghost tried to make her feel better about it.

"You didn't really have a choice, you know."

"You've already said that," was her only answer.

He shut back up and rode. It wasn't long before they ascended the western side of a steep, barren mountain several thousand feet high. The only vegetation in sight was scrub grass pushing through red and brown rocks. It reminded Green Ghost of Afghanistan. They led their horses up a faint game trail that zig-zagged up the slope, and were about to go over the crest when Jane grabbed his arm and stopped him.

"Let me do it," she said. "They might shoot you on sight."

"They who?"

"The people we're looking for."

She handed him her horse's reins and stepped over the top. Standing in one place, she waved her arms for nearly five minutes. Green Ghost saw her cup hands around her mouth and yell to someone on the other side. Then she waved for him to join her.

Standing beside her atop the ridgeline, he squinted against the sun's glare, reflecting off several metallic surfaces within the sprawling complex below. A man in a Jeep, an honest-to-God World War Two model Jeep, waved up at him.

The main feature of the complex, on the floor of the broad valley spread out below, was an aircraft runway, running northwest to southeast. It was crossed by several shorter runways, and on the eastern side of the main runway stood a series of five huge hangars. Tarmac taxiways connected all of them to the runways, along with a dozen smaller buildings.

The area surrounding the airport on all sides was the bright green of healthy crops and fresh grass. Cows grazed in one quadrant, with a large barn in an enclosed area. He also saw horses, goats, and chickens. A large shed stood near what had to be the main house, with another large building on the other side. Scattered around the area were people working at various jobs in the fields.

"What the fuck am I looking at?" he said, forgetting his own self-imposed restriction against cursing around Jane.

"The home of Allen Pohl," she said.

He pointed at a tall man picking his way up the rocky slope toward them. "That him?"

"That's Allen."

1528 hours

Shadows fell early in the valley as mountains blocked the westering sun, chilling the afternoon air. Inside the main house, several loud *cracks* came from the huge stone fireplace as Allen Pohl knelt and fed more broken bits of furniture into the fire. Some still had coats of old oil paint or varnish, which flared up and burned bluish white.

"We can't have many fires," he said. "Trees don't grow around here very well. We've tried mesquite trees, oaks, you name it, and orchards with several different varieties of fruit trees. Most won't do well here, but we've managed to grow oranges and peaches. But that's just because we irrigate using the reservoir; otherwise there's nothing here to burn."

"Except furniture," Green Ghost said. He sat at a wooden table opposite Jane, and had to admit that it felt great to rest. But from the moment he'd seen Jane and Pohl smile at each other, he'd felt an irrational dislike of the man. He didn't have feelings for her, he told himself, but was simply being protective of a teammate.

"Other things too, but yeah, broken furniture heads the list. We can't burn wood from houses or fences, because some of it was treated with toxic chemicals and we can't tell which is which. If it was treated with chromated copper arsenate, that stuff was so toxic even the ashes could kill you. And most of it at least had resins containing formaldehyde."

"Then why such an enormous fire pit?" Green Ghost said. "It seems a lot bigger than you need if wood is all that scarce."

"Don't let the greenery of the fields out there fool you. The winters here get extremely cold. My father built this place before I was born. Back then, all you needed for firewood was money to buy it and have it trucked in, and Dad had plenty of money. Before the Collapse, he stocked up on things to keep us going afterward, including a mountain of firewood and fifty thousand pounds of pasta. The firewood lasted five years, but ran out a long, long time ago. Now we rely on scrapers like Jane for things we need."

Once again he smiled at her, and once again she returned it. Green Ghost's irrational dislike of the man grew, side by side with Pohl's gregarious hospitality.

"Did you say fifty thousand pounds of pasta?"

That brought a chuckle. "Not only that, but we've still more than half of it left, along with dried beans, peas, lentils, honey, and a whole cave full of liquor. None of that stuff ever really goes bad."

Pohl rose from attending the fire and went into the kitchen, returning with a pitcher filled with a clear brown liquid. He set out three glasses, filled them, and then put on the table a squeeze bottle in the shape of a bear that contained, by the look of it, honey. "I'm sorry I don't have any lemons. They're about four months off still."

"What is this?" Green Ghost said, sniffing the liquid. "It smells like... tea. Real tea."

"Yes, that's right."

"Where did you get tea?" Despite the hostility he felt toward Pohl, he couldn't help asking the question.

"We don't get it, we grow it in our hothouse. Do you like it?"

Green Ghost sipped it without adding honey, hoping it was bitter. It wasn't. Grudgingly he said so.

"I'm glad you like it. Jane?"

"Delicious, Allen. Drinking your tea is always a treat." Her voice carried an underlying tone of... of what, exactly? Green Ghost couldn't tell, and didn't like that he couldn't tell. He felt very ill at ease.

"So... not that I'm not always glad to see you again, Jane, but what brings you this far to the east? You're not usually here until mid-summer or later."

She laid out the situation as quickly and in as much detail as she could, with Green Ghost filling in what she missed.

When they were done, Pohl leaned back in his chair, thinking. "And you think that this general — he's your father, right? You think he's still alive"

"Yes."

"How can you be so sure he's not... not dead? I don't want to seem harsh, but it sounds like wishful thinking to me."

"Not if you knew him. He... well, like I said, you'd have to know him to understand why I *know* he's still alive. He's not gonna die driving into some ravine. When Dad dies... well, it won't be like that. I don't know how else to explain it."

"Do you know the location of this ravine?"

"Vaguely."

By that point, Pohl's brows had furrowed and he'd taken on a serious expression. "And you came to me because I have airplanes, and you want to use those for an aerial search, is that it?"

She nodded. "I know it's a lot to ask."

"You're damned straight it is. We could look forever out there and never find him, you know that, right?"

"We do."

Pohl scowled at them, and Green Ghost wondered if they were about to be thrown out. He didn't answer for nearly ten seconds. "Do either of you realize how precious aviation fuel is?"

Jane and Green Ghost both looked down.

Then Pohl clapped his hands so loud it startled them, and followed that with a laugh. When Green Ghost jerked his head up, their host grinned like a young boy on Christmas morning.

"This sounds like more fun than I've had in decades. Want to see my planes?"

Despite having ridden nearly one hundred miles in less than two days, Green Ghost's fatigue evaporated at the prospect of seeing the collection Jane had raved about. He hated himself for what he said next. "Sure!"

From atop the ridge overlooking the valley, Green Ghost had seen the four hangars that flanked the eastern side of the main runway. What he hadn't seen were the wide doors leading into the opposite ridgeline, on its western-facing side, where a vast hollowed-out space acted as hangar, workshop, and parts fabrication center, with doors leading to residential quarters, greenhouses, and other support facilities. It was an engineering masterpiece that would have shocked him, had he not first seen Operation Overtime.

Pohl proudly pointed to the hangar's support scaffolding high overhead, where a complex set of mirrors reflected daylight into all sections, thereby limiting the need for artificial lighting. When it became necessary to switch on the lights, an arrangement of segmented and powerful LEDs allowed him to illuminate large or small sections, one at a time. Electricity came from solar collectors and wind-powered turbines.

Green Ghost wanted to not be impressed with Pohl's collection of vintage aircraft. After all, he'd awakened from Long Sleep in one of the most impressive engineering projects ever built by man, but in the face of so many famous military airplanes he couldn't help gawking.

Most were from the Second World War and were arranged by nationality, with placards on stands to explain each aircraft, its model and specifications. The American section had 22 types, including a P-51D Mustang, a P-47D Thunderbolt, and a B-25H, in the standard factory configuration with eight forward-firing fifty-caliber machine guns. When Green Ghost saw an A-1J (AD-7) Skyraider, and Pohl explained it was the last series built, he thought but didn't say that such an aircraft could be put to very good use by the 7th Cavalry. A flying dump truck loaded with ordnance could be a game-changer.

The British section contained a Spitfire Mark I, "an honest-to-God veteran of the Battle of Britain," a Sopwith Camel reproduction, and a Bristol Blenheim. The Japanese part only contained four planes, and none were a Zero, but there was one of the even rarer Kawanishi N1K2-J Shiden, Allied code name 'George.' Pohl's eyes brightened when they stood beside the large fighter.

"I've only flown her twice," he said. "That is one hot mama."

Green Ghost blinked twice in a row, the *tell* he could never get rid of that showed true surprise. "It's flyable?"

Now it was Pohl's turn to be surprised. "Of course it is. They're all airworthy. That's the whole point of having them."

"Where do you get parts?"

"We make them. Load our own ammunition, too."

"The *guns* work?"

"Yes... fifty years is a long time. More than two hundred people now live on the ranch, and they all know their jobs quite well. That leaves a lot of free time for working on airplanes and their weapons."

When they strolled into the far end of the vast chamber, Green Ghost noticed that Jane didn't appear overly impressed, and said so.

"I've seen it quite a few times before," was all she said.

The German section was by far the largest, with 27 examples. "Dad loved flying Luftwaffe airplanes," Pohl explained.

Although he'd never been a Second World War history buff, even Green Ghost recognized the iconic aircraft types on display there. For a moment he stood back and scanned the collection. Two Messerschmitt ME-109s, a Model E and a Model G, stood closest to him, with oil stains spattered on the concrete under both.

"If you don't see oil, it means there isn't any in the lines," Pohl said.

There was a Focke-Wulf 190A next to those, along with various bomber types, including a Junkers JU-88A-4, which the card noted had been used by the Finnish Air Force, two Dornier DO-17As, and three different variants of the Heinkel HE-111, all of which came from the Spanish Air Force and had been used in making the movie *The Battle of Britain.* Rounding the tail of the third HE-111, Green Ghost stopped in his tracks and gawked at the next aircraft. Jane lifted an eyebrow at his expression, but Pohl grinned.

"Everybody has that reaction," Pohl said.

"Is that..."

"A *Stuka*? Yes, but not just any *Stuka*. That's a Junkers JU-87G-1, the plane that inspired the Warthog. I'm sure you're familiar with Warthogs, right?"

"They've saved my ass more than once," Green Ghost said.

"Really?" This time Pohl's voice carried a hint of admiration. "So you've seen them in action? In person, I mean."

"Sure, lots of times."

"Now I *do* envy you."

Green Ghost walked over to the *Stuka* and ran a hand over the pod slung under the left wing, and then down the long barrel of the 37mm cannon pointing forward from that pod. "There are supposed to be some Warthogs crated up at Operation Comeback," he said in an offhand tone. "Do these cannon work, too?"

Pohl ignored his question. "You have crated Warthogs? Fairchild-Republic A-10 Thunderbolt IIs, is that what you're saying?"

Now it was Green Ghost's turn to play it cool. "That's what I've heard."

"I have *got* to see those aircraft. I can help you get them flying!"

Crossing his arms, Green Ghost lapsed into military mode. "Not unless my father is still alive and we can find him, you're not. The man who has seized control of Overtime might order you shot as a spy, and his security chief is a psychopath who would enjoy pulling the trigger."

"A spy? For who?"

"It doesn't matter. Paranoia doesn't have to make sense."

Pohl frowned and looked at Jane. "Is he telling me straight?"

"From everything I've seen and heard, yeah, Allen, he is."

After considering for a moment, Pohl nodded once. "Then I guess we've got to find your father. Oh, and the cannon on that Stuka? Yes, they work, and yes, I've got ammo."

#

Chapter 17

Flying isn't dangerous; it's crashing that's dangerous.
5th rule of flying

Pohl Ranch, Northern Nevada
1720 hours, May 3

Green Ghost couldn't help gawking at the bizarre aircraft they saw next. The single engine was at the nose of the fuselage, with a short wing on one side and a longer wing on the other. A nacelle of framed glass sat astride the longer wing section like a seed pod, while the tail plane was only on the side with the shorter wing.

"What the hell is that?" he said.

"One of the rarest airplanes in the world, even back when there *was* a world. It's a Blomm und Voss BV141, in the original markings. The Luftwaffe never paid for more than a few prototypes and a small production run, before deciding to go with the Focke-Wulf 189 for their standard recon aircraft. They said it was under-powered, which it was, and although B and V upgraded to a bigger engine, it didn't matter.

"But more important for our purposes, one thing it did have was range. If the quality of your fuel is good, and you know how to cajole the mixture just right, you could get close to twelve hundred miles of range out of this aircraft."

Running his finger along the underside of the starboard wing, Green Ghost felt a difference in the skin from modern aircraft. It was thinner, or that was what his sense of touch told him, more pliant. But the offset cockpit was what seemed like something of a movie. "And this thing really flies, huh?" he said.

"Oh, it flies, Colonel. And it's going to fly tomorrow morning, with us in it."

Green Ghost pointed at the plane. "*This* is what you meant about having a plane that could help us find General Angriff?"

"That's right, it's perfect for the job, that's what it was designed to do, reconnaissance. What's more, I just overhauled the engine not two weeks ago."

"Was there something wrong with it?"

Pohl smiled, but it was a sad smile. "Nothing wrong with the plane, just the world we live in. I was bored, and even stripping weapons to clean them gets tedious after a while. Fueling up one of these gas guzzlers takes anywhere from a few days to a week's worth of production from our little refinery, so I can't fly as often as I want... but tomorrow I've got plenty of time and av-gas to go find this general of yours. Are you in?"

Jane poked him in the arm. "Yeah, Nick, are you in?"

Bundesarchiv, Bild 146-1980-117-01
Foto: Stöcker | 8. Mai 1942

Nevada desert
1749 hours, May 3

Nick Angriff stepped back and wiped his face with his sleeve, although it didn't do much good. Sweat turned the dust caked on his cheeks and forehead into a muddy sludge which, combined with skin oil, resisted being cleaned away.

He pushed the burned-out hovercraft into a crevice between two large boulders and then piled smaller rocks to hide it. But that looked too obvious to his eye, so he kicked and scooped dirt onto the rocks until the deception satisfied him. Once he'd gotten the hang of using the thing, it had greatly sped up his move across the desert. He mentally added finding a way to improve its battery life to the checklist of things he would do after regaining his command.

Given his service in Operations Desert Storm and Iraqi Freedom, and his command of U.S. Army Command Africa, Angriff had spent his fair share of time in the deserts of the world, so crossing the eastern Nevada desert didn't worry him the way it should have. No two deserts have the same dangers. Only those familiar with dangers specific to their desert know how best to survive in those harsh environments.

Angriff's first decision after leaving the two flyboys had been whether to travel by day or night. He'd decided that time was the prime factor, and he could make much better speed during daylight. It turned out to be the right decision, even though rattlesnakes hunted in the daytime, and they worried him more than anything else. Only once had he seen a search aircraft, far off to the west, and his use of the hoverboard had left no tracks for anyone to follow. Consequently he'd gone further, faster, than he'd hoped. A growing worry was how to cross the Colorado River once he got there, but that was still days off. One thing he knew for certain — walking home was going to take a helluva lot longer than he'd first thought it would.

Three miles south of Hiko, Nevada
1752 hours, May 3

On the northern outskirts of the little town of Crystal Springs, Angriff found a few long-abandoned buildings, mostly homes, but also one old combination quick market and gas station, of the ubiquitous sort that had once served food like sausage biscuits, hot dogs, or chicken salad sandwiches. The temperature was on the cool side as twilight settled in, but the exertion of pushing his body past its normal limits had brought beaded sweat to his forehead, which he wiped away so it wouldn't run into his eyes. He drew one of the Eagles and, ready to fire at the slightest sign of danger, he stepped through the smashed glass doors into a half-shadowed interior.

The only inhabitant was a dead snake with bits of skin clinging to its skeleton. Any edible food was long gone. Despite knowing that no food could survive fifty years on a store shelf in the desert, his mind nevertheless fantasized about discovering a box of Twinkies or Slim Jims. By the evidence of the chewed-up packages scattered everywhere, the scavengers had been wildlife and insects, not humans.

He didn't leave empty-handed, though. In the small galley kitchen, he found a stainless steel three-quart pot in remarkably good condition. It even still had a lid. And while it took up a lot of room in his pack, if Angriff had learned one thing during his trek across the desert, it was the value of such relics.

As much as he wanted to press on and scrounge the ghost town of Crystal Springs for food, without binoculars he couldn't tell for certain whether anyone lived there or not. He didn't think so, but even as tired, hungry, and thirsty as he was, he had vowed never again to make assumptions when considering a decision.

Then he froze and by reflex brought the Eagle to a ready position. Looming as if to stare over the buildings at him from the west side of the highway was the round head of an extraterrestrial, its metal face gleaming in the afternoon sun at least thirty feet off the ground. The semi-circular building behind it resembled nothing more than an overgrown Quonset hut.

"What the hell is that?" he said.

Whatever the building behind the giant figure had been, it couldn't have held much worth salvaging, could it? He'd planned to skirt the town on the west anyway, and if he did, he had to walk within a hundred yards of the strange structure. He didn't see any holes in the roof, which in itself was odd after 50 years of neglect. It appeared to have been some sort of museum, maybe in relation to its proximity to Area 51.

Whatever it had been, he lost sight of it when the road bent ninety degrees to the east, putting it at his back. The only road out of Crystal Springs was Nevada Highway 93, which he could either follow to the south or to the east. He picked east.

The low shoulders resembled poured concrete more than rock. Where the desert flattened out, low bushes grew in clumps. Angriff recognized there were different types, but to him they were all sagebrush. For a while he periodically glanced at Crystal Springs, just in case he was being pursued. Eventually, pushing himself through the last of the day's heat radiating skyward from the broken pavement took its toll. Simply taking the next step required all of his energy and concentration. It had been a very long day.

Mountains flanked the highway to the southwest and northeast at a distance of about three miles each way. The highway ran down the center of the flat valley floor. As shadows from the setting sun stretched toward him from the mountains to the southwest, he saw something ahead that he'd never expected to see — open water. There had been several lakes flanking the road as he'd moved past Hiko, and another lake now spread out on the north. Not a big lake, but finding water of any sort was remarkable.

He could barely make out a rusty road sign bearing the seal of the Nevada Department of Wildlife, and which prohibited campfires or overnight camping at Frenchy Lake. He barked a laugh at that, tossed down his gear, and began making a fire pit. The canteens weren't empty because he'd strictly limited his intake to make it last, but a whole lake of fresh water was too good to pass up, not to mention it wasn't long until total darkness swallowed the desert.

Several dead trees near the shoreline provided ready firewood, and rocks to line a fire were plentiful. One big flat-sided rock gave him a start when, as he picked it up, a lizard darted out from under it. A slight breeze made lighting the fire tricky, since it looked unlikely that he could refill the Zippo lighter any time soon and, once it ran out of fuel, starting fires would become exponentially harder. He breathed easier when, during a calm moment of wind, the kindling he'd gathered ignited on the first try. After filling the pot with lake water, he put it on the flat rock to boil.

Unbuckling the twin shoulder holsters removed their weight and the constant tension on his neck and shoulders, which in turn caused muscle spasms and trigger points, especially on his right shoulder blade. Fifty-caliber Desert Eagles weighed four and a half pounds each when loaded. Carrying them in desert conditions for hours on end reminded him of his first job, when he was eleven, in the days when young people earned money with a newspaper route. He'd worn crossed sacks holding forty papers each as he rode his bike from house to house, rain or shine, in the bitter cold or raging heat of Central Virginia.

The desert's nighttime temperature would plunge to near or below freezing, so with the last hints of sunlight turning the western sky purple, he stripped to let his sweaty clothes dry before putting them back on. Pants that had been snug when he'd left Overtime now hung loose, requiring him to notch his belt on the second-to-last hole. A passing thought to wash off in the lake evaporated when he put his big toe in the frigid water. The fire was cheerful, but nowhere near big enough to fight off hypothermia.

Only three MREs remained of the supply given to him by Major Strootman, but they were all favorites. He opted for the cheese tortellini, saving the beef ravioli and maple sausage for last. And he still had the Power Bar he'd saved from the chili-with-beans MRE he'd eaten the previous night.

Such a selection didn't happen by accident, since MREs were usually ratfucked by somebody along the way, meaning the best ones were picked out and the least-desired sent on down the line. The thought ran through his mind that if he ever got his command back — then he corrected himself, *when* he got his command back — Strootman would get consideration for a combat command. He might not be cut out for it, not everybody was, but Strootman had earned a first look.

He slid the meal out and ripped its packing box in half. Then he tucked the heat bag into the box, followed by the meal packet. After pouring in a little water, he laid it against a rock and set the timer on his watch for seven minutes. He wanted to rub his feet next, everybody who had ever walked into battle knew the importance of taking care of your feet, but ingrained priorities caused him to withdraw first one and then the other Desert Eagle. After blowing off dust, he emptied the chambers, worked the slides a few times to clear away any grit, and reloaded the cartridges. Without a cleaning kit, there wasn't much more he could do.

"Ho in the camp," cried a voice from the shadows to the south.

Angriff was on his feet, pistol in hand, within a heartbeat. He thought he saw the form of a man, although darkness made vision tricky, and bent into a shooting crouch with the pistol aimed at where he thought the figure stood. "Be aware that I'm armed and aiming at you," he said.

There was a chuckle to the voice that answered. "Go ahead and shoot, if it makes you feel safer."

"I don't shoot people unless I have to. Who are you and what do you want?"

"Who I am depends on who you ask. And what I want is to meet the traveler who is camping on my doorstep."

"Are you armed?"

"I have a walking stick, if that concerns you."

"Come on in, then."

A tall figure materialized from the darkness. Dressed in blue jeans with patches on the knees, and a stretched-out pullover sweater, the man wore work boots that might once have been black, now colored a muddy brown by years of ground-in dirt.

"Well," the old man said, settling himself on a stone near the fire. He laid aside his walking stick and a canvas bag with a lump in the bottom, and then stuck his hands palms-out toward the fire. "You've come at last."

Angriff's face creased with confusion. He no longer aimed the pistol at the man, instead pointing it ten degrees to the right of the stranger's head. "You were expecting me?"

"I've been expecting you for years."

"How so? I don't know who you are, or even where I am."

Now it was the old man's darkly tinted face that twisted, as if he needed to decipher Angriff's words. "Does that matter?"

"I would think so. It sure does to me."

"Why?"

"Because I need to know whether you mean to do me harm or not, that's why. The safe thing would be just to shoot you, but I don't kill people for no reason. I hate killing even when I have to, and even then it's got to be a last resort. Life's too precious."

"Well said." Flames licked upward as the fire grew. In its light, the white hairs of the stranger's long beard contrasted sharply with the deep caramel of his face. "Especially with as few people as are left in this world."

"Given some of the ones I've met recently, there might still be too many."

"Now, c'mon, don't talk like that. You just said life's too precious to be wantonly shooting people, and I agree. Those are good words to live by, so don't be throwing them away too easy."

"Do you get a lot of folks coming by here?"

"You're the first. Leastwise, the first in a long time. Could you spare a sip of water?"

Angriff considered. The water in the pan had started to boil, so he'd leave tomorrow with full canteens of lake water, but even after being boiled it could still contain pathogens. The water already in his canteens he knew to be potable. Then he thought about the shoe being on the other foot, and passed over a canteen. The man nodded thanks, took one swig, then handed it back.

"You can have some more," Angriff said.

"I'm fine, son. Thank you anyway."

Picking up the MRE, he held it out for the old man along with a spoon. "Hungry?"

The man took it, sniffed, and tasted a tiny bite before handing it back. "You're a generous man. What brings you all the way out to the middle of nowhere?"

For a moment Angriff wondered what to say. "It's a long story."

"It's gonna be a long night."

He decided to tell the whole story, all the way back to Janine and Cynthia being kidnapped on Lake Tahoe. It seemed odd even to him that he opened up like that to someone he didn't know, was never likely to meet again, and who might be a delusion created by extreme exhaustion and rapid weight loss. Then he realized those were all the reasons *not* to hold back.

Angriff got so caught up in telling his story that it was only after he'd finished that he realized the MRE was still in his hands, uneaten. He scooped a cold mouthful and swallowed. Cold meatballs were still meatballs.

"That's some story," the old man said. "And you mean to resurrect the country using this brigade of yours?"

"That's the plan."

"Uh-huh... and you're re-establishing Constitutional law as you go."

"Correct."

"Mmmm..." The old man rubbed his chin. "Help me get this straight in my head... I'm old and my mind gets fuzzy sometimes. When the colonies broke away from England, did they write the Constitution first and *then* declare independence?"

Angriff sensed a trap. "No."

"They did it the other way around?"

"Yeah..."

"Why?"

Now he could visualize the trap closing around him. "Because their style of government wouldn't matter if they lost the war."

"Anything else?"

"I don't follow you."

"What I mean is, when they finally got around to writing the Constitution, on figuring out what kind of government they wanted, did everybody agree right away, or did they have to squabble a while?"

"It was contentious."

"Uh-huh... and which way are you doing it?"

Had the man slapped him it would not have had a greater impact. "You're saying I should reclaim the territory first, and then grant people their Constitutional rights?"

"I'm not saying anything. I'm just asking questions. Do the people understand the rights you're trying to give 'em? Under the Constitution, I mean?"

"I get it."

"Oh?"

"The people we liberate haven't been educated to know what it means to *have* rights, much less how to exercise them in a responsible manner."

"Did I say all that?"

"You didn't have to."

"Oh."

"Who *are* you?"

"I've been called all sorts of things. Call me whatever suits you."

"You must have a name."

The old man just smiled. "One other thing you mentioned in your story... The people who've wronged you, the ones you've shown mercy like that Claringdon man and General Steeple, did they ask for your mercy or forgiveness?"

"No..." Angriff drew out the word, already sensing what was coming.

"So you gave them something they didn't ask for?"

"Again, I get your point."

"Do you?"

"Yes."

After studying him for a few seconds, the man rose. "I appreciate your hospitality, but I'll be going now."

"It's nighttime. Why not stay until dawn? I'm enjoying our talk."

"I appreciate it, son, but I have other things to do."

"You live around here?"

The grin that split the white beard couldn't have been larger, framed as it was against the blackness of night. "Sort of." After taking a few steps, he stopped and twisted, looking back over his shoulder. "Something tells me you won't be on foot much longer." Then he resumed walking away into the night.

"What is that supposed to mean?"

The man turned, waved, and became one with the darkness.

The pile of firewood lay near where the old man had sat. Half an hour later, Angriff started tossing more branches onto the fire and saw that his strange visitor had remembered his walking stick but left behind the canvas bag with a lump in the bottom. Reaching inside, he pulled out a heavy leather jacket, broken in but not worn out, with fleece lining and a faux fur collar.

"Hey!" he yelled, hearing his own voice fade into the night. "You forgot your jacket!"

Despite repeated cries, there was no answer, and Angriff had the distinct feeling the jacket was meant for him. Since he was already shivering as the temperature plunged toward freezing, he put the jacket on to see if it might fit. Although it was a little big in the shoulders, he realized that with his shoulder holsters on, it would be a perfect fit. Almost like it *was* meant for him...

The instant the thought flashed through his brain, the truth of it struck him like a hammer. *Almost like it was meant for him...*

#

Chapter 18

Remote in the desert of Araby lies the nameless city, crumbling and inarticulate, its low walls nearly hidden by the sands of uncounted ages.
H.P. Lovecraft, from "The Nameless City"

Southern Nevada desert
1902 hours, May 3

"Remember the day I agreed to join you on this endless vacation?" Bunny Carlos said, licking his dry lips.

Joe Randall was too tired to give the question any serious thought. "No."

"Yeah, me neither."

"You have my permission to go back."

"Thanks, you're a fuckin' prince. You ready to make camp?"

"I'd rather push on for a little while. We haven't made great time today."

"I don't care, man. I'm fuckin' tired. If we can't eat somethin', at least we don't have to die of exhaustion."

They kept walking south toward Creech, always, as they had been for most of three days. They were down to half a canteen of water each, and the sun had long since dipped behind a ridgeline to the west, when Randall stopped and pointed dead ahead.

"Am I seeing things, or is that a town?"

"It's hard to tell, but I think it's either a mirage or a town, and if it's a mirage, don't tell me."

"You need daylight for a mirage. C'mon, maybe somebody's still living there."

They hurried through the darkness, following a two-lane road that had clearly not been built for heavy traffic, and which was now mostly covered by the desert. With twilight dimming fast, they didn't see the sign beside the road until they had almost passed it.

"Can you make it out?" Carlos said.

Randall reached up and wiped off layers of dust, sneezing when he inhaled some. "You are... now?... yeah, you are now entering the Nevada National Security Site, no trespassing... by... order of the United States Department of... Energy."

"Any idea what it means?"

"None. I don't see any lights on, but let's be careful. That might not mean anything."

"So we're gonna check it out?"

Randall grunted a half-laugh. "Yeah."

"It's about fuckin' time something went right."

A new moon left the landscape lit only by stars, yet even in the darkness they could tell that whatever the place was, it had once been a military base. A small one, but military all the same, and probably Air Force given its proximity to so many other Air Force facilities. The buildings were utilitarian in design and equally spaced.

Carlos decided to risk checking out one of the first buildings they came to. Randall warned him it could be dangerous, but Carlos waved away the objection. The door was closed but not locked, and although it squealed upon opening, it didn't offer much resistance. He was about to step inside when both men heard one of the most chilling sounds you could hear in a pitch black building in the middle of the Nevada desert — the buzzing of a rattlesnake's tail.

"Fuck!" Carlos said, slamming the door and jumping back. He unslung his rifle and aimed it at the door, as if the snake would knock it down and chase him. Randall couldn't stop laughing.

Mercury, Nevada
0540 hours, May 4

With no way to make a fire, they spent another cold, hungry night under a blazing canopy of stars. Neither of them wanted to dare going into another building until daylight, so they huddled against the outer wall of one that blocked the winds coming from the northwest. It helped a little, although what sleep they got wasn't deep or sound.

When dawn was still half an hour away, they went looking for water. Both had finished their canteens during the night, so now it was a matter of survival. If they couldn't find any water, the clock would start ticking until dehydration put them down for the count.

The first thing they learned from a rusted-over sign was the town's name, Mercury. Without a map it didn't mean much, although daylight had restored some of Carlos' bravado.

"At least I know the name of the place if I die here."

"You're too ugly to die."

"Jealous much? But if I don't get something to eat pretty soon, it won't matter how pretty I am."

"Let's go look for that rattler. I hear they're good eating."

"You think you're kidding, but if that slimy bastard shows his fangs and I see him, I'm gonna blow his rattle off and cook him for breakfast."

"Cook him with what? We can't make a fire."

"Then I'll eat him raw."

The biggest building on the north side of town had a definite government-industrial look to it, the kind of place designed by an architect who was specifically chosen because he or she had no sense of humor. A depressed concrete area held a stagnant puddle, but it was covered with a film of algae and a dead bird floated on the surface. Even with a way to boil it, Randall would never have drunk that water.

They passed a power station, what might have once been a church of some denomination, a sign pointing to the post office, and the entertainment complex. *That* could have possibilities.

Unlike most of the ghost towns they'd passed through or heard about, Mercury did not have debris heaped in piles everywhere. There was evidence of some looting, but not much. It was as if the town had been evacuated in an orderly fashion. They ducked into some of the buildings and found things that had great value in the post-Collapse world, such as notebooks and pencils. One place even had a manual pencil sharpener screwed to the wall.

The entertainment complex had all the usual facilities, a basketball court, an empty swimming pool, tennis courts, and locker rooms. They tried the faucets but nothing came out. It seemed obvious that Mercury had used well water, but the pumps must have all been either gasoline or electric powered. Then, as they headed back out the main entrance, they found something even more important. Framed on the wall, where decades of sunlight had faded it, was a map of Nevada, with Mercury prominently marked within a red circle. Unable to read it because of the glare, they took it off the wall.

"That road out there is called Mercury Highway," Randall said, once he'd found exactly the right angle for viewing. "And it leads directly to Highway 95. Bunny, that's the highway Creech is on."

"Isn't that Creech right there?" Carlos pointed to a particularly washed-out area.

Randall held it up, tilting it this way and that until he could read the faint ink. "Son a bitch, you're right. It is Creech. It can't be more than another twenty miles, maybe twenty-five. We can do that in one day!"

"Maybe if we'd eaten lately or had some water. But if we push too hard, Joe, hell, we might not get there at all."

"Wouldn't you rather go through hell for one day, then spend tonight taking a bath after eating a hot meal? And don't forget Frances. I'd guess she'll be damned glad to see you."

"Yeah... yeah, I'm sure she will be."

"So what d'ya say? One last push?"

"One last push," Carlos said.

Randall studied his friend. He knew Bunny Carlos better even than he knew his own wife, so he wondered why his best friend sounded like food, drink, and a willing lady gave him the scowl of a man who had just been told that he needed all of his teeth pulled.

Creech Air Force Base
1637 hours, May 4

"Head's up," one of her crew stage-whispered to Master Sergeant Frances Rossi. "Wang's coming."

Rainwater dripped from *Tank Girl*, the AH-72 Comanche put into service by the missing Captain Joe Randall and the father of Rossi's gestating child, Lieutenant George Carlos. A pop-up shower hadn't set her back enough to move the helicopter into the nearby hangar, and gave her an excuse for not painting over the image on the gunship's side. Everyone else had given up hope that Randall and Carlos were coming back, since they'd last been seen flying a C-5 Galaxy into combat nearly two weeks earlier. Such an enormous aircraft couldn't just land anywhere or on any runway; it could crash anywhere, though. Regardless of how improbable it seemed, Rossi refused to write off the two men, not yet, not ever. And painting over the *Tank Girl* logo implied a finality she wasn't prepared to deal with.

Lieutenant Wang had always been a pain in the ass to the squadron's ground crews. He and his co-pilot, Lieutenant Pra Sakoya, were part of the relief rotation. Most of the relief flight crews shared nine of the squadron's remaining eleven Comanches without complaint, with only two machines assigned to permanent crews. One was Lieutenant Alisa Plotz's *Hell's Hammer*, currently at Sierra Army Base, with the other being *Tank Girl*. But now, with Randall missing, that left his Comanche up for grabs. At least, that was how Wang saw it. And if possession was nine-tenths of the law, he intended to act like it was *his* personal aircraft until told otherwise.

Rossi watched him strut through the hangar, headed her way. He had the air of a man who commanded the entire base, nose slightly in the air, wearing his arrogance like a favorite jacket. When he got close enough to see that the *Tank Girl* logo had not been covered over yet, Wang stopped, put hands on hips, and shook his head in a slow, exaggerated movement.

"Master Sergeant Rossi, would you care to explain why you have not yet followed my order to obscure that disgusting picture on the side of my aircraft?"

Because you're a pompous jackass, she thought. *And you can fuck off for all I care.* "The paint to cover it only arrived with today's supply convoy, sir."

"And?" How anybody could imbue that one word with so much arrogance was more than Rossi could understand.

"It rained, Captain."

"I can see that, Master Sergeant."

"Can't paint in the rain, sir."

"But you can in a hangar, can you not? A hangar like the one right there?"

"Yes, sir."

"Then I suggest you move my aircraft into that hangar, just in case it rains again, and cover that image!"

"Yes, sir."

"And while you're doing that, cover over those names and put mine there instead." He pointed to the stenciled names of Captain Joseph Daniel Randall and Lieutenant George Carlos.

Rossi's face took on a mask of stone. "Congratulations, sir."

"Thank you. For what are you congratulating me, Master Sergeant?"

"I assumed the captain had been permanently assigned to this aircraft."

"Oh. Not yet, but it's inevitable, only a matter of time. So, get to work."

"Yes, sir," she said, hoping that Wang would recognize the anger in those two words. He didn't. "What about Lieutenant Sakoya, sir? Should we paint her name below yours?"

"No, that will not be necessary."

Wang turned on one heel and walked briskly back into the shadows of the hangar. One of her crew flipped him the finger. Rossi appreciated the gesture, but frowned and shook her head. She'd had arrogant commanders before and pegged Wang as the vindictive sort. Besides, noncoms weren't supposed to allow enlisted personnel to show open contempt for their officers, no matter how much they might deserve it.

"Let's get her inside," she said.

#

Chapter 19

I'd always thought the world was a wish-granting factory.
Caesar Augustus

Creech Air Force Base
1955 hours, May 4

Three hours later, the hangar lights fully illuminated *Tank Girl* when Ted Wang sauntered back onto the cavernous work floor. His smile faded and his pace quickened when he saw most of that blonde woman sitting on a bomb still painted on the side of the Comanche, along with the name *Tank Girl*. The muscles of his face went tight with anger. "Didn't I order you to paint over that image, Sergeant? Didn't I?"

"You did, sir." Rossi said, seemingly unconcerned.

"And what excuse do you have for not doing it this time?"

"Your order was countermanded, sir."

"Countermanded by whom?"

"By *me*, Lieutenant." Joe Randall stepped from behind the helicopter, arms folded, scowling at the smaller Wang. Bunny Carlos followed him into view.

"Joe!" Wang blurted.

"That's Captain Randall, Lieutenant! Come to attention!"

Wang's body went rigid as he snapped to attention. Randall approached him, unsure what exactly to do next. He'd rarely ever chewed out a subordinate. It just wasn't in his nature, unless it was absolutely necessary for keeping him alive. Besides, he was a pilot, and after flying, the only other things that mattered were girls and alcohol. Until Morgan came along, anyway.

The thought of Morgan, of Wang ordering her image to be painted over, gave him the words he sought. "The United States Army assigned the responsibility for keeping this aircraft in fighting condition to *me*. Not to you, to me. So by what right did you order my ground crew to do *anything* to an aircraft for which I am responsible?"

"I... I don't know, Captain."

"You don't know why you gave my ground crew orders, Lieutenant? Are you delusional? Do I need to inform the flight physician to ground you pending a psychological examination?"

"No, sir!"

Randall leaned in close, mimicking what he'd seen his father-in-law do. He knew that he smelled terrible after four days in the desert, and dared Wang to show any sign of disrespect or discomfort. An itchy face came from not having shaved lately and dirt matted his clothes. He dropped his voice so only Wang could hear him. "If you ever come near my aircraft again, or any of my ground crew... if you even *look* at *Tank Girl* cross-eyed, I will make you wish you'd never signed up for this duty. Do we understand each other, Lieutenant?"

"Yes, sir."

"Get out of my sight."

Wang wheeled and walked out with as much dignity as he could muster. Carlos watched him go, too, shaking his head. He walked beside Randall and muttered, "What a dick."

"Lieutenant Carlos, may I speak to you a moment, sir?"

Carlos turned to Rossi. "You may, Master Sergeant."

"In private, sir."

Somebody on the ground crew giggled. Carlos followed her through a doorway and into a storage area. Randall heard something metal hit the floor, followed by rustling.

Randall stayed in the hangar while one of the ground crew brought food and water. He was too tired to find the mess hall. Showers had been set up near the old BX and he really, really wanted to take one, but food and hydration came first, and then he'd report to General Kando, or whoever was in command of Creech now. Only after that would there be time for some blessed sleep. His whole body ached with fatigue and halfway through an MRE his eyes started to grow heavy.

He had already planned to leave at dawn to scout for Angriff and, if and when they found him, to transport him to Overtime. He would go whether the flight was approved or not, and whether the general wanted him to or not. Maybe he could at least fly him closer to Overtime. They had a general idea of Angriff's intended course, but it was a damned big desert out there. And he wanted *Tank Girl* loaded down with extra fuel, lots of water, emergency medical kits, and food. But that was for tomorrow morning; for that night he was going to sleep.

While he ate, the rest of the ground crew caught him up on events up north, at Sierra Army Depot. When they reported that *Hell's Hammer* had gone and not come back, Randall's fatigue vanished. Then he heard about the V-22s that came through to refuel, and went north carrying artillery pieces. When they told him that artillery was intended for use to support the Chinese against the Americans, Randall lost his appetite.

"Who told you that?" he said.

"General Steeple did, Captain. He announced it to all units."

"Damn."

That changed everything.

He only gave Carlos and Rossi ten more minutes before he knocked on the door and told them to come out. Both were disheveled and Carlos looked pissed, but Randall didn't give him the chance to speak.

"Get her ready for combat, Frame," Randall said to Rossi. "Ordnance package E. I want her loaded with as much spare ammo as we can take, plus food and water for a week. I need this done now."

"You're leaving?"

"We are. I'm very sorry, I know how hard this must be, but we've got to go help at Sierra, and with General Steeple in charge, that might be scratched. We've got to go before we can be grounded." As much as he wanted to search for Nick the A... that would have to wait. And besides, Angriff *had* ordered him not to search.

"At first light?"

"No, half an hour, tops, so I need you to get to it."

Rossi blinked back tears and glanced at Carlos, but nodded at Randall. "On it, sir."

When nobody was within earshot, Carlos got close. "What the fuck, Joe? What happened to pigging out and screwing all night?"

"Change in plans, Bunny. Looks like we're going back to war."

"By 'going back to war,' you mean there's a chance we might die?"

"That's always a possibility."

"And who are we going to war against?"

"I'm not sure yet."

"So we're going to fly hundreds of miles to the north, to maybe fight against an unknown enemy, for unknown reasons?"

"That's about the size of it."

"I wanna go home."

#

Chapter 20

"I've always had a weakness for lost causes, once they're really lost."
Margaret Mitchell

Over the Nevada Desert
0947 hours, May 2

Two hours into the flight, the heat of the day began to create thermals. Not violent updrafts like what would come with the heat of July and August, but enough that the warm, rising air caused instability in the atmosphere which translated into a jarring ride for the two men in the old German airplane. Green Ghost had ridden for the first two hours in the observer's seat at the rear of the glass nacelle. Suspended over something translucent made him queasy, but nausea was an old friend familiar to any combat veteran. What he couldn't ignore was the urgency of his bladder with every jolt.

He could have used the interplane communication system, but he was also stiff and wanted to stretch out. Unbuckling his seatbelt, he crawled down the nacelle to the pilot's seat and tapped Allen Pohl on the shoulder. When Pohl removed his right noise-cancelling headphone, Green Ghost had to shout over the roar of the engine.

"I need to piss!"

Pohl nodded, reached to one side of his seat, and handed Green Ghost a glass bottle. "Tighten it real good, but don't throw it away," he said. "Glass bottles are better than gold. Oh, and put your ears on."

Green Ghost looked at the bottle, then back at Pohl, who grinned. It wouldn't be the first time he'd peed in a bottle, but he really, really hated doing it.

Once back in his seat, Green Ghost donned his headset. Red and tan mountains continued slipping away below them, as if the world consisted of nothing else. Occasionally a patch of greenery flashed by, mostly scrub bushes, and, of course, flat brown desert.

"Heads up back there," Pohl called, the first words he'd said in half an hour. "We're in the area where that ravine might be, so I'm going to throttle back and gain some altitude so we can take our time and see farther. But even if he's down there, seeing him isn't a lock."

"How much time do we have?"

"An hour, maybe a little more... but if we find a trail, I might be able to squeeze out another few hours."

"How?"

"We'll worry about that when and if."

"I've got my binoculars ready. Let's do this."

The topography tended toward ridgelines arranged in parallel lines from northwest to southeast, with wide swaths of flat desert between them. Pohl flew up one valley and down the next in a systematic pattern. After forty-five minutes, Green Ghost had to close his eyes and wipe away tears. Silver and red sparkles filled his peripheral vision.

"How are you doing back there?" Pohl said in his headphones.

Blinking, Green Ghost sat up straight. The sparkles were still there. "I'm good."

"If we haven't seen anything in fifteen minutes, I've got to think about turning back."

"Roger that. What's that town down below?"

There was a delay before Pohl answered. "The map says it's Hiko... and hey, there's an airstrip!"

"Are you gonna land?"

"No, but it's never bad to have an emergency strip stashed away."

"That makes sense."

Even with the binoculars up to his eyes, Green Ghost still had tunnel vision. Rubbing them felt so good, but the clock was ticking and... what was that? "Pohl, can you take her down some?"

"See something?"

"I don't know, maybe."

"Hang on, it might be a little bumpy."

They'd been flying at only 500 feet, which limited their range of view but made sure they wouldn't miss a long figure on foot. At Green Ghost's request, Pohl took the Blomm and Voss down to 200 feet. Green Ghost ignored the kaleidoscope of color and the turbulence to try and find what he'd seen again, a smudge of black somewhere near the highway... there!

"Pohl, did you see that? Just off the right... wait, I'm backwards, it was your left. Take her back around again."

"What did it look like?"

"A campfire, a very recent campfire."

One foot in front of another... one foot in front of another...

Nick Angriff had vowed not to stop again until he reached the edge of a ridgeline on his left, which appeared to be no more than half a mile away. With no way to measure distances, he could only guess that he'd walked more than a mile since then, and now the sun shone directly overhead. He wasn't dehydrated because of the lake water, but would be in a few days unless he found more. Food was more problematic. Thanks to the jacket, at least he could sleep during the night.

He'd become accustomed to the sounds of the desert, the wind blowing through brush and an occasional mesquite tree, the birds and coyotes. Like any modern American soldier or Marine, he was no stranger to deserts, but only once you were immersed in one could you understand how different that particular desert was from all the others. This one, he thought of it simply as the Nevada desert, felt and sounded familiar now. Even the drone of an insect, growing louder like a swarm filled the sky. Except his tired brain realized that it wasn't an insect at all; it was a prop-driven airplane.

Shading his eyes, he watched it growing larger as it came toward him, using the highway as a guide. Glare made it hard to make out details, but it flew low and slow, and there seemed no doubt that it was out there looking for him.

There was no time to do anything except act. Surveying his surroundings, Angriff saw nowhere to hide, not even a big rock to get behind in case of a strafing run. He moved off the highway about thirty feet anyway, to avoid ricochets off the pavement. Wiping sweat off his right hand by running it down the side of his pants, he drew an Eagle and began to draw a bead on the plane.

The scene in the movie *Patton* came to his mind, where the general shot at attacking German bombers. Angriff knew it to be pure fiction, it was ridiculous to engage aircraft with a handgun, but as stupid as it might be, he wasn't going down without a fight. He squinted to minimize the distortion of the sunlight on his aim, and lined up the aircraft in his sights. As it grew larger, he concentrated on aiming at the cockpit area... which was off center to the fuselage.

What the hell?

Is that something homemade? he wondered, because he'd never seen an airplane like that before. And yet something tickled his memory. He *had* seen it before, but where?

The plane waggled its wings and slowed even more. Instead of passing directly over him, it went over the highway to his right, and he could see the pilot in some sort of glass pod hung on a wing beside the engine. Then he saw its three-tone tan, brown, and green camouflage pattern, the yellow band around the fuselage behind squadron lettering, a black cross outlined in white, and a swastika on the vertical stabilizer. He forgot about shooting it. Instead, he gawked, and saw someone waving from a glass-framed area at the back of the cockpit pod.

The memory where he'd seen it before had come to him the instant he saw the plane's identifiers. Not the model, but he knew it was a Luftwaffe observation plane of some type, which meant it had to be a hallucination. Nothing else made sense. World War Two German airplanes just didn't fly in the skies of post-Collapse America.

The plane made a wide circle and headed back toward him. As it did, it slowed and lost more altitude. Angriff was so convinced that it couldn't be real that he didn't react when the landing gear lowered and the airplane flared to a landing. Bouncing on the rough highway, for a second it appeared the plane might tip a wing into the dirt and cartwheel, until the pilot settled it onto the makeshift landing strip and taxied toward him. A rattlesnake crossing the highway slithered off the hot pavement to avoid being squashed.

Angriff pulled his shirt up over his nose and mouth, and turned away as prop wash threw dust and gravel into the air. When he spun back to the plane, a lean figure walked toward him wearing American uniform camouflage pants (UCPs), a black T-shirt, and worn black boots. He holstered the Eagle and shook his head. "Who wears black in the desert?" he said, extending his hands to either side.

"I didn't know if I was going to a funeral or not," Green Ghost said.

"You're going to a funeral, all right, but it won't be mine."

With the afternoon shadows lengthening, Allen Pohl climbed out of the cockpit and began unloading five-gallon plastic gasoline containers from the cargo hatch. He assumed that Green Ghost would bring his father over for an introduction, but when that didn't happen, he called to them. "Hey, guys, a little help?"

"Sorry, Allen," Green Ghost said.

The older man was heavier than his son, with thick, wide shoulders. When Pohl shook his right hand, the skin felt rough and calloused.

"Nick Angriff."

"I've heard all about you," Pohl said. "My father was a great admirer of yours. I'm Allen Pohl."

"Now I understand the plane. I know all about your father. We met once, did he tell you that?"

"He did, yes, several hundred times."

"He was a great man... that's a Blomm and Voss, right?"

"Correct, a BV 141."

"Is it hard to fly?"

Pohl shook his head. "Just the opposite. It's surprisingly well balanced and easy to handle. I love flying it."

"Huh, I never would have guessed. How have you kept it airworthy all these years?"

"I gave up TV." They both laughed. Even Green Ghost smiled. "Seriously, there's not much else to do, and we've got a machine shop that can make just about any part I need."

"His compound is amazing," Green Ghost added.

"It's getting late. Would you mind giving me a hand refueling?"

"It's the least we can do."

Using a ladder Pohl had brought, Green Ghost climbed onto the wing and poured the aviation fuel through a funnel into the tank. Pohl stood at the top of the ladder and Angriff handed up the containers to him. Once they'd finished and tossed the empties back into the cargo hatch along with the ladder, Angriff broached the subject he'd been practicing a pitch for in his head.

"We need you to fly us across the Colorado River," he said, without preamble.

"I thought you might ask that," Pohl said. "But if I do that, I'll never get home before dark, and I can't fly at night. If it was open desert the whole way, that'd be one thing, but I'm going to have to navigate multiple mountain ranges, plus my landing strip is surrounded by ridges and isn't lit. I'm sorry, it's just too risky."

"Spend the night here," Green Ghost said.

Angriff smiled. "We'll tell campfire stories."

"Gentlemen, I really do want to help, but I'm expected home. I'm afraid if I don't show up, Eduardo will send people out looking for me."

"General Angriff is the man who can put you in the seat of an A-10."

An instant change came over Pohl's face, from a scowl to wide-eyed interest. "Oh?"

"That's right," Angriff said, playing along. "We've got some that have been crated for five decades. I'd love to have an expert like you to help get them into the air, test fly 'em, you know, that sort of thing."

"Is that a promise?"

"You get us east of the river, and that's a promise."

"In that case, what do we have to eat?"

Pohl had given Green Ghost some jerked antelope, hard biscuits, and dried beans, and had more of the same stored on the aircraft as emergency rations. Angriff had two MREs left and shared one, the beef ravioli. He and Green Ghost each had a pan in which they boiled water, with the jerky in one and the beans in the other. After boiling the beans, Green Ghost covered them with a rock to soak until breakfast.

Once the jerky had softened, they dipped the biscuits in the water until they'd absorbed enough to be eaten without breaking a tooth. With hunger pangs abated and a fire crackling in a pit of stones, the three men felt more like talking. They shared some of the beans' cook water, and then Pohl tossed in some salt so they'd taste decent in the morning.

"You boys make sure you're downwind tomorrow," Angriff said.

After small talk, the conversation turned to recent occurrences concerning the Seventh Cavalry. Green Ghost filled him in as best he could. Angriff pegged the situation at Sierra as being particularly volatile, and said so.

"I'm very disappointed in Bob Young," he said.

"Don't be so harsh, Saint. He's only doing what Steeple ordered him to do."

"That's what disappoints me."

"Steeple controls all the fuel, food, and ammo to keep Colonel Young's regiment in the field. There's not a lot of choice."

"There's *always* a choice."

"What happens if the Chinese take Sierra?" Pohl said.

"I imagine they'll move into Western Nevada, take Reno and who knows what else. There won't be anything to stop them."

"How many men do you have defending the depot?"

Green Ghost pursed his lips. "Maybe three hundred on their feet, able to fight. There's about four thousand Chinese and another five hundred to seven hundred in the 2nd Mechanized Regiment. Not counting artillery."

"So you're outnumbered ten to one?"

"Or worse. Plus, they've got some tanks and self-propelled artillery."

"Any timetable on the attack?" said Angriff.

Green Ghost turned away and stared into the dark desert. "They're waiting for artillery support to come up."

"Artillery? Steeple is sending artillery to shell his own troops?"

"Yeah."

"He's not a very nice guy, is he?" said Pohl.

"Nice isn't a word that's ever described Tom Steeple, but I never in my wildest dreams thought he would turn on his own people. He was once the highest-ranking officer in the U.S. Army. Those are his tribe, and if he's willing to kill them... I've got to get to Prime ASAP. I've got to put a stop to this insanity." Nobody spoke for a minute, and then Angriff added, "I wish now that you had that A-10, Allen."

"Maybe I do," Pohl said.

"Huh?"

"Nothing."

#

Chapter 21

An angry man is again angry with himself when he returns to reason.
Publilius Syrus

Highway 93 east of Crystal Springs, Nevada
0636 hours, May 4

    The sunrise blinded Nick Angriff as he sat crammed into the center of the BV 141's long cockpit. He was a big man and the seat had been designed for someone no bigger than 140 pounds, so he sat with bent back and knees in his chin. Regardless of his discomfort, it beat the hell out of walking.
    Pohl flew a direct route over a series of mountain ranges. They couldn't risk getting too close to Hoover Dam, or too far east. Aside from the chance of discovery, Pohl was pushing the reconnaissance plane to the limits of its range for him to reach home after this detour. So when Nevada Highway 93 appeared 8,000 feet below, they scanned for any oncoming traffic and, finding none, Pohl lost altitude. Angriff shouted final directions for which strip of highway to land on. He had a very definite destination in mind.
    They bounced to a stop along a desolate stretch of road, between two ridgelines barren of anything except rock. Angriff and Green Ghost climbed out while Pohl kept the engine running. There was enough room on the shoulder of the highway for him to turn the aircraft for takeoff back in the direction they'd landed, to the east, and the two men watched as he

climbed into the rising sun and banked away to the northwest.

"I'd guess we'd better get going," Green Ghost said. "We've still got a helluva long walk."

Angriff stood silent a moment, orienting himself. "Maybe not."

Leaving the highway two miles southeast of where Pohl had left them, Angriff led Green Ghost over a high ridge to the north. The day grew hotter and dust caked their nostrils, but after a few hours they found a small ravine in the side of another ridge that provided shade to rest in.

"What's the name of this place we're heading to?" Green Ghost said. Drinking two mouthfuls, he swished the second around before swallowing.

"Ma Kelly's."

"What is it?"

"It's a trading post. People bring in things they've found and barter it for other things they need."

"No money involved, I assume."

"That's the irony of this whole thing, isn't it? So many people spent their lives chasing something that, at the end of the day, didn't really exist. Money was never more than an idea, a token that represented stability so we didn't have to kill each other over food and shelter. But when everything that made modern life possible grew scarce, the people that had food, or gas, or ammo, weren't so willing to trade it for those little pieces of paper any more. Don't get me wrong, son, I've got nothing against money. You've probably had somebody tell you that money is the root of all evil, haven't you?"

"I have."

"That's from the Bible... Timothy, I think... it's been a long time and I can't remember for certain. But see, that's not the whole quote. Money's not the root of all evil — the *love* of money is the root of all evil. Money was created to spend, not to hoard."

Green Ghost smiled. "Wanna hear something funny? During one of her sober periods, Mom managed to buy a house; she got a mortgage and everything. It wasn't much of a house, and it wasn't in much of a neighborhood, but it was hers. Then... then she lost it. She couldn't pay the mortgage and the bank threatened to foreclose, but they never did, because by then the area had gotten so bad it was a liability. If they foreclosed then they'd be responsible for it, and they knew that nobody'd ever want to buy it, not in Little Hell. She finally lost it because the city took it for back taxes, but even then we kept living there.

"After you went missing and we thought you were dead, I decided to get it caught up on the taxes. Then I went to the bank and negotiated a buyout, and paid that off, too. I owned it outright. I thought it was important to do that for Nikki. It was the only bit of stability she'd ever had in her life."

"And? Did she live there?"

"No, it wasn't habitable. You don't know this part, but do you remember right before the op in the Congo, I took a leave, and then requested for my squad to join me? And you okayed it?"

"I remember. Lake Tahoe happened during that op in the Congo."

"Yeah, that's right. What you don't know is that Nikki had gone back to the old house. Part of the roof was caved in and it was in terrible shape, but she'd worked for months turning it into a fortress. See, she'd found Mom's journal. We always thought Mom had relapsed, but her journal made it clear that's not what happened. She'd kicked the drugs, but a leader of the biggest gang in Little Hell spiked her drink to get her hooked on heroin again, and then made her pull tricks to get drugs. When Nikki read that... something changed inside her. That's when Nipple first showed up, and Nipple went to war with that gang. She was determined to kill the guy who took Mom away from us. The problem was that gang leader's father was the Memphis chief of police, so she couldn't go to them about it."

"What about the FBI?"

"She didn't think about that, which might be a good thing, looking back. Remember, Bettison was FBI. I don't think we were on his radar, but if he'd started poking around, who knows what he might have found."

"Yeah," Angriff said, thinking about it. "You're right, but he didn't know you were my kids. The chances of him making the connection would have been slim."

"Maybe, but there was so much corruption I wouldn't have wanted to take the chance. I don't think Nikki even thought about it. Instead, she took the money I'd been sending her and learned how to shoot. Nikki's like me, and I guess Morgan, too... I don't know about Cindy. Nikki's a natural-born dead shot, and just as fast. She only called me after she'd killed nine of the gang members and the entire state was looking for her."

"*Nine!* By herself?"

Green Ghost nodded.

"But you obviously got her out of it."

"I got her out of the country, with the help of my squad. We left a lot of bodies behind, too."

"All of them deserve it?"

"Every last one."

"Good. All enemies, foreign and domestic, right?"

"Yeah."

Angriff pointed to the east. "Somewhere way off that way, a few thousand miles, is the Angriff family farm outside of Charlottesville, Virginia. That piece of land would have been your heritage, you and the girls. The Angriffs have lived there since the early 1700s, when our great-great-however-many-greats-back-grandfather came to America from Bavaria. Most German speakers settled in New England, but the Angriffs picked Virginia. I have no idea why."

"One thing I've always wanted to know is how we got the name Angriff."

"You mean because it's German for attack?" Green Ghost nodded. "The story goes that during the Thirty Years' War, one of our grandfathers impressed the king of Bavaria so much that he granted the man and his family the honorific surname *Angreifer*, which is German for attacker."

"Kind of like the names Krieg and Krieger."

"Yes, that's it exactly. That man's son was the father of our ancestor who emigrated to America. There were four boys, but the father was killed during the Siege of Vienna in 1683, and only our granddad left Europe for the New World. All of that is family lore, although I don't know how true any of it is."

"Based on his descendants, I believe it's probably true," Green Ghost said.

His father smiled. "I'm sure as hell not going to argue the point."

Ma Kelly's

Green Ghost lay atop the crest of a ridge, peering with his binoculars into the valley below. "You said it didn't look like much."

Beside him, Angriff used his own binoculars to observe the ramshackle buildings. Four horses stood in a small holding pen, still saddled. "You'd be surprised what all they've got in there. But right now I'm more interested in those horses."

"You think they're ours?"

"No, those aren't Army saddles. My only question is whether or not they belong to Rednecks."

"So you think Steeple pulled Wincommer's men out of here?"

"I do. No reason to commit scarce resources to some insignificant shack at the ass-end of nowhere."

"You did."

"It's not some insignificant shack to me."

Half an hour later a man came out of the main door and headed for the outhouse in the back. Around his neck was the telltale red scarf that gave the Rednecks their nickname.

"Plan?" Green Ghost said. "Lure them out?"

"I'm going in there. When that guy comes out, put him down."

"You're not going in there. I am."

"No."

"*Yes.* If something happens to you, Steeple wins. Stop acting like you're a lieutenant, Dad! You're not, you're the one irreplaceable person in the whole brigade, whether you like it or not."

Angriff used his right middle finger to rub the bridge of his nose. It wasn't a gesture he used except in trusted company, since it could be easily misconstrued, but Green Ghost recognized it for what it was, a signal that he was thinking.

"Sometimes I liked it better when you weren't my son."

Green Ghost felt like John Wayne about to push open the swinging doors of an Old West saloon. The biggest danger was the man in the outhouse coming out before Green Ghost had slid down the ridge and run to the first building. His luck had held and the Redneck was still in there, but that could change at any second, and a gunshot would alert those inside. He'd left his rifle with his father, so with the Sig Sauer up to his right eye, he pushed the door open with his boot.

The cluttered main room appeared empty, but he took no chances, clearing each area before moving on to the next. Although he'd affixed a silencer to the pistol, the distinctive *thwitt* sound would be instantly recognizable to anyone familiar with weapons. It would be much better to catch all three Rednecks together, although the 226 Legion RX Full-Size had a 15-round magazine, fully loaded.

He'd crept to the wide door leading into another room when a single rifle shot echoed outside. Seconds later, it was matched by one from another room inside the building.

Stepping to his left, Green Ghost used the wall to shield his body, while leaning forward at the waist to shoot anybody who appeared. Within seconds, three Rednecks stumbled into the room, one of them pulling up his pants. All carried AK-47s. He let them get close until the lead man spotted him and tried to raise his rifle. Then Green Ghost put two rounds into each of them, one in the chest and the other at the base of their necks. It was easier than a training run.

Blood pools covered the floor as the men bled out. One moaned. It was the guy with his pants down, and Green Ghost put a third shot into his head. He'd killed people in his life that he regretted having killed, but a rapist didn't make the list, and it seemed clear that was what the man had been.

He cleared the rest of the complex. In the last room, he found the older man he'd been told about, the one who could only be Dave Weiner, hugging the limp body of a young girl who'd been shot in the chest. Next to Weiner knelt two weeping young boys, with the oldest boy perhaps twelve or thirteen. Green Ghost lowered the pistol.

Weiner looked up, eyes puffy. "You animal! Why did you have to kill her?"

"I'm not one of them. I'm with General Angriff."

"Angriff!" Weiner shouted the word like a curse. He gently laid his daughter back on the floor and pushed to his feet. "That son of a bitch promised to protect my family. Where is he? Where is the bastard?"

Green Ghost's eyes never left the girl. Something didn't look right about her. Absently, he pointed toward the door. "He's outside."

In his grief, Weiner ran out of the room, forgetting his sons and daughter. Green Ghost knelt beside the girl and felt her neck, then laid his hand between her breasts. He felt the slightest rise and fall. Ripping open her shirt, he put his ear close to the gunshot's entry wound and heard a faint sucking sound. She wasn't dead yet.

"Go find me some clean rags," he said to the boys, who only blinked in response. "Now! And a tube of some kind. She's not dead! Go find me this shit, and hurry!"

He'd treated such injuries several times before, and knew the first priority was to seal the wound and stop the bleeding. The bullet had entered the right side of her chest. He felt her back and found the exit wound, which meant the bullet had to be lodged in the wooden floor. That was both good and bad. Exiting the body had done more damage, but the round wouldn't have to be surgically removed.

The boys came back with a two-foot-long piece of half-inch PVC pipe and a pile of rags. At his request for alcohol, the older boy retrieved a jug of clear homemade something. A sniff told Green Ghost that whatever it was, it had plenty of alcohol in it. He used the liquor to sterilize the PVC pipe and clean the wound, and then poured some over his hands.

As he worked on the girl, Weiner ran back into the room. "Get away from her!" He tried to pull Green Ghost away, but the older boy intervened.

"Venni's alive, Father. He's trying to save her."

"What?" Weiner's entire demeanor changed as hope flooded his face. "How did I miss that?"

"Forget it!" Green Ghost said, as he taped the PVC in place "She's got a sucking chest wound and has lost a lot of blood."

As he worked, Weiner stood behind him. Every now and then he fetched something Green Ghost asked for. At some point, Angriff entered the room but kept quiet. With her father's help, Green Ghost taped rags into place on her back, but her pulse remained weak.

He looked up at Angriff. "She lost a lot of blood. If we knew blood types, I'd try and rig a transfusion, but if we get the wrong one, as weak as she is, it could kill her. She needs a hospital."

"Take my blood," Weiner said, holding out his forearm.

"It's too dangerous," Angriff answered. "I know it's hard, Dave, but the best thing to do now is to wait. Come on, let's see to your boys."

Weiner turned a stunned face to Angriff. "I thought she was dead... but she wasn't. How did I miss that, Nick? If you hadn't showed up—"

"Hey, you didn't do anything wrong, Dave. The scumbags who shot her did. Now come on, let's be ready in case any more show up."

#

Chapter 22

*Send me not again into the chasms of my mind,
For there dwells only darkness.
Oscar O'Connor, from "Cumha"*

Ma Kelly's
1311 hours, May 4

Angriff quickly explained what had happened with Tom Steeple, and why the cavalry troop had been ordered to leave. Even as he told Weiner what had happened, he felt guilt welling inside him again, along with the urgency of getting back to Prime. This was his fault, and Weiner's daughter needed medical care urgently, but first he offered to tie the bodies of the Rednecks to one of the horses and drag them out of the valley so scavengers wouldn't be attracted to Ma Kelly's. It would take all afternoon, but he felt he owed Weiner at least that much.

Weiner, however, had another idea. "You go on. I'll take care of this trash," he nodded to the Rednecks, "I'll feed 'em to the pigs. Me and the boys can do that. You've done all you can do here, but you said that when you get back to your base, you'll send a doctor back for Venni?"

"Not just a doctor, Dave, a whole team. I'll send a helicopter that's rigged specifically to help gunshot victims. I promise."

Weiner met his eyes. "Then you'd best get going. Take their horses; they're already saddled. Let me get some food together and fill your canteens, and then you get back to your base. The sooner you do that, the sooner you can send that doctor."

There were still a few hours of daylight left when they climbed onto the horses. They took all four, loading the spare two with their supplies. Green Ghost checked the four AK-47s to make sure they were operable, gave one to Angriff along with three extra magazines, all loaded, and left the other three with Weiner. Then they waved goodbye and rode like hell for as long as they could.

#

Part Three

Positioning

Chapter 23

Thunder in the black skies beating down the rain,
Thunder in the black cliffs, looming o'er the main,
Thunder on the black sea and thunder in my brain.
  Robert E. Howard, "Red Thunder"

In the skies above Sierra Army Depot, Herlong, CA
1835 hours, May 4

The gathering darkness cast shadows from the huge vehicles directly under the BV 141's left wing, but Allen Pohl had seen everything he'd needed to see. Junker Jane had made it clear that the Americans held Sierra Army Depot, and the Chinese were to the west, while some other Americans camped to the south might or might not be helping the Chinese. Everything lined up just as she'd said, and now he knew who was who.

With the sun setting, he turned for home. Having seen the Chinese with his own eyes, Pohl had no doubt that if the Americans didn't stop them at Sierra, nothing would stop them from driving as far to the east as they wanted. And that put his compound squarely in their path. Off his right wing, he passed a prairie falcon, and for a brief second he felt a kinship with the creature of the air, and wondered if it, too, feared that the men below would destroy its home. Then it was gone.

He already knew what he was going to do. It was stupid and crazy, even desperate, and Eduardo would do everything humanly possible to dissuade him, but Pohl's mind was made up. If a man wouldn't fight to defend his home, then what was the point of owning weapons? No, he was going to do it with or without Eduardo's help, which meant that the sunset visible off his right wing might very well be the last one he would ever see.

0410 hours, May 5

They didn't make camp until three hours after full darkness fell, and were up before dawn. Both men turned their attention now to figuring out how to get back inside the mountain, back inside Overtime Prime, without being seen. Even approaching it was problematic.

"My own early warning system is working against me," Angriff said as they wolfed down a fast breakfast. Camping on the bank of a tiny stream meant the horses could forage on a small patch of greenery, but the risk of building a fire meant the humans ate cold food in waning moonlight.

"There *is* a way to get in, if I can find it again," Green Ghost said.

"That's a start. Where is it?"

"Do you remember Rita?"

"She the one who had the glass knife?"

"Yeah, that's her. Do you also remember when we tracked down the rest of the RSVS to that room in the unfinished section? We thought there were ten of them, but once we got inside we found that some had left?"

"I vaguely remember it."

"The way they got out was... well, there's a shaft that goes straight down, with a ladder—"

"Another one?"

"Yes. It goes down a long way, and then splits into two different tunnels. One comes out in the east, and that's the way those RSVS people went. But the other one exits on the west. I followed it that way once, all the way out. They're all connected together inside the mountain."

"Can you find the western exit again?"

"That's the question. I think so. I remember there are these two small spurs at the base of the mountain, and in between them is a crack. And inside of *there* is a hatch that leads into the base."

"Does it lock?"

"From the inside."

"Then let's hope nobody thought about that. All right, so now we might have a way in once we get there, but two riders approaching from the west *will* attract attention. We'll stick out, even if we travel at night."

"I know. I had all those cameras installed in the western approaches to prevent what we're going to try doing, but I can't think of any way around it."

"I can't either, and with this new moon, the nights are too damned dark to be hunting for landmarks. That's also when all the predators hunt and we can't see holes in the desert… there are a lot of negatives to waiting until tonight to try it. And then there's Dave's daughter. She needs a hospital, and quick."

"And Steeple. We don't know the combat situation or what's he planning."

"I don't see any way around it. I think we have to go during daylight and hope for the best."

Green Ghost nodded. "It sucks, but yeah, I agree."

#

Chapter 24

"If we lose freedom here, there's no place to escape to. This is the last stand on Earth."
Ronald Reagan

Sara Snowtiger's cave
0709 hours, May 5

Zo Piccaldi approached the cave entrance and dropped to his stomach, squirming forward the rest of the way onto the ledge. They had built a rock wall to provide cover from small arms fire, using loose stones from inside the cavern, and it now reached nearly 18 inches in height. Several tiny holes had been left for shooting through, and Lara Snowtiger lay prone behind one of them, the barrel of her rifle extending through the wall just in case a Seven on the desert floor became careless. Piccaldi glanced up as he crawled, directly at her backside, and then turned his head and shook it. That brought a chuckle from the old Cajun guy, Thibodeaux, sitting with his back to the mountain and watching Piccaldi from the cave's mouth.

After giving Thibodeaux a dirty look, Piccaldi called out softly. "Hey, Lara, relief time."

She didn't respond, but instead stayed rigid. He didn't say anything else because he knew what that meant. Seconds later she fired, once, then pulled the rifle from the hole and rolled onto her back.

"Get him?" Piccaldi said.

She shook her head. "No, but I scared the fuck out of him. He's their sniper. He'll be back, so keep an eye out around the rock pile on your left."

"Got it. Anything I should know?"

"About an hour ago, a rider came in with a couple of boxes. I couldn't get a clear shot." She met his eyes, trying to convey the importance of her words, but all he noticed were the depths of her green-flecked brown eyes. Piccaldi could stare into them all day and never get tired. "They could have been mortar rounds."

That brought him back to the present. The Sevens had fired off six mortar rounds before they'd apparently run out of ammo. The first five had been ranging shots that kept getting closer, while the sixth had barely missed the ledge and exploded against the mountain thirty feet below the cavern.

"Shit."

"Yeah."

Snowtiger crawled into the cave mouth before standing up and disappearing inside. Piccaldi wanted to watch her — if he couldn't stare into her eyes, then her backside would do just fine — but with Thibodeaux watching, he forced himself to keep his eyes front. He used the time to take readings and adjust his settings.

"You gots it bad," Thibodeaux said, laughing. "She don't know, does she?"

"You're out of your mind, old man."

Thibodeaux's laugh came out as a cackle, and Piccaldi could tell he was doing that on purpose.

"Yeah, I'm old, but I ain't blind yet, an' I ain't forgot what a woman can do to yer insides, neither. Why ain't you told her how ya feel?"

"You're still out of your mind."

"Never figured a Marine to be scared of a girl."

"And you talk too much, too."

"I seen her look at you... it's mutual. You might not believe me—"

"Ssshhh!"

"All right, if you—"

"Shut the fuck up! Something's going on down there and you're distracting me!"

Thibodeaux moved like a man half his age. Throwing himself down behind the little wall, he used binoculars to peer through another opening in the rocks. "What're you seeing?"

"Right in the center, I saw two heads pop up, but I couldn't get a shot before they went back down. I've seen mortar crews do that same thing."

"I don't like the sound o' that."

Piccaldi didn't respond. After another minor adjustment, he scanned the Sevens' position for any potential targets and finally settled on the very top of a man's head, where he thought the mortar crew might be. There wasn't enough of a target to justify taking a shot, but if the man raised his head just another inch...

All of his senses shifted into combat mode. Nearby sounds made no impression on Piccaldi's brain; nothing in his peripheral vision distracted from the sliver of a target in his scope. It was like he could reach out and touch the man he'd chosen to die. Only another sniper knew what it was like.

Then, as he concentrated, his mind registered a faint, distant shot, like a muffled shotgun, and knew it was a mortar firing a round. Simultaneously, the target's head moved upward no more than half an inch, but it was enough. Piccaldi squeezed the M40A7's trigger, like he was caressing a lady, and the rifle recoiled into his shoulder. In three-quarters of a second, the 7.62x51mm round impacted the target's head just below the crown, knocking him backward and out of sight. But after the echo of his shot finished ringing in his ears, a whistling sound reminded him that the mortar had gotten off a round.

"Incoming!" he yelled. Jumping up but staying hunched over, he grabbed the slower Thibodeaux's arm and half-dragged him toward the cavern entrance. Bullets whizzed over their heads, making it clear this was a coordinated attack and the Sevens had anticipated them standing up to run. With Piccaldi's help, they were a foot inside the cave when the mortar round hit twenty feet above them.

Most of the blast force went out from the cliff's face, raining stones and splinters onto the ledge. Piccaldi's left hand had grabbed the cavern mouth's rim for support, and a rock shard cut a bloody but shallow gouge into the back of the hand. A second round struck the ledge directly on the left side, while two follow-up rounds hit well to the left of the cave mouth.

Once inside, Piccaldi shoved Thibodeaux ahead of him down the short tunnel and into the common area beyond. Dennis Tompkins stood with his arm around Sara Snowtiger's shoulders, but ran over to check on Thibodeaux. Paul Hausser, Sig Zuckerman, and Derek Tandy had been asleep against one wall, and after seeing that everybody was still on their feet, they all laid back down.

Lara Snowtiger came over to check on Piccaldi after she saw him fumbling with his IFAK. Lifting his hand, she moved him closer to the flaring fire at the center of the chamber. Both squatted down, and she held Piccaldi's wounded hand close to inspect it.

"I took one out," he said. "I think he was the loader."

"Nice. Maybe that's why the last three rounds were off target. Hand me your IFAK."

"While you're handling things, I might have taken a hit in the groin."

"If you did, we may have to amputate," she said.

He'd never heard her joke around with others like that. Everyone else thought she was an ice queen, but with him she seemed like a different person. "I'd rather we try something else first, to see if it still works."

She used the back of the combat gauze bandage to wipe dirt from the wound, then flipped it over and used tape to wrap it in place. "What did you have in mind?" she said. It was nothing more than an offhand remark while she worked.

"I heard the Choctaw have a healing ceremony where everybody gets naked."

She glanced up, moving only her eyes. "You heard wrong."

"It couldn't hurt."

"If you keep talking like that, one of us is gonna get hurt, and it won't be me."

"I miss the sunshine, Dennis," Sara Snowtiger said. When she snuggled deeper into his right armpit, Dennis Tompkins didn't have the heart to tell her that his arm had gone numb.

"You haven't left this cave for decades, my love," he said. It felt strange, calling somebody his love at age 83. He hadn't had a girlfriend since... since when? Who was the last one? Was it Dodi? If it was her, that would have made him 30. Fifty-three years between girlfriends and he'd gotten pretty rusty at this kind of banter, but both he and Sara felt the pressure of time as their lives neared their ends. The days of beating around the bush were long gone now.

"That is not technically true, Dennis. I leave the cave every day to meditate on the ledge, or watch the birds fly overhead. The sun greets me as it would a dear friend, and I miss my friend."

"I hope he doesn't get jealous of me."

She gave him a very serious look. "If he does, I will have a stern talk with him."

For a second, Tompkins thought she meant it, until a wide smile exposed her bright, white teeth. Reflecting the firelight, they almost seemed to glow in the dark. "You've lost too much weight," he said, running his finger over her left cheekbone. "I'm going to give you my share today, and I won't take no for answer."

As she always did when he showed concern, Sara Snowtiger smiled. This time it was sad. "I cannot see my own end, Dennis, yet I am not afraid."

"What is that supposed to mean?"

"Just that I know death is a transition to something else, something more, something... wonderful. It holds no fear for me."

"You've seen this?"

She nodded. "For others."

"Have you seen my death?"

"No, and I hope that I do not."

"Could you if I asked you?"

"It does not work that way. I never know why I see what I see, or when I will see it."

"Can you refuse the visions, shut them out?"

"I have never tried."

"If you don't want to fall in the river, stay off the bank."

She giggled. "You say the strangest things."

Before he could respond, her sister called out from the front of the cave. "They're coming!"

Tompkins pulled his arm away from Sara Snowtiger, grabbed his M16, and promptly dropped it from nerveless fingers. He shook his arm, trying to restore circulation, meanwhile grabbing the rifle with the other hand. By the time he got to the cavern's mouth, four people lay at the shooting ports in the wall. The left two feet of ledge had collapsed from the mortar round that hit four days ago.

Automatic weapons fire spattered the wall and the mountainside all around the cave's entrance. Tompkins crouched in the cavern mouth, feeling his knees burn but not willing to risk standing to see what was going on down below. "What do you see?" he called out to no one in particular.

"They's sneakin' up, Skip, hidin' and coverin' each other," Thibodeaux said. "Maybe fitty of 'em, maybe more. Them Marines is keepin' 'em pinned down. You boys can shoot like nobody I ever saw, me."

Tompkins knew that when Thibodeaux said 'fitty' he meant fifty. Nor did he bother to explain that Thibodeaux called everybody 'boys', even girls.

Beside him, Sig Zuckerman called out, "Ha! Got one!"

"Aw, shit!" It was Thibodeaux again. "PRG!"

Tompkins dropped flat as his brain instantly translated more of Thibodeaux's jargon, knowing that 'PRG' was his way of saying RPG, rocket-propelled grenade. The missile hit the top of the little rock wall above Zuckerman and exploded, showering them all with steel splinters. Seconds later a second rocket smashed into the wall right of the cavern's mouth, barely six feet over Tompkins' head. To his shock, he wasn't hurt, but Zuckerman hadn't been so lucky. As his friend rolled around in pain, Tompkins saw a slender piece of stone sticking out of Zuckerman's calf.

Crawling to his wounded friend, Tompkins grabbed his arm and dragged him back inside the cave. Once Zuckerman was out of the line of fire, Tompkins returned on hands and knees to take his place on the firing line. Vibrations from the rocket blasts and bullet impacts had shifted the stones in the wall, enlarging the hole through which he could shoot. It gave him a panoramic view of the Sevens' attack.

Five bodies lay in plain sight, testament to the accuracy of the two Marines' fire, since he assumed they'd taken out four of the five. One of the dead Sevens had an empty RPG next to his body. Two men on the left leapt to their feet and ran forward. One had an RPG and everybody in the cave concentrated their fire on him. Struck multiple times, he spun around and his finger must have jerked the trigger, since the RPG launcher fired and its warhead went skipping over the desert, exploding far to the south.

But those two had been a distraction. As the Americans poured fire down on the left, on their far right six men sprinted directly for the mountain wall, covering half of the two hundred yards before anybody could shift their fire. By that time, Piccaldi and Snowtiger, on the ledge's left-hand side, had too great of an angle to get a shot. That left only Thibodeaux and Tompkins.

The ledge and wall faced south and the Sevens' attack moved north. When the six men neared the wall, they were west of the cave and ledge. Thibodeaux and Tompkins had to pull back from the wall to fire from the ledge's western edge, where they had no protection. By the time they sighted on the Sevens, one man with an RPG was already kneeling to fire.

Both sides opened up with rifles set to full automatic. Bullets zipped over, under, and all around the two prone Americans. Before the two bolts on the M16s hit the bolt catch when the magazines emptied, three of the six attackers had fallen over. But they'd missed the one with the RPG. He fired. They saw the puff of smoke from the launcher, then the missile struck the ledge a foot below them.

Even though he was hugging the ledge to present as small a target as possible, the violence of the explosion slammed Tompkins' head into the rock. Stunned, he heard something crack. Strong hands grabbed his ankles and dragged him backward. And that was the last he remembered.

#

Chapter 25

"Do your duty as you see it, and damn the consequences!"
Lt. General George S. Patton

West of Albuquerque, New Mexico
0912 hours, May 4

The Lockheed-Martin M270B-1 self-propelled Multiple Rocket Launch System, the MLRS, was an integral part of the United States artillery forces for more than two decades. Eight M270s, such as were arrayed in the two firing lines in the desert west of Albuquerque, could launch 96 rockets in less than 40 seconds on targets more than 40 miles away. Screened by two companies of mechanized infantry, with their full complement of 28 Bradley fighting vehicles and half of the battalion's organic tank force, seven machines, it was a fearsome array of firepower from such a relatively small force.

Because of the nature of the mission, the battalion commander, Major Letif Ahmadi, had taken personal command. Short, with the dark hair and features of his Iranian ancestry, Ahmadi had proven himself in Iraq, Syria, and Afghanistan as being tough and personally fearless. His seeming indifference to danger had once even drawn a reprimand, citing the lack of unit leadership if he were killed in battle. Ahmadi found that ridiculous and ignored his CO's orders to avoid danger whenever possible. The officer was soon thereafter transferred to the Pentagon.

In accepting the assignment in New Mexico, Ahmadi had promised General Steeple that if ordered to fire on American troops, he would do so. Whether he really would or not was a different story, and he suspected that was why Colonel Mwangi had been flown in that very morning to negotiate with the Emir of New Khorasan. Or, as Ahmadi still thought of it, the city of Tucson.

He wanted to accompany Mwangi to the meeting with the representatives from the Caliphate, but she refused to allow it. Both of them couldn't afford to be killed or taken captive, so if something happened to her, he could defend himself and conduct a fighting retreat. At least, that was the reason she gave. Ahmadi didn't believe it for one second. Mwangi just didn't want him getting any of the credit for bringing peace with the Sevens, but that was fine with him. Radical Muslims had destroyed his ancestral home and it was his fondest wish to grant their wish of martyrdom.

Then, at the last instant, Mwangi changed her mind about going alone with a driver, and asked Ahmadi to come with her and to pack a rifle squad into a Bradley for security.

"May I ask why the change of heart, ma'am?" he said.

"A show of force never hurts, Major." She said it like she had experience in shows of force, and he didn't, like a teacher to a student. Ahmadi wasn't positive it was an insult, but chose to believe that it was. He wouldn't forget it.

Sati Bashara grabbed the emir's elbow before he stepped into the Bradley. He leaned close to the older man's ear so he couldn't be overheard. "You cannot bring her, Uncle. This is men's business. She has no right to be there; it is forbidden."

El Mofty had one foot inside the Bradley, but stepped back out. Taking his nephew by the arm, he led him out of earshot. "Never again tell me that what I do is forbidden. Do you understand, nephew? Not even in private."

"But Uncle, it is written—"

The emir's voice dropped to a whisper that sounded more like a hiss than a voice. "What did I just tell you? *I* am the emir, not you. It is my brother to whom Allah speaks, it is my brother who has written down the words of Allah, it is my brother with whom I discuss deep matters. In matters of interpretation of the words of the New Prophet, it is *I* to whom that responsibility has been given. Do you understand these words as I have told them to you?"

Bashara nodded without meeting el Mofty's gaze.

"Good. Let us speak no more of theology, but instead let us make this a moment to learn. The Americans are sending a woman to meet us." He paused to see how Bashara might react to that. As expected, the younger man's face showed anger. El Mofty held up a finger to stop any response, and then said, "Why would they do this, Sati?"

"To insult us, Uncle!"

"Perhaps," he said, lifting one eyebrow and nodding. "It is certainly a possibility that this whole meeting is a ruse designed to stall our attack on Shangri-La, until they could bring reinforcements to aid their countrymen."

Bashara was surprised that his uncle said that. He wasn't sure the emir had given such a thing its due consideration. "Then why do it, Uncle?"

"Because we have more to gain that to lose. Our forces are spread out now, making them much harder to hit. If the Americans attack, we will retreat. The battle will be lost, yes, but the army will live to fight another day, and our losses, while regrettable, will not leave us crippled. However, if the Americans are serious about this proposed alliance, then we have much more to win. You have read Sun Tzu; I know you have because I gave you that book myself. I am told you re-read it many times. Is there wisdom in that book about the best way to win a battle?"

"There is, Uncle. The best way to defeat your foe is by not having to fight him."

"Now you are learning, Sati. The Americans bring a woman because they wish to unbalance us, so how better can we turn the tables than by bringing a woman of our own? It is something they will never expect, and will give us the upper hand in negotiations, if there are any."

Something still troubled Bashara. He rubbed his lips with his fingertips. "But a woman... alone with men not her husband, her face uncovered. It goes against all that I've been taught."

"That is because you are still learning. I will put General Gollins next to me, on the end, so that no one else has to sit beside her."

"Thank you." Bashara turned for the Bradley.

But el Mofty had one more thing to say. "Always remember, nephew. First, win the war. Then you can worry about the peace."

They met on a bridge of Interstate 40 over a dry river bed ten miles west of Albuquerque. Both Bradleys stopped at their respective ends of the bridge and disgorged their passengers. Both turrets mounted the deadly M242 Bushmaster 25mm chain gun, each aimed at the other. Both TOW missile launchers drew aim at their counterpart. In a firefight, both vehicles would be quickly shot to hell.

Four American infantrymen walked beside Major Ahmadi and Colonel Mwangi, two on either flank. The Sevens only had three riflemen, and put them out in front of el Mofty, Bashara, and General Tracy Gollins. Both groups walked toward the other until they met at about the middle of the bridge.

Mwangi saw a woman with them and had to try very hard not to let her surprise show. The only reason they would have brought her was to elicit such a reaction, and it had worked. Whether she showed it or not, it distracted her.

"I am Colonel Amunet Mwangi, United States Army," she said when ten feet separated them. "This is Major Ahmadi. I am the representative for General Thomas Steeple, commander of all United States armed forces."

Bashara spoke first for the Sevens, addressing Ahmadi and not looking at Mwangi. "Allow me to present Superior Imam Abdul-Qudoos Fadil el Mofty, Emir of New Khorasan. I am General Sati Bashara."

Mwangi waited for him to introduce the woman or look at her, but Bashara did neither. In any other setting she would have reached past him to shake the woman's hand. Instead, she stared at the emir and kept a blank expression. It wasn't easy. If such disrespect continued, she worried about being able to negotiate an agreement.

Fortunately, the emir stepped in. "And this is General Tracy Gollins," he said, motioning to the woman standing beside him. "It is well that we meet here, near the place of battle. So often in life we strive against those who under other circumstances might have been friends. Perhaps this is a first step in that direction."

"Let us hope so, Emir," Mwangi said. Bashara's stony expression made it clear that he disapproved of the emir treating directly with her. Whatever was decided here, she knew that Bashara would be working behind the scenes to unravel it. "Especially when death is a permanent solution to a temporary problem."

"I could not agree more, Colonel. Since you reached out to me, pray tell me what it is you have in mind."

"An armistice, pending negotiations for a long-term solution."

"Do you mean an alliance?"

"Yes."

The tall emir stroked his once-dark beard, shot through now with streaks of white. "Why must we wait? Why can such a thing not be agreed upon here and now? Are you prepared to do that, Colonel Mwangi?"

The words almost left her speechless. Could she really achieve everything she'd come for so easily? "I have plenipotentiary powers to negotiate such an agreement, Emir el Mofty."

"I am pleased to hear this. Yet you come in great force. If we are to be allies, then what is to happen to those of your countrymen who have sided with our enemies, those who have stolen our territory and call it Shangri-La?"

Your territory? she thought. *How in the world is northern New Mexico your territory? How is anything your territory?*

She said none of that. Steeple had not informed her of his future plans, but she assumed they included wiping out this so-called Caliphate. "You speak of the renegade Marines," she said. "Sadly, they are in defiance of their legal chain of command, and have so far refused the orders of their commanding general. If they persist in this mutiny, thus making them a danger to our mutual future operations, we will have no choice except to fire upon them, and to keep firing until they recant their mutiny or are no longer a threat."

"Until they are all dead, is that what you mean?"

It took her several seconds to get the word through her lips. "Yes."

"So that we are both clear in our minds, you are offering to join in an alliance with the Caliphate of the New Prophet, and to support our operations against those who oppose our rightful rule, yes? And further, if that opposition comes from members of your own organization, you are prepared to kill them in great numbers to keep the friendship of the Caliphate, yes?"

He leaned forward, ever so slightly, but Mwangi didn't miss it.

"Yes, Emir, we are prepared to do both of those things."

"With such being the case, Colonel, I welcome you into the brotherhood of the Caliphate as a friend, you and... what is the number of your unit? Since we are now allies, I should know what to call you."

"We are members of the 7th United States Cavalry Brigade, Mixed, Emir."

Bashara finally looked at her, and it wasn't a friendly look. "Refer to him as Blessed One, infidel!"

"Sati!" el Mofty said. Rather than embarrass the younger man in public, the emir's expression promised stern words later. Mwangi had seen similar looks from Tom Steeple many times before. "My apologies, Colonel. General Bashara is sometimes over-protective of his emir."

"It is I who should apologize, Blessed One. May I suggest you give us the deployment dispositions of your forces, so that we do not accidentally fire at them, should firing become necessary?"

"Certainly, Colonel. I will let General Gollins do this. Do you have a map?"

"I do, Blessed One."

"Very well, I will leave you to do this, then. Oh, before taking my leave, have you given your recalcitrant subordinates a deadline, beyond which they endanger their lives by continued disobedience?"

"We have, Blessed One. Fourteen hundred hours tomorrow. That's two in the afternoon."

"Excellent. We will prepare our attack for that time, after your bombardment ends. I suggest you send a liaison with a radio so that we might coordinate our efforts."

"I will do that, Blessed One. Expect a Humvee from our position tomorrow morning."

"It is done. And let me say how pleased I am to be the ally of such a great military organization. Together we will rebuild this nation into something greater than it ever was before."

Bashara and the emir turned and walked back to their Bradley, covered by the three guards. Once they entered the vehicle, the guards followed them, leaving Gollins alone with the Americans. Mwangi tried to engage her in conversation, woman to woman, but the only thing Gollins wanted to do was mark out their positions on the map provided and get out of there. The last look she gave Mwangi actually sent ripples down her spine. Gollins' eyes shone with a madness she had never in person seen before.

Walking back to the Bradley, Ahmadi couldn't help asking, "Did you really mean all of that?"

"All of what?"

"Everything you said back there. You're prepared to wipe out two full companies of Marines to ally with those people?"

Mwangi stopped and made sure none of their troops could overhear them. "If you cannot follow your orders, Major, say so right now and I'll find someone who can."

"Those people are... are... insane. They're murderers, cold-blooded killers. You've heard the stories."

Mwangi crossed her arms. "Major, we have devoted our lives to resurrecting the United States from the dustbin of history, right?"

He nodded, and crossed his own arms. Recognizing the inherently defensive nature of that pose, Mwangi uncrossed hers and put her hands behind her back. Within seconds, Ahmadi did the same.

"North America is a damned big place, and in case you haven't noticed, General Patton's Third Army isn't coming over that hill. We are alone in a world where our country no longer exists, and there are only twelve thousand of us. If you spread us equally throughout all forty-eight of the contiguous states, that would put less than three hundred brigade members in each state, and that's not a lot of people. Because of General Angriff, we are engaged on two fronts, against the Chinese and the Sevens, we fought against the so-called Rednecks throughout the region of our home base, *and* we have a potential conflict against the Mexicans at Yuma. It is likely that we are facing off against millions of people, while our numbers are small and finite. Each man or woman killed cannot be replaced. Whether we like it or not, General Steeple is doing what must be done for us to have any chance at all to accomplish our mission."

Ahmadi kept staring but said nothing.

"Now," Mwangi said. "Will you follow my orders, or won't you?"

"I'll follow any legal order you give me, Colonel."

"I'll accept that answer for now, Major, but if the time comes when I tell you to open fire against a target inside of Shangri-La, you'd better accept that as a legal order."

"Yes, ma'am," Ahmadi said. "I understand."

#

Chapter 26

You have to quit confusing madness with a mission.
Flannery O'Connor

1057 hours, May 4
The desert west of Albuquerque, New Mexico

Before stepping back into the Bradley, el Mofty stopped his nephew. "General Muhdin is in no condition to command his regiments. I want you to turn over your command to General Gollins—"

"Uncle!"

"Shut up and let me finish, Sati! Because of your youth, I grant you a lot of leeway, but stop interrupting me before I become truly angry. Now, I want you to take over Muhdin's command. I am also giving you my Guard troops, all of them except my personal bodyguard. That's four thousand men. They are the finest we have, and I want you to deploy them in such a way that, if we are double-crossed by our new American allies, the Guard can attack and destroy them quickly."

"Our casualties will be very heavy, Uncle. We have only infantry and have seen what happens when we attack their armored fighting vehicles over open ground."

"Yes, that is true. But you have more than twenty-four hours to get your men in place. Deploy them in such a way as to attack the Americans from all sides. Divide their fire. I will give you our last remaining tank, the one I have been holding back. It has twenty-two rounds of main gun ammunition. That gives you two tanks, if you count the one remaining from

Muhdin's command. We also have four mortars that you may use."

"Your trust with these precious assets honors me, Uncle."

"I am also giving you the rockets."

"The Qassams?"

"Yes."

"I was not aware that you brought them, Uncle."

"When our Hamas brother showed us how to build them and how to make the fuel, he intended them for use against infidels. But their inaccuracy requires a large target area. I intended them as a last resort for use against Jemez Springs, the so-called Shangri-La, but I now give them to you for use against the Americans if they betray us."

"Did you bring them all?"

"No, I brought eighty. That should be enough. If you have to use them, nephew, use them well."

"May Allah and his New Prophet guide my hand."

The emir smiled a rare smile and grabbed both of his nephew's shoulders. "No one in the Caliphate honors our beloved New Prophet more than you, my nephew. I know that you will make us proud."

#

Chapter 27

Every new beginning comes from some other beginning's end.
Marcus Annaeus Seneca

1st Mechanized Regiment headquarters, south of Sierra Army Depot, Nevada
1925 hours, May 4

Major Dieter Strootman scanned the headquarters tent for his C.O., Colonel Young. Not seeing him, Strootman asked a staff sergeant where he'd gone.

"The colonel said he was going outside for a while, Major."

Strootman found him standing alone in the dark, hands in his pockets, staring up at the stars. "There you are, Colonel. Is everything all right?"

"How's the dog?" Young said, deflecting his question.

"Kona's fine, sir. She barks a lot, but that's a damned smart puppy."

"Where did you put her?"

"I had a pit dug for her, deep enough that she can't climb out. If it comes to a fight, she's safe against anything other than a direct hit. But you didn't answer my question, Colonel. Are you okay?"

Young didn't look down. "I went cold in 2007, Dieter. Before that, I'd been in the Army for twenty-three years. I served all over the world, from Thailand and South Korea to Afghanistan and Iraq. I never got married, because I grew up an army brat. I loved my dad, but I saw the toll all that moving around had on my mother, and I just couldn't do that to my own wife and kids. I thought I'd retire at forty-six with twenty-five years in, and I'd still be young enough to have a family. Then Tom Steeple recruited me for Overtime and that dream vanished.

"I volunteered, though, so that part's not on Steeple. He convinced me that by preserving my knowledge in Long Sleep, I would be serving my country in a special and unique way. I believed him. But now, he wants me to send troops under my command into battle against their fellow Americans, alongside an ally that I trained most of my career to defeat as an enemy. The Chinese were and remain hardcore Communists, and there is nothing in the world I despise more than communism. It's an all-devouring ideology of fear, yet now I am supposed to call those people friends. He wants me to kill my countrymen for the benefit of my enemy."

"He has *ordered* you to do that, Colonel," Strootman said.

"Yes, Dieter, he has, and there's the rub. If I defy him, we are cut off from resupply, and without fuel, ammunition, and food, this regiment will be hors de combat in short order. Then what? There's four thousand Chinese less than two miles away who would gladly shoot every one of us. But if I obey... if I obey I lose my soul." He finally lowered his gaze and turned to Strootman. "What would you do, Dieter?"

"I don't know, sir. I'm not sure there's a good answer to that question."

"Well, you'd better come up with one, because if I get arrested, that decision falls into your lap."

Jerome, Arizona
0953 hours, May 5

Many of the houses that once hugged the hillside had collapsed and slid downhill. In places, their horses had to pick their way through weed-overgrown rubble that partially blocked Highway 89A, and here and there, rusted-out cars sat on the roadside as they had for five decades. Jerome was like all of the former United States, a ruin of the once-greatest civilization in human history, now rotting, its glory long forgotten.

With the sun well up in the eastern sky, they came to a fork in the road, where Highway 89A separated from Main Street. The old buildings thinned out so the only obstacles were cracks and potholes. Once they passed the crest of the mountain, the road switched back twice. After the second turn, they had an unobstructed view down the slope and could follow the line of the highway for several miles. Less than a quarter mile away was the head of a cavalry column, one flying the American flag.

"That's Major Wincommer," Angriff said.

"We've gotta double back and find cover. There's an old house back up there we can hide behind."

"No." Angriff stood in the stirrups. "I am not hiding from my own men."

"That's a helluva gamble. One radio call back to Prime, and we're screwed!"

But Angriff only shook his head. "The French Army didn't shoot Napoleon when he returned from exile, and mine won't shoot me."

"I didn't say they'd shoot you."

He cut a familiar glance sideways at his son. "Even though I'm your father, I still outrank you."

Arizona Highway 89A, east of Jerome, Arizona
1024 hours

The stiffness in Major Edward Wincommer's neck wasn't a surprise. He'd known it would happen if he didn't prop his head on something to sleep last night, but after a full day of riding all he'd wanted to do was close his eyes, so his mind had convinced him otherwise. Now, the shooting pain down the back of his spine reminded him of the lesson he already knew but had ignored.

"Major?" said the executive officer of the 7th Cavalry Regiment, Captain Ron Lozano, who rode beside Wincommer at the column's head. When Wincommer looked up, Lozano pointed with his chin. Some riders blocked the road ahead. Since it hugged the hillside, there was no room to go around them.

"They're heading this way, Major." Lozano pulled his binoculars out of their case and focused on the riders. "Coconino, take two men and... wait a minute." He dialed in the binoculars a little more and leaned forward in his saddle.

"What is it, Captain?" Wincommer said.

Lozano lowered the binoculars. His face had a questioning look, as if he'd seen something impossible. "I think you should look for yourself, Major. I don't trust what I'm seeing," Lozano said, handing him the binoculars.

Wincommer reached for them and felt a muscle spasm down the right shoulder blade.. Damn, that hurt! Lifting the binoculars, he dialed them into focus for his eyes and started with the man on his right. "They're Americans, all right. That man looks a lot like... hell, it *is*, it's the colonel named Green Ghost."

"Our S-5?"

"Our former S-5, yeah. And the other one..." His voice dropped to a whisper. "The other one— it's... it's not possible."

By now the two horsemen had closed within twenty yards. Shading his eyes, Lozano didn't need the binoculars to recognize the second man. "I don't believe in ghosts, sir."

"Neither do I."

The two riders stopped ten feet in front of the column. Behind him, Major Wincommer heard the troops murmuring to each other, passing back the word. *It's Nick the A! He ain't dead!* The excitement in their voices found an echo inside him.

"Good morning, Major," Angriff said. He saw a man two rows behind Wincommer reaching for something on his back. A black antenna stuck up over the man's left shoulder. "Major, would you please ask your radioman not to contact Overtime Prime until we've talked?"

Lozano turned in his saddle without waiting for Wincommer's order, and told the man not to make any calls without specific instructions to do so.

"Thank you, Captain," Angriff said.

"General, I... we heard you were dead."

"I'm happy to report that news of my death is premature. What I need to know from you right now, right this minute, Major Wincommer, is whether you will take orders from me as your commanding officer."

"Sir, General Steeple—"

"General Steeple illegally seized, by force, the command of a United States Army unit from the commanding officer appointed to that duty by the Constitutionally appointed commander-in-chief. He is a criminal and a mutineer, and has stained with innocent blood the reputation of his brother and sister officers in the armed forces. Now I once again ask whose orders you will heretofore follow, those of a traitor, or of the man duly appointed by legal authority to lead the 7th Cavalry? Make your choice, Major."

Wincommer could feel every eye in his regiment staring at his back. Shooting pain rolled up and down his back and neck, and he'd never thought that a day which started in such an ordinary fashion would so quickly escalate into a decision that would likely change the rest of his life. If he arrested Angriff, the gratitude of General Steeple would likely catapult him to colonel, and maybe even a staff job. He loved his regiment, and he loved being in the saddle, but he'd underestimated the physical toll it would take on his body. Sitting behind a desk held an allure it never had before.

Measured against that was the adoration his troopers felt for the legendary General Angriff and, if he was honest with himself, his own deep-seated respect for the man. It was probably a lot like serving under Patton. You could hate him, but you could never betray him.

"Welcome back, General. Sergeant Riotto, front of the column."

Four ranks back, a man of Angriff's size and bulk, with dark, close-cropped hair under his helmet, trotted up beside the major.

"General, this is Sergeant John Riotto. He's one of my best men. Riotto, until further notice you're the orderly for General Angriff."

"Yes, sir," Riotto said.

"General Angriff, what are your orders, sir?"

Operation Overtime, the Crystal Palace
1052 hours, May 5

Adder entered General Steeple's office to find him on the phone with Colonel Claringdon. Steeple held up a finger meaning 'hold on,' and then pointed to a chair. Instead, the beefy ex-Zombie crossed his arms and stood at the corner of Steeple's desk. The commanding general wasn't a man of action, he was a man of words, and his tendency toward examining an issue from every direction before making a decision drove Adder nuts. It was true that method eliminated a lot of mistakes, but it also eliminated a lot of possibilities that a faster response might have taken advantage of. He once again found himself admiring Angriff's Patton-like damn the torpedoes, hard-charging attitude, when compared to Steeple's pedantic style.

"I want you in here when the balloon goes up," he heard Steeple say. Their eyes met and the general mouthed *Claringdon*. "That shouldn't be a concern, Fitz, Colonel Santorio will have all channels patched in up here. You can do anything here that you can do there, but our communication, yours and mine, must be instantaneous... right. Be here by thirteen-thirty so we can go over the details one more time."

Once he'd hung up, Steeple sipped coffee before turning his attention to Adder. "There is never enough time when an op is hanging, is there?" he said. "Is there something I should know?"

Adder smiled, but didn't express his first thought. *How the fuck would you know about ops hanging?* Steeple watched ops from thousands of miles away, while Adder saw them firsthand. He doubted Steeple had any clue what combat was really like. "I'm usually bored before things kick off," Adder said. "Once everybody is set up, I don't worry about it. If people don't do their jobs, I'll kick their ass 'til they do, or do it for them. When you're in a metal storm, plans don't matter, actions do."

"That is when plans matter most. Men have to know what is expected of them."

Rather than tell the general he was a clueless peacock, Adder changed the subject. "You asked to see me, sir?"

"I just wanted to make sure we're buttoned up tight. This is not the time for internal security problems."

"We *were* buttoned up, but sending all the Chinese to Prescott left some holes in the lockdown I had planned."

"I'm sorry I had to do that, but it was necessary. It's one thing to support allied forces with artillery, where the crews never see who they are firing at, but it's quite another to kill a fellow American face to face. That is why I have grounded our helicopter gunships, because of your report that they might not carry out a strike mission against Americans. And once the bombardment is over, the Chinese will need to occupy the town. At Sierra and New Mexico, we don't have to do that. All we have to do is give support to our allies."

Adder knew there was no point to further discussion, as they had already argued about this more than once. "I understand your logic, and as you know I don't agree with it, but I guess it's too late now. I've put in place every security measure that I can, but I'd feel better having Chinese sentries in every corridor and elevator landing." Then he mentioned the subject he'd avoided bringing up before, waiting for exactly the right moment. "I *would* like permission to preemptively arrest any potential internal enemies."

"Do you have anybody particular in mind?"

"I want the Angriffs confined to quarters until this is over, and I want to station one of the remaining Chinese outside of those quarters. I'll personally escort them there. I also want to confine the Zombies."

Steeple turned his head with a confused look. "I thought you sent them to investigate Phoenix?"

"That's right, I did, all except Green Ghost's sister."

"Is she the one they call Nipple?"

"That's her."

"Then lock her up. She has no status. She's not even supposed to be here."

"I'm on it."

Adder turned to leave but Steeple stopped him. "No surprises today, Colonel."

"No surprises, General Steeple. You can put that in the bank."

#

Chapter 28

"When I despair, I remember that all through history, the ways of truth and love have always won. There have been tyrants and murderers, and for a time, they can seem invincible, but in the end, they always fall. Think of it — always."
Mahatma Gandhi

Operation Overtime, Security Center
1138 hours, May 5

Adder resisted the urge to find Nipple right away, telling himself that business came before pleasure. And he had to admit that Green Ghost had done a good job getting the security center sorted out, which he didn't really find all that surprising. Green Ghost wasn't cut out to lead men in combat, but something routine like getting a security center organized was much more his speed.

The security control room measured thirty feet long and twenty wide, with banks of flat-screen monitors on all four walls showing pictures of the mountain outside in real time. Ten cameras pointed west, ten to the east, and five each to north and south. Ten people currently watched the video feeds for anything out of the ordinary, although there were seats for up to thirty.

The cameras sending those images had always been part of Overtime's design, but hadn't been installed ahead of time because of the danger of damage due to weather or rock slides. Nor had placement been diagrammed for the same reason, and the angles he now watched left very little dead space for potential enemies to stay hidden.

"Seeing anything interesting today?" he said to a very pretty corporal with auburn hair.

"Just a coyote, Colonel, and a prairie falcon."

He smiled when she looked up at him. He'd have to remember her. "What's going on there?" he said, pointing to another monitor where a large dust cloud moved over the desert.

"That's Major Wincommer's cavalry, sir. They're patrolling to the west."

"Oh," he said. Something about that bothered him. They seemed to be riding pretty fast, but then, he didn't know jack shit about handling cavalry, so he forgot about it and turned his attention back to the pretty corporal.

1216 hours

"That's it," Green Ghost said.

Angriff followed his point, but at such a distance it all looked like one big jumble of rocks. "Where?"

"See those two spurs? Right in between them."

"If you say so... Are your eyes really that much better than mine?"

"I can't see it from here. I just recognize the spot."

"I'll take your word for it."

Angriff ordered Major Wincommer to continue patrolling north along the western edge of the mountains. The regiment closed within one hundred yards of the place Green Ghost said housed the tunnel entrance. Without stopping, he thanked Wincommer.

"Do you want Sergeant Riotto to accompany you, General?"

Green Ghost answered before Angriff could. "Yes, Major, he does."

"I do?"

"With all due respect, General, you do."

With raised eyebrows, Angriff nodded to Wincommer. "I guess I do, Major."

Breaking off from the mass of riders, where they'd been hiding in plain sight, Angriff and Green Ghost galloped to the side of the mountain, Riotto behind them. Angriff had grown up riding horses. His great-great-grandfather rode with J.E.B.

Stuart and the family had always raised horses, so he and Riotto found the brief dash exhilarating. Green Ghost, on the other hand, had first sat in the saddle during team training and, while genetically predisposed to be a good rider, he twice almost fell off and came in well behind the other two.

Angriff smirked as his son tried to suppress the fear he'd felt. "Wasn't that fun?"

"Yeah, it was great."

"Do we have time to do it again?"

"I don't think so... sir."

Riotto glanced between them, wondering what he'd missed.

Angriff noticed. "The colonel doesn't have a sense of humor, Sergeant, so I'm helping him grow one."

"Uh, yes, sir, whatever you say, sir."

"I need your jacket and helmet, Sergeant."

"Sir?"

"Your helmet and jacket? Take them off and give them to me."

Realization lit up Riotto's face. "Gladly, General."

Green Ghost led the way. The crevice in the mountainside wasn't as wide as Angriff had envisioned. The hatch was two feet off the ground and back about fifteen feet, which required him to turn sideways to get there.

The hatch was rectangular, with rounded corners, three feet tall and two feet wide. Rust spots showed through where damage marred the stainless steel surface. Angriff knew that it latched from the inside, so if somebody had locked it they would have to risk bashing it open, or even blasting, if it came to that.

Once Angriff had squeezed close enough to reach the hatch, he grabbed the lever handle in the center. "Sergeant, this is probably a one-way trip, so I'm not going to order you to come with us. You can stand guard here and make sure nobody else comes at us from the rear."

"With all due respect, sir," Riotto said, "I thought we were in a hurry."

Angriff smiled. "You're right, we are. Here we go."

The lever moved down. He pushed using his right shoulder and the door squeaked inward on rusty hinges. Five feet inside the tunnel, after the ambient light faded, was only blackness.

"You still remember everything?" Green Ghost said.

"I'm not that old."

"Age has nothing to do with it. Repeat it back to me."

"You keep forgetting that I'm your C.O."

"And I'm in tactical command of this mission, *sir*, so repeat your mission parameters... please. Sergeant Riotto should be aware of the game plan, too."

Angriff didn't argue the point, since Green Ghost had actually done what they were attempting to do. Rank or not, his son really was the man in command of the mission. "This tunnel dead-ends into a cross tunnel. At that spot, there is a shaft that leads straight up, and that shaft meets another cross tunnel but keeps going up. I turn left at the second cross tunnel and go nearly a mile under the mountain, until I come to a second shaft. That's the one that leads up to the Clam Shell. Once past sub-level eleven, each succeeding level is marked. I climb nearly a thousand feet and get off at level eight. This is the point where I could potentially be recognized, so utmost caution must be used. Once I locate the entrance for the emergency escape shaft that leads to the hatch under my office desk, I climb that and put a bullet into Tom Steeple's brain."

"I'll leave that last part in the category of mission options, sir."

"Or," Angriff said, as if Green Ghost hadn't spoken, "I can just follow your ass."

---

12 miles west of Albuquerque, New Mexico
1244 hours, May 5

Being inside of a headquarters tent was something Amunet Mwangi had experienced before, but not often. Being in one behind the front lines, in close proximity to a battery of artillery and several dozen dug-in armored vehicles, was new. The buzz and hum from dozens of people coordinating the coming bombardment both terrified and thrilled her. She had never before realized the breadth of the gulf between career staff officers like her and like Tom Steeple, and combat commanders like Khin Saw or Nick Angriff. The exhilaration surprised her, although she showed nothing on her face except grim business, as if she'd done this a thousand times before.

"Colonel Mwangi?"

She turned to face Major Ahmadi. "Are your people ready, Major?"

"They are, ma'am. It's me that's not ready. I have thought about this all night, Colonel, and I cannot order my crews to fire on their own comrades."

Mwangi squinted, exploring his face. He hadn't done the thing she'd feared he might, namely, have her arrested. She didn't see mutiny there, only conflicted emotions. "This is a serious violation of your oath, Major, refusing the direct order of a superior in a combat situation. You *do* realize that, don't you?"

"Yes, ma'am, I do."

"Are you aware of the potential consequences, Major? Think hard before you answer."

"No need, ma'am. I'm aware that the penalty could be death. But I will not fire on troops who are doing their lawful duty."

"But they aren't doing that, Major. They are in defiance of the direct order of a superior officer, which is the path you're on right now."

"I don't see it that way, ma'am."

Mwangi bit her lower lip. "Will you inform your battery commanders that I'll be giving the order to open fire?"

"I can do that, ma'am."

"If we are attacked, will you defend your command?"

"I will, ma'am, to the best of my ability."

"Very well. You may retain your command, Major, pending review by General Steeple once we are back at Prime. And Major? Thank you for telling me in time."

"You're welcome, ma'am, and Colonel... what you're doing is flat-out wrong."

Adder took a wrong turn trying to find the Deuce. Every member of the brigade knew the location of the Clam Shell and the Crystal Palace, but many weren't even aware that a secondary control center even existed, or that it was the official office of the brigade executive officer, formerly Norm Fleming. Now, with General Steeple ensconced in the office of the brigade commander, Colonel Claringdon had no choice except to set up shop in the Deuce.

Most of the people who passed Adder in the corridors didn't make eye contact, and the few who did got a hard stare back in return. He had finally been given the leadership position he deserved. The power was all his now, and Adder had every intention of enjoying it.

When he eventually found the entrance, he realized the Deuce was identical to the main headquarters called the Clam Shell, only smaller. A glass wall fifty feet long gave way to a ten-foot-wide entrance. The titanium blast door had been slid to one side. Two Chinese guards flanked the doorway but didn't check his ID, since he'd brought them with him from California in the first planeload.

Unlike the Clam Shell, the Deuce had no gigantic picture window to let in natural light. Nor was there a ramp to a round platform that resembled a flying saucer. Instead, Claringdon's office was to the far right, with the same electrochromatic technology that allowed the glass to become opaque using an electric charge. His staff worked in open cubicles to either side.

A young female corporal with close-cropped blonde hair looked up from her desk at his approach. "Colonel Adder?"

"That would be me," he said, imbuing the words with innuendo.

The corporal smiled but otherwise ignored his obvious flirt. She rose and walked over to the closed office door. "Colonel Claringdon asked that you come right in, sir." Knocking twice, she stepped into the doorway and announced him. "Please go in, Colonel." She stepped aside to let him enter.

But Adder stopped beside her. "I think later we need to discuss your security clearance for this job."

She said nothing with her lips. Her eyes, however, said *Eat shit and die.* He laughed and went inside. Claringdon pointed to a chair and he sat down.

"Thanks for coming, Colonel. We've never worked together before, and I thought it might be a good idea to get to know each other."

Adder had no intention of playing nice, however. He'd waited too long for this, and put up with way too many pompous idiots who fought their wars from behind a desk. "Why?" he said.

"I beg your pardon?" Claringdon said.

"Why should we get to know each other? I know my job and how to do it."

Adder noted that Claringdon's left eye twitched and then he blinked, both signs of agitation. Good.

"Because I'm your commanding officer, for one thing," Claringdon said.

"I think you're operating under a false assumption, Colonel. You think that I'm going to take orders from you, just because you're technically the brigade commander, right?"

"Why would I believe otherwise?"

Adder grinned; he believed he knew Claringdon's type, and that if it came down to him or Claringdon, General Steeple would pick him. Combat veterans were always at a premium, but a highly successful special ops team leader brought irreplaceable skills to Steeple's disposal that political officers like Claringdon didn't. In the corridors of power, the White House, the Pentagon, Congress, in those environments, men like Claringdon could be invaluable as allies. They knew the right and the wrong way to kiss ass. Now, however, such skills were useless.

Clasping hands on top of his head, Adder leaned back and crossed his left leg. "My job is to keep this base safe, Colonel, and I'm gonna do just that. When our interests align, I'll obey your orders. When we're in public, I'll show the deference due a commanding officer. But don't for one second think you can order me around, because you can't."

Claringdon tried to keep his hands clenched and still on the desk, but Adder noticed the thumbs move a little. The man's face showed less emotion that it had before, which was interesting. *This is why Steeple recruited this guy.* When he had to, Claringdon's self-discipline let him keep control of his emotions. Good to know.

But Adder believed he could read people; he thought of it as his superpower. Claringdon was not the sort to explode in rage at such an insult. He was the far more dangerous type, the ambush predator, as Adder thought of it. Whatever conciliatory words Claringdon might say next would be pure bullshit. They were now mortal enemies, and that played right into his hands. Discrediting Claringdon as unfit and unstable was how Adder planned to take Claringdon's job as brigade commander for himself.

"You're going to regret saying that," Claringdon finally said.

"I don't think so."

"Do you know what my job was before this?"

Adder raised his eyebrows. "I've heard. Do you mean failed assassin or disgraced prisoner?"

Claringdon's eyes nearly closed, they became so slitted. "I was the executive officer of the 1st Armored Battalion, the unit that stopped the Chinese armored thrust and won the Battle of Prescott last year."

"And I once shot an unarmed woman in the head. What do you want, a cookie?"

Once again Claringdon paused before continuing. "Can we leave our personal quarrel for later? General Steeple wants me in his office in fifteen minutes."

"So why did you ask me to come all the way over here? It's kind of at the ass-end of nowhere."

"Angriff. He might be dead, but there are family members to worry about."

Adder's eyebrows went up in surprise. Maybe he'd misjudged Claringdon. "Tell me what you're getting at."

"His daughter is a decorated tank commander. That makes her dangerous, because if the armored battalion goes rogue, our position becomes untenable. She will be able to spread dissension without us even knowing about it."

"You're growing on me, Claringdon."

"Such a potential threat needs to be quarantined, do you agree?"

"I do, but arresting her could get ugly. Are you prepared for that?"

"Meaning?"

"Meaning somebody might get hurt, or killed."

"That would be tragic, of course, but the safety of this brigade is my first concern. I'm sure you will only do what you must."

"What about Nipple?"

"Is she that psychotic blonde?"

"Yes, and Green Ghost's twin sister."

"Is she even in the Army?"

"No, she was like his pet. She only got to hang around because Nick let her. She was never an official member of the team."

"In that case, given the danger her brother represents, and her lack of status, I would think she poses a grave and immediate threat to the operations of this brigade. Therefore, I order you to arrest her, too."

"Colonel Claringdon, that is one order I will gladly carry out."

#

Chapter 29

"I have built my organization upon fear."
Al Capone

Prescott, Arizona
1019 hours, May 5

It seemed like twenty years since Lester Earl Hull had last walked more than fifteen feet in one direction, and to suddenly be not only free but in charge of Prescott again seemed miraculous, or maybe providential. At his age, he'd certainly never expected another chance to do what he did best, command other people, and yet there he was.

In theory, he commanded the Chinese forces arrayed in a defensive ring around the old Prescott Mall on the east end of town. In reality, the Chinese colonel named Zhang Shongjang had made it clear that Hull, or General Patton as he had been introduced to the Chinese officer, could give all the orders he wanted, but the Chinese only listened to their colonel. He had looked Hull up and down with a sneer of disrespect, but once he was back in charge at Prescott, Hull would show him all about respect.

The commander of the four M109 Paladins was civil and correct toward him, even if cold. That was fine, too. All those people were there to put him back in power, so if they did that, he really didn't care about anything else. While rotting in that cell, he'd rehearsed the conversation he would have with Rick Parfist, the so-called mayor of Prescott, if he ever got the chance. Hull would enjoy that talk very, very much, but he doubted the opportunistic Mister Parfist would feel the same way. Without realizing it, Hull smiled, because in just under four hours his dream would become a reality. He could almost hear himself laughing as Parfist and his precious family bled out.

1231 hours

Half of the newly renamed 2nd Marine Raider Battalion lay behind the hill across a four-lane street, south of the ruined Prescott Gateway Mall, with Colonel Berger in tactical command. Directly east of the mall were the ruins of a large neighborhood, which provided excellent cover for the other half to get into attack position. Berger recognized the Chinese uniforms immediately on seeing them, and could only rate their perimeter security as poor.

Berger saw four U.S. M109 Paladin self-propelled 155mm guns formed up in the parking lot, with their guns aimed to the west toward downtown Prescott. Various other vehicles were parked nearby, including six M992 ammunition supply vehicles, or CATs, for Carrier, Ammunition, Tracked. Their presence surprised Berger. Just how much ordnance was

Steeple planning to throw against Prescott, anyway? If those were all full, and the Paladins had a full complement of shells, that totaled close to one thousand rounds of 155mm ammunition, enough to flatten the courthouse and most of the structures near it, or to blast the Marines into pancakes. Apparently Berger had well and truly pissed General Steeple off.

But the flip side was that if those Paladins fell into his hands, he would have a powerful bargaining chip to use against Steeple and the Chicoms. Now the only thing left was to capture them.

"Drone in the air, Colonel," a sergeant said in a low voice. Berger followed where he pointed and saw it flying over the city several miles to his left. He only had to capture those guns... and yet a drone with a camera could still ruin everything.

"Sergeant, send a runner to Colonel Cranston. Tell him there's a drone airborne and to go right away, not to wait for thirteen-thirty hours. Tell your runner to run!"

Eastern Prescott, Arizona
1246 hours

Captain Alejandro Chávez stalked back and forth between the four M109s and his headquarters vehicle, where live camera shots from the drone were shown on a monitor. He wished they had more than one, but one was better than none. The whole operation made his skin crawl and he sure as hell didn't want to screw it up by hitting a hospital or school, although his orders were to maintain fire until the garrison at Prescott surrendered. Theoretically, that meant flattening the city, hospitals and schools included, but if he could avoid that he would.

"Anything, Chief?" he said to the chief warrant officer overseeing the battery's electronics array.

She pursed her lips and glanced up at him. "Negative, not a thing, Captain. The city appears to have been evacuated. I haven't seen anything bigger than a squirrel."

Chávez was known for being taciturn, but firing on other Americans really called for a higher ranking officer than a mere captain, and his anxiety manifested itself by him using even fewer words than usual. "Ambush?"

"If that's it, they have some serious positional discipline."

He paused a moment to watch the screen, where Prescott slowly slipped by in the overhead view. The scars from last year's Battle of Prescott remained visible in shattered trees, broken buildings, and shell craters. Chávez was bent over staring at the screen when the man named General Patton strolled over like he was their commander. The captain didn't bother to recognize him.

"Everything ready, boys?" Patton said, ignoring the fact that half the battery command staff was female.

"Yes," was all Chávez said.

The warrant officer looked up. "Earlier I walked the perimeter and all the Chinese were on our western flank. I suggested they move some assets to seal the other flanks. Do you know if they did that?"

"Is that how you talk to a general?" Patton said.

The warrant officer and Chávez exchanged a look that meant *Is this guy serious?*

"You're not a general in our army," the captain said.

"Huh... you both are gonna be sorry about this. No, they didn't move anybody to those flanks, I told 'em not to. We'd be stretched too thin, and we came from the east, didn't we? If somebody was there, we'd have seen 'em."

Is this guy really that stupid? Chávez thought.

1257 hours

In all the years he'd led the security forces for the Republic of Arizona, Norbert Cranston had never felt as nervous as he did in that moment. The past ten months had been one long lesson about leading men in battle, and while undergoing Marine boot camp, he'd learned what it meant to be a *real* warrior. But training was over and now it was all real, and Cranston didn't want to let Colonel Berger or his Marines down.

Hunkered down on the roof of an old hotel east of the mall, Cranston gave hand signals for his men to advance. The building's once bright pink stucco had faded to pinkish-white, with multiple holes in the facing. What had once been a cheerful resting place in the Arizona sun was now a derelict ruin. An artificial slope of land surrounded the mall itself, limiting his view even from the top of the hotel. Three scouts slipped out of ground-floor exits on each side of the hotel, covered by ten Marines on the roof with Cranston. His men had no heavy weapons, only small arms, which made the seizure of the artillery guns that much more critical.

The scouts made it up the thirty-foot slope without drawing fire. Cranston used his binoculars to read the hand signals from the sergeant leading them, and when he spotted an upturned thumb he relayed that to a man on the other end of the roof. In his turn, that Marine waved forward the half battalion hidden in an old neighborhood across a narrow street.

Hundreds of Marines climbed over a low brick wall surrounding the houses. They crossed another street marked with a still-readable sign that named it as N. Lee Boulevard. Cranston left orders for the force on the roof to remain in place and cover any potential retreat, and then went down three flights of stairs to the old lobby. The glass front doors had long since been smashed, so he trotted through them and climbed the slope. He had never been afraid to lead from the front, and embraced the Marine code of officers sharing hardships with the rank and file.

They faced the back of the mall. From their position, they had no view of the Paladins, which had been set up in the parking lot on the opposite side, with the mall between them. Directly to their front was a white building, part of the mall but painted differently to contrast with the mall's red brick. As one, the Marines rose and ran across a narrow parking area into the double doors of the old clothing store's entrance.

The plan called for his entire force to use the mall for cover while approaching the rear of the 'enemy' artillery. Cranston knew the old mall well, having overseen the systematic looting of anything that could potentially be reused. Every bit of clothing had long since been taken, along with the metal racks, shelves, hangers... even the mirrors in the dressing rooms. A few broken mannequins littered the floor as the Marines silently ran past them.

Berger's mission orders and rules of engagement left no room for misunderstanding — securing the Paladins was priority number one. Engaging in combat was an absolute last resort where other Americans were concerned, but the Chinese were fair game. Prisoners were not a primary concern.

The Marines moved forward as they'd been taught, in column, with a six-man squad on each side of the wide corridor. One group moved forward while a second and third covered them, then the second moved while the first and third provided cover, and so on. Cranston went with the first group. As it happened, they were in the middle of the other two groups when the men in front held up a fist, which meant *stop*. Cranston leaned out from behind a curved support column to see four Chinese soldiers working their way toward the Marine position. At first he thought they were a patrol, but then realized they were looking for things to loot.

Cranston extended his right arm toward the floor, palm down, and moved it in a circle, the hand signal for *commence firing*. The squad leader relayed his instructions across the corridor using hand signals. Ten seconds later, all four Chinese reappeared in the corridor and moved closer to the Marines' position. At a range of sixty feet, the forward squad opened fire.

None of their M16s had noise suppressors. Operations Overtime and Comeback both had plentiful numbers of M16s, made surplus after being replaced by the M4. Suppressors had never been available in enough quantities to be made surplus, so the *crack* of twelve rifles, each firing one three-round burst, echoed down the empty corridor. The four Chinese dropped like dead men cut down after a hanging. Assuming the element of surprise was gone, Cranston signaled for the entire battalion to move forward at the run.

#

Chapter 30

"Man is the cruelest animal."
Friedrich Nietzsche

Prescott, Arizona
1306 hours, May 5

Still watching the display screen for signs of human life in Prescott, Captain Chávez heard what sounded like rifle fire coming from inside the mall. Although distant and muffled, he was pretty certain that was what he'd heard, but instead of reacting, he didn't move. Either the Chinese had found something to shoot at, rats most likely, or it was the Marines coming for his guns. If it was the Chinese, he had no command authority over them, but if it were the Marines... he commanded an artillery unit, not infantry. Nobody could fault them for being overrun by Marines, and that would solve his problem of firing on fellow Americans.

The man called General Patton stalked toward him over the hot pavement. "Did you hear gunfire?" he demanded.

"No, I can't say that I did. What about you, Chief?"

She glanced up at her captain and then back at the display. "Not me, no, sir, didn't hear a thing."

"Bullshit!" Patton said, jabbing his finger at Chávez. "General Steeple's gonna hear about this, you can bet your ass on that."

Chávez knew that Patton might actually be right, and that disrespect toward the man might have blowback, but in that moment he just didn't care. "Do you need me to spell my name?"

1312 hours

In his guise as General Patton, Lester Earl Hull had only slightly better luck ordering the Chinese into the mall to investigate what he'd heard. Since they were deployed several hundred yards west of the mall, they'd heard nothing. The looseness of his uniform couldn't have helped them take him seriously, either. He'd lost so much weight in prison that even a new set of ACUs gave him a slovenly appearance. Colonel Shongjang listened in silence for three minutes before finally detailing ten men to go check out the inside of the mall, just to shut the old American up. Hull knew that was why he did it, because the Chinese officer told him so.

Following the ten Chinese, Hull held his own M16 in the crook of his right elbow. The side entrance had a covered patio that led to two sets of double glass doors. As usual, the glass had been shattered at some point in the distant past, so their boots crunched on the broken shards as the Chinese entered the mall. None of them seemed concerned about Marines lurking in ambush. Hull hung back on the patio, putting a square column between him and any bullets coming from inside. It wouldn't do to get killed only minutes before regaining power.

When he peered around the column, all he saw was darkness inside. Had he been hearing things? Then, without warning, muzzle flashes lit up the interior in snapshots of color, like lightning flashes in the night. Screams echoed from inside the mall, along with dozens of gunshots. Five Chinese stumbled back out through the smashed doors. Two men supported a wounded comrade, while the other two fired backward into the shadows.

Some bullets whizzed into the parking lot, some struck the door frames, and some struck Chinese flesh. The two men covering the rear fell in quick succession, while the other three limped toward Patton. Seeing him peeking around the column, one of them yelled, "Cover us!"

At that moment, the shooters found his position and bullets riddled the column. Patton put his back to the bricks, heart pounding and breaths coming fast and shallow. The three struggling men had gotten equal to his column when a fusillade of bullets ripped into them from behind. They fell on sculpted concrete, where millions of people had walked into the mall to buy Christmas gifts or some new underwear. A blood puddle grew rapidly around them.

Hull looked up to see the Chinese running toward him across the parking lot, all 200-odd of them. He decided it was safest to stay in place until they got there. In no way would he risk his life now, when his restoration to power was so close at hand.

1319 hours

At the first rifle report, Captain Chávez knew he'd been right; the Marines were behind them. Now he had to avoid any friendly fire incidents. Running down the headquarters line, he yelled, "Take cover! Do not engage friendly forces!"

The Paladin crews were more than happy to button up inside, while the crews of other vehicles rolled under them to get out of the line of fire. Chávez joined two others, including the chief warrant officer, under a Paladin. They could see the Chinese running toward them, and once they got close enough, some took cover behind the huge armored vehicle. Chávez drew his pistol and nudged the warrant officer to do the same. There was no telling what might happen next.

1320 hours

Every Marine in Colonel Berger's half of the battalion lay prone on the hill over the parking lot. They'd all watched some sort of argument a few minutes ago between a Chinese officer and a tall American wearing a general's star. Berger assumed that had to be the man who called himself Patton. When Patton whirled and strode toward the mall, preceded by ten Chinese soldiers, Berger made the connection that Cranston had to have been discovered.

"Mark your targets and prepare to fire," he said, and word was passed both ways down the line. The distance to target was about 150 yards. The ten Chinese entered the mall, Patton taking cover behind a support column outside, and seconds later rifle fire echoed over the parking lot. American personnel manning the guns ran for cover, while the Chinese still deployed to the west broke cover and ran toward the mall. The fastest had reached the Paladins and knelt down when Berger squeezed off the first round and saw his target pitch forward. Hundreds of keyed-up Marines followed within a second and a metal storm ripped through the Chinese ranks.

1323 hours

From his position under the Paladin, Chávez saw sparks light up the asphalt before he heard the chattering of M16s. Men fell on all sides. The one kneeling behind the Paladin dropped to his belly and tried to crawl under the armored vehicle, but stopped when he saw the two Americans. In his panic, he didn't care *which* Americans they were, and tried to bring his rifle to bear, so Chávez and the warrant officer each put two rounds through the top of his skull. Brain matter and blood sprayed their outstretched arms.

1324 hours

Cranston's advance squad leader signaled more Chinese heading for the mall, moving fast. The ones who'd survived the firestorm outside ran for the shattered doors. As they neared the mall, the fire from the hillside slackened as vehicles blocked Berger's line of fire.

The first few men through the doors were cut down. The rest, Cranston guessed there were at least fifty, took cover behind the columns and against the outside wall. He had heard the firing outside, but without radios he didn't know the situation. When more Chinese came through the doors, it forced him into a decision. Was he under attack by superior forces? Would the Paladins lower their cannon for direct fire at the mall and blast his Marines out? His men engaged the Chinese with their rifles and drove them back, but then something bounced down the hallway.

"Grenades!" someone shouted.

Four explosions flashed in the shadows, followed by renewed automatic weapons fire. Cranston heard men moaning and knew he had casualties. He either had to advance or retreat, because if he stayed in place much longer, his men would be cut to pieces.

Cranston had taken cover in a storefront with smashed windows, about one hundred feet from the entrance, and used the wall to the adjacent store as a shield. At least fifty men were in the empty store with him, and two squads had leap-frogged ahead before they got pinned down. Now, whatever he did would likely result in casualties, and he considered withdrawing. But although Cranston hadn't been a Marine for very long, and unlike when he led Patton's army against civilians and outlaws because it was either that or be enslaved, for the first time in his life he'd found something he *wanted* to fight for: his fellow Marines. He'd led them into this mess, and it was up to him to get them out again.

"Improvise, adapt, overcome," he whispered to himself.

"I didn't hear you, sir!" a lance corporal nearby said.

"I said let's give 'em hell, son!"

There was no time for a scheme of maneuver. More grenades bounced down the corridor. One detonated beside two Marines on the other side of the corridor, blasting them into the brick wall, where they left bloody streaks as they slid to the floor. He had to do something, so he did the only thing he could think of. Cranston jumped to his feet, shouldered his rifle, and stepped out of the building.

"Follow me, Marines!"

Colonel Shongjang didn't start running toward the mall until a nearby hill erupted with pinpoints of light, like fireflies winking on and off on a hot summer night, followed within tenths of a second by a hailstorm of 5.56mm bullets. Only when a bullet hit a man ten feet in front of him in the head, knocking him sideways off his feet, did Shongjang realize what had happened. He'd been flanked and decoyed into the open, and there was nothing to do now except run.

Although 49 years old, he prided himself on keeping in top condition, and he outpaced many younger men in the dash for safety. Some took refuge behind the big American self-propelled artillery vehicles, and returned fire on the hill. Shongjang made it behind one of them, where three other men had already taken refuge. Kneeling in the big machine's shadow, he sucked down the warm afternoon air and looked back at the asphalt he'd just traversed. Scores of his men lay dead or dying.

Most of them had made for the entrance into the mall, and he sprinted the short distance to join them. He had maybe sixty men left. Rifle fire from the darkened shadows inside explained the heap of bodies lying in the shattered doorway. Taking cover behind the fourth square column in a row of six holding up the entryway's roof, he spotted the American General Patton across the twenty-foot-wide path behind another column.

His men were throwing grenades into the building and using them at a high rate, but his shouted orders to stop went unheard in the din of battle. Then one of his men pointed toward the hill. Shongjang turned to see hundreds of Americans attacking down the hill. The American trap had worked to perfection. He was caught in a crossfire and had only two choices, surrender or attack into the mall where he might have a chance to escape. If he surrendered, General Zhang Wei would doubtless hear of his disgrace, and the general was not known as a man who tolerated failure. If he wasn't lined up against a wall and shot, he'd spend the rest of his life working in a cabbage field.

Cupping hands around his mouth, he yelled "Gōngjī!" in the simplified Chinese taught in California schools. It meant *attack!* Holding his CF-07 9mm pistol in both hands, he stepped out from behind the column and advanced at a fast walk. Shongjang wasn't used to being in the middle of a firefight; he commanded from the rear. The visual spectacle of explosions and muzzle flashes in the dark ahead, combined with the aural assault of automatic weapons firing at close range, the reek of sulphur from burnt gunpowder, all overwhelmed his senses.

Bullets zipped all around him, sounding like high-speed mosquitoes. Something tugged at his uniform pants, and he felt wetness on his right side, but the rational part of his brain that governed self-preservation had shut down. He had completely lost situational awareness and strode forward, squeezing off shots at anything that appeared to be a target. When the pistol's magazine was empty, he pushed the release and inserted another one, as if on the practice range.

Passing the frames of the doors, Shongjang dimly realized that other Chinese soldiers ran past him into the mall. In his peripheral vision, he saw a man knocked backward. Stepping over bodies, he entered the mall itself, searching for targets. He tried to take a step but stumbled. For some reason his left leg didn't work and he lost his balance, again stumbling sideways.

Standing seemed too hard, so he dropped to one knee. Men ran past him going in both directions, young men, healthy men, all carrying guns and wearing uniforms. What was going on? And why did his head seem so heavy? Looking up, he saw a man walking directly toward him, carrying a rifle, but this man was older, with close-cropped white hair. The gun aimed right for his head. Why? What was the man going to do with it? His brain registered the flash of light caused by exploding gunpowder, but his synapses didn't have time to process the information before a 5.56mm bullet struck just above his left eyebrow and blew them out the back of his head.

Chapter 31

The universe is transformation; life is opinion.
Marcus Aurelius

Prescott, Arizona
1328 hours, May 5

Echoes from the last gunshots had faded. The only thing Norbert Cranston heard was men crying and moaning, shouting orders and cursing. Never in his life had he been through anything like that, and as his adrenal gland stopped pumping adrenaline into his veins, slowing his heart rate, he felt drained. Blinking, he inspected the last Chinese soldier, the one he'd shot in the head, and wondered what had driven the man to point his pistol at Cranston, even after he'd been hit a dozen times already. The gray hair at the Chinese soldier's temples, and three stars on his shoulder boards, meant he was likely a high-ranking officer.

Puddles of blood made the floor sticky and slippery. Metal fragments sharp enough to cut through a boot sole injured more than one man who stepped on them. The haze from exploded gunpowder not only interfered with his vision, but the gritty particles made his eyes water.

No less than thirty bodies clogged the mall's entrance. Beyond the doors, Colonel Berger's men frisked Chinese troops for weapons and then pushed them into a group. Corpsmen rushed from wounded man to wounded man, doing whatever they could with whatever they had.

Then Colonel Berger appeared. "Well done, Colonel Cranston," Berger said. "That was textbook."

"Was it?" Cranston said, still dazed.

"Hell to the fuck, yes! We caught those bastards in a vise and cut off their balls. How are your men?"

"Uh... my men... damn." Cranston shook his head as his thinking cleared. "I need to see to my men, Colonel Berger."

1339 hours

Captain Chávez crawled out from under the Paladin and immediately ran from vehicle to vehicle to see if there were any casualties. Colonel Berger found him inspecting the battery command post for damage. The two men had never met, but Chávez had heard of Berger's gruff and profane manner, which made him predisposed to like the colonel.

"Nice to meet you, Captain," Berger said. "So are you my subordinate or my prisoner?"

Chávez didn't have to think about his answer. "Colonel, it would be my honor to serve under you, sir."

1341 hours

Prescott's only medically trained doctor, predictably nicknamed Old Doc Thomas, had been standing by in a house not too far from the mall. Along with his two protégés and the two medics assigned to the artillery battery, he set up a triage station in the parking lot. Cranston helped carry several men to the doctor, wiping his bloody hands on his blouse. He was still trying to get an accurate count of casualties when he spotted a tall, familiar figure among the enemy prisoners.

His hands began to shake and a roaring filled his ears. Dodging men running this way and that, he stalked over to the knot of prisoners and raised his rifle. The Chinese who saw him all shrank back, while the Marine guards just watched him without interfering. But the tall man was looking the other way and only turned when Cranston's gun poked his chest.

"Bert!" he cried. "Thank God! Would you tell these idiots who I am?"

Cranston's eyes narrowed. His nostrils dilated as he drew deep, fast breaths. "His name is Lester... Earl... Hull, and he likes murdering women and children."

Hull's face paled. "My name is Patton! I'm your general!"

"These men know who you are, Lester," Cranston said. "They got taken in by you, and believed slavery and rape were normal because you taught them it was. They have since learned otherwise. You see, you called them marines in your army, but now they know what it means to be a United States Marine."

Hull regarded the men, blinking, and Cranston could tell he was trying to remember them. He wondered how he could ever have followed a man like Hull, and felt his anger rising again. The rifle still lay over Hull's heart and the Marines watched with curiosity, but made no move to stop him from killing the Butcher of Prescott. But before his finger tightened on the trigger enough to fire a round, somebody called his name. Turning only his head, he saw Colonel Berger waving him over.

"Colonel Cranston, come here, on the double! You're not gonna believe this!"

#

Chapter 32

Fear is pain arising from the anticipation of evil.
Aristotle

Operation Overtime
1343 hours, May 5

The northern end of Motor Bay C was the parking and maintenance area for Alpha Company, 1st Armored Battalion. Morgan Randall's M1A3 Abrams, named *Joe's Junk*, had finally rotated into the service bay where Master Gunner Kenji Kohan's team began routine checks of all major systems. But no sooner had they begun working on the tank than the digital multimeter went down, and without it they couldn't run-test the systems. Kohan gave his crew mess call while he disappeared into a workshop he called the Inner Sanctum.

"I think it's got a cold solder joint," he said.

Randall and her gunner, Joe Ootoi, were on hand to help work on *Joe's Junk*. Their lives depended on the proper functioning of their tank in battle. During the previous summer's attack on Prescott, code named Operation Kickass, the Abrams had performed better than anyone could ever have hoped, but sustained heavy damage in the process. Despite being cleared for a return to combat, little things seemed to keep going wrong that worried Randall, especially now that she was pregnant.

She hadn't yet told her crew that part, though.

And those days, anywhere that Joe Ootoi was, Randall's half-sister Nikki wasn't far away. Fortunately, she'd proved adept at using her hands and had actually been a big help. When Kohan left, she walked to a blind spot behind the tank and motioned for Joe Ootoi to join her.

Randall raised her eyebrows and shook her head. "Hey, you two," she said, "I'll be in the latrine if Master Gunner Kohan gets back and wants me."

All she could see over the rear of the tank was Nikki's handwave, showing that she'd heard her. Randall laughed and headed for the bathroom halfway down the length of the immense motor bay.

Although the base had been operational for almost a year now, Randall never ceased being amazed by the sheer scope of such a huge engineering project. No part of Overtime Prime bespoke the genius of those who'd built it than the four motor bays. Motor Bay C was only the second largest of the ground-level caverns, which were essentially garages, with maintenance and repair facilities, refueling stations, and parking areas. The dimensions were 874 feet long, 290 feet wide, and sixty feet tall. The height allowed for use of heavy cranes mounted on gantries for moving items like engines. One was even rated to move an Abrams.

As impressive as Randall found all of that, she didn't stop to admire the scenery. She'd tried to will her recent nausea into submission but that hadn't worked so well, and now she just hoped she made it to the latrine in time. The motor bay was mostly empty since the battalion had no ops on the board, so she was able to cover her mouth. Blessedly, she made it in time.

After ten minutes of heaving she felt better, and rinsed her mouth out five times with cold tap water. The sour taste still filled her mouth, but wasn't quite so bad. Coming out of the latrine, she spotted a large man walking toward her very fast, a pistol in his fist. His head turned toward her and he raised the pistol to high ready position. She started walking back toward *Joe's Junk* and he veered to his right, which put him trailing in her wake, and sped up.

Randall sensed the danger and broke into a trot. Glancing over her shoulder, she saw him start running, and then she did, too. The motor bay ended with a wall, which had a number of doors, a massive service elevator, and two more for personnel. Heart beating hard in her chest, she ran like her life depended on it, because she thought it might. But more, the life of her child depended on it. Reaching *Joe's Junk*, she intended to seal herself inside until help came. At a dead run, she grabbed the cannon's barrel and swung herself up onto the front right corner. She took a half step toward the turret, but a hand grabbed her ankle and threw her to the concrete floor.

Motor Bay B, Operation Overtime

A man in ACUs came out from behind the tank, followed by a disheveled woman in uniform. Adder's chest heaved after the chase, but his gun arm was steady.

"What's going on here?" the man said. He took a step toward Randall. "Lieutenant, you okay?"

"Go get help, Toy!"

"Don't do it," Adder said. "I hate shooting a man in the back. Your name is Toy?"

"Ootoi, Joe Ootoi. Who are you?"

Despite his threat, he pointed his Sig Sauer M17 at Morgan Randall, not Ootoi. It was apparent he hadn't recognized the other blonde woman with the streaked mascara and smeared lipstick.

"He's a degenerate asshole," Nikki said.

"Well, well, well, if it isn't my favorite psychopath. Looks like our boy Toy his been having some fun with his little slut."

"You need to shut your mouth," Ootoi said.

But Adder just laughed. "I didn't come here to shoot you, butthead, but I'll be glad to if you take one step." Staring Ootoi down, he glanced back at Morgan Randall. "I always heard you were hot, and fuck me, they weren't kidding."

"Come here and find out," she said.

Adder only smiled. "Don't tempt me. I might just do that."

"Leave her alone, you fuckin' ape!" Ootoi said, and took another single step forward.

Adder pivoted, fired twice, and brought the gun back to his original aim. Morgan leapt the instant he moved, but the distance was too great. He swiveled the gun back and fired at a range of six feet, aiming for her lower stomach. With impossible reflexes, she spun left and caught the bullet on the saddle of her right thigh. The impact knocked her back down and blood immediately darkened her pants.

"Ahhh!" she screamed. Adder glanced at the man he'd shot but couldn't see him. The blond woman knelt beside him, sobbing and begging him to wake up. Adder couldn't see her face but dismissed her as a threat and turned back to Morgan Randall. "I guess it's time to have some fun with you before it's too late," he said, grinning.

The bullets struck Toy in the sternum and left breast. Nikki's combat experience kicked in by reflex. She knelt beside him and stripped off his shirt, but knew the instant she saw his eyes that Toy was dead. Blood covered her hands. Stunned, she simply knelt there and blinked as more of it oozed from the holes in his chest.

Time stopped and her mind went blank. She never knew how long it stayed that way, but looking back, it could only have been milliseconds. Nikki Bauer had been madly in love with Joe Ootoi. She had put his needs before her own and realized for the first time in her life what it meant to be human. The instant she'd met him, she'd suppressed the demon inside her, the twisted spirit named Nipple, but it never completely vanished. It was always there, lurking in the deep shadows of her inner rage, kept hidden because the love she felt for Joe Ootoi was too strong for it to overcome.

But now, the man who'd taught her the meaning of love lay dead. No, not dead... murdered. Shot in cold blood by a ruthless asshole she'd always hated. And then she heard it again, the voice inside her... the demon, the one who haunted her dreams, the one she called Nipple.

But that wasn't his name.

Long, long ago, a shriveled old Haitian voodoo priest told her the demon was called Congo Savanne, and he would never leave her, not for good. He would live inside her, and only her toy could silence him. Now her Toy was gone and Congo Savanne was back. And for that she was glad.

'Toy's death demands revenge,' he whispered, 'and it's your fault. If you had killed this man when you first wanted to, Toy would still be alive. You might as well have pulled the trigger yourself.' Nikki Bauer would have recognized his lies and resisted them, but Nikki Bauer wasn't her, not any more.

Nipple was back.

Adder stood over Morgan Randall for a few seconds and watched her bleed. He nudged her with his boot and smiled. Then with his free hand he began unbuckling his belt. The pistol he shifted to his left hand, pointed now in Nipple's direction.

"You're not gonna die for a while," he said to Randall. "There's plenty of time for me to show you what I think of your father."

Morgan grimaced and rolled. Excruciating pain sucked the breath from her lungs as fire burned in her side and stomach. All she could think about was the baby. She didn't see her sister approach Adder from behind, and for a brief moment he was too busy enjoying her suffering to notice.

A long flathead screwdriver filled her left hand. She could easily have stabbed him at the base of the skull, but Nipple liked seeing the eyes of the people she killed, so instead she balanced on the balls of feet, ready to strike. "Hey, dickbreath," Nipple said. "Remember me?"

Adder wheeled faster than a man of his bulk should have been able to manage and pointed the gun right at Nipple's face, but she had anticipated that exact move and, despite his uncanny speed, she was still much faster.

Still clutching the screwdriver, she grabbed his thick forearm, put her heels together, and used it as a fulcrum to slide under him. He fired but she was no longer there and the bullet ricocheted off the far wall. Nipple slid between his wide-braced legs until she stared up at his crotch, and then shoved the point of the screwdriver upward with all her strength. She wasn't sure where it hit but it must have hurt like hell, because Adder screamed and swiped at her head with the back of his hand. This time he was faster.

He was a powerful man and, fueled by pain and rage, the blow caught her on the jaw and knocked her backward to the ground. Stunned, she rolled left by sheer reflex as Adder squeezed off three rounds. All missed and sparked off the concrete.

"What the hell's going on out here?" yelled Master Gunner Kohan, emerging from the workshop with a pistol in his hand.

Bending over in pain, Adder felt blood running out of his pant legs into his boots. He squeezed off two shots at Kohan, firing blind. Then, still shrieking, he made for the elevator, squeezing off the last rounds in the magazine over his shoulder and leaving a long trail of blood.

Nipple stood, still dazed, and wanted to go finish him off, but the blood soaking Morgan's shirt took priority. She ripped off her own ACU blouse and knelt beside her stricken sister with only a sports bra covering her chest. Putting pressure on the wound was hard because the bullet gouged the flesh near her hip, and it kept bleeding. Kohan rounded the corner of the tank and, seeing the two fallen tankers, ran to Ootoi.

"He's dead!" Nipple yelled. "She's not! Call the medics and get me a medical kit, right now!"

#

Part Four

Game in Play

Chapter 33

I faced my foe without fear.
Tomb of unknown Macedonian hoplite, circa 330 b.c.

Operation Overtime
1344 hours, May 5

They had arrived at the danger point, where the shaft dead-ended one level below the Crystal Palace. Access to the corridor, which traversed Officer's Country, was through an unlocked hatch disguised inside a laundry chute. The door to Angriff's personal quarters was only forty feet away. He detailed Sergeant Riotto to stand guard beside his door and not to let anyone except family members inside.

Fortunately, nobody was in the corridor. They climbed from the hatch and went straight to the one leading to the escape shaft under the Crystal Palace. It was so well hidden that unless you knew to look for it, you'd never find it. But Angriff and Green Ghost knew where it was, and in seconds they were safely inside. Hand over hand, they climbed the final rungs.

Excitement made it hard for Colonel Claringdon to sit still as the emvee wove in and out of foot traffic approaching the Clam Shell. Today was the day they all crossed the Rubicon. Once General Steeple gave the order for the deployed artillery batteries to open fire on their comrades, they would know which units could be trusted and which couldn't. Circumstances might change, but human nature never did. Those who killed their fellow Americans would share the collective guilt. Psychologically, he knew that any commander who gave the fire order would never again challenge Steeple's authority. It had worked in Nazi Germany's SS, and it would work for the 7th Cavalry.

The Chinese guards at the main entrance snapped to attention. Claringdon scanned them and didn't like what he saw — shirts partly untucked, dirty boots, beard stubble. That would all have to change, but for the moment he was glad to have them protecting him. Two more stood at the base of the ramp and two more at the top. Sergeant Major Schiller saw him coming and stood to rigid attention. *His* uniform was impeccable. Despite them having exchanged gunfire less than a month ago, if Schiller could swear loyalty to him, Claringdon was willing to overlook it.

Schiller announced him and held the door as Claringdon entered.

"Fitz, right on time," said Tom Steeple. "Are you excited?"

"I am, sir. It is a portentous day."

"It is indeed. Pretty soon we will know, beyond the shadow of a doubt, who we can count on and who we cannot. Colonel Adder is taking care of another security matter."

Claringdon knew Steeple's reputation for knowing when he was being lied to, so he smiled and told a half-truth. "I'm sure it's a critical matter, sir."

Steeple's return smile held a hint of suspicion, but he said nothing more about Adder. Instead, he checked his watch. "Ten minutes."

Green Ghost went up the ladder first, holding a flashlight in his teeth. One of his father's attributes, although he was extremely agile for a man of his age and size, was not stealth. The hatch in the Crystal Palace floor opened downward. If the desk chair was pushed up under the desk, it would be on top of the hatch. Even if unoccupied, it would take great care for it not to partly fall into the hole created by the open hatch, thereby making a lot of noise. They had agreed if Tom Steeple was sitting in the chair, Green Ghost would try to shoot him.

The hatch's locking mechanism could be manipulated from above or below. Green Ghost lifted the bolt from its locked position. Gently, with the lightest touch he could manage, he slid it back. The squeal of metal on metal made him stop. Exposed as they were on the ladder, thirty feet from the floor below, anybody with a pistol, even Tom Steeple, could kill them both from above with a couple of shots. If the bullets didn't kill them, the fall would. And even if they did manage to crawl out into the office, they would be vulnerable until they could get out from under the desk. Only the desperation of the moment drove them on.

More light squeals marked the opening of the hatch, magnified by the tight confines of the shaft. Green Ghost could hear someone speaking above, which masked the noise he'd made. It sounded like Tom Steeple rambling on about something. Later, it would make a great story, how Steeple himself covered the noise Green Ghost made sneaking up on him, that if he hadn't been so long-winded he might have heard them. But that was later, this was now, and before he could tell the story, he had to survive.

Very slowly, he lowered the hatch, feeling no chair's weight on it, and crawled through the opening.

Hands behind his back, bouncing on his heels, Steeple stared at the blast shutters as if he saw the desert beyond. "I understand Angriff a little better now, Fitz."

"I am not sure what you mean by that, sir."

"How do I explain this feeling? It's like I'm the conductor of an orchestra whose parts are scattered over multiple music halls, but the various components all have to play the same symphony at the same time in perfect harmony. And there's no way to practice first; all you can do is plan and pray it goes off well."

"I see what you mean."

Steeple smiled without turning around, keeping his back turned to Claringdon. "Today we put the Seventh Cavalry on the track it should have been on a year ago, if Angriff hadn't been such a bullheaded fool. We've had to coordinate the attack on Sierra with the Chinese, and the attack on the so-called Shangri-La with the Sevens, while planning a sweep of disloyal members here at Overtime and holding back the Mexicans in the south. Not to mention the mess over at Comeback. That's a lot of coordination and planning, and to know that it moves into action in less than half an hour is exhilarating. Surely this is how Angriff must have felt before the launch of an operation. So many things can go wrong, and yet it's that fear that makes it all so exciting..."

"Yes, sir."

"I envy you, Fitz. You've been in combat; you know battle up close and personal. I've never had that opportunity."

"Never, General?"

"Never. I'm been in combat zones many times, but nobody ever shot at me. Which is just as well, because as attractive as the idea sounds to me now, I have a very real understanding of where my talents lie, and it's not in directing men in battle. Nick Angriff could stand toe to toe with an enemy and give better than he got, but not me. I'd be dead at the first shot. I'm a macro warrior, not a micro one. I'm a planner; my genius lies in organization and logistics. And strategic politics — I'm not ashamed to admit that."

"Sounds like you miss him a little bit."

"Who, Angriff? The man was a royal pain in my ass, but people like him only come along once in a generation. He was larger than life, and even the people who hated him also respected him. He was a force of nature. Do I miss him? Maybe I do."

In his mind's eye, Steeple pictured his far-flung command preparing for battle. Never mind that it was their own countrymen they prepared to fire upon.

He glanced at his watch again, a gift from the 44th president. "It's almost fourteen hundred hours... the wait is over. I've given Fleming, Berger, and Sully plenty of time to come to their senses. Lieutenant Colonel Santorio is standing by on line one to relay an order to all commands to give the order to open fire, and to keep firing as long as necessary. But you're the brigade commander, so you should be the one to give the order."

Steeple stared out at the desert he couldn't see, listening for Claringdon to issue the fateful order.

"Did you hear me, Fitz?"

When no response came this time either, he turned on his left heel, prepared to chew Claringdon out for daydreaming. Instead, he stared down the barrel of a gun he'd stared down before, in the hand of the same man who'd held it then. Behind that fist, bright blue eyes arched downward in a very angry scowl.

For one of the only times in his life, Tom Steeple was taken completely by surprise. His mouth dropped open and his eyes widened. "You're dead," he said, the way someone might when speaking with a ghost.

"Dyin' ain't what it used to be," Angriff said.

Angriff noticed Steeple cut his eyes sideways to Claringdon, but there was no help there. Green Ghost held a knife to the colonel's throat. Steeple said nothing, but stared back at Angriff, expecting him to speak, but he was too angry. What he really wanted was to kill the man.

"Put it between my eyes and get it over with," Steeple finally said.

"Don't tempt me, Tom. Now here's what you're going to do. You're going to use the intercom to call Schiller in here. You're going to do it in a normal tone of voice, so nobody gets suspicious. Got it? If you're a good boy, you'll live through this. If you're not, I'll splatter your brains all over those blast shutters. Which is it?"

"You know I'm not a hero."

"Then don't do anything stupid."

"I've already done it... I brought you into this."

"Schiller, get in here."

General Steeple's voice sounded like a nail being dragged across a blackboard, but Sergeant Schiller had worked for too many assholes and been in the army too long to let it show on his face. With an almost bored expression, he picked up his tablet. Ignoring the two Chinese guards eyeing his every move, he made for the door into the general's office.

With the blast shutters closed, he had to knock and wait for the door to be unbolted so it could open. He slipped through and it closed behind him with a slam, but the tableau inside wasn't what he'd expected. General Angriff pointed a Desert Eagle at General Steeple, while Green Ghost stood to one side of Colonel Claringdon holding a knife. Schiller's heart immediately pounded like he'd run a mile, but his facial expression didn't change.

"Nice to have you back, General Angriff," he said.

"Hello, J.C. Not surprised to see me?"

"Actually no, sir. I've been expecting you."

Angriff couldn't help chuckling. "What's it like out there?"

"You mean, aside from all the Chinese everywhere?" He cut his eyes to Steeple for just an instant.

"How many here at the Clam Shell?" Green Ghost asked.

Schiller turned to him. "It's nice to have you back, too, Colonel. There're two guards outside on the catwalk, two more at the base of the ramp, and one on either side of the headquarters entrance. Some of their technicians are being briefed by the computer people."

"Are they all armed?"

"The guards have rifles and sidearms. I don't think the technicians are armed."

"Here's what we need you to do."

Both guards were young and neither was actually Chinese, but they were clearly enjoying pushing the Americans around. When Schiller stepped back out of the office, one of them blocked his way. "Where do you think you're going?"

"To carry out General Steeple's orders."

"What are they?"

"If he'd wanted you to know, he would have told you."

"I don't like you, old man," the guard said, trying to sound tough.

"I'm heartbroken. Now move, unless you want to explain to General Steeple why you're standing in my way."

"You'd better watch yourself." He stepped aside to let Schiller pass, but called after him as he walked down the ramp. "This is all ours now!"

Schiller just kept walking. Once off the ramp, he turned right toward Dupree's station. The young tech had two Chinese leaning over his shoulders, watching something on his monitor as he clacked away on a keyboard. Schiller tapped Dupree and nodded with his chin. The Chinese gave him dirty looks but didn't say anything. Dupree followed him.

They moved into the main hallway, far enough toward the mess hall so the guards at either side of the main entrance couldn't hear them. He waited until there were no passersby in earshot. "Where's your weapon?" he asked without preamble.

Dupree tilted his head. "My rifle?"

"Yeah, where is it?"

"Beside my desk, as you ordered, Sergeant."

"You're a sergeant now, too, so call me J.C. What about a sidearm?"

"In my drawer. What's this about, Sergeant... I mean, J.C.?"

"It means we're gonna get rid of these Chinese cocksuckers."

"Won't that piss General Steeple off?"

"Probably." Schiller dipped his head, but then cut his eyes to look up. "But it'll sure as hell make Nick smile."

Schiller waited until the Chinese technicians had moved down the row before slipping Dupree's Sig Sauer P226 under his belt and retucking his shirt to cover it. After a quickly whispered plan in Dupree's ear, he picked up a clipboard off the desk and pretended to study it as he walked back up the ramp. Once at the top he scooted past the guards and ducked into the Crystal Palace, then turned around and went back down. Once at the bottom, he turned left into the warren of cubicles to the right of the ramp. Sitting in a vacant chair, he opened desk drawers as if searching for something. With his back to the guards, he slipped the Sig out of his waist, and waited.

Exactly two minutes later, he walked out the main doors into the hallway. Two Chinese guards were posted on either side, roughly fifty feet apart. He walked two paces past the one on his left, whirled, and stuck the pistol barrel behind the guard's left ear.

"Say one word and you're dead," Schiller whispered.

The man's eyes darted back and forth. Probably without meaning to, he yelled something unintelligible and tried to knock Schiller's gun away, but it was futile. One round blew out the right side of his head. Even as he slumped over to the right, the other guard reacted by shouldering his rifle and aiming in Schiller's direction. He was also too slow, as Schiller fired four rounds. Three hit him, while the last ricocheted down the hallway.

Schiller had started to run back inside when a third guard, one of those at the foot of the ramp, came out of the door ready to shoot. He never got to fire. Two shots from an M16 knocked him forward and exited his chest, smacking the wall across the corridor and fragmenting. The man twisted to face Schiller and his AK-47 clattered to the floor. He fell to one knee and then toppled backward. In the meantime, three shots rang out inside, followed immediately by two thundering reports from a weapon Schiller had never thought he'd hear again, a fifty-caliber Desert Eagle.

#

Chapter 34

> *"Human beings are made up of flesh and blood, and a miracle fiber called courage."*
> George S. Patton, Jr.

The Crystal Palace, Operation Overtime
1402 hours, May 5

"You need to let *me* handle this," Green Ghost said. "You're too valuable to die a third time, maybe for real."

Angriff grunted. "I have no intention of dying again. But if either of these bastards so much as sneezes, don't hesitate to cut him down, with extreme prejudice."

Steeple tried to return Angriff's glare, but soon averted his eyes. Claringdon stared back, face filled with hate. Then the first shot rang out, and everything happened within seconds.

Angriff opened the Crystal Palace door with the pistol extended, turning toward the ramp. The two guards had both gone to one knee, aiming downward and not looking back. Angriff saw one of the guards at the foot running toward the doorway when Sergeant Dupree cut him down with two shots in the back. He then engaged the other guard at the ramp's bottom.

The two at the top swung their aim at Dupree, but Angriff was faster. He aimed at the one on his right and put a round into the back of the man's head, which exploded like one of the watermelons he used to practice with in his backyard in Virginia. The other half turned before Angriff put his second shot into the small of his back, just above the coccyx. With the soldier lying on the grated steel, blood dripped through the mesh to the floor below.

Meanwhile, Dupree kept the last guard pinned down so Schiller could flank him at the doorway. Three shots put him down, too. As the reports echoed through the Clam Shell, Angriff walked over to the wounded Chinese soldier. Despite his rage, his righteous rage, Angriff felt only pity for the dying man. He knelt beside him. The man seemed to be mouthing something.

"You trying to tell me something, soldier?"

"F-fuck you."

"Too late for that now. You had your chance."

"And fuck your whore wife."

Angriff's eyes widened and he stood up. "You shouldn't have said that. I think it's time for you to get off my headquarters."

Using his boot, he shoved the man over the side and off the balcony. Flailing as he fell fifty feet to the tile floor, he hit with a wet *smack* and the *crack* of splintering bone.

Without more than a glance down at the dead man, Angriff saw Schiller looking up at him and waved the sergeant major up the ramp. "All right, J.C., find Colonel Walling and see if he's in shape to get up here. In the meantime, what should I do first?"

"If I were you, General, I'd call Colonel Coughlan first. He's got orders to provide artillery support for the Chinese attack on Sierra."

"He *what*?"

"It's true, General. He issued the same order to fire on Prescott and on the Marines in New Mexico."

"Put me through to Colonel Coughlan. I'll take it here."

"He also cancelled your order for air support for General Tompkins."

"After you get me Colonel Coughlan, call the air operations dispatcher and send General Tompkins whatever we've got ready to go, over my name. If the officer gives you any static, hand him over to me."

Colonel Young rubbed his eyes and wished the whole thing was over. Any second now, he expected to hear General

Steeple give the order to open fire on his brothers in arms, knowing the rounds from John Coughlan's artillery tubes would scream over his head seconds later. The explosives would then rip apart men that only two weeks before had been the heroes of the brigade. It was all so wrong and there was nothing he could do about it short of mutiny in the face of the enemy, and yet that was the very thing on his mind.

"What is taking General Steeple so long to order the attack?" Captain Chen Yi said. Young couldn't stand the arrogant little prick, but by Steeple's direct order he had to show their new ally every courtesy.

"I don't know."

"If we do not attack soon, it may be dark before the battle ends. If that occurs, some of your mutinous countrymen could escape under cover of night."

"I'm well aware of that, Captain."

"The People's Army is not so indecisive."

"Your general is welcome to start his attack any time he feels like it, but that's not how we do things in the U.S. Army. Besides, since when does China give any initiative to individual officers?"

"We have always believed it on the battlefield."

"Stier scheisse."

"What?"

"Nothing."

"Sir, it's Prime."

Colonel Coughlan stared as a corporal handed him a headset. All eyes in the headquarters tent were on him. He could feel them watching and wondering what he'd do. He didn't want to take the headset, didn't want to hear the words he dreaded — *open fire*. But there wasn't any choice. Holding the set to one ear, he closed his eyes and mouthed a silent prayer. Then he stepped to one side and stared out the tent flap as a prairie falcon circled in the distance. "This is Colonel Coughlan."

The voice on the other end came through perfectly clear, but it wasn't the nasal New England accent of General Steeple. It was a deeper voice with a raspy quality and a mild but distinct Southern accent. "Colonel, are your guns in range of the Chinese regiment?"

"Yes, sir!"

The low buzz of the headquarters personnel quieted at his enthusiastic answer.

"Do you recognize my voice?"

"I do for a fact, General."

"Good. You have new orders. The Chinese are not, I repeat, *not* to be considered allies or friendlies. You are to retarget to the Chinese forces in your area. Target selection is at your discretion, as is your ordnance package. I understand you only have light guns? One-oh-fives?"

"That's correct, sir."

"Do what you can with what you've got. Coordinate your support with 2nd Mechanized Infantry Regiment. This attack needs to be made today, if possible. Do you understand these orders as I've given them to you?"

"Hell, yes! Sir."

Coughlan heard Angriff chuckle. "Excellent. Good hunting, Spud. Tear 'em a new one."

The Chinese liaison officer, Captain Tian Tao, moved closer. Short, with a pot belly, Tao had obviously been part of the original expeditionary force to invade California. Although close-cropped, the hair that remained was steel gray. He'd only arrived half an hour before, to observe the U.S. artillery in action.

"Have you finally been given the attack order?" He tilted his head back when he spoke, which gave him a condescending air that had made Coughlan want to shoot him the instant they'd met.

"Yes, I have, Captain. Guard!"

A private rushed in from the tent's entrance.

"Place this man under arrest as a prisoner of war, Private."

"You cannot do this!" Tao protested. "We're allies now. Your General Steeple agreed!"

"Yeah," Coughlan said. "About that... he's not running the show any more." He turned to his headquarters staff and put hands on his hips. He tried but couldn't stop a smile. "Ladies and gentlemen, we have new orders. Nick's back!"

The guard jabbed Tao in the back with his rifle, motioning for him to leave.

But instead the Chinese officer leaned forward. "What does that mean, *Nick's back*?"

Wearing a broad grin, the guard answered. "It means you're goat-fucked, asshole."

Colonel Coughlan couldn't help venting his own pent-up emotions. "Captain, you and your buddies are about to get your asses kicked, and it couldn't happen to a nicer bunch. Now get this piece of shit out of my headquarters."

Major Dieter Strootman rushed out of the large headquarters tent, glanced both ways, and found his C.O. walking back from the latrine. "You all right, Colonel?"

"No, Dieter, I'm not. Not even a little. The idea of killing my fellow Americans makes me sick. But that—" He pointed backward with his thumb to indicate the latrine tent. "—that was just nature calling."

"Good to hear, sir."

"Why were you looking for me? Have we heard from General Steeple?"

"The general's on the horn."

"I guess this is it. Damn that man... damn him!"

"It's not General Steeple."

Young squinted. "Fleming? Is he surrendering?" At that, he started walking again, faster.

"Not General Fleming, not General Tompkins, not General Saw..."

"Then who the hell is left?" But as soon as he said it, Young stopped. "No." He looked into Strootman's face, and the major couldn't help grinning. "It can't be."

Strootman nodded. "It can, sir. It's General Angriff."

After handing the receiver back to the radioman, Colonel Young turned to Captain Chen Yi. "You're about to get your wish, Captain."

"You are finally going to attack?"

"Soon, yes."

"What is the delay now?"

"See, we've had a change of target." He turned to his exec, standing beside Yi. "Major Strootman, redeploy the regiment to attack west after artillery support lifts. We go in half an hour, so get to it. And relay this information to General Fleming at Sierra. Ask if he wants to take over tactical command."

"Yes, sir!"

Yi looked at the floor, then back up at Young, confused. "But if you attack west, you attack us."

"You catch on quick."

Angriff handed the receiver to Schiller. "Any grief from the air dispatcher?"

"I'm not sure, sir. I used your name like you told me to..."

"But?"

"Sir, my brother General Schiller called from the Air Force Annex at Operation Comeback. I... I took the liberty of authorizing an A-10 sortie in support of the Marines in New Mexico. I used your name, sir."

"Good call, J.C. Why is he in the Air Force Annex?"

"General Steeple ordered him apprehended at all costs. They've been using thermite over there to break in..."

He went on for twenty more seconds, filling in the details, but Angriff had stopped listening. He felt his face burning, and all he could do for a moment was blink. His reputation of being Nick the A had been well earned, but never in his life could he remember being so angry, so absolutely outraged. Not even when the Secretary of State had arranged for Stingers to be sold to terrorists had he been that infuriated.

"J.C., I need an immediate call to all units in the field. Right now."

It took almost a minute for Colonel Santorio's communications department to patch the call through to all commands outside of Prime. Angriff used the time to calm his breathing. He stared down at the man he'd rolled off the balcony, who lay face down below in a spreading pool of blood.

"To all commands, this is General Nicholas T. Angriff. I repeat, this is the commanding officer of the 7th Cavalry. I'm calling you from my headquarters at Overtime Prime to let you know that I am still alive and in command. Any and all orders given to you by General Steeple are hereby null and void, and under no circumstances are you to fire on friendly forces. Do not, I repeat, do *not* fire on U.S. troops. If enemy formations are in your area, you have tactical freedom to engage at your discretion. All personnel at Operation Comeback are to immediately acknowledge General Schiller as your commander. I am back in charge, and you have my full backing to take whatever measures you deem necessary to prevent General Steeple's orders from being carried out. If you choose to ignore this message, may God help you, because I won't."

The whole time he spoke, all he could think of was his people in harm's way because of Tom Steeple's personal ambition. A man could only take so much and for the first time in a long time, his anger got the better of him. Angriff handed the receiver to Schiller, marched back inside the Crystal Palace, and without hesitation smashed his fist into Tom Steeple's face.

"There's something else, General," Sergeant Major Schiller said. "General Steeple sent a company-sized force to Comeback armed with Stingers, to prevent any attempts to stop the Sevens in New Mexico using fixed-wing aircraft."

Angriff's chest already heaved as he suppressed a rage that could only be sated by killing Tom Steeple. When he replied, he didn't take his eyes off the man he'd just knocked senseless. "He sent Americans to shoot down American aircraft?" Then he held up his right hand. "Never mind. Radio those men and tell them not to fire on Americans under any circumstances. Make it *very* clear that any hostile act will be judged by me as mutiny under wartime conditions. Get me on if you need to."

"I'm on it."

"And get a MEDEVAC to Ma Kelly's. Tell them to expect a sucking chest wound."

"Yes, sir!"

Steeple was coming around. Angriff held his right thumb and index finger a hair's breadth apart.

"That close, Tom... you're that close to having me shoot you right here, right now. And Claringdon, you'll be next."

Prescott, Arizona
1419 hours, May 5

Colonel Berger had been right. It was hard to believe.

Standing beside the TA-838 field telephone, Norbert Cranston's mouth gaped, and he didn't care. It didn't matter how stunned he might look, because so did everyone else. Then, along with Colonel Berger, the open maw transformed into a grin. General Angriff wasn't dead!

"That man must be related to Chesty Puller," Berger said. "Or Lazarus. Let's let him decide what to do with the mighty General Patton."

"I don't mind shooting him, Colonel," Cranston said. "I did some terrible things on his orders, because he told me that's how the old U.S. Army operated. I wanted to help rebuild the country and he took advantage of that. He needs to be shot."

"Maybe so, but that's not our call."

"Can I at least gag him?"

"*That* you can do."

The ledge outside of Sara Snowtiger's cave was gone. The Sevens had gotten four more mortar rounds from somewhere, and three of them had scored directs hit on the rock. Sig Zuckerman had been on watch when the first one struck between his feet and the cave mouth. It was likely that he was dead before that section of the ledge broke away and fell three hundred feet to the desert, but Dennis Tompkins didn't know that for certain. Paul Hausser had been too near the entrance and got a chest full of splinters, none fatal, but he lost a lot of blood and the danger of infection was high.

Tompkins himself was still sore from the near-miss with the RPG round, while Thibodeaux wasn't hurt at all, and they still had the two Marines and about one third of the ammo they'd started with. But the food was long gone and they hadn't eaten anything in two days. The two Snowtiger twins spent all of their free time together now, as if in preparation for the end. Sara, in particular, worried Tompkins; where before she had appeared so strong, now she seemed frail.

He sat with his back to the cave wall. Just beyond his boots, the fire had died to little more than a flicker as their store of wood ran out.

John Thibodeaux leaned against the wall beside him, and then slid to the floor. "I think this time might be the last time, Skip."

"Didn't you say the same thing last year, right before we got rescued?"

"Maybe I did, but this time there ain't no Nick Angriff to save our asses."

"You never know."

Thibodeaux laughed, once. "I guess we don't change much, huh? I heard you say that afore. Me, I don't see no downside to you doing the same thing you did then."

"You mean I should call for help? Call who?"

"That Steeple fella... don't know anybody else you *can* call. Maybe beg him. I ain't askin' so much for me, but Zig's leg is bad infected, and I'm really worried about Sara. Maybe he'll send help, maybe he won't, but we won't know lessen you ask him."

Tompkins drew in a deep breath and let it out in a sigh. "Hand me the radio, will you please, John?"

Angriff stood behind his desk, back turned to where Claringdon supported a sitting Tom Steeple. Steeple shook his head and wiped blood away from his lip. Angriff hung up the phone and heard Claringdon say, "Only a coward sucker-punches someone half his size."

Before he could answer, Green Ghost did. "He should be glad it wasn't me. I'd have shot you both by now."

Angriff was about to speak when Schiller came in. "Urgent call from General Tompkins, sir! Line 1."

Tompkins heard a click as the call was transferred and someone picked up a phone. Sig Zuckerman chose that moment to yell out in pain, so all he heard was somebody say "Dennis?"

He was determined to say everything without being interrupted, and so it came out in a rush. "General Steeple, you may not want to help me but please there's innocent people dying here for God's sake show them mercy even if you don't show me any."

"What's your situation, Dennis?"

Tompkins blinked. What he thought he'd heard wasn't possible. "General Steeple?"

"Hell, Dennis, you call me that one more time and I'm gonna reconsider our friendship!"

Tompkins went rigid, his face slackening with shock. Thibodeaux leaned around to look at him straight on, worried.

"Nick?"

Angriff disconnected the call but kept the phone receiver in his hand. "J.C., get me aircraft dispatch, now!"

Schiller ran out to his desk. It took nearly two minutes for the dispatcher to pick up with a bored sounding "Dispatch, Warrant Officer Coleman speaking."

"Warrant Officer, this is General Angriff! How many birds are in the air to General Tompkins?"

"General... *Angriff?* You really are alive, sir?"

"How many helicopters, Warrant Officer Coleman?"

"None, sir. General Steeple cancelled the order to keep crews ready twenty-four-seven."

Once again Angriff glared at Steeple, as if his stare could kill. "What about Sergeant Major Schiller's call a few minutes ago?"

"I— I didn't believe him, sir. They said you were dead and all—"

"I want four gunships airborne within five minutes, Warrant Officer Coleman, and if they're not, it's your ass on the line! Get 'em up there! I'll have Sergeant Major Schiller send you the coordinates."

"What ordnance package, sir?"

"Anti-personnel. Now get to it! Timing is mission critical, Coleman."

"Yes, sir!"

#

Chapter 35

Remember, upon the conduct of each depends the fate of all.
Alexander the Great

Sierra Army Depot, Herlong, CA
1409 hours, May 5

    Sunlight partially washed out the magnified view of his M22 binoculars as Norm Fleming inspected the American position south of his forward line of resistance. One hundred yards out from the main line, his line served the same function as skirmishers did in the American Civil War, namely to warn of and break up incoming attacks. He'd left the defensive setup in the hands of Major Samuel Ball, C.O. of the 1st Airborne Battalion, who'd deployed 75 of his roughly 300 men facing their brethren in the 1st Mechanized Infantry Regiment, and the rest had dug in west against the Chinese.
    Standing beside Fleming, Major Ball spoke while peering through his own binoculars. "You think they'll really attack, General?"
    "I wish that I could give a definitive answer, one way or another, but Major... your guess is as good as mine. Colonel Young is a fine man and commander, and while it seems incomprehensible that Americans are about to kill Americans, history teaches that we have done this before. But *if* they are going to attack, it will come soon. Both of us have night vision gear, so waiting until dark would supply no tactical advantage to them, and since I doubt the Chinese do have any NVGs, that would be a major disadvantage. It—"

Fleming stiffened and adjusted the binoculars.

Ball had lowered his while they'd talked, but now raised them back up. "That's a Humvee, sir."

"Yes, Major, it is. And it bears a white flag."

"What could it mean?"

Fleming smiled as the face of his dead best friend, Nick Angriff, flashed into his mind. He knew exactly what Nick would have said to that question. "Maybe they want to surrender."

The Humvee pulled to a stop thirty feet from where Fleming stood waiting. The dust cloud that followed it boiled upward, once it stopped, in a yellow mushroom cloud that looked like a tiny tactical nuke had gone off. Fleming averted his face as the outer edge of the cloud washed over him and Major Ball.

A paratrooper in the closest foxhole aimed his rifle at the vehicle.

But Fleming gently pushed it down. "No shooting, Corporal. Not unless they fire first."

"Yes, sir," the man said. "Sorry, sir."

"Never apologize for doing your job."

Unlike Nick Angriff, whose mood could usually be read on his face, Fleming's expression when faced with surprise was less expressive and more sanguine. Now, however, he found it hard not to react when Colonel Young himself got out of the passenger seat, strode up to him, and saluted, while the driver remained behind the wheel. Fleming gave his best West Point salute in return.

"Good afternoon, sir," Young said.

"A pleasure as always, Bob. To what do I owe this visit?"

"I'm here to coordinate our attack on the Chinese, General Fleming."

Fleming nodded to give himself time to think. "What has changed?"

"General Steeple's no longer in command, sir." Now a grin began playing at the corners of Young's mouth, a grin he had trouble containing. "We have a new C.O. Or, rather, the old one is back."

Fleming's brain processed the words quickly, but in microseconds realized that if Young meant his words literally, they could only mean one thing. "What are you saying, Colonel? We've only had one other commanding officer, and he's dead."

"Actually he's not, General Fleming. Rumors of his death have been greatly exaggerated."

"This is twice you've done this to me," Fleming said into the radio headset. He'd stepped away from Young and Ball so he couldn't be overheard, and told the officers that his watering eyes came from all the dust. Wiping them with the heel of his left hand, he saw the fast-moving shadow of a prairie falcon race over the ground. "It's getting old."

"Trust me, Norm," Angriff said. "If I'd had another choice, I would have taken it. The only reason I got away at all is help from Bob Young."

Fleming glanced up to see the colonel watching him. "He's a good man."

"The best. I didn't think so at first, but now I do. What's your sitrep?"

"My wounded need help ASAP, Nick. We've lost two in the past three days, with four more who are touch and go. Food, water, fuel, you name it, we need it."

"I'm setting up an air relay. Do you have a useable runway?"

"There is an old landing strip called Amedee to the north, but I have insufficient forces to secure it."

"What kind of shape is it in?"

"It is outside of our perimeter, so I have not seen it up close, but I cannot imagine any damage could render it unusable for long."

"Good, make that a priority so we can get those people out of there. What else do you need?"

"Aside from a shower?"

"Ha! Yeah, aside from that."

"A couple of cold beers would go down nice about now."

"I'll tell the Ag people to hurry up with the hops."

"You'd better... and Nick?"

"Yeah?"

"Don't die a third time."

"That's one bullet I can't dodge, but I promise to put it off as long as possible."

Sierra Army Depot
1428 hours

After telling the commander of the platoon deployed along the southern MLR to radio for all company commanders to meet them at headquarters on the double, Fleming and Ball trotted back to the small building near the center of camp. Sweat ran down Fleming's torso and he had to keep pulling up his pants. At first, losing a few pounds had sounded like a side benefit of being cut off from supply, but the reality wasn't all that great.

Both men stopped at the old-style pump outside the headquarters. Ball worked the handle as both men gulped water before going inside. Two captains had already showed up, along with Lieutenant Alisa Plotz and Sergeant Andy Arnold, the pilots of *Hell's Hammer*. Their AH-72 was low on fuel and mostly out of ammo, so after doing whatever maintenance they could, Plotz and Arnold had volunteered to work as headquarters staff to free up combat personnel for the front lines.

Several of the company commanders noticed Major Ball grinning, until Fleming cut him a side glance and he turned away. *Nobody* was going to steal this thunder from him. It was not the sort of attention-drawing thing he usually worried about, but this was a unique situation.

One of the company commanders handed him a cracker with a smear of peanut butter. He took it, but stopped before eating it.

"Is this your lunch, Lieutenant?"

"It's yours, sir, one per man. I didn't want you to miss out."

"Thanks. You're not kissing my ass, are you?"

"No offense, sir, you're not my type."

Fleming chewed while the others filed in. Once they had all gathered inside, he crossed his arms and walked around as if delivering more bad news. With his peripheral vision, he saw his audience either raising their eyebrows in the question *Do you know what's going on?* or shrugging the answer *I don't have a clue.*

Fleming's voice had a naturally bass timbre, deep and resonant. Over the years, he'd learned to modulate it for various occasions, from a deep baritone for happy occasions to a rumbling bass for solemn ones. Now, as he scowled, he used the lowest voice possible without making it sound false.

"Ladies and gentlemen, as you know, the Chinese have assembled an armored task force of indeterminate size to assault and capture this facility. It appears they have at least one or perhaps more self-propelled artillery pieces. Our best estimates of numbers are between two and three thousand men, spread out in an arc to our north and west. None of this takes into account the 2nd Mechanized Regiment to our south, which is on hand with half a battery of M119s. I think you all know what that means... mortar teams, Bradleys, and Strykers. Somebody's going to catch hell..." He paused and glowered at each man in turn. Then he cracked a little smile. "But it won't be us.

"The 7th Cavalry has a new commander. Or, rather, it has its old commander back. Never count out Nick the A... he's back, ladies and gentlemen, he's in command, and we're about to make the Chinese pay for setting foot in our country!"

Gapes and laughs gave way to cheers, and Fleming let them go on for twenty seconds or so before waving for quiet.

"Listen up! We go in half an hour. The Chinese are expecting a coordinated assault on our position, supported by the First Mech, so we have to go quick before they become suspicious that something has changed. There's no time to develop the area of engagement or determine the enemy scheme of maneuver. We don't know if they will attack, stand fast, or retreat. You should already have determined likely attack routes forward to your positions, but we have no idea about their path of egress. There's no time to plan or integrate indirect fire, either.

"Look for opportunities to advance with supporting fire, and be prepared for enemy counter-movements." He turned and indicated their battalion commander, Major Ball. "The major may redress your positions according to our new priorities. The airfield to our north is our number one target. Take it, and we might get more than a cracker for lunch. After Major Ball has given you your orders, get back to your companies ASAP and get your people ready. Major."

Fleming stepped aside to let Ball speak. "All right, listen up, here's how we're going to cut the Chicoms' balls off. First thing, there are a lot of arroyos out there with Chicoms in them, so remember your dry gap crossing principles—"

Arms crossed, Fleming listened to Ball briefing his people, and tried to remember exactly how you crossed a dry gap by the book.

Operation Overtime, the hall outside of the Angriff Quarters
1530 hours, May 5

A sticky blood trail panicked Nick Angriff for a split second, until he saw Sergeant Riotto standing beside his door. A dead Chinese soldier lay slumped down the corridor twenty feet to Riotto's right, a neat hole in his forehead and his brain matter splattered against the wall.

Green Ghost felt the man's neck. "Dead as a rock."

"What happened?"

"He thought I was here on the orders of Colonel Adder, and said we got to execute the woman inside but could have some fun first. I played along until he got too close to miss."

Angriff clapped him on the shoulder. "Thank you, Sergeant."

"It was my pleasure, sir."

Lying in bed, unable to nap, Janine Angriff couldn't stop crying. The anti-nausea medicine dispensed by Colonel Friedenthall had done little to alleviate her pain, and while she never actually threw up, she felt like she would. Between the worsening fits of coughing, and an overall feeling like the worst hangover she'd ever had, Janine couldn't bear the thought of eating anything. To avoid dehydration, she forced herself to drink a glass of water every two hours.

Whatever she had, Cynthia had it, too. Otherwise, without her girls to fret over, Janine wasn't sure if she could go on living with Nick gone. Even now she could hear Cynthia coughing in the other room.

When the lock on the door to her quarters clicked, she wiped her eyes and sat up on one elbow. It was probably Morgan, or maybe Nikki, and Janine didn't want either girl to see her like this. But the footfalls were too heavy to be one of them, and that didn't bode well. An hour earlier, she'd heard a single gunshot, and she put nothing past Tom Steeple. Suddenly afraid, she wished there was a pistol within reach.

The bedroom door squeaked open and a large man stood in the doorway. There were no lights on in the apartment, so she couldn't make out details, but his size was intimidating. Then he spoke, and her entire world changed.

"Hi, Nini, I'm home," he said.

#

PART FIVE

SACRIFICE OF KNIGHTS

Chapter 36

> *Into the bullets I dodged and weaved*
> *As I felt them tug at my arm and sleeve;*
> *I wanted to turn, I wanted to flee,*
> *I didn't because my brothers needed me.*
> Sergio Velazquez, from "As I Die"

1547 hours, May 5

"Skip, they've got a machine gun!" Hausser called from the cave mouth. Seconds later a stream of bullets hit just above the cave entrance. Hausser hit the dirt as the gunner walked them into the cave mouth and held down the trigger. Light caliber rounds poured into the cave and struck the ceiling. Sparks lit the darkness as the bullets ricocheted throughout the tunnel beyond and into the main chamber.

Lara Snowtiger had been standing, talking to her sister, when the shooting started. Taken by surprise, she'd hesitated an instant before throwing herself down. Zo Piccaldi tackled her, covering her with his own body.

Dennis Tompkins was across the chamber from Sara Snowtiger. Their eyes met and he ran to do the same thing, protect the only woman he had ever truly loved. But a ricochet hit his right ankle and he collapsed. The whizzing of bullets didn't stop for ten more seconds.

Moans filled the chamber. Tompkins' ankle felt like it was on fire, but he dragged himself over to check on Sara Snowtiger. Their eyes met once again, only this time she seemed to be showing pity for him. His eyes went to her chest, where a darker stain showed on the already dark material.

"No!" he said.

The machine gun opened fire again. More bullets ricocheted through the cave. And then, without warning, they stopped. Tompkins heard *something* outside, a tearing sound. In his pain, shock, and grief, it took his brain several seconds to recognize fifty-caliber Gatling guns spewing havoc. Then others joined the cacophony, and explosions.

For the second time in less than a year, the cavalry had ridden to his rescue. Only this time it was too late. He crawled again, harder, and scooted up next to Sara.

She had slumped over to the left, looking up at him, but she was still alive. Her lips formed soundless words. "I love you."

She only had one hope. "Hang on."

Pushing to his feet, he ignored the agony lancing up his leg. Bracing himself with one hand on the cavern wall, he hopped to the cave mouth. An Apache hovered fifty feet out, looking for more targets, and Tompkins started waving his arms. The chance that a Seven might still be down there never entered his mind. All he knew what that Sara was going to die without immediate help.

The Apache had shark's teeth painted on the nose. The pilot and co-pilot scanned the ground for long, agonizing seconds, before the co-pilot finally saw him waving and alerted the pilot. When the Apache hovered mere feet from what remained of the ledge, blowing dust and grit back into the cave from its rotors, Tompkins shouted that he had casualties in need of emergency transport to Prime. He had to say it four times before the co-pilot heard enough to understand. Reaching down, he displayed a medical kit with a large Red Cross, and gave a thumbs-up to ask if Tompkins wanted it. He did. The Apache gained altitude and the co-pilot leaned out, throwing the case into the cavern. "Dustoff two minutes out!" he yelled.

Tompkins nodded. *God bless Nick Angriff*, he thought. With a full medical staff on board, Sara had a fighting chance. Hobbling back, he knelt beside her and began tearing strips off the bottom of her robe to use as bandages. He looked up to see Lara standing nearby, hands covered in blood.

"Lara, I need your help!"

She looked at him with a vacant expression.

"Lara, your sister needs you. Come here."

She took two faltering steps and stopped. "Zo's dead," she said.

Sierra Army Base, Herlong, CA
1603 hours, May 5

As the seconds ticked away until jump-off time, Private Marcus Lamar licked his lips and tried not to show his raging fear. Huddled in the trench, his imagination pictured hundreds of expert Chinese marksmen all waiting for him to show the slightest target, so they could riddle him with bullets.

"You gonna be okay?" said the man next to him, Private Tamil Noruk.

"Y-yeah, I'm cool."

"It's always been like this, y'know. Before a battle, I mean. Your mouth gets dry, your mind plays all kinds of mind games with you, a lot worse than any woman ever did—"

"Hey!" yelled a female corporal a few feet down the trench. "A little respect, Noruk!"

"Sorry, Corp, present company excepted. You can't see any way you're gonna survive the fight, but then you do, and sooner or later, there's another fight, and you feel the same way."

"Do you feel that way?" Lamar said.

"Fuck, yeah. Every time."

"He pees in his pants, too," someone else said. "That's why we stuck him down there with you, Marcus."

"Thirty seconds, people," the corporal said. "Good luck and good hunting."

Lamar forgot the banter when four distant *booms* echoed over the desert, the signal for the platoon to advance and capture the airfield. Even at a weapons depot like Sierra, some things were in short supply, and nothing was more precious than machine guns, rifles, and hand grenades. When the original garrison had fled in the time after the Collapse, those three types of weapons had been the most popular to take along. Only at the end did those people intending to stay on the base manage to save some of them.

A heavy weapons squad manned three of the precious M2 fifty-caliber machine guns, the fabled Ma Deuce. The intent of so much heavy firepower, for such a small assault force, was to try and compensate for a platoon being assigned a job that really needed at least a company.

The Americans slipped out of their trench and began moving forward at a crouch. It wasn't getting shot at that scared Lamar — he'd been wounded but survived the brutal battle that killed his father and grandmother a few weeks before — it was purposely exposing himself in open terrain that made his hands shake. He'd fought the First Battle of Sierra from the protection of a rifle pit, and wished he could crawl back into the dirt now.

He watched the corporal's hand signals as they advanced. The only sounds were the scuffing of boots on the desert floor and the ever-present wind. Halfway to their target, the corporal raised her left fist and Lamar went to one knee along with the rest of the platoon.

A loud cry came up from the trench ahead and Lamar thought he was about to die. But instead, a wave of Chinese troops rose and climbed over the trench top, running straight toward them. In the instant he had to judge numbers, Lamar guessed they faced hundreds of Chicom troops.

Far to Lamar's right, the company sergeant waved them down, and the corporal repeated the gesture. The entire platoon dropped flat in the dust, freeing up a field of fire for the machine guns. All three opened up. If Lamar needed a reason to keep his head down, the heavy fifty-caliber rounds zipping by overhead gave it to him.

"Let 'em have it," the corporal yelled. Lamar turned his head enough to see the rest of the company lying prone and firing. It took a few seconds to realize that if he stayed perfectly prone, he could fire his M16 safely even as the machine gun bullets passed inches over his helmet.

Centering his sight on a Chinese soldier, he started to squeeze the trigger, but the man fell before he could fire. Fifty-caliber rounds ripped into him and everyone around him, filling the air with a red mist and slamming them backward. Lamar shifted targets and joined the storm of lead cutting the Chinese to shreds.

From somewhere a Chinese machine gun fired and the battle devolved into a series of individual gun battles. Bullets hit the ground near Lamar's face and kicked sand into his right eye. Closing it, he kept shooting until he emptied the 60-

round magazine. As he reached for a reload, the first Chinese soldier turned and ran for the safety of the trench, quickly followed by others.

Something in Lamar's brain switched gears. Forgetting fear, he jumped to his feet and charged the Chinese trench one hundred yards away. Bullets buzzed by like stinging wasps, but none hit him as the fleeing Chinese themselves spoiled the aim of those already in the trench. Jumping over the bleeding bodies lying in the desert made him an even harder target. Not until he was ten feet away did the first round hit his left shoulder, but by then it was too late. Adrenaline filled his veins and blocked his pain.

Cradling the M16 in both hands, he hosed the confused mass of Chinese soldiers at point blank range. Every round hit flesh until the new magazine also ran out. Then two rounds caught Lamar in the stomach and he toppled forward. Inside the trench lay a heap of dead men. Body armor stopped the rounds but not the pain. All he could do was scream.

Unknown to Lamar, the rest of the platoon had followed his charge and hit the Chinese before they could organize their defense. It had been the most feared kind of military encounter, a meeting engagement, when both sides attacked without knowing the other was doing so. The Americans had struck first and showed better discipline. Now, the platoon stood at the edge of the Chinese trench and fired until there was no enemy left alive to fire at.

West of Sierra Army Depot, Herlong, California
"What is taking so long?"

As General Zhang Wei stalked among the APCs parked four hundred yards behind his front line facing east, he outwardly waved clenched fists in anger, but inwardly he reveled in once again being on a field of battle. The exhaust and rumbling engines of the APCs provided the perfect backdrop for his strut among the assault troops, trailing his staff. He'd once seen a video of the American General Macarthur, and thought he displayed the perfect combination of arrogance and *sangfroid*. That image was foremost in his mind as he waited impatiently for the Americans to open fire on their own comrades.

Wei was careful to never expose himself to enemy fire for more than one second, using the armored vehicles as shields.

Fifty years ago, as a young captain eager to prove himself, Wei had gained a reputation for fearlessness in combat that bordered on reckless. Now in his mid-70s, he could still stick his chin in the air, but couldn't do anything about the loose folds of skin that hung from his lower jaw.

Six of the seven APCs were standard Type 90s, armed with a 12.7mm dual-purpose anti-aircraft gun, while the seventh was his only operational self-propelled howitzer. Its 122mm gun would, when combined with the American artillery, blast a hole for the APCs to carry his troops through. Those would be quickly followed by the four Type 98 Main Battle Tanks.

The Americans had showed during the last fight that they had some of the deadly Carl Gustav recoilless rifles, so Wei expected to lose all of his armor in the attack. But no matter; the hundreds of mothballed American tanks and APCs would more than make up for any losses. But as the moment of the planned attack grew imminent, Wei wondered why he hadn't heard from his liaison officers in the American headquarters.

"General, the Americans appear to be moving into attack position," said his adjutant.

"Finally! They are late, but no matter. The battle will be short."

"But... but sir. I don't mean our American allies. I mean the Americans defending the depot."

"What?" Zhang put his own binoculars up to his eyes. Unable to see anything, he pointed at the nearest man. "Help me up." The man cupped his hands and Wei used them as a ladder, half climbing, half rolling onto the top of an APC. The vehicle commander saluted but Wei ignored him. Focusing the binoculars, he spotted the telltale movement along the American lines, where reserves moved forward into the front positions. "What are they doing?" he whispered to himself. Four distant *booms* answered him. "So begins victory."

"Sir, I need you to get down before I can advance," the APC commander said.

"Good luck to you, Lieutenant!" Sliding down the metallic hull tore his pant leg, but that mattered nothing at all. The attack was underway!

His mind registered a familiar whistling sound and he reacted by reflex, dropping to the ground and covering his head. Four explosions ripped into the nearby desert, followed by the screams of wounded men. Dirt showered him from a near miss, and Wei barely had time to raise his head before more rounds screamed down on the Chinese position.

The armor had been concentrated for a breakthrough role, and it was clear they were the target, but who was doing the shooting? Then he covered his head with his arms as the second salvo impacted to his left. One of the APCs took a direct hit, setting off secondary explosions. With 12.7mm rounds zipping and skipping in all directions, Wei's adjutant helped him to his feet, and together they ran, bent over, behind a series of boulders.

"Who is shooting?" he screamed, infuriated by the sudden attack.

"I believe it's the Americans, General."

"Which Americans?"

"All of them!"

Despite having only four tubes supporting the 1st Mechanized Infantry Division, Colonel John Coughlan had insisted on being with his men when they received orders to fire on their fellow Americans. It was a terrible thing to do, unimaginable, and only a coward would order others to do it. Coughlan hated the whole thing, but if someone had to give the order to open fire, it was going to be him.

Then came the miraculous order to target the Chinese armored grouping to the west, which brought whoops of joy from his men. *That* command he would allow the battery commander to give, and gladly. Let that young officer do what he'd been trained to do. Coughlan stood in his headquarters tent watching his people perform. The reports of the four howitzers sounded like *whunk, whunk, whunk, whunk*. He grinned, knowing the deadly rounds were aimed at the right target.

After the second volley, he heard a deeper, distant boom, knowing it instantly for what it was. "Incoming!" he yelled. "Into the trenches, out, out, out!"

Coughlan stood beside the tent flap, waving his people toward the slit trenches thirty feet away. There was no panic as everyone dropped what they were doing and bolted for the exit. The high-pitched scream of the approaching Chinese round grew louder. Five out of eight soldiers had made it out when the 122mm round landed forty feet to the other side of the tent. Steel splinters sliced through the tent's polyester walls and struck a female technician named Stovall as she ran to leave. Coughlan pushed two people toward the tent as his battery fired a third salvo, blocking the fainter noise from a second Chinese shot.

Stovall was on all fours, trying to stand, as blood poured from a dozen wounds. He rushed to her side and bodily picked her up by the waist.

"Come on Stovall, you're gonna be fine."

That was when he heard the second round coming, except this time it sounded different. To his experienced mind, it was the sound of a direct hit on the listener.

Him.

Still holding Stovall around her middle, he'd taken two steps toward the exit when the shell struck the tent roof, tore through, and blew everything inside into bits.

Wei and his staff ran for the cover of a boulder fifty yards from the armored assemblage. A shell landed near one of his aides and blew off the man's right arm, while another hit beside an APC and knocked it on its side. Then the world erupted in fire when a 105mm shell scored a direct hit on the self-propelled howitzer.

The initial blast threw the vehicle ten feet in the air and blew off four of its eight tires. Secondary explosions rent the hull and filled the air with shrapnel as the 122mm shells cooked off. By the time flames licked at what was left, it resembled a skeleton after a swarm of piranha had stripped it clean.

"What is going on?" the general screamed over the blasts. "I must know what is happening!"

One of his officers took a hand-held radio away from his ear. "The Americans south of the base are attacking us, General. They have us flanked on the right. We must pull back."

Stunned, Wei knew that he had committed every piece of operational armor left to this operation. If it failed, he could not defend most of California. And if the Americans could only put 20 percent of the tanks stored at Sierra back into operation, that would be more than enough firepower to throw the Chinese back into the sea. All of those thoughts flashed through his mind as men yelled over the tumult of battle asking for orders.

But one thought stuck out among all the others... he knew that at his age, this was his final chance for ultimate success. The Americans had crushed his attempt to capture Arizona and killed many of the men he'd come to California with all those decades before. Wei had sworn vengeance, but suffered another ignominious defeat in the First Battle of Sierra. This was his final chance, using the last army he could put in the field with any hope of defeating the Americans. It was time to gamble everything.

"General, you must give the order to withdraw!"

"No!" he bellowed, as loud and deep as he could. "Any man who retreats is to be shot! Order the armor forward as planned, supported by mortars and infantry. The right flank is to bend ninety degrees and hold the enemy while the armor penetrates into the base. I repeat, any man who disobeys these orders is to be executed immediately!"

#

Chapter 37

"Only he is lost who gives himself up for lost!"
Hans-Ulrich Rudel, Stuka Pilot

Allen Pohl's compound
1620 hours, May 5

Painted dark green and buffed to a high sheen, the upper surfaces of the JU-87G-1 *Stuka Kanonenvogel* shone in the afternoon sun like a mirror. Slung under each wing in a long pod, the barrels of its 37mm guns protruded forward like the outstretched horns of a bull. The aircraft had been obsolescent when it went into combat over Poland in 1939, and by the end of World War Two it was target practice for enemy fighters. And yet, in the hands of a veteran pilot like Hans-Ulrich Rudel, it had remained a deadly gun platform against Russian armor.

Allen Pohl hadn't rushed his preparations or his pre-flight check. Time was short if he was going to help stop the Chinese, but crashing with engine trouble wouldn't do anybody any good, and the aircraft hadn't flown into combat in more than 130 years. Still, he couldn't be *too* careful. If the Chinese took Sierra Army Depot, then sooner or later they'd overrun his compound, too, and everything he'd spent fifty years building would be lost. It wasn't so much his life that concerned him, although he reveled in living, but rather all the people who lived at his compound, the old and the infirm, the women and the children. The Chinese showed mercy to no one, and Pohl had no illusions what would happen if they got that far.

"This is a really bad idea, Allen," said Eduardo, chief mechanic of the compound and Pohl's right-hand man. The idea of an employee-employer relationship had vanished along with the United States, leaving only groups who cooperated or died.

"You didn't see what I saw."

"That's not the part I'm arguing about. If the Americans win, then you think we'll be safe, and if the Chinese win, we're screwed. That part I understand. But this plane was built more than one hundred years ago. It's one thing to fly it around at low altitude over flat desert, where you can make an emergency landing if you have to, but it's something very different to dive bomb tanks while somebody's shooting at you. Hell, man, you can't even be sure the ammunition is good."

"Those rounds cost my dad two thousands dollars apiece."

"Who gives a shit about that? He bought 'em sixty years ago, and they were manufactured in 1944. For all you know, a misfire is gonna blow your wing off."

Pohl put a hand on his friend's shoulder. "I have personally reloaded every round with fresh powder, Eddie. I inspected every shell casing, and took measurements to make sure it wouldn't misfire in the barrel. You know all this, and you also know that I'll be fine." He put a foot in the step ring on the left side of the fuselage, behind the wing. From the corner of his eye, he saw Eduardo shaking his head, and turned his head back before climbing into the cockpit. "I'm coming back, you'll see. Hans-Ulrich Rudel got shot down dozens of times and came back."

"That book again," Eduardo said, still shaking his head. "He was a Nazi, and you told me the Nazis were evil."

"Yeah, he admired Hitler, which I'll never understand. But he also survived twenty-five hundred combat missions flying a plane just like this one."

"You're not Rudel."

"I'm not a Nazi either."

"What does that have to do with anything?"

Pohl smiled and shrugged. "I don't know."

"Since you're determined to kill yourself, Allen, you know that if you don't—"

"I'm coming back!"

"—if you don't, I want you to know that I'll keep this place running as if you were still here."

Once he'd strapped in, Pohl took a few seconds to refresh his memory on the controls. He flew the Stuka enough to know it well, but the layout was quite different from the German aircraft he'd been flying, the BV 141. Once he was ready he stuck his head out the side window. "Clear!"

The Junkers Jumo 211J-1 engine balked, as usual, coughing several times before finally catching and driving the three-bladed prop at increasing speed. Pohl taxied the plane onto the end of the runway, gunned the engine, and sped northwest. As air rushed under the wings, faster and faster, first the tail wheel lifted off and the plane leveled out. Then the fixed landing gear lost contact with the concrete of the runway, and the slow, ungainly aircraft climbed for altitude. Passing the ridge on the northern edge of his compound with five hundred feet to spare, Pohl kicked the rudder left and banked until the compass read two-eight-zero degrees. For the first time in more than a century, the old German plane was on its way to again fulfill its designed purpose of destroying enemy tanks.

Sierra Army Depot, Herlong, CA

There was no point remaining at his headquarters away from the front line, so against Major Ball's pleas not to get too close to the fighting, Norm Fleming moved into the burned-out ruins of Colonel Lamar's old office. Timbers, boulders, and sandbags had all been piled up as a makeshift barricade, behind which Fleming could see the battle as it formed on the west. Captain Ruiz didn't need to remind him to wear his body armor as a precaution, or to clean and load his rifle.

"I've been doing this for a little while," he said, with his usual laconic tone.

Once he heard the four booms of the American artillery and knew the battle had been joined, Fleming used his binoculars to peer through all the smoke and dust rising in a pall from the Chinese lines. Two hundred yards to the west, Fleming saw the American Airborne troops rise from their subsurface hiding places and move forward on the attack. All seemed to be going well until he saw a series of flashes, and then rocket trails heading into the cloud. Without warning, a Chinese tank burst into view, heading directly for him at its full speed of 40 miles per hour. Then another one followed it, and then a third.

"Tanks!" he yelled, and began pushing his staff out the back door, which was now just a big hole in the wall. Alisa Plotz grabbed the AN/PRC-25 radio and began helping Andy Arnold slip his arms through the straps, but Fleming stopped her. "Go! Forget the radio!"

He went out last, sprinting toward a long building eighty yards to his left front. He'd only made it fifty feet when a 125mm tank round hit the front barricade of the shattered building. Following a microsecond later, another shell blew out the walls and collapsed the whole structure. The blast waves knocked Fleming flat on his chest. More explosions followed, plus gunfire, and then, through the flames and smoke, the front end of a Type 98 tank nosed around the burning rubble like an alien machine from *War of the Worlds*. Fleming scrabbled up and stumbled forward on hands and feet as machine gun bullets ripped into the desert near his right side.

Allen Pohl's heart pounded as he skirted Reno on the north. Light winds aloft made the flight smooth, and unlike the heat in southern Nevada that created thermals, the temperature so far north remained cool enough to stabilize the atmosphere. The instruments all showed optimal engine performance, he had plenty of fuel, and the controls responded perfectly to his touch. All in all, it was the best flight he could remember, and there was an excellent chance it would be his last.

Sunlight reflected off Pyramid Lake on his right, while he followed a valley west of the Virginia Mountains toward Sierra Army Depot, maintaining an altitude of 500 feet. The bare, rounded hump of Tule Peak, standing as it had for millennia, offered a permanence he didn't feel at that particular moment.

Smoke rose directly ahead as he flew northwest, so he pulled back on the controls and took the Stuka up to 3,000 feet. It was hard to make out much of anything as a pall of dust and smoke hung over the battlefield. Speeding vehicles trailed clouds of dust and Pohl could make out tiny figures running across the desert, but he couldn't tell who was who.

Then he spotted the orange and red of fire coming from the base itself, and through the haze of smoke came flashes. It took a few seconds to realize it was a tank firing a machine gun at a solitary figure zig-zagging to avoid being hit, and the only tanks he'd seen during his earlier overflight were Chinese.

This was it. His hands shook as he eased the controls forward into a shallow dive. He couldn't swallow because his throat felt constricted, but then his flying reflexes took over. The ridgeline on his right ended and only flat desert remained between him and his target, the shadow of his predatory aircraft racing over the parched soil.

Concentrating fully on his target, Pohl fired before the sight was fully lined up. The two Bordkanone BK 37mm Flak 18 guns each fired one round of tungsten-carbide-cored armor-piercing ammunition, which sailed over the tank and sent great geysers of dirt into the air. Due to the Stuka's slow speed, he still had time to line up the tank better. White globs rose from the ground and flashed by the cockpit unnoticed. He fired again, and watched as the shells sped away from the Stuka, two bright dots growing smaller and smaller as they raced toward the tank.

Norm Fleming ran three steps left, pivoted and ran five steps right, then two left, six right. Bullets dug into the dirt and zipped overhead, and once flashed by either side near his waist, missing him by inches. The building he ran for was still more than one hundred feet away when he spotted a slight depression in the ground and threw himself flat. More machine gun fire chewed up the ground inches in front of his helmet and the Chinese tank clanked onward toward him. Panting, he gulped a breath and jumped up again, running straight for the open doorway ahead. He expected to be cut down, but then he heard two explosions.

Risking a glance over his shoulder, Fleming saw the tank's gunner, who stood in an open hatch, swivel the ring-mounted machine gun toward a new target, one up in the air. The tank skewed right in a violent turn. Two shells exploded less than a yard from its right rear sprocket. Running with his head turned, Fleming stumbled and nearly fell, but finally staggered through the doorway into the building. The others were nowhere in sight.

Inside, the Chinese couldn't see him, at least, and he knew that he really should run out the other side. If the Chinese tank commander used his 12.7mm gun against the building, the cinder blocks would barely slow down the big slugs. Instead, he watched something that challenged his sanity. Was he hallucinating?

Some sort of aircraft skimmed toward the tank at a thirty degree angle, but it couldn't be what Fleming's brain identified it as being. Gull wings and fixed landing gear meant only one thing, a thing utterly impossible to believe. Flashes came from the ends of two long gun tubes. Two shells moving slow enough that he could watch their flight sped toward the tank. One struck it at the base of the turret, where it met the hull, while the other impacted against the top rear.

The next seconds passed in what Nick Angriff called "the slow motion of combat," where many things happened at the same time and the mind recorded them all, but only later could they be sorted out.

A gout of flame jetted skyward, and then another, larger fireball mushroomed into the air. The tank stopped maneuvering as secondary explosions began ripping it apart from within. The tank commander climbed out of his hatch and bent over to help his crew escape. Fleming had no qualms about sighting his M16 on the base of the man's spine and firing two three-shot bursts.

He found no satisfaction when the man staggered and fell, rolling off the side of the tank into a puddle of flaming fuel. Nor did he feel anything more than sadness when a man who had crawled halfway out the top hatch disappeared in a massive internal explosion. Even in the moment, Norm Fleming felt empathy for the dying men.

But when the aircraft lumbered overhead at a speed slower than he had sometimes driven on the open road, he clearly saw its markings and wondered if he'd imagined the whole thing, after all. Maybe he was dying in the headquarters building and these were his mind's last fevered hallucinations, because a Balkan cross on the fuselage and swastika on the vertical stabilizer couldn't possibly be a real part of a post-apocalyptic battlefield.

The Stuka's sluggish response made it hard to pull out of even such a shallow dive, and it took all of Pohl's strength to keep it from nose-diving into the tank he'd just destroyed. He zoomed so close overhead that flames licked past his right wing root, and a column of smoke blinded him for a few seconds. A fast glance out both sides of the canopy showed holes in both wings. Only the Stuka's rugged airframe kept it flying at all.

Coming out of the smoke, he saw another tank racing straight toward him at a distance of less than one hundred yards. At least a dozen times while flying the old German plane he'd imagined just such a scenario, as if he were Hans Ulrich-Rudel attacking a T-34, and now that practice let his hands fly over the controls. At less than 80 feet altitude, he throttled back to only 80 miles per hour, near the Stuka's stall speed, and lined up the tank in his gunsight. It was point blank range. He pushed the trigger button twice, sending four rounds into the tank's glacis plate.

Three of the shells struck the sloped front and ricocheted away. The fourth smashed into the tank's gun mantlet, where the base of the barrel entered the turret. Hopping over the wounded machine, he immediately saw four APCs and fired at one of them, another down-the-throat shot. Two rounds sailed over the APC, so he fired again and this time both smashed into its front, blowing it on its side.

Yanking back on the stick to gain altitude for another pass, he throttled up, expecting to climb quickly, but the Stuka was even more sluggish than before. More holes had appeared in the wings, and half the left aileron had been shot away. Violent shaking rattled Pohl momentarily, and he knew by instinct that the Stuka would never make it home. Tracers flashed past on all sides, and not all missed. Then they stopped. He flew over a group of parked vehicles, and then only open ground sped by underneath him. He'd flown west over the entire Chinese army.

The southern fork of Honey Lake ended at old California Highway 395, which itself abutted a high ridgeline. Given the Stuka's damage, he doubted it could make it over the hills. But the highway had long, straight stretches, and with such a slow stall speed, the JU-87 only needed a short landing strip.

The airframe vibrated as he pushed the right rudder pedal. It was like wrestling an unbroken stallion, and Pohl assumed the tail had to also be shot up. Sweat poured down his forehead as he fought to get the plane down in one piece. Now if the highway just didn't have any big potholes…

#

Chapter 38

> *"Action breeds life, inaction breeds demons."*
> Lt. Colonel Kevin Ikenberry, US Army (Ret.), from Peacemaker

Sierra Army Depot, Herlong, CA
1628 hours, May 5

    Against Major Strootman's advice, Colonel Young stood on a low rise, waving his Strykers forward like a traffic cop. Speed was what mattered now. One look at the map and Young had understood the trap the Chinese had put themselves into. Their position west of Sierra meant their backs were against Honey Lake. If Young could move fast enough, and his spearheads could reach the lake's southeastern tip before the Chinese could set up a defense, he could cut off the whole enemy army.
    Cupping hands around his mouth, he shouted to the passing vehicles. "Move it, boys and girls!" Between the roar of the engines and the sounds of battle coming from the north, nobody could hear his words. But that didn't matter. What did matter was the sight of him standing in the open, waving them forward. More than one passing Stryker commander saluted, and several gave him a thumbs-up.
    His staff had gathered on the protected side of the little knoll and worked the radios as Major Strootman coordinated the attack. The only other person atop the hill with Colonel Young was his driver, a young corporal named Persephone Bee. Standing beside the hill, Strootman wore noise cancelling headphones. Whenever he used the radio, he would slide the

cup off his right ear to listen, and shout into the transmitter to be heard. Both headphones were in place when something heavy hit the back of his ankles.

Half-turning at the waist, he looked down into the dead eyes of Corporal Bee as they stared at nothing. Blood soaked the front of her uniform from a long gash under her left ear. A trickle ran from a hole in her forehead.

Ripping off the headphones, Strootman tossed aside the hand-held radio and scrambled up the hill on all fours. Colonel Young's body lay face up on the other slope, with most of his left shoulder missing. Shrapnel had mangled the left side of his face. Strootman checked the pulse at his neck, but Young was long past having a pulse. For a few seconds, he knelt beside the body in shock, until one of the staff called down to him from the hilltop.

"Major, Alpha Company requests fire support!"

That meant shifting targets, which only the regimental commander could authorize, so why was the man asking *him*? Then the reality hit him; now, he was the regimental commander.

Events moved too fast for General Zhang Wei's staff to follow. For too many years he'd let his men languish in a sedentary lifestyle, and not bothering to stage drills had led to the destruction of his armored force the year before. Now, when the set piece battle plan did not survive contact with the enemy, they lost effective command and control. A dozen men surrounded him, yelling into radios and issuing orders, but Wei could sense their growing panic as events moved too fast for them to understand.

With his armor driving hard straight up the middle, Wei personally ordered the six remaining 82mm Type 87 mortars to concentrate their fire on the American trenches blocking the armor's way into the base. Using his binoculars from ground level made it hard to understand what was happening at the front. He saw rocket trails here and there; without a doubt they were American Carl Gustav recoilless rifles, with explosions and rifle fire everywhere. Then, out of nowhere, a bizarre-looking airplane appeared and shot up one of his tanks and an APC.

Wei drew his sidearm and emptied it as the plane flew right over him. What the hell kind of markings were those? Crosses? He knew they were old German markings, but World War Two ended more than one hundred years ago. He stared as the plane flew west.

A frantic radioman interrupted Wei's reverie. "General, the Americans are behind us. They've cut us off!"

Wei immediately snapped back to the present. "What? Where?"

The man pointed almost due west. Wei focused the binoculars and saw men and vehicles trailing southeast in a long line. At least twenty of the eight-wheeled American APCs called Strykers were in sight. Mixed in might have been eight or ten Bradleys. If he had his Type 98s, Wei might have tried to blast through the American line. Without them, all he had left were his trucks and his NJ/2045s, the hybrid of a truck and SUV, with a lightly armored body and 12.7mm machine gun. It would be suicide to attack with nothing heavier.

With chaos all around, Wei realized the moment had come to live or die. Seemingly out of options, he would do the one thing the Americans wouldn't expect. He would launch everything he had left in a final attempt to take the base.

When the Chinese tank blew up, Norm Fleming didn't waste time staring. He ran out the building's other side to a narrow open area separating it from another long building. To his left, facing west, through a stand of trees, he saw the American front line under heavy attack.

"General!" The staff he'd pushed out of the headquarters ran toward him from wherever they'd taken cover.

"Has anybody seen Major Ball?"

"He's up front," answered Alisa Plotz.

"You stay here. I'm going to find him. The rest of you, find cover and set up a command post."

Plotz and Andy Arnold both held out M16s, as did the rest of the little group. As senior officer, Plotz spoke for them all. "General, if they get through that line, we're all dead anyway. If it's all the same to you, sir, I'd rather die fighting."

Fleming wasn't known as a fighter, and his emotional response was to send Plotz into the line. But he'd made his reputation as a cool-headed staff officer, advising aggressive commanders like Nick Angriff when the situation was tense, and that served him well now.

"Negative, Captain. You and Lieutenant Arnold fly your Comanche out of here. Go join Colonel's Young regiment. If they have fuel and ammunition, then join the fight. Otherwise, your prime objective is to not let that gunship fall into enemy hands."

Plotz clearly didn't like it, but she and Arnold took off away from the fighting at a trot.

"The rest of you, follow me." He wondered what Angriff would say at a moment like this, and said it. "Let's go kick some Chinese ass!"

General Wei stood beside the machine gunner in his personal NJ/2045, holding onto the frame as the truck bounced over the crater-pocked desert toward the American front line. When they passed the tank the strange German aircraft had attacked, it seemed undamaged but all the hatches were open, indicating the crew had abandoned it. Another Type 98 burned to his left, while a third had disappeared behind a flaming building. The fourth, and last, lay stationary ahead, the turret still firing but with one of the treads blown off.

The aging general watched his staff vehicles racing forward, like the cavalry charges he'd seen in old Western movies. All around, vehicles blew up as the Americans hit them with rockets, but the rest kept going. He envisioned himself atop a horse, his pennant in the wind as he pointed toward the enemy with his sword.

The American line materialized through the smoke and dust, a simple trench and rifle pit system. Next to him, the machine gun hammered away without stopping, the hot spent casings clattering off his shoulders and onto the truck's floor. Even when the truck bottomed out in a crater, the driver kept spraying bullets without seeming to care what they hit. Wei saw the man's young face twisted in terror.

Fifty yards directly ahead, the APC they followed took a direct hit. The explosion tossed it in the air, while its forward momentum left it rolling into the American trench. Wei leaned into the car and screamed at the driver not to slow down, but keep going. That breach was exactly what he needed.

The release of tension left Marcus Lamar exhausted. He lay against the side of the trench, as far from the mangled bodies of the dead Chinese as he could get. Flies already crawled on their flesh, looking for places to lay their eggs. It didn't seem to bother the Airborne troops, but in Lamar it triggered all the fear and terror he'd felt during the first battle. His wounds weren't fully healed yet, the two rounds his body armor had taken earlier might have cracked some ribs, and yet there he was killing and risking death again. It was too much. He turned away from the others and vomited, while they pretended not to notice.

"Incoming infantry!" someone down the trench yelled. Lamar scrambled to the other side, poked his head over the edge, and ducked again as bullets ripped into the dirt all around him. A man ten feet away toppled backward, hit in the head. Lamar recognized Noruk, the man who'd been kidding him earlier.

The female corporal spotted him shivering. "They're not gonna take prisoners, Lamar, so you might as well shoot back!"

He glanced up to see the corporal staring at him, then she winked and went back to firing at the enemy. For some reason, her bravado cut through his fear. If he was going to die anyway, then what the hell, he'd take some of the bastards with him. Charging his M16, he stood, brought the rifle to bear, and with his rifle set to auto, cut down a soldier no more than fifty feet from the trench.

"Burst fire, Lamar, burst fire. You're using up all your ammo!"

He nodded and adjusted the selector. There was no shortage of targets. He hit at least three, and some got close enough to hurl grenades. There were screams and explosions and shots everywhere... and then it was over, as the surviving Chinese ran the other way. Sporadic shots rang out at the backs of the retreating enemy until no targets remained.

Panting, he slid on his back to a squatting position inside the trench. He'd survived, again! And they'd beaten off the Chinese.

"You okay, Lamar?" the corporal called.

"Yes, ma'am!"

"I'm not a ma'am. Corporal will do just fine."

Then he heard the sergeant yelling from further down the line. The attack had overlapped their right flank, and an unknown number of Chinese had penetrated into the base. They needed volunteers to go after them, so the corporal volunteered five men before they could object, and then pointed at Lamar.

"C'mon, Lamar, you know this place better than anybody."

Alisa Plotz had moved *Hell's Hammer* to a paved area on the eastern edge of the base when it had looked like the 2nd Mechanized Regiment might be hostile. Now, running east for their gunship, she and Arnold didn't worry about keeping under cover, since they assumed the Chinese were all at their backs. They were taken by surprise when they crossed into the open space around the Comanche and drew gunfire from the left, which was north.

Caught in the open, they could only hit the ground and return fire. The shooters had taken cover behind a dumpster fifty yards away, and a few more near a dilapidated truck.

"Dammit!" Plotz yelled. She coughed. They'd kicked up a lot of dust and, lying prone, she breathed in a lungful. She tried to hold her breath long enough to fire back, but coughed anyway.

"What if they target the bird?" Arnold said.

"Shit." He was right. *Hell's Hammer* was an irreplaceable asset, not to mention her only child. Plotz loved that helicopter more than any human being, except maybe Arnold. If those fuckers shot it up... she couldn't bear thinking about that. A desperate idea came into her mind. "Cover me!"

Scrambling up, she sprinted for the gunship. It wasn't far, but she was still two steps from the cockpit when something tugged at her right ankle. It took another second to open the door and several rounds hit just behind her left hand, holing the fuselage.

Then, behind her, she heard Arnold yelling at the Chinese. "Hey dickheads, over here!"

As they shifted fire away from her, Plotz scrambled inside and turned on the instruments, fast as her fingers could move. The telltale whine when it powered up couldn't be avoided, and she heard a *thunk* that sounded like a rock on a metal roof. One hit in the engine and it would be the shortest flight of her life.

Glancing to her right, she saw Arnold on one knee, firing. She started the engine and the rotor blades came to life, kicking up clouds of dust that she hoped might blind the Chinese.

Thunk, thunk.

Two more hits... damn! She looked over to motion Arnold to run for it, but he was gone. *What the—? Maybe he made it back to that building*, she thought, and took the gunship up. But instead of picking up speed and flying south, she turned and used the rotors to kick dust and rocks at the Chinese, blinding them.

And that was when she spotted him lying in the dirt, halfway between where they'd dropped prone and the dumpster, and she knew what he'd done. To distract the shooters, the crazy fool had charged them, and they'd cut him down. Still coughing, tears flooded her eyes as she turned south and picked up speed. There was nothing she could do for her longtime co-pilot now, except find some ammo and come back to avenge him. And avenge him she would.

#

Chapter 39

> *"The term 'good bureaucrat' is an oxymoron."*
> Liberty Fields

Headquarters, 1st Mechanized Regiment, south of Sierra Army Depot
1700 hours, May 5

The partially obscured image on *Tank Girl's* side already had Joe Randall ready to hit somebody, even before the officious supply sergeant refused to allocate him fuel without Colonel Young's written authorization. The man had been happy enough to offload the extra ammo he'd brought for the weapons' pods, but balked at giving him fuel in return.

"Sergeant, I'm trying not to lose my temper, but you're pushing it."

"Captain, without the proper authorization, I am not going to allocate you any fuel. We are a *mechanized* unit, sir, and *mechanized* translates to 'drinks a lot of gas.' When a Stryker or Humvee runs dry, it's my job to fill it up again, but without Colonel Young's say-so, choppers aren't on that list."

"A chopper is a motorcycle; a helicopter's a bird."

"I'm sorry, sir. The answer is still no."

Randall towered over the diminutive sergeant. Leaning forward, he pointed to the north. "Can you hear all that shooting, Sergeant? There's a battle going on up there, a battle where Americans need air support, and my Comanche *is* that air support. I've got ammo. I only need fuel to go help our mutual friends stay alive. I—" He stopped in mid-sentence and straightened. Shading his eyes he looked north into the sky. "Do you hear that?"

"Yeah," answered Bunny Carlos, who had been content to let Randall do all the talking. "That sounds like a Comanche."

"It does. It must be Plotz and Arnold."

"Before the issue comes up, sir," said the sergeant, "if I can't give you fuel for one helicopter, I sure can't give you fuel for two."

Randall ignored him as *Hell's Hammer* settled to the dirt one hundred feet away. Without waiting for the dust cloud to settle, Alisa Plotz climbed out of the cockpit and ran toward them.

"Man, am I glad to see you!" Randall said when she got within earshot. "Where's Andy?"

When she stopped, gasping for breath, he didn't need any words to know the answer.

"Aw, hell," Carlos said.

"Chinese broke through on the north," she said, between gulps of air. "Arnold held them off while I started her up... when I looked again, he... he..."

"I get it," Randall said. "How many Chicoms?"

"I don't know, could be a squad, could be a battalion. I just don't know. I need fuel and ammo."

Randall turned back to the sergeant. "Do you hear that? The Chinese have broken through and the base is about to be overrun."

"No can do, sir."

"What's the problem?"

Randall pointed at the sergeant. "We brought ammo, but the sergeant won't give us fuel without written authorization."

Plotz's flushed face went blank as she processed his words. Then she nodded. "I've got authorization." Drawing her Beretta M9 sidearm, she aimed it at the sergeant's forehead. "Don't I, Sergeant?"

The 1st Airborne Battalion's forward command post now consisted of a radioman, one rifleman acting as a guard, Major Ball, and General Fleming. Everybody else was in the trenches, fighting.

"Major!" The radioman handed Ball the handset.

Fleming could only listen to his side of the conversation, but it was enough.

"Can you hold? How many? All right, you have permission to pull back if necessary, but whatever you do, you *have* to keep your platoon intact."

"Breakthrough?" Fleming said.

Ball shook his head. "Not that bad, but an unknown number of hostiles slipped around Third Platoon's right flank into the base."

"Any reserves you can send?"

"Yes, sir... me!"

"You're the battalion commander, Major."

"I'm all there is, General, and at the end of the day, I'm a soldier like everybody else. If those Chinese find the battalion aid station, they're going to kill a lot of helpless people... *my* people. Will you take over tactical command of the battalion until I get back?"

Fleming hesitated, and then jerked his thumb toward the base. "Go! Take him with you." He pointed at the guard. "If you go near the BAS, alert Claw and Vapor they might have company coming and to stay put." Ball grabbed his M16 and started to leave, but Fleming grabbed his arm. "We need you in one piece, Sam."

The major gave a short nod before running toward the buildings.

"Well, son," Fleming said to the radioman, "looks like it's you and me running this show. We can do it, right?"

"Uh, sure, General."

Fleming smiled. Then a fifty-caliber machine gun, twenty yards to the west of the command post, opened a continuous fire that went on for two seconds... three seconds... four... then a huge explosion shook the ground, and the gun was silent.

General Wei could sense that victory was close. Despite being virtually surrounded by the enemy, his attack on the base had been the right move. Losses were terrible, but he had too many men for the Americans to stop them all, and now they were about to break through. His truck bounced past an American trench filled with hand-to-hand fighting, and now only an American fifty-caliber machine gun directly ahead of Wei's vehicle blocked their way. At least one hundred of his men followed in his wake.

The American gun opened a continuous fire, pouring shells into his truck's engine and windshield. With the engine and driver both dead, the truck lurched to a stop. His own gunner returned the fire, and for one second tracers sped by in both directions, at a range of only forty feet. Wei ducked inside the truck just as the gunner shook from multiple hits in his head and chest, and the gory remains collapsed on top of him. Smelling smoke, he opened the side door and scrambled out just as a grenade went off and silenced the American gun. They must have had a Carl Gustav in the pit with them, because a much bigger blast almost knocked him down.

The explosion stunned him. Bending over and shaking his head, he waved his men forward. The moment had come to capture the base. Once they were in among the buildings, it would be much harder to dig them out, and if they could find a cache of those American rocket launchers, they could yet be victorious.

Smoke and flames boiled up from the machine-gun pit as Fleming braced his M16 against his right shoulder. The radioman crawled up beside him as both waited for targets to materialize. When they did, Fleming's brain realized there were far too many to stop.

Both Americans set their selectors to auto and opened fire. Bullets ripped into the direct targets around the edge of the pit. Chinese soldiers fell in heaps but more came on. The radioman fell backward as something knocked off his helmet. Fleming was the last man between them and the battalion aid station, and he had no illusions about how the Chinese would treat wounded Americans.

He fired until his magazine ran out. The nearest Chinese soldier was thirty feet away. As he changed magazines, in his peripheral vision he could see the man taking aim. And then everything disappeared in a gigantic mushroom of dust. Rocks and steel splinters rained on him and Fleming slid below ground level to the bottom of the pit. Covering his head, it took him a moment to realize what he'd seen — the unmistakable impact of hundreds of 30mm cannon rounds tearing the Chinese to shreds.

Hell's Hammer crept over the ground at a height of only one hundred feet. Below, she saw Arnold lying right where she'd left him, but there was no sign of his killers. So she hovered in plain sight, making *Hell's Hammer* an easy target to draw them out.

It worked.

Tink, tink.

Plotz jerked the helicopter around to see four men firing at her, using the corners of a building and the dumpster as cover. She clearly saw their muzzle flashes. A bullet struck the windshield and bounced off, leaving it cracked but intact. She didn't fire until she'd lined up the shot perfectly, and when she pressed the trigger she didn't let go for three full seconds.

The M73 30mm autocannon had a rate of fire of 4,000 rounds per minute. One hundred-twenty rounds of such massive shells blasted through the cinder block walls of the building and shredded the men hiding there. The dumpster flew up in the air and smashed down, twisted like an old soda can.

She was breathing so hard that her vision fuzzed out from hyperventilation. Red sparkles shone at the edges of her vision. As her breathing slowed and a light wind dissipated the smoke from her cannon fire, nobody else shot at her. Satisfied that the Chinese were all dead, she landed *Hell's Hammer* near Arnold's body.

A gnawing fear had eaten at her that maybe he wasn't dead when she'd left, that maybe he was only wounded and she somehow could have saved him. But kneeling beside him, she could tell that wasn't the case. Blood soaked the back of his flight suit. When she gently turned him over, there were two wounds in his neck and at least ten more to his chest. If he hadn't died instantly, he had within seconds. That was some comfort.

Bending down, she kissed his forehead. Then she cried.

Blood seeped into Zhang Wei's eyes from a scalp wound that burned as if his hair was on fire. All around him, bits and pieces of humans that seconds before had been his men lay in heaps like the discards from a butcher's cleaver. Here and there he heard a groan, but nobody remained standing.

Wei tried to push to his feet, but only his right arm responded. Blinking, he looked at the bleeding stump that should have been his left arm and wondered where it went. He needed to find it, to stick it back where it belonged. Struggling to his feet, he stumbled forward through gore deeper than his knees, scanning the ruined flesh for any sign of his missing limb. Glancing up, twenty feet away he saw a black American with three stars on his helmet aiming a rifle at him, and wondered what the man was doing.

Then he saw some flashes from the end of the rifle, and felt light thumps in his chest. His knees buckled and Wei wondered *Why?* And why was everything getting dark, all of a sudden?

And then he didn't wonder about that, or anything else, ever again.

#

Chapter 40

> "The world is filled with winners and losers, but ofttimes even losers win. This day, however, shall losers lose, and never be seen again."
> Maj. General J.E.B. Stuart, CSA

Sierra Army Depot, Herlong, CA
1804 hours, May 5

The shooting didn't stop all at once. Distant rifle fire continued for quite some time, but the Comanches broke the back of the Chinese attacks. Norm Fleming searched for targets, but any Chinese still on their feet had had enough. Hands raised, they knelt and waited to be collected as prisoners of war.

The first thing he did was check on the radioman in the pit with him. By a miracle, the Chinese round that knocked off his helmet seemed to have ricocheted without penetrating his skull, probably because it struck at an oblique angle. He was out cold, though, with a nasty gash over his right eye near the hairline. Fleming used his own IFAK, individual first aid kit, to tape a combat gauze dressing over the bloody wound.

Major Ball found him as he propped the unconscious man's head on his ruptured helmet to keep the bandage clean. "General, are you hurt?"

"Not this time. Give me a hand. We need to get this man to the aid station."

"Maybe we should let a medic check him out first, sir."

Fleming was still in combat mode, his veins filled with adrenaline and the urgent need to *act*. But Ball's words got through and he nodded. "You're right, Major, good thinking. What's our situation?"

"I've got teams combing the base for any Chinese infiltrators; otherwise they're done as a fighting force. A few swam across the lake, some others took off to the north, but not many. We killed a lot of people today, sir."

"Our losses?"

"Heavy. I don't have any numbers yet."

Fleming's expression was grim, and he knew it, but if ever there was a time for it, it was now.

"Did you…" Major Ball started.

"Did I have to use my weapon?"

"Yes, sir."

"I did." Fleming nodded toward the battle area. "He was almost on top of me."

A soldier outside the pit had overheard them and called down. "Hey, General, is this the guy you tagged? He looks like some kinda bigwig officer… sir."

Fleming climbed out and got his first look at the aftermath of the battle. Mangled bodies, blackened vehicles, and twisted equipment lay everywhere. Within sight were at least one hundred dead Chinese, most of them young. The body the soldier pointed out lay no more than twenty feet from the position he'd defended.

Kneeling beside the dead man, Fleming inspected his face and uniform. The front of his uniform showed four holes where Fleming's rounds had torn into his body. He had definitely been important, and his age appeared to be at least in his sixties, maybe older. A paunch indicated he'd been well fed, but the most telling indicators of rank were the black shoulder tabs, with three gold stars and gold oak leaves.

"He was the commander." Fleming stood, still looking down at the man. "He's a general. A senior general."

"Dayum," said the soldier. "I wonder when the last time was that a general killed a general?"

Fleming was sitting on the edge of a trench when a corporal led a civilian toward him. The right side of the soldier's face had dried blood that ran all the way down to his neck. He saluted. Dust and sweat grimed the civilian, but that was true of anyone who'd spent more than ten minutes in the desert. What weren't normal were his trembling hands.

"General, sir, have you seen Major Ball?"

"Not in the last ten minutes, Corporal. I believe he's out checking his command. Who is this?" Fleming nodded at the civilian using his chin. His voice sounded wooden and flat, even to him.

"Sir, he says his name is—"

"Pohl, General," the man said, interrupting. He put out his hand. Fleming didn't move. "Allen Pohl. You may have seen me earlier, or at least, you may have seen my airplane."

"I saw a hallucination earlier, one that looked like an old German *Stuka*. Is that what you mean?"

Pohl grinned. "This whole thing sure feels like a dream." He left his hand extended.

Fleming finally shook it. "I'm Lieutenant General Norman Fleming, Mister Pohl. That really *was* a JU-87?"

"You know your airplanes, General Fleming. I'm impressed. Yes, that was indeed a JU-87G-1, a tank buster. It's part of a collection of warplanes my father amassed before the Collapse of the United States."

Fleming rubbed his chin, thinking. "Why does the name Allen Pohl sound familiar?"

"He founded a software company and later sold it for six billion dollars; that's probably it."

"Yeah, I remember him now. What was the name of his company?"

"CCS."

"Right... is he still alive?"

"No, we lost him more than twenty years ago. But Dad saw the Collapse coming. He said the COVID-19 panic in 2020 convinced him that if there was ever a bigger catastrophe, the people would not survive, and no people meant no country."

"Smart man."

"He prepared so that his family could keep going. Many of his Hollywood friends made fun of him. I'm old enough to remember some TV show where three actors spent a few minutes ridiculing him for being a prepper. Once money became worthless, I'm sure they did, too."

"I'm tired now, Mister Pohl, but when we have time, I want to hear the whole story of how you managed to fly a one-hundred-thirty-year-old airplane into battle. And also *why*."

"The *why* part is easy. Green Ghost told me that if I helped him find his father, he'd convince General Angriff to let me help rebuild your Warthogs."

#

Part Six

The Battle for Shangri-La

Chapter 41

True friends stab you in the front.
Oscar Wilde

12 miles west of Albuquerque, New Mexico
1400 hours, May 5

Everything was ready. Like horses in the starting gate, all Amunet Mwangi needed now was General Steeple's order to open fire. Only a light breeze rippling the tent walls disturbed the silence, as the entire headquarters company stood by, barely breathing. No one spoke at all. But as seconds ticked away past zero hour and no order came, Mwangi furrowed her eyebrows, wondering what could have happened.

Then the radio operator turned and broke the quiet. "Message alert, Colonel."

"On speaker."

There was a hiss from the loudspeaker on the radioman's table, and then a voice spoke out. Mwangi raised her hand, ready to point to a lieutenant who stood by to relay her order to fire to the battery crews. The instant she heard the first word, she lowered her arm, but before the lieutenant could relay the order, everyone heard the first sentence and froze in place.

"To all commands, this is General Nicholas T. Angriff..."

Mouth agape, Mwangi stared at the speaker as Angriff's voice filled the tent. As he continued speaking, she squeezed her eyes shut. She wanted to put her hands over her ears, but retained enough composure not to. When it ended, she felt something hard poke her in the back. A corporal stood next to Major Ahmadi, with the barrel of a pistol pressed into her spine.

"Colonel Mwangi, you are under arrest for suspicion of treason," Ahmadi said. "I am taking command of elements of the 2nd Mechanized Regiment that have been under your command." Then, to the radio operator, "Send to all batteries and to the elements of 2nd Mechanized Regiment. Shift targets to troop concentrations of the enemy force known as the Sword of the Prophet. If they come within range, engage to destroy."

1406 hours

"Why have our American allies not opened fire?" Counselor Ibrahim Yaseen's sarcastic tone rankled the emir of New Khorasan, Abdul-Qudoos Fadil el Mofty, but while the man enjoyed the protection of el Mofty's brother, the Caliph, he was beyond retaliation. But el Mofty promised himself that one day, the worm would pay for his insolence.

Sitting in the living room of his residence in Albuquerque, el Mofty had no intention of betraying the anxiety racing through his mind at that moment. Why, indeed, had the Americans not opened fire? Or had they, and he was too far removed to hear the rockets firing or exploding?

"You know as much as I do, revered counselor. Perhaps there is some technical difficulty that we have not heard about."

"Yes, perhaps so."

Protection or not, Yaseen's continual sneering and condescension made el Mofty seriously consider killing the man anyway. He was about to respond when distant *whooms* rippled through the walls. El Mofty smiled in triumph. "I think our allies have answered your question, Yaseen."

The two men walked out to the house's front porch, which some of their men had propped up with surplus lumber. A wasp's nest had been removed and burned, although some men got stung in the process. From the porch, they heard the distant explosions of the rockets, like a thunderstorm over the horizon. They went on for twenty seconds, stopped for half a minute, and then resumed. The sequence repeated itself three times.

"These are life's precious moments, Yaseen," el Mofty said with a wistful tone. "When doing Allah's work pays off, and you know you are giving him a gift in accordance with the laws he passed down to us. It is very satisfying."

"Yes, o Great Emir, I am certain that is your motivation."

El Mofty felt too satisfied to react to such inflammatory words. His slight smile lasted until a man ran out from the old house's interior.

"Blessed One, it is General Gollins on the radio for you!"

"Perhaps the Americans have made it unnecessary for us to attack at all." He went inside and put on the radio operator's headphones. The cups were so old the material had dried and cracked, and the sharp edges irritated his skin. "I am here, General."

"The Americans are firing at us!" she said. In the background, he heard screams and explosions. "They have ripped my regiments to pieces with their damned rockets. What has happened?"

Stunned, he said nothing until she had repeated her question for the third time. "I don't know," was all he could think of.

"What should we do?"

He had to give her an answer, but had no idea of the overall situation. Was this a mistake? Were they also firing at General Muhdin's men? "Withdraw one mile, General," he finally said. "That should put you out of the target zone. I will call you with further instructions."

"I sure as hell hope so!" Gollins said.

#

Chapter 42

> *"Liberty is best delivered at 3,900 rpm."*
> Lieutenant Shannon Hartmann

Operation Comeback, Air Force Attachment
1426 hours, May 5

Captain J. Babb ran his hand along the undersurface of the A-10, relishing the tactile thrill of its cool metal skin. Since coming out of Long Sleep, he'd only had the briefest time in the simulator to remind his brain how to fly the legendary Warthog. He had a dozen reasons to worry about flying it against a real enemy. Not only was he still acclimating to being awake again, but so was the plane. Lieutenant Hartmann had promised that she'd run every conceivable test to measure its performance, and swore that it exceeded minimum performance levels across the board. But the truth was that nobody could say with absolute certainly how it would fly until somebody flew it, and he'd been elected.

Babb took extra time during his flight check to inspect any exposed connection surfaces, such as at the wing flaps. Out of long habit, he checked the ordnance package for any obvious bad connections.

"No offense to you, Lieutenant Hartmann," he said to the head of the technical staff. "It's just something I've always done."

"I'm glad you're doing it, sir. My only concern is you coming home safe, and it never hurts to have another pair of eyes."

"We're going to get along just fine," he said.

"We're not sure of what you're hunting, Captain, so we had to guess at the ordnance load. Based on our intel of the Sevens, you're unlikely to run into much armor, so we mixed Mavericks, five-hundred-pound GPs, and Rockeyes. The gun has HEI for the same reasons. I had to make that call, so I hope it was the right one."

"Whatever you know, Hartmann, it's a helluva lot more than I do. Ready to get this show on the road?"

"Let's do it, Captain."

He ascended the rolling ladder and climbed into the cockpit. It felt like snuggling under the covers of your childhood bed. The A-10 cockpit had a beautiful symmetry to it. The pilot sat inside a titanium bathtub up to one and one-half inches thick. Between his or her legs was the joystick. The instrument panel had rectangular displays on the upper part of each side. On the right-most of the instruments were black dials with white numbers and hands, while the left side had more switches than dials. At each elbow were consoles with more controls that extended well beyond the back of his seat.

First he moved the battery switch on the right-side console to power, and then the inverter switch on the same console. As AC current flowed through the Warthog's wiring, he almost felt like the electricity moved through his own nervous system, too. Next he pressed the lamp test button on the auxiliary lighting panel on the left console, to make sure that any cautions or warnings during startup would be displayed. As much as he instinctively trusted Hartmann, with the aircraft newly put back into commission, Babb knew that anything could happen. While holding the button down, he glanced around the cockpit to verify that all warnings and tones worked.

Glancing to the lower right, he checked his fuel status. The readout indicated 3,000 pounds, while the digital tonalizer readout said 5,800 pounds, both perfect. Next he went to the oxygen regulator panel on the right console and switched the supply on, verifying in the flow window that it worked. Just behind that on the same console, he pushed the oxygen test button to check the amount of oxygen remaining. The oxy-low indicator would turn off if his oxygen supply dropped below half a liter. Babb wasn't planning on needing oxygen, but ingrained habits wouldn't allow him to skip even such a probably unnecessary step, even when time was of the essence.

Below his left elbow were the radio controls. He set the VHF-AM frequency dial to TR, or transceiver, and heard the reassuring static he always heard when the radio was first powered on. He right-clicked the squelch switch to get rid of it. He then repeated the process for the VHF-FM frequency radio, and set the UHF radio switch to main. Blinking, he rubbed his eyes and drew a deep breath. It was time for the fun to begin.

"Initiating engine start sequence," he said into the helmet mike. Beyond his left wing tip, Hartmann raised her thumb.

On the right side bulkhead, he right-clicked and held the canopy control switch. As the canopy closed, he had a moment of panic, having forgotten the next step. *What the hell?* He'd done this a thousand times! But then he remembered, and exhaled. He had to power up the fuel pumps in each wing, and in the left and right fuselage tanks. The four switches were located near the top of the left console, on the fuel system control panel. He flipped all of them to the up position. Also on the left console were the left and right engine fuel flow switches on the throttle panel, which he put to norm.

The APU, auxiliary power unit, was also on that same console. It required him to monitor the exhaust gas temperature and the RPMs on the engine monitoring instruments panel on the right front dash. Flipping the APU to start, Babb paid close attention to the EGT, which needed to stay around 425 degrees Celsius when idling. It would spike when he used it to power the engine starter, but he expected that. Once the EGT and RPM had stabilized, the latter at 100 percent, he looked at the electrical panel and set the APU generator switch to the power setting. The APU would supply electrical power during flight operations, with the battery acting as a backup. Outside of his right elbow, Babb set the right and left AC generators to power. After engine startup, they would replace the ACU and supply electrical power, thus giving the aircraft triple electrical redundancy.

And now it was time for engine startup. The throttles were located on the left console and Babb moved the left one from off to idle. If all went right, that would automatically start fuel flow, use bleed air from the APU to turn the fans, and ignite fuel in the combustion chamber. A whine began to grow in volume as Babb watched the engine monitoring instrument panel on the front dash, paying close attention to the engine interstage turbine temperature, engine core speed, fan speed, and fuel flow gauges. He said a prayer that everything worked the way it was supposed to. The core fan stabilized at around 55 percent, which was a little on the low side but not enough to abort. Left hydraulic system pressure began to come up. It stabilized around 2,900 psi, again in the normal range but slightly below average.

The joystick vibrated as the left engine powered up to full idle. Satisfied with left engine powerup, he repeated the sequence to start the right engine. Once that was done, he tested the flight controls for stick and rudder input, the responsiveness of the speed brakes and flaps. The whine of the turbines was like the cooing of a baby to his ears as he visually inspected the flaps moving up and down.

Sitting straight in his chair, Babb realized the time had come for take-off. Adrenaline pumped through his body as he thought about what was to come. He'd never before taxied up an incline, even with a pushback tug towing him, but what the hell? He'd never slept for fifty years before, either. Once topside, he would only have a wind sock and flagman for takeoff assistance, but again, so what? He'd signed up for adventure and now he had it.

"Give 'em hell, Captain," Hartmann said.

Holding up his right thumb, Babb closed his visor and prepared to go back to war.

A thousand things could have gone wrong with the takeoff, and Babb expected any or all of them to happen, but none did. The A-10 lifted off into a perfect spring afternoon with a light headwind providing lift. Passing a thousand feet, he glanced out the right side of the cockpit, where a line of a dozen or more vehicles stood several hundred yards southwest of the runway. Banking right, he flew near enough to verify they were Americans, and most waved at him. What the hell were they doing there? There had to be a story behind it, but he'd have to find out later. With no more time to waste, he headed east toward New Mexico.

Shangri-La
1427 hours, May 5

Johnny Rainwater couldn't take his eyes off the blackened lumps lying in heaps two hundred yards beyond the wall. Because of the exhausting effort led by Abigail Deak, they had managed to bury all of their dead and had an unofficial list of their names, with plans to erect a permanent memorial to stand over the mass graves. But for him, there were no tears left, no emotions left, only the nightmare memories of those innocent women and children burning to death while the Sevens laughed, which would haunt his dreams forever. Although you couldn't tell it now, one of the piles of bodies off to the right had been a mother trying to beat out the flames on her little boy, until the fire burned her hands away. He couldn't tell which pile it was, but he knew they were there.

"How could anyone do that in the name of their god?" said Mohammad Qadim. His voice had a detached, neutral tone that brought a glance from Rainwater. "How could any human being do that to another human being?"

"I don't know. I don't want to know. But I would think you'd understand them better than me."

"It's not my religion... although I think now that I understand the motivation behind the Crusades."

"Why do you say that?"

"Islam spread at the point of a sword. I never really thought about it before this, but they took lands away from Christians and Jews and Zoroastrians and pagans. They killed those who opposed them. Now that I'm on the receiving end... they can get fucked."

"I wouldn't let—"

An unfamiliar sound interrupted him. It wasn't loud, but it was unlike anything he'd ever heard before. And a weird whistling sound followed it, growing louder and louder. By sheer reflex, everyone along the wall dropped down and covered their heads. Some people tucked their heads between their legs while others curled into the fetal position.

Huge explosions shook the ground and deafened Rainwater, who covered his ears with the heels of his hands. At first he thought the Sevens were using mortars again, but then he realized the blasts were much bigger than mortars. Glancing both ways down the defensive line, he could see no explosions, even though the sounds of the detonations continued. Peering through a firing port in the stone wall, he saw the Sevens' front lines obscured by dust and smoke. The echoes of the explosions faded away and an ominous silence came over the desert.

It took a few seconds for Rainwater to work out the only possible explanation for the devastation that must lie behind the obscuring cloud — the Americans had turned their guns on the Sevens instead of Shangri-La. The only question was why? Was it a mistake?

More faint *whooshes* meant his question would soon be answered. Had the Americans corrected their aim, or was it already correct? Rainwater stood to watch. He realized that if the Americans launched such a barrage at Shangri-La, hiding behind some rocks wouldn't save him.

The roar of incoming rockets grew loud, fast, and Rainwater knew he'd have his answer in seconds. It might be the last answer he ever got.

Smoke trails appeared over the ridgeline to the west, on his right, arcing down toward their target. Eight M26 rockets detonated in a line above the enemy positions and scattered more than 4,000 sub-munitions that exploded half a second later, living up to its nickname, steel rain. That was what Captain Sully had called it, and now Rainwater understood why. He could only gape at the destruction.

The process happened five more times. Beginning east of Highway 4, a systematic progression of blasts blanketed the Sevens' trenches and bunkers with ordnance. As Rainwater watched, a Seven missing an arm staggered out of a smoke cloud with his robe and hair on fire. He rejected the fleeting thought of putting the man out of his misery... let the bastard burn.

The headquarters platoon for Dog Company, 1st Marine Recon Battalion, ringed Shangri-La's central meeting place, where the flagpole stood, in a widely dispersed formation. When the first salvo of rockets launched from 15 miles west of the ridgeline, Company Commander Captain Martin Sully assumed his men were the target. All of his people knew the sound of an M270 firing a rocket salvo, and he'd left standing orders for them to take cover if that happened. And then it did.

Sully buttoned up inside his LAV-25, knowing that a direct hit would wipe out him and his crew, and a near miss might tip the vehicle over. If the Sevens had coordinated their attack with the Americans, however, they might come in right

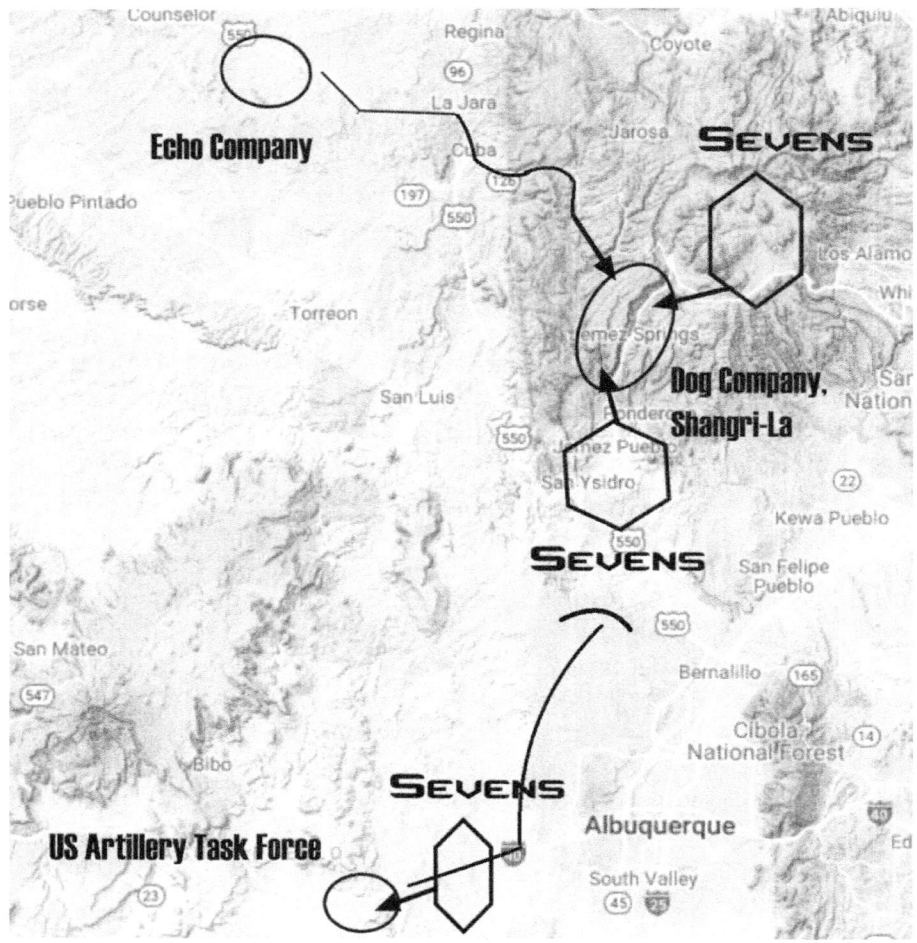

after the first salvo and Sully would need to be mobile as soon as possible. Then the first salvo landed outside Shangri-La's defensive perimeter and blasted the Sevens, quickly followed by so many more that he lost count.

"Kicker Real, this is Kicker One One, do you copy? Over."

"Kicker One One, this is Kicker Real. Sitrep, Onni, over."

"I'm at the northern gate on Highway Four. I observed multiple direct hits on enemy lines directly in front of my position. Has the situation changed? Over."

"Unknown at this time, but circumstances indicate yes. From my position, I can observe enemy positions hard hit all along our perimeter."

"Roger that, Kicker Real. Kicker One One out."

Seconds later, his radioman patched through a call from the commander of the Army MLRS batteries.

"Kicker Real here."

"Kicker Real, this is Badass Six. We are under new management, do you copy? Over."

"Roger that, Badass Six, Kicker Real acknowledging your message. Congratulations, glad to hear it. Over."

"We have to cut support for now, Kicker Real. We are under heavy ground attack. Will keep you informed of our status. Badass Six out."

Sully pushed out of the hatch and stood atop the turret, using his binoculars to scan what he could see of the perimeter. The Sevens might have pulled troops away from his sector to try and knock out the artillery, or they might have used reserves. If it was the latter, then Shangri-La could expect renewed attacks soon.

The flagpole area sat atop a ridge, but other ridges limited his line of sight. The southern line was about a mile south and he could see most of it, along with all of the ridgeline to the west. Half a mile east, the line was a series of strongpoints built over decades at the crest of a steep ridge. Below, the terrain was relatively flat. Assaults on that flank would be costly in the extreme.

The most worrisome area was on the north, where the rugged country gave defenders inherent advantages by restricting routes of advance by attackers, and properly sited guns could have excellent fields of fire. But the area was huge, and the very terrain that gave them advantages also negated mutually supporting strongpoints. It was also their longest flank. Even though the defenders had withdrawn three miles south of the junction of Highway 4 and Highway 126, the front still arced down the ridgeline of the west, then straight east for three miles, before turning south again to link up with the strongpoints scattered along the eastern ridgeline. In total it stretched more than six miles.

Shangri-La could only field about 800 people in defense now, having lost more than 200 in the first battle, including some of the fittest. As partial compensation, those who survived had scavenged automatic weapons off the dead Sevens so the compound's firepower had actually increased. Sully had 13 LAV-25s left, and had given the second one from his headquarters section to replace the one lost by Alpha Company.

Sully had deployed Alpha Company evenly spaced along the southern flank, with Bravo and Charlie supporting in the north. He kept the company's specialized LAVs with him as a reserve, including both LAV-Ms, which carried 81mm mortars; four LAV-Ats with TOW missile launchers; three LAV-Ls, designed for logistics and packed with food, fuel, and ammo, but also armed with a 7.62mm machine gun; and an LAV-R recovery vehicle. His own LAV-C2 command and control vehicle stood close by the LAV-25 he commanded in a combat role. It should have had its own commander, but casualties from last year's battle had limited the number of qualified crewmen. Last year's loss of Lieutenant Embekwe, First Platoon's C.O., left one LAV-25 short a commander and, after it was put back in fighting condition, he'd taken it for himself.

That left Sully commanding two different vehicles at the same time. The rear door of LAV-C2, his command vehicle, stood open only ten feet from his combat LAV-25. This allowed for communication without the need for radio. When he wasn't aboard the command vehicle, First Sergeant Meyer was in charge.

"Staff Sergeant Monroe," he called down to a female Marine standing half in, half out the back of the LAV-C2. She turned and shaded her eyes to see him. "Send to all units — button up and expect enemy assault. Report any movement to your front."

"On it, Captain." The small sergeant turned and relayed his orders to the radioman inside.

Instead of following his own order to get inside and close the hatches, Sully kept sweeping the enemy lines for signs of movement. The cloud of dust and smoke stirred up by the rockets still hung close to the ground, obscuring everything, but Sully could *feel* something happening out there.

"Captain," Staff Sergeant Monroe called up, "message just in from Echo Company. Captain Jones wants to coordinate our movements."

"Send to Captain Jones — stay clear. Do not want you also in violation of orders."

Two minutes later he still had the binoculars up to his eyes when Monroe called up Echo Company's answer. "Captain Jones says that General Angriff rescinded all of General Steeple's orders, and asks if we didn't hear the transmission. We've received no such report, Captain."

"General Angriff's dead."

"That's what I said, Captain, but sir, Captain Jones sounded pretty sure of herself, and she said he wasn't as dead as everyone thought he was."

Sully stared at her for a few seconds, and then began to climb off the turret. Once clear of the vehicle, he climbed into the command vehicle. Jittery excitement raised his voice half an octave. "Any contact yet with Colonels Strickland or Berger?"

"Negative, Captain."

"Get me Prime."

Wearing a headset with retractable mike and close-fitting earphones, he felt his heart racing while waiting for Prime to acknowledge the radio request. It felt like it took hours for them to answer, although it was really about twenty seconds.

"Kicker Real, this is Overtime Prime. What is the nature of your call? Over."

"Prime, we've heard reports of a broadcast by General Angriff, negating General Steeple's orders. Can you confirm? Over."

"Stand by, Kicker Real."

Several clicks later, Sully heard the voice of a dead man.

"Captain Sully, this is General Angriff. What's your situation?"

Sully could never remember how the words came to him. He was stunned, but his training kicked in and he continued on like Angriff hadn't been reported killed. "Sir, we are inside the fortified perimeter of the compound known as Shangri-La. Estimates are between eight and ten thousand enemy infantry surrounding this position, with small numbers of armor in support, including M1 Abrams. Previous fighting inflicted heavy casualties on both the people of this compound, and the Sevens. Remaining defenders number in the range of eight hundred, not counting Dog Company. We suffered the loss of one LAV-25 with crew in the previous fighting. The MLRS batteries located twenty-two klicks west of our position laid down multiple heavy salvoes on enemy positions around our perimeter. We are unable to see through the lingering smoke cloud, but I would estimate their losses as being very significant. Fire support has ceased, as Major Ahmadi reports being heavily engaged with a large force of infantry. Over."

Sully heard Angriff turn away and say something he couldn't make out, and then the general came back to him. "What do you need from me, Captain? Over."

"Air support, General, and reinforcements. Over"

"You'll get everything I can spare. I'm turning you over to Colonel Strickland now, Captain. I'm damned proud you're part of this brigade, Sully, you and every Marine in your company. Give 'em hell! Over."

"Yes, sir!"

#

Chapter 43

If we come to a minefield, our infantry attacks exactly as if it were not there.
Marshal of the Soviet Union Georgy Zhukov

The desert west of Albuquerque, New Mexico
1434 hours, May 5

Because his new command had deployed so far to the west, his uncle had given Sati Bashara one of their precious few radio sets. When the bombardment started, he expected a message that the Americans had betrayed them. Some part of Bashara might even have hoped they would, not only so he could prove his worth on the battlefield after two defeats, but also so that el Mofty might value his opinion more in the future. But as the minutes ticked by, it became more and more apparent that he had misjudged their new allies, which meant that not only could he not redeem himself, he would also miss overrunning the infidels in Shangri-La.

Then one of his men climbed the dune where he stood, watching the Americans launch their rockets more than one mile away. One of their three remaining tanks, an M1A1 patched together from other machines of the Texas National Guard, remained hull down behind him, engine off and the crew standing in its shadow.

"General," the man called when halfway up, "the emir wants to talk to you."

He half slid, half walked down the loose soil of the hillside and found the radio set up in the back of an old pickup truck.

Taking a deep breath, he prepared the words of apology in his head. "General Bashara here."

"Sati, we are betrayed. The Americans fired on our positions, not their own, and casualties are heavy. Withdraw back to Albuquerque to cover the army's retreat. I will meet you at my headquarters."

For a few seconds Bashara said nothing. Despite expecting it, the actuality of the situation shook him. But then an idea emerged. "Uncle, no! Now is the time to attack!"

"What?"

"Their rocket launchers have already fired off much of their ammunition, and I have four thousand of your best troops in position to make the Americans pay for their betrayal. Attack Shangri-La now, Uncle, as I attack them here, and we will divide their firepower. We can yet turn this into a victory!"

"It is a high risk gamble, nephew. They have tanks there, do they not?"

"Yes, they do, but we have RPGs. Uncle, if we withdraw now, we will never again be in this position. We will have run from the enemy, and the next time we may face many more than we do now. It is a chance to defeat them en masse, but if we do not seize this chance, which may be our *last* chance, if we retreat now when we have them outnumbered ten to one or more, then we acknowledge they are the superior army. The Sword of the New Prophet was created to cut the enemy, was it not? Let it cut, Uncle, let it shed American blood."

"Very well, Sati, you shall have your war. Go win it, and may Allah go with you!"

Bashara handed the radioman the mike and ordered messengers to the other regiments. He was with the westernmost force, and sent word to the east and north that they would attack in half an hour. The designated men mounted their horses and rode away at the gallop.

1435 hours

Major Ahmadi stood in the top hatch of his Bradley command vehicle, scanning the horizon. With little time to readjust the batteries' targets, he could only hope their fire had landed on the enemy and not a bunch of black-tailed jackrabbits. All he could see were faint smoke columns on the horizon that diffused into an amorphous gray cloud.

"Badass Six, Badass Six, this is Apache Red Six. I've got incoming foot traffic to my front and both flanks, range one-eight-zero-zero, approximate number two-zero-zero-zero. Over."

Shit!

The fourteen Bradleys of Alpha Company were echeloned on the left in an arc facing east and bending west to protect the M270s, with an equal number of Bradleys from Bravo Company in the same position on the right. Ahmadi had two BCVs organic to the M270 battery, situated one hundred yards to the rear. Dismounted infantry had two lines of rifle pits and reinforced machine gun positions in front of and close to the Bradleys. Now he missed the battalion's organic tank company more than ever; with the firepower of fourteen M1A2s, he wouldn't be so anxious.

"Apache Six, do you see armor? Over."

"Negative, Badass Six, infantry only, but a lot of them, over."

Ahmadi paused, thinking, which gave someone else a chance to break in. "Badass Six, this is Bedlam Black Seven

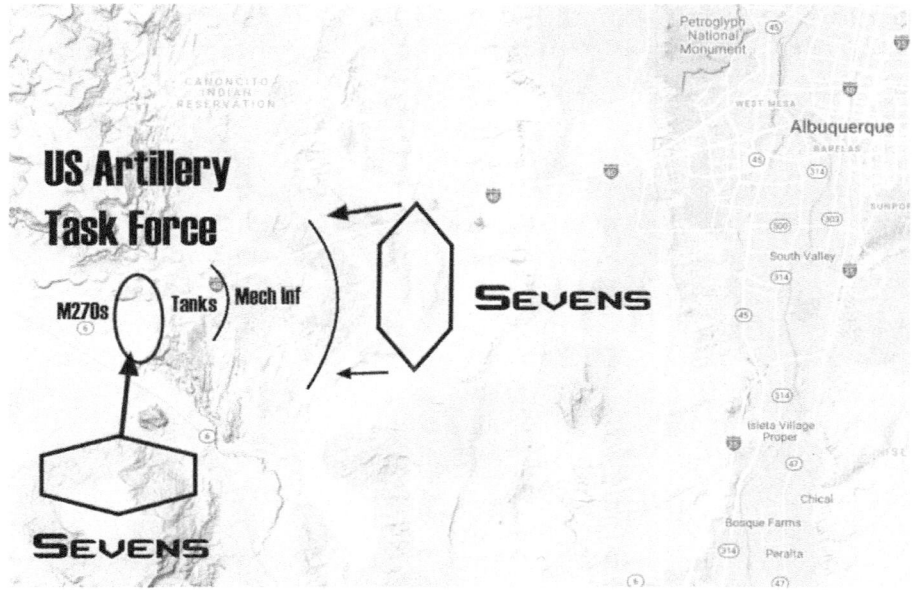

One. Infantry moving this way, two-zero-nine degrees true. Armored support in sight, three Abrams, repeat, three Abrams positively identified, over."

"Bedlam Black Seven One, this is Badass Six, numbers and range, please, over."

It went on like that for another minute, after which Ahmadi had a clearer picture of the tactical situation. The Sevens had obviously expected a double-cross, and deployed thousands of men in a semi-circle around the American vehicles. The nature of the terrain meant they could inflict horrific casualties, but it was unclear whether that would be enough to break up the assault, or if the Sevens would get close enough to deploy handheld antitank weapons. If they did that, things could get dicey quick. Worse, if they were defending themselves, they couldn't support the Marines, which he felt certain was the whole point.

Using the intercom, he called to the BCV's radio operator. "Get me Prime."

Within one minute of the last rockets impacting on her forward regiment's position, Tracy Gollins was out of her headquarters camp west of Los Alamos and into her personal Bradley. The explosions were loud even from miles away. She couldn't imagine what kind of artillery could fire such large caliber shells, but she was glad they were aimed at the enemy and not at her men. She now had three regiments under her command, her original Mecca Regiment, plus the two from that little shit, her cousin Sati, the Rasūl and Ayyub Regiments. He didn't know they were related, and she couldn't wait to see his expression on the day he found out.

That put nearly 5,000 men at her disposal and she meant to use them. She'd read every book they'd scraped out of the ruins of dead America on war and military tactics. There were many things she didn't know about commanding troops in battle, particularly troops who looked at women as inferior, but one thing she did know was to attack immediately after an artillery bombardment is lifted. They'd known the timing of the barrage, but she had last minute details to take care of and now had to make up for lost time.

At first she urged the driver to ever greater speed, but when he still didn't go fast enough she threatened to have him executed. That did the trick and he floored it, taking sharp turns at dangerous speeds and twice nearly rolling the armored troop carrier. Blood pounded in her ears from the excitement of being so close to smashing their enemies. She didn't give two shits about killing infidels for the Caliph, or any of that nonsense; Gollins just liked the feeling of power that was part of being a battlefield commander. Most of all, she liked the blood.

As they got close to the lines, drifting smoke cut down on visibility and she allowed the driver to slow down. The wind had to be out of the southwest, she thought, but then they came to a section of highway where splintered pines had fallen into a gaping crater. One of the American shells must have been errant, which wasn't surprising with artillery.

But there was no driving around it. Thick woods on either side of the highway blocked them, so the general had no choice but to get out and walk, accompanied by two guards and two of her lieutenants. The smoke had an odd, acrid taste and smell. Wood, yes, she could distinctly smell burned wood and pine resin. And dust; fine particles of the powdery soil mixed with the smoke and hung in the air, stirred only by light breezes. But there was another odor, too, something Gollins knew all too well... charred meat. Once you knew what burning human flesh smelled like, you never forgot it.

That was to be expected and truthfully, the thought of the defenders roasting to death made her smile. Then one of her men staggered through the smoke toward her, both arms missing below the elbow and the stumps nothing more than raw and blackened meat. His eyes stared at something no one else could see.

Her lieutenants shied away from the man, as if he carried a curse, but not Gollins. She couldn't have cared less about his grievous wounds; she needed information, because she had a nauseous suspicion that the man hadn't been wounded by accident.

"Soldier of Allah, what happened?"

He only kept shuffling down the highway in silence.

A second man stumbled toward them, dazed but not obviously wounded. He recognized his commander right away, which wasn't hard given that she was the only woman on their side of the front lines. "Whistling..." he said. "We heard... whistling and then explosions... big... Junaid and Kashif were in a trench next to me. No more than fifty feet away." The man's rapid blinking and wide-eyed, questioning stare told Gollins more about the severity of the bombardment than his words. "After it ended they were... they were gone. Not dead, just... gone. Where did they go, General? Where are my friends?"

"What's your name?" she said. There was nothing comforting about her tone, because Gollins saw her soldiers as tools to be used. If a man was wounded or broken, she had no more need of him. She allowed medical teams to keep up the façade that she cared about them, and she did *that* only to keep up morale.

"Owais Abdelnour."

"Soldier Abdelnour, why do you blaspheme our beloved New Prophet?"

Her lieutenants stiffened when she said that, and the two guards turned so their rifles pointed in his direction. Abdelnour blinked twice, and Gollins watched sanity return to his eyes. In her experience, threats usually had that effect.

"I don't understand, General. I love our New Prophet with all of my heart, all blessings be upon him."

Since childhood, Gollins had instinctively paid attention to her surroundings. As the illegitimate daughter of the emir, who could never publicly acknowledge her, and being a female in the repressive Caliphate, knowing what happened around her had kept her alive in a world where the lives of women counted for little. Now Gollins saw the men watching from outside their circle, some in the trees, others on the highway. She sensed that her troops were on the verge of panic and word would spread quickly of what happened here.

"If your words are true, Soldier Abdelnour," she said in a menacing tone. She raised her voice so others could hear. "If you truly love Allah's chosen New Prophet, then why do you doubt that your friends are in heaven at this very moment, enjoying the rewards of serving Allah?"

"I— I... I'm sorry, my General, I meant no—"

"What is your regiment?"

"Ayyub Regiment."

"By leaving your post, you have betrayed your regiment. I give you this one chance to redeem yourself, Soldier Abdelnour. Go back and perform your duty, and seek a glorious death in battle. You may still find the glory of heaven."

Abdelnour bowed his head, turned, and ran back to his unit. He lurched from side to side, unsteady on his feet, but Gollins couldn't have cared less. Her words had had their desired effect on all of the others listening to the exchange, and word would spread quickly to the rest of her army, that they would either triumph or die. It was brutal leadership; she knew that was true. She also knew that it had worked for many others over the centuries, including Josef Stalin, as she'd learned from a book she'd read about World War Two in Russia.

After ordering one of her lieutenants to clear the highway and fill in the crater, she went forward on foot to inspect the damage and see how many men remained on their feet, and how many would never stand again. More craters and splintered trees blocked Highway 4, but as she faced south toward the front lines, Gollins saw that the road hadn't been the main target. Only overshots had landed that far north.

Flames licked through a smoke cloud that partially obscured a belt of smashed and burning trees. Traversing the rolling and mountainous terrain was difficult enough in normal circumstances. Now it seemed almost impossible.

"General," said one of her lieutenants. He held out a radio handset to her, trying hard to mask his distaste at treating a female as his superior. "The emir wishes to speak with you."

She squinted, trying to remember the man's name. Sohail Mohammad? He'd been with her for months now, but Gollins never cared much about those beneath her.

"This is General Gollins, Blessed One. How may I serve you?"

By the way he replied, she knew he was alone. "You've got to attack, Tracy, right now, with everything you've got. The Americans fucked us over."

"Yes, Blessed One, I am walking through the evidence of their treachery."

"Here's the deal. Sati is attacking them right now using the Life Guards. He thinks he can defeat them, but I'm not so sure. They've got tanks, Bradleys, and artillery. But you've got a small window where they're too busy defending themselves to fire at you, so you've got to take advantage. Can you do it?"

"Is there no alternative?"

"No. If we withdraw, they might catch us on the road and that'd be the end. We'd lose the whole army."

"Very well then, Blessed One, you may rely on me and my regiments." She habitually wore a scowl, which deepened now into a frown. They had continued walking south through the debris of the artillery barrage, climbing over fallen trees and avoiding red smears that might once have been human. Survivors dug to free trapped comrades. Turning to the man with the radio, she was pretty sure his name was Lieutenant Mohammad, she started issuing orders. "Radio the commanders of Mecca and Rasūl Regiments to attack at once down Highway 4, using all available assets, including the tank. Do you understand? Make it clear that they *must* break into Shangri-La regardless of the cost."

"Yes, General," the man said, and stepped away to use the radio.

"You," she said, pointing at another man standing beside her. Hashir something. "Find Major Ozid. Tell him to rally Ayyub Regiment and attack south without delay. Make it clear that I don't care how difficult this may be, or how many men he has. Do you understand my order?"

The man nodded.

"Go. And may Allah be with you."

What a fucked-up deal this is, she thought. What she really wanted was a drink.

U.S. Encampment, west of Albuquerque

The first mortar round hit less than one hundred feet from where Colonel Mwangi stood beside an Army specialist, who held a rifle pointed in her direction. Major Ahmadi had ordered her arrest and told the E-4 to hold her, but he hadn't said what to do next before incoming mortar rounds sent everyone scrambling for cover. The past few minutes had changed her entire life, and now she might get killed before even learning what the hell had happened.

Her guard licked his lips and glanced around, making it obvious that he didn't like standing in a shooting gallery any more than she did. After 24 years in the Army, this was the first time she'd ever been under enemy fire, and it overwhelmed her senses. Aside from the visual, she'd never realized how *loud* combat was, or the vibrations of cannon firing and vehicles moving in the ground underfoot, or even the smell of gunpowder and rocket fuel. For the very first time in her career, Mwangi realized that she had no idea what it was really like to be a combat soldier.

Standing in the middle of such pandemonium, she wanted to scurry into the nearest Bradley and curl into the fetal position. But she did something entirely different.

"Go find Major Ahmadi," she said to the specialist. "Tell him I want to fight."

#

Chapter 44

"At the first scent of blood, I forget all else except killing the man before me, and when the battle is ended, I pray that it were not."
Centurion Venitus Derri

The desert west of Albuquerque, New Mexico
1512 hours, May 5

The local radio net was like a crowded bar on Saturday night, with everybody calling out at the same time.

"Bedlam Black Six, I've got Ali Babas at one-nine-five degrees true, range nine-four-zero, engaging with twenty-fives."

"Watch out, they're working their way through that little gulley."

"Apache Red One Three, I don't have eyes, repeat, I do not have eyes. Over."

"That's one helluva lot of Jimbangs."

"Badass Six, fire support mission urgently requested, two-two-three degrees true."

They kept coming like that, but it was the fire support mission that got his attention. Two hundred twenty-three degrees was nearly behind them. He'd buttoned up the BCV when mortar rounds had started hitting their position. Using the vehicles periscopes, however, he couldn't get enough elevation to see behind them to the southwest and west.

"Badass Six to all units, does anyone have a visual on enemy moving into our rear, over?"

Several seconds passed with only the sounds of battle outside the hull. A mortar round exploded close aboard, and they all heard the *ting* of metal splinters bouncing off the BCV's armor. Meanwhile, Ahmadi plotted some of the requested fire missions, but someone called him before he could issue the orders.

"Badass Six, this is Badass Red One Eight. Large force of enemy infantry moving toward the highway at our rear, range one-four-zero-zero, over."

"Badass Red One Eight, any sign of armor? Over."

"Negative, Badass Six, no... hold." Two seconds of silence left Ahmadi's heart beating hard and fast. "Correction, Badass Six. One AFV, possible tank, over."

"What is your ammunition status, Badass Red One Eight?"

"Forty-five percent."

"Any tubes hot, Badass Red One Eight? Over."

"Roger that, Badass Six, half load. M26A2."

"Coordinate with Badass Red One Seven, put two full loads up their ass. Do you copy, Badass Red One Eight?"

"Roger that, Badass Six. Hamburger's on the menu, over."

"Keep me advised. Badass Six out."

"Badass Six to Stinger Six, over."

"Stinger Six copy."

"Possible enemy armor at our rear. I need a section to secure that flank and keep open possible withdrawal route, over."

"With pleasure, Badass Six! Over."

"Badass Six out."

Despite the heat inside the BCV, his second-by-second command responsibilities, and thousands of an enemy who wanted to kill them, Ahmadi grinned. Telling a tank commander an enemy tank was out there for the killing was like throwing red meat to a tiger.

Sati Bashara had learned much from his ignominious defeat the year before. Then, they had tried to overwhelm the superior American firepower with sheer numbers, and had been slaughtered in the process. Now, he used a different plan, and watched the battle unfold exactly as he'd envisioned it. He'd lured the Americans into thinking the Sword of the Prophet would use the same tactics as last year, and as General Muhdin had used again this year, with the same result: failure.

Bashara knew his infantry had no chance in a direct assault against the American tanks and Bradleys, not to mention their rocket launchers and dug-in infantry. He'd ordered them to advance en masse again, only this time they were ordered to take advantage of the terrain and not expose themselves unnecessarily. Only when the Sword of the Prophet's rocket barrage hit were they to rise up and charge, and hopefully by then they would be close enough to get among the Americans before the effect of the homemade rockets wore off.

Those infantry assaults would hit the Americans on three sides, supported by the four 120mm mortars. But all of that was to distract them from his picked force of 1,000 men and all vehicles, the three M1s, two Bradleys including his, and a handful of pickups with machine guns mounted in the bed, all of which would then race north to cut the American retreat route to the west. As this force moved out, he would fire all of the Qassam rockets. The dangerous homemade devices were as likely to blow up on their launcher as to fly safely, and were guaranteed to hit anything except their target. But 80 of them fired, all at once, were bound to hit something. If nothing else, they would act like a smoke screen to block the Americans from seeing the blocking force's advance.

The Bradleys sped across the desert, leaving a wake of dust, with both M1s close behind. The pickups came next, their drivers and gunners breathing through cloths tied tight around their noses and mouths. Last came the infantry, but Bashara made them advance in groups of 100 men, leaving 300 yards between each group. They would take a long time getting to the highway, but recklessness would lead to defeat and it was much safer that way.

A deep but narrow ditch on the shoulder of old Interstate 40 caused the Bradley to bounce hard, nearly throwing Bashara and the driver out of their hatches. Gunning the engine, the driver pushed it past the ditch and onto the roadbed. A light wind dissipated the dust cloud that boiled up from all of the vehicles following him up on to the Interstate.

"Radio to fire the rockets," he called down into the vehicle, since the intercom didn't work. Focusing his binoculars, he spotted a flash from the American position three miles to the east. He'd seen the same thing earlier and knew it meant rockets launching. Turning, he waved at the other vehicle commanders to close their hatches, shouting as he did so. Then he and the driver dropped down and closed theirs. There was nothing to do now but wait.

It only took a few seconds. Multiple explosions ripped the desert simultaneously, followed by so many smaller ones that Bashara knew they numbered in the hundreds, if not thousands. But they were muffled, which confused him until he realized they hadn't struck his position; they'd hit further south.

The infantry.

Opening the hatch, he stood and scanned back the way he'd come. A huge pall of smoke and dust rose into the air like a mushroom cloud. The strike had impacted about a quarter mile to his south, and he knew right away that nobody could have survived such an inferno. And if the Americans fired again, shifting to aim at him...

Where are our rockets?

Powered by cane sugar and fertilizer, the Qassam rockets left an unmistakable smoke trail. Then, as if Allah himself answered Bashara's unspoken question, dozens of such smoke trails rose into the sky four miles to the south. Like arrows loosed on an ancient battlefield, they rose in one large grouping, hit the apex of their climb, and then plunged back down again. The rockets appeared as nothing more than dots at the end of a contrail. He followed their rise and fall and grinned as the flashes of explosions rippled across the American position.

He waved the two Abrams forward to block the interstate as the Bradleys pulled off onto the shoulder. This way, the first thing that any fleeing Americans would encounter was one of their own tanks. Bashara could feel the hand of Allah in such irony.

American position west of Albuquerque

Major Ahmadi watched with satisfaction as his salvo of rockets hit their target. Without eyes overhead, he couldn't tell what damage had been done, but nothing within half a klick of the impact could have survived. But yet another dust cloud led to the interstate directly to his west a few miles, which meant they'd struck the middle of the enemy column, not the head.

"Badass Red One Eight, this is Badass Six. New target due west, range three—"

"Incoming!" warned a voice on the radio net. "Bearing two-two-five true. Appear to be numerous rockets."

"Button up!" Ahmadi ordered as he dropped into his own hull and dogged the hatch after him. The driver had never re-opened his.

So many rockets detonated within seconds of each other that Ahmadi couldn't distinguish between them. It was like a MOAB going off in their midst. And at least one scored a direct hit on the BCV.

The sight of the specialist being vaporized by a mortar round left Amunet Mwangi stunned into inaction. Never in her entire career had she seen someone die, and her brain couldn't process how a man could be alive and running one second, and then gone the next. Not just dead — blown into a million pieces. The only thing left to bury was a boot with the foot and half the shin still in it.

Somewhere she heard the cry of "Incoming!" and glanced up. The trails of incoming rockets crossed the sky. For whatever reason that snapped her back to reality, and she ran for the nearest cover she could find, an M270 that had just launched a pod of rockets. It was the southernmost of four MLRSs lined up in the second row of the battery. None of its hatches was open, and there wasn't time to bang on the hull. Inhaling the fumes of burned fuel, she dropped to her knees and rolled under the machine.

As Sati Bashara watched the rockets hitting the Americans, he couldn't make out any details aside from the yellow and orange explosions amid an obscuring cloud. Then he saw a much, much larger blast come from something nearer his own position. More secondary explosions made it clear they'd either hit an ammunition vehicle, or the onboard rounds of an American vehicle were cooking off. Either way, it was glorious to see.

Being in combat had been a terrible idea, the stupidest thing she'd ever done, and if Amunet Mwangi survived, she vowed never to volunteer to be shot at again. Ground vibrations ran up her spine as Mwangi stared at the underside of the M270. Hands splayed to either side, her fingers dug into dirt as she held her eyes tightly shut. Terror brought prayers to her lips that she hadn't thought of in thirty years.

"You're gonna be fine, Amy, you're gonna be fine," she said, the words coming out one on top of another. "You're under an armored vehicle, they're armored to keep people safe during battles, you're safe, you're gonna be fine, please, God, keep me safe." She kept talking as explosions rocked the area all around the M270, never daring to even crack her eyes open. As long as she kept praying, everything would be fine, it just would be, it *had* to be. Other people died, not her.

Closing her eyes didn't block out the whistling made by incoming rockets, though, and her subconscious kept track of them without Mwangi knowing it. So when one sounded louder and shriller than the others, her brain alerted her conscious mind. It only lasted a few seconds before Mwangi realized it was going to hit the armored vehicle eight inches above her nose.

"No, oh, God, no, no, no, no, no, no, no—"

Her brain processed the rocket hitting above her, driving the M270 downward into her chest, but the shock absorbers kept it from crushing her. Her eyes opened involuntarily, to see flames whooshing down either side and scorching her hands. She opened her mouth to scream in agony, but never got the chance before the stored rockets in the vehicle overhead detonated. A massive blast lifted the 28-ton vehicle six feet in the air, vaporizing Mwangi and burying her when the wreckage slammed back to Earth.

A blast wave rocked Ahmadi's BCV like a child playing with a toy, slamming his head into the hull to his left. Helmet or not, it hurt. "Damage?" he said into the intercom.

"Fire control is down, Major. Checking other systems now."

He switched to the battery net. "This is Badass Six. Damage report."

One of the M1A2 Abrams had taken a hit on its gun mantlet, dismounting the barrel of its 120mm gun and rendering it useless until fixed. Another had damage to a sprocket which limited its speed and maneuverability, while a Bradley got a jammed turret. Most of the infantry came through okay, except for a fifty-caliber machine gun position that took a direct hit. None of the four men manning it came through alive, or even in one piece.

When none of his battery reported, Ahmadi called them.

"Badass Six, this is Badass Red One Four." The voice quavered just a little. "Badass Red One Eight took a hit and... I don't know what happened, Major, but Red One Eight blew up. The rocket must have set off their ready ammunition. There's not much left. Badass Red One Seven is on its side, casualties unknown."

Damn, damn, damn! Where had all those fucking rockets come from?

There was no time to worry about the what or where, though. Ahmadi had no idea whether they had more, and if his people stayed here they were sitting ducks. But if they didn't, the Sevens could concentrate everything on the Marines at Shangri-La. "Badass Six to Stinger Six, any word on that section you sent to clear the road, over?"

"Stinger Green One Two and One Three are on their way, Badass Six, over."

"Prepare to cover the withdrawal of the battery, Stinger Six, using all assets. Report to me when you're in position. Badass Six out."

Before he could even take a breath, more warnings crackled over the net.

"Enemy infantry three hundred yards to my front and closing."

"Radio discipline!"

"Taking heavy fire on the right."

"Shit, where'd they all come from?"

"Urgently request artillery support!"

Ahmadi once again opened the hatch and stood up. He started to lift the binoculars to his eyes, but didn't need them now. Across the whole front from northeast to southwest, large clumps of Sevens charged forward, using shallow depressions to hide whenever American fire caught them in the open. The infantry, entrenched in an arc, took a toll as white-robed men tumbled or were knocked backward by American bullets, but there were too many. Then Ahmadi saw what he most dreaded, the faint smoke trail of an RPG rocket. The first one missed an M1A2 moving out on the left and exploded harmlessly in the dirt, but where there was one, there had to be many more.

#

Chapter 45

> "When you surround an army, leave an outlet free. Do not press a desperate foe too hard."
> Sun Tzu

Albuquerque, New Mexico
1608 hours, May 5

"Could this be a little premature?" the old man said.

The emir of New Khorasan eyed him and went back to throwing his clothes in an old hard-sided suitcase. "Let's hope so, but I'd rather have plenty of time to unpack again instead of running out of here with the Americans on my ass."

"You're such an optimist."

"I'm a realist. I don't know what the hell happened with the Americans, whether it was a trick the whole time or something changed, but packing up eighty trucks and cars takes time. I gain nothing by taking a chance."

Running feet in the hallway outside the den alerted them that someone was coming. A young man from el Mofty's headquarters dashed into the room, eyes bright and face grinning. "General Bashara says the Americans are surrounded on the highway and the rockets hit them hard. He expects victory soon, o Blessed One!"

At sight of the man, el Mofty had automatically lapsed into his regal emir persona. The tone of his voice and his word selection shifted into the formal diction of the number two man in the Caliphate. "Thank you, and please relay to General Bashara that we are deep in prayer for his success."

The man nodded and ran back out. El Mofty turned back to packing.

"Your confidence is inspirational," the old man said.

On Interstate 40, west of the American battery position

Stinger Green One Two rolled over the pitted surface of the old roadbed without a problem. The tank's commander, Platoon Sergeant Emerald Tuckahoe, could barely sit still. Adrenaline pumped through his veins and filled his entire body, knowing that within minutes he might be shooting at a real enemy tank. Even if it was another Abrams, it was in the hands of the bad guys and he was authorized to kill it. That was enough to give any tanker a hard-on.

Being inside an Abrams when the main gun fired was beautiful because, less than two feet from his head, an explosion would occur that could rock the huge 68-ton tank like a dog shaking a toy. If they didn't brake the sprockets when the 120mm main gun fired, it shoved the whole tank backward.

This was a once in a lifetime opportunity and Tuckahoe intended to have his head outside the hatch when the gun fired. The shock wave from the blast went out in a spherical pattern and vibrated your teeth. It flattened your hair and eyebrows. It was awesome.

The tank's electric whine drowned out most other sounds. A vagrant wind kicked dust up over the highway. As it drifted off, he saw sunlight glint off something in the road ahead.

"Targets in sight," the gunner called out, "zero-zero-four degrees relative."

"Exacto round," Tuckahoe said. He saw the gunner tilt his head. It was slight but noticeable. They only had three Exacto rounds, and once they were gone, they were gone.

Taking a shell from its storage rack, Tuckahoe pushed it into the barrel and sealed the breech. A different-pitched whine came in on top of the first one as Tuckahoe stood up in his hatch. He barely had time to focus down the road before the gunner fired. The glowing shell raced downrange, corrected a few degrees left, and smashed into the first enemy tank with a gout of flame and boiling smoke. Best yet, there was a second enemy tank behind that one.

Training took over before it struck and Tuckahoe ordered a second Exacto round, which left the tube four seconds after the first. This time he watched the streak of light and had enough time to wonder at the second shell that passed it going the other way, and then the top of his body exploded as shrapnel ripped it apart.

Sati Bashara's Bradley idled on the roadside fifty feet to the right of the nearest Abrams, but even there the blast wave when both tanks fired felt like getting slapped in the head. Microseconds after flames shot out the ends of their barrels, both tanks flared and blew up.

"Reverse! Reverse!" he screamed at the driver, who immediately shifted gears. The Bradley lurched backward as ammunition detonated inside the closest tank, which led to a huge blast that sent the turret spinning sideways. It hit the desert and rolled over the spot the Bradley had just occupied.

All three M1s sent boiling black clouds into the sky as flaming fuel surrounded the hulks. Bashara's Bradley stopped forty yards to the west. The *crack* of machine gun ammunition cooking off sent the nearby infantry diving for cover. The other Bradley was still operational, which was good news, and one of his tanks had gotten off a shot before being destroyed. Maybe they'd stopped the Americans long enough for the infantry to get there with their RPGs. Between them, the Bradleys, and the pickups, they might yet trap the Americans.

"Say again, Stinger Six," Major Ahmadi said. Even inside the BCV, the noise level made communication nearly impossible.

"Engaged enemy armor. Stinger Green One Two is out of action. Stinger Green One Three reports both enemies destroyed. I am advancing with the rest of my command, over."

"Copy, Stinger Six, good hunting, over."

"Stinger Six out."

Using periscopes, he inspected the combat zone. Still forms clad in white littered the desert beyond their firing line, but two of his Bradleys were on fire and a third damaged. Desultory mortar fire still hit the area. The Sevens had lost a lot of men while advancing to within one hundred yards of their position. It was time to withdraw. Or maybe past time to withdraw.

Six American tanks stood off at 1,000 yards and fired explosive rounds as Sati Bashara's men tried to dig in, and with his own tanks destroyed he couldn't shoot back. One of the pickups had taken a direct hit and cartwheeled backward, blowing up and leaving a trail of fire in the dirt. After that he'd ordered all surviving vehicles, including his own, to retreat behind a low ridge that intersected the interstate from the south, about 80 yards west of the blocking position.

They had taken refuge on the western side of the ridge, near the cut made the by the highway as it moved east–west. The rest of his forces fought the Americans east of the ridge, as they tried to use that highway to flee the area, but the trap had been sprung and now they had the infidels surrounded. Now they had to find a way to destroy them.

Without radios for all his units, Bashara couldn't direct a battle he couldn't see. Only after climbing 300 feet to the top did he get his first look at the damage caused by the initial American rocket strike. Scores of white-robed bodies lay in a blackened area hundreds of yards long and at least half as much wide. At such a distance he couldn't count the numbers, but it looked like at least 200 men. Seeing the carnage, his uncle's warning came back to him — if they fought this battle and lost, they might lose everything. Having taken and inflicted heavy losses, there was no backing out now. If they tried to withdraw, the Americans would chew them up. It had now become a fight to the death.

By now most of his infantry had come up and dug shallow trenches or rifle pits on either side of the interstate. At his direction, they formed three lines of defense back to the ridge. He'd kept 20 men armed with RPGs with the pickup trucks as a rapid deployment force. There was nothing more Bashara could do now, except wait.

He didn't wait for long.

The dull *thunk* of bullets bouncing off the Bradley kept Major Ahmadi buttoned up during the withdrawal. Once he'd issued the general order to pull out, there wasn't much he could do to control the battle. The support system for the advanced electronics which gave the BCV its reason for existing had vanished along with the country that put them in place. Not that it mattered all that much; he was an artillery officer, not an infantry one. Ground fighting tactics weren't his strong suit.

He had only a brief moment to consider the situation and plan the fighting retreat. The Sevens had chosen their blocking position well. Going around their line of entrenchments wasn't realistic, since ridges on either side limited their room for maneuver.

The six surviving tanks formed a firing line to blast a way through the Sevens' road block, although only five had a functioning main gun. The two wrecked Abrams blocked part of the interstate, and even in their ruined state, enough remained intact to make it impossible for the American tanks to shove them out of the way. There was room to drive around them, but with deep ditches on either side of the road, the Bradleys and M270s would have to slow down, which made them vulnerable to RPG fire. That job required infantry, to clean out the enemy one rifle pit at a time, except he only had less than two companies, and one had to act as rear guard.

Worse, the Abrams reported having only a few M908 HE obstacle reduction rounds left. Each had three canister rounds, but those didn't work against entrenched targets, and the rest of their ammo loads were armor piercing. Stinger Six told him they had access to AMP rounds, which could have been set for airburst over the open trenches, but since they were in very limited numbers, General Steeple had nixed their use. So as Ahmadi visualized the battle in his mind, he realized that his command was becoming something the Germans called a *kessel*, a pocket of troops moving through enemy territory. It other words, they were surrounded.

The sound of steps crunching up the slope behind him alerted Sati Bashara and the radioman beside him of a third person joining them. Keeping the binoculars in place, he only turned his head.

"Haleem! What are you doing here? I thought you were aiding General Gollins."

"She believed me to be a spy and sent me away, so I sought you out. That was easier said than done."

"You have come at just the right time, my friend! We have the Americans trapped."

Bashara's best friend smiled and nodded. "It is a day of glory!"

"Indeed it is. How goes the battle against the stronghold of the infidels?"

Haleem's good humor faded. "It is a hard fight. I was close enough to our southern forces, those of General Muhdin, to observe the American rockets hitting our lines. Our losses must have been terrible. I asked your uncle where you might be and he sent me here. When I asked about the fighting at the place called Shangri-La, he said it was very difficult."

"Once we crush them here, we can help our brothers finish off their stronghold." Lowering the binoculars, he pointed into the distance. "They cannot get around us here; they have no choice except to fight. Our men to the east are herding them into our trap here. We have many RPGs left, and two dozen of Allah's Chosen."

"They are praiseworthy men," Haleem said.

"They are destined for paradise. If we can hold this place, we will win, and we *will* hold here." Even as they watched, Bashara became aware that something had changed. It took half a minute for him to realize what. "Their tanks have stopped firing. That was my only concern, that they could stand off long enough to open a hole they could escape through, but now they have stopped firing. It can only mean they are out of ammunition. If that is true, then we can expect their infantry soon." Bracing his friend's shoulders, he looked Haleem in the eyes when he spoke. "Carry a message to Captain Nusallah, if he still lives, to expect the enemy assault very soon. Tell him the eyes of our beloved New Prophet are upon him. It is dangerous, Haleem, but I trust Allah to keep you safe. Will you do this thing for me?"

Haleem nodded, but couldn't hide his fear. "I will, Sati. Please pray for me."

"You know that I will."

Watching his closest friend descend the ridge's reverse slope, Bashara never expected to see Haleem alive again. He'd always known the time might come when he would have to sacrifice his friend for the greater good of the Caliphate, and he had dreaded that moment, but now that it had come he felt nothing. Haleem was just another tool for him to use on his climb to replacing his uncle as the emir of New Khorasan, and one day, his other uncle as caliph.

#

Chapter 46

"Nobody kills me and lives to tell about it."
Lt. General Nathan Bedford Forrest

The desert west of Albuquerque, New Mexico
1649 hours, May 5

There were too many Sevens. Major Ahmadi tried to form a laager to hold back the pursuing enemy infantry long enough for the M270s to reload. If they could do that, then the barrage from 84 rockets would not only blast a hole through the road block ahead, it would likely annihilate anyone within a mile of the center aiming point. The whole task force could drive through unhindered.

But they couldn't buy enough time. One M270 that tried to reload wound up with two wounded crewmen for their efforts. A Bradley trying to cover them took an RPG round dead center on its right side, and only survived because it was a dud, and another rocket barely missed the ammo truck.

The radio was alive with commanders wanting orders, fire support requests, and calls of damage or enemy positions. It was overwhelming.

"Stinger Six, this is Badass Six. Provide close support to infantry on the way to your position, over."

"Badass Six, I have enemy closing on my position now. I have already had RPG rounds fired in my direction. If I move forward, more casualties are likely. Over."

"Stinger Six, copy that, but pressure on our rear is—"Ahmadi felt a nudge on his right arm. "Hold, Stinger Six."

Moving his helmet to uncover his ear, he leaned close to the radioman, who shouted into his ear.

"Incoming message from T-Bolt One on tac three, Major."

Screwing up his face, he indicated for the radioman to turn his head so Ahmadi could answer him. "Who the hell is T-Bolt One?"

"No idea, sir."

"Patch me in." Ahmadi waited a few seconds until the radioman pointed at him to speak. "Badass Six for T-Bolt One, do you copy? Over."

"This is T-Bolt One, Badass Six. Need target assignment, am approaching from two-niner-four degrees true, over."

"T-Bolt One, who or what are you? Over."

"Badass Six, I am a Fairchild Republic A-10 Thunderbolt Two, with a full load of bad news for whoever you tell me to dump it on, over."

Even using his binoculars, Haleem appeared tiny to Sati Bashara as his friend ran from one rifle pit or trench to another. Using the shattered tanks on Interstate 40 as cover, Haleem crossed the wide highway at a dead run, but seemed to stumble as he approached a hole on the other side. Bashara zoomed in, expecting him to get to his feet, or at least to crawl toward safety. Instead he lay still. Bashara knew right away that his childhood friend was dead, but he felt nothing. Haleem had been with him during a time when Bashara needed him, and now that he was no longer needed, Allah had called him to paradise. In truth, Haleem was a lucky man to die in battle.

Re-focusing on the Americans, he thought they seemed less distinct than they had a moment ago. The smoke pall hanging over the battlefield hadn't grown thicker, if anything it had lessened, so what happened? A dozen Bradleys had moved within 500 yards of his forward line, and some of his men had gotten close with RPGs. The trap was set... had his men pushing them from behind faltered? This was when having no communication with his various units crippled his ability to conduct the battle.

The radioman beside him then did something he had never done before, namely, speak directly to Bashara without being spoken to first. "My General, look!"

He pointed to the western sky, and Bashara assumed that it would be an American helicopter. After all, if they'd betrayed the Sevens with their rockets, why not also with their helicopters? That was why he'd brought the only case of Stingers in the army with him to this place.

Shading his eyes, Bashara was about to warn the man never again to speak to him first, when he noticed something strange about the aircraft. As he watched, it grew large much faster than a helicopter. It took a moment find it in his binoculars, but when he did his heart raced and his hands shook. Wings protruded to either side, and two round things seemed affixed to the upper fuselage. And smoke streamed back from something under its nose... he opened his mouth to scream a warning to the vehicles parked below, but it was too late.

The instant Babb heard Badass Six give him targeting data, the veteran pilot slipped back into that state of automatic response only possible after hundreds and hundreds of hours in the cockpit. Finding the enemy only required flying east above Interstate 40 and looking for smoke and wreckage. Eight miles out, he spotted the pillar of smoke and throttled back to 250 knots. Dropping to 900 feet AGL, above ground level, to drop his dumb bombs would require flying through ridgelines on either side that could be problematic if anybody had shoulder-fired SAMs. And at that speed and distance, he couldn't see individuals on the ridge. But what was that at the base?

From six miles out, he visually acquired a new target, a group of parked vehicles ten degrees right of center in his electronic gunsight. The GAU-8 Avenger 30mm gun didn't have armor-piercing rounds loaded, but for anything short of tanks that shouldn't matter, and he didn't see any tanks. Maybe some Bradleys, though. "Badass Six, this is T-Bolt One. Do you have assets behind a ridge? Urgent, over."

The response was immediate. "Negative, T-Bolt One."

"Out."

At three miles, his right thumb moved over the red firing button on the left side of the joystick. The range clicked down in the gunsight, until at 3,000 yards he sent a one-second burst downrange. Rate of fire had been set to 2,400 rounds per minute, so 40 rounds of HEI raced toward the unsuspecting Sevens. Without conscious thought, he shifted right and fired again, and then twice more. As he sent the last rounds downrange, the first ones had already ravaged their target. Smoke and dust billowed up amid dozens of explosions. Babb banked the Warthog right to circle back for a second run.

"No!"

From the crest of the ridge, Bashara watched in horror as scores of cannon shells ripped into his carefully hoarded vehicles. Fuel tanks blew up and ammunition detonated. Ones that hadn't been hit caught fire from those that had. A man ran out of the raging fire and flung himself to the ground, rolling in the dirt to extinguish the flames. Within thirty seconds, everything was lost.

"Shouldn't we go help?" the radioman said.

Bashara wanted to slap him, but instead grabbed the radio and shoved him away. "You'd rather be down there with them? Go on, then, go be with your friends!"

The strange-looking airplane banked and circled, lining up for another attack. Bashara wished he had a Stinger, just one Stinger, to make the American pay for ruining his victory. Because he had no doubt the battle was now lost, despite his brilliant planning.

The Bradleys had had a few TOW missiles left, but they couldn't slug it out on the battlefield with main battle tanks and they were aflame now, in any case. But when the Americans got close enough for the infantry to engage them with RPGs, then he would launch his counterattack. The hated infidels would be caught between all of his forces and crushed. But then the aircraft banked around for another pass, and it was all lost.

Rocketing straight down the interstate, the aircraft ignored the vehicles this time. It flew through the smoke cloud and raced by the ridge where Bashara stood. Inevitably, it dropped bombs all over his dug-in troops, but the young general didn't stay to watch. Picking his way down the reverse slope, Bashara went to find a vehicle that still worked. The window of escape would close very soon.

Only after he'd dropped and fired off the last of his ordnance, and turned for home, did Captain Babb allow the images of his attack runs to play in his mind. All had gone off better than the best training runs he'd ever made, and without a doubt he'd killed a lot of bad guys. Exactly who they were, and why there were America's enemies, was still fuzzy, but in the end it didn't matter. They preyed on the weak and that was all he needed to know.

Outside Counselor, New Mexico

April Jones paced back and forth, arms crossed, her brown eyes nearly shut from her frown. She wasn't tall, and sometimes her helmet seemed too loose on her head, no matter how much she tightened the strap. Nor was she a typical Marine company commander; instead of some fierce nickname, behind her back they called her Easter Bunny. But it wasn't derogatory; it was a term of endearment, because none of her company doubted that when it came to a fight, she'd be leading from the front, like a Marine C.O. should.

"Anything from Kicker?" she asked her E.O., Lieutenant Marquita Tomas. They were well away from the LAV-C2, where they couldn't be overheard.

"Nothing. I think he's ignoring us, April."

"Why would he *do* that? It doesn't make any sense."

"He doesn't want to get you in trouble."

Jones shook her head. "That made sense when General Steeple was in command, but now that General Angriff is back... it doesn't make sense."

"What are we gonna do? We're just using up gas this way."

"I knew we should have kept going all the way to Shangri-La after the first battle. I *knew* it!"

"Except you were ordered not to. So what are your orders now? Do you want to stand the company down until we have definite orders?"

Staring into the distance, Jones didn't answer for nearly a minute. "No. Saddle up, we're Oscar Mike. We'll take Highway 550 to Cuba and pause there to gauge the situation, but if we haven't met opposition or see no signs of the enemy, we're moving immediately toward Shangri-La."

"I hope you know what you're doing, April."

"We're Marines, Marky. If fellow Marines are in a fight, then we are, too."

"Oorah, Captain."

The Warthog's second bomb run had dumped more ordnance on the dug-in positions to their front. Then, at Ahmadi's request, two strafing runs at the Sevens to his east had left a pile of broken bodies scattered over the desert. He needed no further encouragement to order the Bradleys forward to within 300 yards of the Sevens' road-block position, there to disgorge the infantry for an assault. The IFVs would provide close support, with the five operational Abrams using their last HEI rounds to subdue strong points.

Regardless of their casualties, the enemy still badly outnumbered his command, and he urged his men forward before the Sevens could recover from the shock of the bombing. He needn't have worried. Even the finest troops in the world might crack under such an attack, but regardless of their religious fervor, the Sevens weren't highly trained soldiers. By the time the Americans got into their positions, nearly everyone left alive had fled into the desert. One man, after playing dead, jumped to his feet and managed to fire an RPG even as bullets riddled his body. His aim was spoiled as his body twitched from the bullets, and the rocket hit a corporal standing next to a Bradley in the chest. It was a dud, but that didn't matter. The impact crushed the man's chest and killed him instantly.

Ahmadi's BCV arrived at the blocking position and he dismounted. Craters, rifle pits, and trenches turned the area into a moonscape. Visibility was still reduced, but he watched as riflemen poked each Seven to make sure they were dead. Several weren't, and then they were. He issued orders and waved vehicles past the position, grimacing as tracks and tires rolled over flesh and bone, turning it into a gruesome paste.

A recon patrol investigated thick smoke boiling up from behind a ridge several hundred yards to the west and reported no live enemies, just a score or more wrecked vehicles. Working fast, Major Ahmadi re-entered his BCV and directed that a defensive line be set up, one that he dared the Sevens regrouping to his east to try and break. The remainder of the two infantry companies occupied the Sevens' old positions, with the Bradley in close support, the tanks behind them, and the M270s well to the rear. Half an hour after being strafed, they came on again and were hit by full salvos from the seven M270s. Eighty-four M26 rockets dropped in excess of 5,000 M77 grenades over an area one mile long and a quarter mile wide. Nothing within the area survived.

Stinger Six, call sign for the commander of the two tank platoons, was a captain, and second in command of the task force. Ahmadi had removed his helmet to mop sweat from his face when the radioman indicated that Stinger Six was on the radio. Blowing out his breath, Ahmadi put his helmet back on and flipped down the mike.

"Badass Six, it's clear to the west. Do you wish to continue the withdrawal, sir? Over."

Ahmadi could think of a dozen reasons to say yes. Everybody was low on ammo, they'd been fighting for hours, losses were heavy… but there was one overriding reason not to retreat. He might not have been a combat infantry commander by trade or training, but that didn't matter now. The Marines at Shangri-La were still under attack, and his unit were the only reinforcements who could get there in time.

"Negative, Stinger Six. Organize a counterattack that will take us all the way to Shangri-La. Speed is a critical factor. When you give the signal, we'll let go another barrage and you punch a hole in whatever is left of the enemy to the east. We're not about to let those Marines grab all the glory. Badass Six, over."

"Yes, sir! Stinger Six out."

#

Chapter 47

> *"We're surrounded. That simplifies the problem."*
> Lt. General Lewis B. "Chesty" Puller, USMC

The desert west of Albuquerque, New Mexico
1721 hours, May 5

The Marines' LAVs formed a second line of defense to bring immediate fire on any Sevens that might break through, and to give the defenders of Shangri-La cover in case of a retreat. But they had to limit their fire to critical situations because of ammunition constraints. The LAV-LOGs were empty, except for a little bit of food and medical supplies. Captain Sully's LAV-25 only had half an ammo load left for the M242 25mm Bushmaster, and slightly more for the coaxial 7.62mm machine gun. The Bushmaster's loading system had two storage bins for ready-use 25mm ammo, one that held 150 rounds and the other 60 rounds. Both were full, but only 15 rounds were stowed elsewhere. The pindle-mounted 7.62mm machine gun, on top of the turret, still had over 600 rounds. Unfortunately, using it required exposure to enemy counterfire.

The vehicle's position on a low rise 350 yards behind the stone wall gave him a field of fire over most of the front, which interlocked with the other three LAVs of First Platoon. In the minutes after the rockets lit up the enemy positions, Sully had wondered if they might break. Such a saturation barrage typically shattered the courage of whoever survived, causing them to flee in terror. The Iraqis did, ISIS did, the Taliban usually did… but the Sevens did not. The Sevens regrouped, and came on with more ferocity than ever.

The focal point of their attacks remained the same as during the first fight, Highway 4 and the low stone wall. Mortar rounds came in clusters, but aim was poor and not all of the rounds exploded. Unless things grew worse, the defense would probably hold here, but he needed to know what was going on elsewhere.

"Field Goal Real, this is Kicker Real. Sitrep, over."

Onni Hakala's immediate response encouraged him. "Kicker Real, Field Goal Real responding with sitrep. SGL holding the gate under heavy pressure. Scouts report enemy attempting to flank on the west. Rainwater led a force up the ridge to hold the crest, over."

"What's your ammunition situation, Onni?"

"Forty percent on the M242, better on the MGs."

"Roger that, keep me informed. Kicker Real out."

Seconds later, a gigantic explosion blasted a hole in the stone wall, cutting down all defenders in a fifty-foot diameter and showering rocks for a hundred yards.

"What the hell?" said the LAV's gunner in his helmet's speaker.

"Maintain radio discipline," Sully said into the intercom. "Anybody see what happened?"

Nobody answered. Then Sevens began pouring through the gap and Sully had other things to worry about.

Abigail Deak had spent the previous night wondering what drove the Sevens to kill in the name of their god. Two years earlier, she had met a cousin from Texas named Istvan, who'd traveled north with his father on what they said was a hunting trip, although now she realized it had been a scouting mission. Istvan had grilled her about religion, and warned her that unless she accepted the New Prophet as the true messenger of Allah, she would die a terrible death.

As chief of the Jemez Pueblos, she understood the importance of God in the lives of her people, and had always assumed it was similar with the Sevens. But after meeting her cousin, she wasn't so sure. Within Walatoa, or Bear Village, the name they gave their chief community, the thought of forcing someone to change their religion or face death was insane. Because of the Spanish, most of her people were Catholic, but even those who clung to the old beliefs didn't try to convert anyone, much less by force. Even after all the fighting, it hadn't sunk it just how fanatical the Sevens were, until she saw three men clutching huge bundles running toward the wall. Two fell, but despite being hit by bullets, the third hurled himself atop the stones, and one second later an enormous detonation blasted a hole in the wall.

Deak didn't know she'd been hurt until someone helped her stand up. When she shook her head, she felt something run into her left eye and thought it was sweat. It wasn't; it was blood. Something stuck out of the meat on her left thigh, and she pulled out a long sliver of stone.

Someone tugged at her arm from behind. Squinting, she recognized Billy Two Trees.

"Chief Abigail, come on or they'll get you."

He led her away and rifle fire erupted all around them. Bullets threw dust into the air around their feet as they topped a three-foot rise. Billy Two Trees pushed her down behind it, but even as he dropped beside her, his body was knocked backward by automatic weapons fire. He fell, twisted, with his legs bent under his body and blood rapidly soaking his shirt.

The sight of his broken body roused her. Deak checked the pulse at his neck and didn't find one. Grabbing his rifle, an AK-47 he must have looted from a dead Seven, she lay prone and sited over the lip of the little rise. Forty yards away, Sevens poured through the gap and over the wall. Picking out a white-robed man with a blond beard who had one leg over the wall, she pulled the trigger. Pink mist sprayed into the air where the 5.45mm bullets ripped through his body. He rolled backward, off the wall, and she shifted to find another target. There were plenty to pick from.

The Bushmaster sounded like someone banging on a sheet of metal with a hammer. Three-round bursts sent high explosive incendiary-tracer (HEI-T) 25mm warheads into the mass of Sevens pushing through the breech in the stone wall. Five such bursts left a mess of red-spattered gore and torn white robes clogging the breakthrough point.

"Twenty-one rounds of HEI-T left, Captain," the gunner said, yelling to be heard.

Sully nodded. "I'm going up. Don't use the chain gun unless you have to."

Without waiting for a response, he unlocked the hatch and stood up. Without hesitation, he put the stock of the M240E1/G machine gun into his right shoulder and poured 7.62mm fire all along the wall and into the gap. Spent shells casings, from both his gun and the coaxial one fired by the gunner, clattered onto the exterior of the LAV's hull. Sully fired by reflex whenever a target appeared at the wall, but unknown to him, another breech had occurred further east. A firefight erupted to his extreme left when a group of defenders opened fire on approximately two dozen Sevens. Sully swung the machine gun to help suppress the latest threat just in time to see an RPG rocket streak toward his vehicle.

The lookout atop the ridge to the west of Highway 4 waved for Johnny Rainwater to hurry and reach the crest. Fifteen men followed Rainwater, including Mohammad Qadim, all armed with rifles. They also had four homemade hand grenades, which were nothing more than hand-thrown ceramic pots filled with scrap metal and gunpowder in two small chambers. A simple fuse was designed to give five seconds before detonating the powder, but it didn't always work out that way, and more than one man in the community had lost a hand, or an eye, or both.

Lying on his back a foot below the slope, the lookout started yelling at Rainwater from thirty feet away. "Must be hunnerts of 'em coming up that hill, Johnny! I tried to warn Shandoria but I think they got her. What're we gonna do, Johnny, what're we gonna do?"

Rainwater threw himself down beside the man and laid a hand on his shoulder. "We're going to fight, Montel. You hear me? This is our home, and we're not going to let those bastards hurt our families, are we?"

"No... hell, no!"

"All right, check your rifle and let me take a look."

"Let me do it, Johnny," Qadim said. He lay in the dirt on Rainwater's other side. "Shangri-La can't afford to lose you."

Before Rainwater could stop him, Qadim crawled to the top of the ridge and peered over. With a loud cry, he brought his rifle up just in time to shoot a Seven who stepped to the crest. The man toppled backward out of sight.

"Grenades! Grenades!" Qadim yelled.

The four men carrying them passed a glowing brand to a young boy, no older than fifteen, on the end. An older man next to him held the grenade out for the fuse to be lit, but the boy's hand shook so badly he couldn't touch the fuse at first. After a reassuring word from the older man, he lit the fuse and the grenade arched over the crest. Two seconds later they heard a loud *bang* and then screaming. A second grenade followed the first, but the third one's fuse burned too fast. Realizing he couldn't get rid of it before it detonated, the older man clutched it to his chest to muffle the explosion. It worked.

The blast knocked him backward from a sitting position. Rainwater turned at the explosion, and was close enough to see that, for a few awful seconds, life remained in the man's eyes. Then they glazed over. Horrified, the boy stared, entranced, at the red gore that had been the dead man's torso.

"Brian, get down!" Rainwater yelled, but too late. A bullet struck the boy in the forehead and knocked him over. He rolled all the way to the bottom of the hill. The Seven who'd shot him leaned over the crest and aimed at a new target, until Rainwater puts two rounds into his throat. More Sevens topped the hill, only now they'd been alerted that opposition awaited them on the reverse slope. Rainwater knelt on one knee and looked for targets.

The man with the last grenade grabbed the burning stick, lit his fuse, and lobbed it just over the top. The blast was close enough for a few metal shards to rain on them.

Rainwater realized this was a battle for the crest of the ridge and that whoever controlled it could fire down the other side at the enemy below. If the Sevens controlled it, they could bring enough fire on the gate defenders and others on the wall to make it indefensible. So he had to keep them from seizing it, but he had only a handful of men, with no idea how many Sevens were on the other side.

"Follow me!" he yelled. Holding the rifle at his shoulder, he dug into the powdery dirt and charged ten feet to the crest. The others followed. Halfway up, he saw the first Sevens to his left, a long line of them stretching in both directions, a hundred at least, with more pouring up the slope. A few bodies lay in the dirt. He had caught them moments before they swarmed over the top in a coordinated attack of their own, and there, standing on the crest, for a microsecond, he locked eyes with the nearest Seven, a young man with only a wisp of beard. And then he opened fire on full automatic.

Both sides stood and fired, at a range of no more than twenty feet. Blood, bodies, and bullets filled Rainwater's senses, until something slammed into the side of his head, shoving him backward. He waved his arms to keep from falling, but his sense of balance was off and he fell, rolling over and over down the 300-foot slope to the bottom. Groggy, through blurry vision he saw a line of white-clad figures far above him on top of the ridge, and then nothing except darkness.

Lieutenant Onni Hakala's LAV-25 idled on a small hill fifty feet south of Highway 4, near the main gate of Shangri-La, where the huge tree still blocked the road from the previous fighting. From his vantage point, he had a view of most of the southern defenses, and stood ready with the pindle-mounted machine gun to support anywhere it was needed. Except the direction that trouble came from.

"Loot, the ridge," called out his gunner, Sergeant Dajuan Wiseman, over the intercom. It took Hakala a second to realize what he meant.

Oh, shit!

One hundred white-robed men topped the ridge and started down the other side. The turret whirred as the gunner brought the Bushmaster to bear.

"Engage," he said to Wiseman. *Bam, bam, bam.* Three 25mm rounds struck amid a cluster of Sevens, all leaning backward to descend the steep hillside, and exploded on impact. Fountains of dirt hid the carnage caused by fragmentation of the HEI rounds. Wiseman kept firing in three-round bursts, as Hakala sprayed the hillside with the machine gun. Bodies rolled downhill all over the ridge. At least 30 Sevens fell under the fusillade, but dozens more kept coming.

"Ammo's almost gone, Loot!" Wiseman said.

Hakala took down two more men who crested the hill, steadying his shoulder against the machine gun's recoil. Then he ran dry. "Me, too. Use the coax and keep 'em off."

"I'll do what I can."

From their vantage point, the bottom of the ridge was masked by a line of bushes and trees, mostly splintered now but still thick enough to block line of sight. Using that cover, the Sevens could close within 75 yards of their position, and if any of them had an RPG, it could get ugly quick.

Reloading the ammunition box required remaining exposed to enemy fire. Hakala licked his lips before calling Sully as he worked.

"Kicker Real, this is Field Goal Real. I've got a hundred bogies over the ridge on our west. We are flanked, repeat, we are flanked. Need immediate reinforcement, over."

He waited several seconds before resending the message. Nothing.

#

Chapter 48

"It's like déjà vu all over again."
Yogi Berra

Shangri-La, Jemez Springs, New Mexico
1755 hours, May 5

"Captain, Captain, can you hear me?"

Sully felt his head loll to the left, and then realized that his driver, Corporal Douglas Evereaux, was shaking his leg from below. Squatting, Sully rubbed his eyes. "What happened?" he said.

"We took an RPG round. The LAV's dead. We gotta get out of here."

"How is Hodges?" he said, meaning the gunner.

"He's out of it."

"Okay, get out. I'll get Hodges."

"Captain, let me get Hodges. You cover us."

The mere fact that Evereaux ignored his order shook Sully enough for him to regain his situational awareness. The corporal was right. Standing, he found a knot of Sevens running toward the disabled vehicle, no more than twenty yards away. They saw him at the same time and started shooting on the run. For one second, bullets whizzed by each other on opposite trajectories. The rifle shots ricocheted off the turret or missed wide of the mark, while the M240 machine gun put three men down and left the last bending over with a shoulder wound. Another trigger pull took care of him.

Others had come over the wall and, as Evereaux pulled the unconscious Hodges out the gunner's hatch, Sully sent two long streams of HEI rounds at them. He could hear Evereaux straining beside him. There wasn't much room to get a grip on Hodges, so it was like pulling dead weight straight up. Bullets pinged off the LAV's hull and Sully leaned into the machine gun, squeezing the trigger until it ran out of ammo. The last stream of tracers brought screams from behind a small pinion juniper tree. Then Sully climbed out, and then helped Evereaux lift Hodges and carry him toward his LAV-C2 command vehicle.

Once they were inside, Company Sergeant Meyer leaned toward him, holding a phone receiver. "Field Goal Real is in danger of being overrun, Captain. Lieutenant Hakala says the Sevens came over the western ridge, and they can't hold the gate without reinforcements."

Sully's vision was still blurry at the edges, but there was no time to recover. "Get me Punter." Somebody handed him a canteen and he drank two big swallows. Nodding his thanks, he handed it back and knelt beside Hodges. "How is he?"

"Blow to the head, sir. Must have been when the RPG hit. I think he'll be all right. The helmet took most of it."

"Sir," Meyer said, extending the phone, "it's Punter One. Punter Real's out of action."

Taking it, Sully said, "Punter One, this is Kicker Real. Can you reinforce Field Goal at the gate, over?"

"Negative, Kicker Real, request permission to pull back. Enemy has an M1, I say again, enemy has armor support, over."

"Roger that, Punter One. Kicker Real out."

Things were moving too fast to use either a digital or a paper map, so Sully tried to visualize the battlefield in his mind. If the enemy had flanked them on the west, and the northern and southern flanks were crumbling, then it didn't matter that so far the east looked solid. That was 3rd Platoon's area, and if they were undamaged and still had ammo...

"Put me through to the company," he told the radio operator who had given him the canteen.

She flipped a switch and then looked over at him. "You're on, sir."

"To all units, this is Kicker Real. Coordinate with friendly forces and withdraw to the central meeting place they call The

True. We will set laager defense in that position. Conduct a staged withdrawal but do not hesitate. Execute immediately. Kicker Real out."

Holding the phone straight out from his side, Sully felt Meyer take him from his hand. For a moment he stared at nothing.

"Captain?" Meyer said. "Haven't we done this before?"

For one of the rare times since any of them had known their captain, he smiled. "I thought you might like an encore, Sergeant."

"No offense, sir, but I got shot the last time."

The western ridge that the Sevens had breached ran north and south, like a rampart wall protecting the valley of the Jemez Pueblo, and the larger community of Shangri-La that had been built up around it after America collapsed. The ridge dead-ended abruptly into a higher peak with a sheer western facing, and prevented anyone walking along the crest from going any further. After several thousand feet, the intruding hill ended, like a canine tooth protruding from the gumline, and the ridge picked up again.

The founder of Shangri-La, Winston Ballinger, had chosen that stone anomaly as the place around which to center the life of his new refuge. Ballinger had studied history and knew better than to trust to the outer walls of such a large area to hold forever, so at the center of this bastion was The True, a bastardization of the Latin word *teatru*, meaning 'theater.' Like an ancient Greek amphitheater, The True had been hewn from the rock of the surrounding hill.

To either side of the curving stone benches were the openings that led into the underground greenhouses. A complex series of shafts and mirrors brought sunlight into chambers located below ground level. There were also living quarters down there, temporary shelters for emergencies just like this one.

Ballinger had always intended for the area around The True to be a defensive zone of last resort, like a castle's keep. To that end, he'd insisted on continuing to build it up even after the outer defenses had become strong and the people thought additional work was unnecessary.

Now, a long wall of cut and fitted stone, nine feet high and four feet thick, surrounded the whole area, its total length running to 600 yards in a semi-circle that began and ended against the hill on the western side. Like a medieval walled city, the battlements allowed the defenders to shoot through regularly spaced square openings. Two twenty-foot-wide gates facing north and east provided access, with thick doors of mesquite wood. A large open area, surrounded by adobe buildings, acted as the marketplace.

LAVs that still had ammunition formed a loose ring around the entire wall, providing covering fire as the entire population of Shangri-La retreated into the fort. The Sevens made one concerted effort to rush the lines of women and children, but they hit the zone covered by Onside, the 3rd Platoon, which still had nearly full ammo racks. A group of sixty or seventy men rushed forward to fire on a group of women who were carrying and shooing small children along Highway 4. Opening fire, they cut down at least a dozen of their helpless targets before two LAVs blasted them with Bushmasters and machine guns. At least forty of the tightly packed Sevens went down before the rest retreated to safety. After that, the Sevens seemed content to let the defenders move into their sanctuary, from which there could be no escape.

It took less time to evacuate the defenders than Captain Sully had feared it would, because the people of Shangri-La had practiced this very thing many times. The threat of the Sevens had long been known, and Johnny Rainwater, in particular, had insisted on monthly evacuation drills, with the full agreement of Abigail Deak. But as their people filed into the relative safety of The True, neither Rainwater nor Deak was anywhere to be found.

Even Tracy Gollins smiled as her men jumped up and down on the makeshift roadblock of stones piled around a felled tree, which blocked Highway 4 on the north side of Shangri-La. Fighting in the rough country east of the highway continued with occasional single shots and bursts of automatic weapons fire, but none of that mattered now. The defenders of Shangri-La had abandoned their field fortifications and fled, leaving her the field of battle. Best of all, she hadn't had to use the Abrams, which only had three rounds of armor-piercing and one round of high explosive ammunition left. They could now use that to smash anything else the defenders threw in their way.

Bodies piled in front of the barrier had already attracted flies, and the first vultures circled overhead almost the instant that shooting stopped. Carrion eaters wanted their fill before something else ate their free meal, not realizing that on such a day, there would be plenty for all to eat.

"My lord General, what are your orders?" asked one of her lieutenants.

Gollins' good humor turned sour again. Celebrating could come *after* the battle was won, and that wasn't now. Their enemy had retreated in good order.

"Get those idiots down from there!" she said, pointing to the men dancing on the bole of the tree. "Move south. There are plenty of infidels left to kill before this day is over."

The man hurried to do what she said, kicking butts and pushing men down the road. Within a minute, hundreds of white-robed figures slouched off to the south, with many a scowl turned her way. They had seen too many of their friends die, but somehow they had lived and thought the fighting was over. Now, learning they might yet die that day, many weren't happy with the thick woman who returned their frowns. Gollins could tell that some of them considered disobeying her, but as long as she stood with a running tank at her back, as she did now, she doubted any of them would act on the impulse.

Finally, when the last of her men had moved out, she waved the tank to follow. It was a precious resource, even without ammunition, and she wasn't about to put it out front where it could be damaged. That idiot Muhdin had gotten his destroyed, and a Bradley, too, but she wouldn't make that same mistake.

Cuba, New Mexico
1803 hours, May 5

At five feet, five inches tall, Captain April Jones couldn't see too much from the commander's hatch of her LAV-C2 anyway, but being behind 1st Platoon left her even more in the dark about what was directly ahead of the Echo Company column. The small town of Cuba lay at their backs, but coming through, they'd seen evidence that Sevens had ransacked the place, including one man who'd been shot in the back. None of them could tell if an American had done it, or one his fellows who wanted something he'd found. Powder burns stained the back of his robe, however, giving strong evidence of having been murdered by a fellow Seven.

The moment of decision had arrived. They still couldn't get through to anybody from Dog Company, so the situation at Shangri-La remained unknown. During the approach to Cuba, some of the forward elements had reported hearing distant gunfire, but that had now died away. Was the battle over? If she moved forward, would Echo face the full force of the Sevens' army alone? And how big was that army, anyway? There just wasn't much intel on what they could expect, so what should she do? Lined up with engines idling, all they were doing now was wasting fuel.

"Safety Real, this is Nickleback One. What are your orders, Captain?"

Without consciously making a decision, her lips moved and made it for her. "Never shall I forget the principles I accepted to become a Recon Marine. Honor, perseverance, spirit, and heart." Jones knew when she said stuff like that, some of her Marines thought she was a motard, and had lately cut back on all the rah-rah stuff. But this time she didn't care.

Nickleback One, call sign for Lieutenant Marquita Tomas, didn't answer right away, apparently waiting for clarification of Jones' answer. When none came after seconds, Tomas got back on the radio. "Safety Real, does that mean we're on the move?"

"Roger that, Nickleback One. We're going to go find Dog Company, and God help anybody who gets in our way."

"Kill, Captain. Nickleback One out."

#

Part Seven

End Game

Chapter 49

"Aim towards the Enemy"
Official instructions printed on the side of a U.S. rocket launcher

Operation Overtime
1721 hours, May 5

Despite everything going on in Nevada, Arizona, and New Mexico, Nick Angriff followed the medical team who wheeled his wife and daughter to the hospital section. He'd known the second he laid eyes on Janine that she had something drastically wrong with her. In just a few weeks she had lost at least twenty pounds, her skin was gray, and the cough had deepened. Cynthia wasn't quite as bad, but she was also much younger.

Colonel Friedenthall wasted no time in taking the Angriff women into an examination room. Angriff made to follow them, but the doctor halted him by holding up a hand.

"General, sir, in my experience, grown women don't like having male relatives around when they're undergoing a thorough physical examination. They don't particularly like male doctors, either, which is why I've asked Captain Noshimura to take the lead on this."

"How long will it take?"

"Likely several hours. I want to run a comprehensive battery of tests. You can wait outside, or I'll be sure to call you the minute we're done."

"All right, do that—"

An orderly burst into the waiting room, spotted Friedenthall, and ran to him. He turned to apologize to Angriff, and then noticed who he'd interrupted. But instead of being nervous or scared, he blurted out his words all at once. "General Angriff you're wanted in the trauma center right away sir!"

He immediately pictured his son lying on a gurney and cursed himself. He should never have left Nick, Jr. alone with Steeple and Claringdon, regardless of his lethality.

Then the orderly said something that chilled his soul. "It's your daughter, sir!"

Operation Overtime Trauma Center

Angriff pushed through the double doors leading into the trauma center. Located on the main floor near Motor Bay B, it was separate from the hospital, although Colonel Friedenthall oversaw both of them. But a military unit needed specialized medical facilities designed for battle casualties, a trauma center, and the closer it was to the entrance point for combat troops, the better. Angriff wasn't there to save a life, however; he was there to end one. All he'd been told was that his daughter had been shot, and after he checked on her condition, Angriff had every intention of killing whoever had done it.

He found Green Ghost in the large waiting area. He didn't ask what happened to Steeple or Claringdon; at that moment he wouldn't have cared if his son had thrown them off the balcony outside his office. "Which one?" He'd assumed it was Nikki, but couldn't bring himself to say it.

"It's Morgan."

"M-Morgan?"

Green Ghost nodded. "They brought her in hours ago, but nobody here knew you were alive. I heard about it from Nikki."

"What happened? How is she? Was it an accident?"

Green Ghost decided to answer the middle question first. "She's gonna make it, probably a full recovery."

"Thank God. Can we see her?"

"Not yet, maybe in a few hours. They want her to rest after the surgery. But..."

"But what?"

"The baby... the bullet killed him."

Angriff scrunched up his face in confusion. "Baby?" Then he understood. "She was pregnant?"

Green Ghost nodded. "He was a boy."

"My grandson... oh, dear God... What happened, some sort of accident?"

"It was intentional."

Angriff's entire demeanor changed. His body tensed and his hands clenched. Green Ghost knew his father pretty well by that point, and recognized the promise of death reflected in Angriff's eyes.

"Who did this? Tell me who did this, Nick."

"Adder."

"Adder killed my grandson?"

"Yeah, and my nephew."

"Where is he? I'm going to kill him."

"He's on the operating table."

"The... they're trying to save that worthless bastard's life?"

"There's more... Dad. He shot Joe Ootoi, too."

"Nikki's Joe?"

Green Ghost nodded again.

"And is he—"

"He's dead. Nikki's the one who handled things. She stabbed Adder in the groin while defending Morgan, but he got away. She wanted to chase him down and kill him, but stayed with Morgan instead. Probably saved Morgan's life — you know how good Nikki is with first aid."

"How did he get here?"

"Called for medical help from an emergency call site. This all happened while we were up in the Crystal Palace getting rid of the Chinese."

"I'm going in there, son, and I'm going to kill him."

"I don't blame you for feeling that way, Dad, but you can't. You're the C.O. You can't kill helpless people, no matter how much they deserve it. He's got a lot more innocent blood on his hands than you even know about. After Lake Tahoe, after you disappeared, we lost Second Squad on a mission into Venezuela..."

Angriff tried to concentrate, but he felt like he'd been run over by a truck. "Are you talking about the Zombies?"

"Yeah. Adder took eleven people into the jungle with him, looking for a dirty bomb. He was the only one who came out."

"You think he sold them out."

"Yeah, I do."

"So what are you suggesting we do now? The man killed my... my grandson. This is going to rip Janine's heart out."

"I suggest we let the father decide what to do with him. After all, it was Joe Randall's wife who got shot and his son who died."

"What about Nikki? She lost someone, too."

"Nikki will torture him. She'll keep him alive as long as she can and cut him up into little pieces, making sure he doesn't die. I think she's back where she was... before."

"You mean that Nipple's back?"

"Yeah. I hate Adder more than anyone I've ever met, but I can't sign off on torture, even for him. There was a time when he was a damned good team member. We wouldn't have gotten out of Egypt without him. Line him up against a wall? Hand me a rifle; I'll fire the first shot. But not torture. I also can't let Nikki do it... that would kill her soul. She's my twin sister, I can feel some of her pain, and I just can't let that happen, not after all she's been through."

"So you suggest we let Joe decide? Because I'm not sure torture's such a bad idea. I'll give her Steeple to work on, too."

"Don't do that, please. Whatever is inside her, letting her torture people is just going to push the real Nikki deeper down and keep Nipple front and center."

"You talk like she's possessed or something."

"Maybe she is. Let Randall handle it. It's his wife and his son. He's not gonna let Adder get away with it."

"And what if he votes for torture?"

"I'm not gonna get in anybody's way over Adder."

"I'll agree to that on one condition," Angriff said, his teeth clenched with a rage unlike anything he'd ever felt before. "That whatever Joe decides, it ends with Adder dead. Otherwise, I swear by all that's holy and righteous in this world that I will blow his head off. Now that I think of it... where is she?"

"I don't know, but experience says that somebody's about to die."

Khin Saw's quarters had the identical setup to those of most other high-ranking officers who rated a private apartment — one bedroom with bathroom attached, a small living room with a desk, chair, and couch, flat screen TV that he'd never turned on, and a kitchenette. He sat now in the chair, his Sig Sauer M17 lying on the desk beside the nine empty bullet casings he had picked up off the floor, after he'd shot the four Chinese guards who had come to arrest him. Somebody must have heard the gunshots, but so far nobody had come to investigate.

If they had sent Americans, he wouldn't have fired. Regardless of how vile Tom Steeple might be, Khin Saw would not gun down a fellow American except in self-defense. But Chinese? That would never be a problem.

The longer he sat there, the stranger the situation felt. Saw wasn't sure what he should do next. He'd never thought that he'd gun down the Chinese and then just sit there. As any fighting man must, he relied heavily on his instincts, and now those instincts screamed that something was fundamentally wrong with this picture.

Then a stray thought came to him unbidden — what if something had gone fundamentally *right?* As if he were psychic, the base PA system came to life, and he recognized Sergeant Major Schiller's voice.

"Attention all personnel, attention all personnel, stand by for the reading of an Order of the Day by the commanding officer. This is a mandatory listening event."

Mandatory listening event? He'd never heard *that* before. Staring into space, he dreaded what he knew had to be coming: the smooth delivery of Tom Steeple informing the 7th Cavalry there was yet another new brigade commander. Part of him wished he'd used the gun on that man.

Then the voice of the C.O. boomed from the speakers, and there was nothing smooth about it, but there was something deep, raspy, and very welcome. As the words continued, Saw could only blink and gape at the speaker in the ceiling. Halfway through the message, he started to grin.

"...after the conclusion of this message, the following officers are to report to my headquarters immediately — Colonel Saw, Colonel Kordibowski, Colonel Walling, and Colonel Wisnewski-Smith. Ladies and gentlemen of the 7th Cavalry Brigade, this is your commanding officer speaking, General Nicholas T. Angriff."

Saw stepped over the dead Chinese and was out the door. His quarters were only a level below the Crystal Palace, so he took the stairs instead an elevator, listening as he took them two at a time.

"All Chinese are to be considered enemy troops and should be treated as such. If they surrender, respect them as you would prisoners of war, but any action that you consider hostile is to be met with overwhelming force. Your personal safety, and that of this base, is paramount. In addition, any and all orders issued by General Steeple are invalid. Take no further action based on those orders."

There was a pause.

"As you have probably surmised by now, reports of my death were slightly premature. That day will certainly come, but it's not *this* day. I'm back, and I'm back to stay."

For only the second time in the brigade's history, Khin Saw heard cheers ringing through the hallways, and couldn't stop grinning. As he came out of the stairwell near the Crystal Palace, he saw American sentries at the main entrance, the foot of the ramp, and the head. Sergeant Major Schiller saw him coming and opened the office door for him. Saw nearly ran inside, stopped before Angriff's desk, and came to rigid attention. He offered the crispest salute of which he was capable. "Colonel Khin Saw, reporting as ordered!"

Angriff seemed puzzled, since they were indoors, but returned the salute. "At ease, Khin. Would you like to sit down?"

"Thank you anyway, sir, but I'm kinda amped up right now."

That brought a nod, although Angriff's expression had a sadness the colonel didn't understand. "I get that, Khin... I guess I am, too."

"There is one thing you should know, sir. General Steeple sent four Chinese guards to arrest me—"

"I'm sorry that happened to you, Khin. Were you injured?"

"No, sir, but I can't say the same about them."

"Oh?"

"Yes, sir. It's a pretty big mess."

Angriff raised his eyebrows. "All four?"

"All four. The cleanup crew is going to need a mop."

"You know, this may sound odd coming from me, but usually when I hear about deaths, even those of our enemies, a part of me cries for them. I hate the necessity of it. But in this case... in this case I'd call it a good beginning."

#

Chapter 50

"After the battle come the tears."
General of the Army Nicholas T. Angriff

The Crystal Palace, Operation Overtime
1814 hours, May 5

Angriff waved Colonel Kordibowski into his office. "Come on in, Rip, we're getting the band back together."

Green Ghost, Colonels Saw and Walling were already there, with Saw in one of the two chairs in front of the desk and Green Ghost sitting on the couch, one leg crossed on his knee, while Walling was in a wheelchair.

Kordibowski took two steps and stopped short of the desk. "It really is you, General."

Angriff's smile showed his fatigue. "It really is, Rip. I'm sorry you all thought I was dead, but I knew they wouldn't stop looking for me if they thought I might be alive."

"Pardon my language, sir, but I am damned glad to see you."

"I think I've heard worse. Have a seat, and let's catch up on what's been going on around here. Colonel Walling was just telling us how he eluded Colonel Friedenthall to get here."

Walling nodded the way people do when they're the butt of good-natured ribbing. "I'm not sure that's exactly how I remember it, General. I think maybe he got tired of having me around."

"Whatever the case, I'm glad you're back. How long before you won't need the wheelchair?"

"Two weeks, maybe less."

Corporal Diaz brought coffee for them all and beside Angriff's he laid down something wrapped in a napkin. Curious, Angriff unwrapped it and found a Habana Especiales Monte Cristo Number Three, with matches and his silver cigar cutter.

Picking up the fragrant tube, he inhaled. "I assumed General Steeple would have ordered these destroyed."

"He did, sir, but Sergeant Major Schiller smuggled them out and hid them, along with your humidor."

"Thank you, Diaz."

He tried to focus as his officers spent half an hour filling him in on all of Tom Steeple's orders, and what they knew of the position of each unit. Kordibowski had been under arrest from the beginning, and Walling hadn't learned much in the hospital ward, so Khin Saw had to fill in whatever gaps he could. Angriff leaned forward on his desk and rested his chin on his hands, scowling in concentration as he always did during meetings, but concentrating on what they said was hard. All he could think about was Morgan.

"General Steeple recruited me into Overtime," said Khin Saw, "so I think since he recruited me, he felt that I would somehow rubber stamp anything he did."

"I'd say he misjudged you," Angriff said.

"Yes, sir, I'd say he did."

"I heard he gave you a star."

"And took it back."

"I want you to put it back on, Khin. I have a very important post for you, and I'd like you to take it."

"I'll do anything I can to help the brigade, General Angriff, even without the star."

"No, you need that star for the job I have in mind. I want you to take over for General Fleming at Sierra Army Depot. It's a damned hard job, Khin. I need you to put as much of that hardware back into service as possible. I'll give you as much technical help as we can afford, but you're going to be making up a lot of this as you go. You'll need to inventory all the ordnance, make repairs, grow your own food to whatever extent possible, train replacements, anything and everything to turn that depot into a functioning base again."

Saw didn't hesitate. "When do I leave, sir?"

"I can't guarantee when you'll be back at Prime."

"No matter, sir. To be honest, that assignment suits me a lot better than brigade S-1."

"Do you want some time to wrap things up here?"

"If it's all the same to you, General, my apartment's a mess right now anyway, so I'll leave immediately."

Angriff understood the grim joke. "At least pack some clean underwear."

"Yes, sir. I—"

Schiller buzzed the intercom, interrupting Saw. "General Angriff, I apologize for interrupting, sir, but I thought you'd want to know. A CASEVAC is inbound with wounded, sir, from General Tompkins' position."

"Who's wounded, J.C.?"

"I'm not sure about the others, sir, but General Tompkins was hit in the foot."

"Any word on other casualties?"

"Three KIA, General."

"Brigade personnel?"

"That's what I was told, sir. Would you like me to have communications reconnect to the pilot?"

"No. ETA?"

"Fifteen minutes. A full medical team is on their way to the hangar."

"Thank you, J.C. Keep me informed." Angriff clicked off the intercom and met his son's gaze. "If you see me heading for the brig, and I have a weapon, under no circumstances are you to stop me."

Operation Overtime Trauma Center

Colonel Harry 'The Hat' Strickland had not expected the trauma center waiting room to be as crowded as it was, nor as quiet. It was eerie. At least two dozen Marines stood or sat around Sergeant Snowtiger, yet his usually loud and boisterous people whispered if they spoke at all. Most of them hadn't served with Snowtiger or Piccaldi, and only knew them from reputation, but there they were, using their off-duty time to show solidarity with one of their own. He was damned proud of them.

Everyone stood when he entered, but he waved them down before anyone could even call out ten-hut. He wasn't there to be a distraction. "As you were."

Snowtiger hadn't moved. Strickland had seen the thousand-yard stare too many times not to recognize it for what it was, sudden acute post-traumatic stress disorder. The man whose life she'd fought and nearly died to save the previous summer had instead died saving hers. He couldn't think of anything worse.

Squatting in front of where she sat, he bent his head down until his eyes were in her line of sight. She blinked twice and met his gaze.

"I'm very sorry that we lost Gunny Piccaldi, Master Sergeant Snowtiger. He was a credit to the Corps, and to all Marines everywhere, living or dead. I want you to know that I'm putting him in for the Silver Star."

Her voice had none of its usual life, but was dull and robotic. She sounded like someone who had given up. "Thank you, sir. Zo would have been very proud."

"Gunny Piccaldi *is* proud."

Now her eyes changed, and widened in an earnest expression, like a child hoping her dad could make it all better. "Do you really believe that, Major?"

"I do, Master Sergeant. I truly do."

"They shot my sister, too."

"I know. I'm praying for her."

"Thank you."

"You're the sinew of the Corps, Snowtiger, you and Piccaldi and every man or woman who ever put on that uniform. We're not just your comrades; we're your family. You take all the time you need to sort this out. And I want you to talk with the brigade psychologist before returning to duty."

"I'll be all right, sir."

"That's an order."

New Mexico Highway 126, 38 miles southeast of Cuba
1817 hours, May 5

"Safety One Four to Safety Real, enemy in sight, taking small arms fire from high ground north of the highway. Infantry engaging, am in support, request backup, over."

Captain Jones was eight vehicles behind Safety One Four, the leading LAV-25 for the column. Fortunately, they were on a short straight part of Highway 126, past the numerous switchbacks, and that allowed for faster deployment at the point of contact. The northern bank of the road sloped uphill at a steep angle, with moderately dense trees, but the southern shoulder had a fifteen-foot-wide verge adjoining the roadbed before it dropped away into a valley.

Jones could hear the distinctive sound of M242 Bushmasters firing, like a carpenter hammering nails into wood paneling. *Bam, bam, bam! Bam, bam, bam!* Machine gun and rifle fire went on continuously for more than two minutes, which was forever in terms of battle time. Using her binoculars, she watched LAVs stopping to disgorge the Marines riding in their troop-carrying compartments, hammering away with their guns as the infantry scrambled up the hill.

By the time her command vehicle got within one hundred yards of the scene, all firing had stopped. Jones dismounted and approached, her personal M16 locked and loaded. Four Marines and the company sergeant went with her. They found Lieutenant Tomas standing in the turret of her own LAV.

"What have we got, Lieutenant?"

"Field hospital, Captain, or at least what passes for one with the Sevens. Apparently it's pretty primitive."

"They resisted?"

"Yes, ma'am, even the severely wounded. I haven't been up there yet, though. Waiting for it to be cleared."

"Casualties?"

"None reported yet."

"You stay here. I'm going up."

"Captain—"

"Get the company ready to move again, Lieutenant. If we've overrun their hospital, the enemy must be close."

Tomas started to protest, but Jones turned and dug into the loose soil of the hill. Signs of a firefight showed up right away in the bullet-chewed bark of the numerous pine trees. The slope angled upward at close to forty-five degrees, so Jones had to dig the toe of her boots into the carpet of pine needles covering the ground. About one hundred feet above the highway, she came to a cleared area covered in bodies.

Flaps of white blew in a light wind. Three smells dominated the scene — blood, gunpowder, and burnt pine needles. Jones showed no emotion as she viewed the carnage, but inside it tore at her heart to see so many young people dead for no sane reason. Marine officer or not, she despised the waste of war. A dozen or so Marines roamed the clearing, rifles at the ready as they poked the bloody corpses in case somebody was playing dead.

The company sergeant, Gunnery Sergeant Hector Quallo, took a fast tour of the site and then came back over to her. "Rough count is a hundred thirty-seven, Captain. I only saw one guy who might have been a doctor; otherwise it's all pretty medieval. It looks like the orderlies killed the severely wounded and we took care of the ones that could shoot."

"No prisoners?"

"No, ma'am, they're all dead."

"Round 'em up, Gunny. I want to be moving in five mikes."

"Rah, ma'am," he said, turning to herd the Marines on the hill back into their LAVs. "Move out, Marines, we've got plenty more people to kill before this day is over!"

#

Chapter 51

"Thirteenth law of air combat maneuvering: "You ain't cheating, you ain't trying."
Commander Chris Kennedy, USN (Retired), A6E pilot and co-founder of the Four Horsemen Universe

Air Force Annex runway, Operation Comeback
1820 hours, May 5

Captain Babb hadn't thought about how he would get the A-10 back underground once he'd landed at Operation Comeback, not until he was halfway home. Thank God the runway had a homing beacon on both UHF and VHF frequencies, so finding it wasn't a problem. The strain of the sortie, coming so soon after he'd woken up, was far greater than the two-hour flight should have been, even given the combat runs. He felt drained, as if he'd been in the air for eight or ten hours, but one thing he knew for certain was that he needed to go back out again, ASAP. There were still targets left, and he'd never gotten close to Shangri-La.

The problem was... the only things above ground were a runway and storage shed, for tools and such. Nor could he imagine taking a Warthog *down* a slope to the underground hangar complex, regardless of how gentle the angle might be. But the air traffic controller for Comeback said to worry about landing the plane, and to let them worry about rearming and refueling it.

A light crosswind wasn't enough to force him around again, and he touched down without incident. Babb expected the retractable doors at either end of the runway to be lowered, and when neither was, he radioed the ATC again.

The ATC said, "T-Bolt, taxi to the north end of the runway and bring the aircraft around."

"Then what, Comeback Control?"

"Then ground crews will rearm and refuel you. You will have approximately two hours and twenty minutes of daylight left, T-Bolt. If you're delayed until darkness, be advised the runway has illumination on each side for its full length."

"Comeback Control, roger."

What the hell did all that mean? Opening the canopy to get some fresh air, he taxied the last thousand feet to the end of the runway and turned around, facing south by southwest, the direction of the prevailing winds. Now what?

To his immediate left, a section of desert sixty feet square slowly sank into the ground. Dirt and pebbles poured in after it, and Babb had to laugh at his own lack of imagination. An elevator! Just like on an aircraft carrier or a mine shaft. He should have known; any agency that could build an entire base underground, complete with a three-thousand-foot hangar deck-runway, would have no problem installing an elevator.

Less than two minutes later a fuel truck, ammunition carrier, and a full reload of bombs in their cradles rose into view, along with Lieutenant Hartmann and enough ground crew to get the plane back up fast. It was like going to a fast-food drive-through and actually getting good service.

When the Warthog took off after service, Babb again passed over that unusual American unit parked beyond the runway. Again they waved at him, and he waggled his wings in response. There seemed to be more of them now, as if some Comeback personnel had come out to join them for a picnic in the desert.

Gollins was in her Bradley when the message came from the emir, so she was able to take it right away. The first thing he did was tell her to go someplace private, so she exited out the back and walked into the woods beside Highway 4 until satisfied nobody could overhear.

"Things have gone to shit here," he said. "Sati apparently had the Americans trapped until a bomber showed up and shot his men to hell and back. What's going on up there?"

"I told you he wasn't ready," she answered.

"There is no time for that now! How are things there?"

"We broke them. They retreated into a walled inner defense place, which we're preparing to attack now. My tank still has four shells left. That should be enough to blow down one of the gates and take out some of their armored vehicles. Once we're inside, it's over."

"You're not inside Shangri-La yet?"

"Yes, but they have this last fortified place. Once we're in there, it's over."

"Hurry. I could have American tanks up my ass any minute now."

"I have to coordinate with Muhdin first. Or whoever's got his command now."

"Muhdin died a couple of hours ago, so I'm giving you his troops. They have a radio. Just tell them what to do and finish the job. I'm counting on you, Tracy."

"Remember you said that when this is all over."

Major Letif Ahmadi could feel fatigue dragging at his limbs. The earlier fight at Interstate 40, and the subsequent breakthrough to Albuquerque, felt like it had emptied his nervous system of adrenaline, leaving him shaky and exhausted. Despite the afternoon sun, a cold sweat soaked his uniform, and he felt nauseous. While dealing with the wounded after the battle earlier, he had allowed the distribution of T-Rats, the B-rations that came in trays, available in company-sized packages. The company mess had heated water to cook them, while everybody not taking care of the wounded had refueled and rearmed. Ahmadi had spent his time seeing to his command and ate nothing, although he still had a Soldier Fuel bar.

Rather than moving through Albuquerque, which was known to be enemy territory, Ahmadi took his force across the desert and skirted the city to the northwest. He worried that the Sevens might still have a mobile force capable of hitting them while they were on the move, and hated the whole idea of advancing so fast. The officers of the mechanized infantry had convinced him otherwise, but it wouldn't be their asses on the line if they were wrong. It would be his.

As they bumped over the bare ground, however, it soon became apparent that he'd been worried about nothing. Dropping back into the BCV, he found a water bottle and ate the energy bar. He stood back up when the rattling stopped and the ride smoothed out, shocked to see houses on either side of a two-lane road. Then they were back in the desert. Straight ahead was New Mexico Highway 550, which they would take to Highway 4, the direct route to Jemez Springs and Shangri-La. And as the food calmed his stomach, Ahmadi began to plan for the coming fight.

The angle of the sun had reached a point low enough on the western horizon to cast shadows stretching west of the ridgeline and past Highway 4. Night was falling and Tracy Gollins knew they had to finish this here and now. She stalked the area behind the main gate to the south, where the troops of General Muhdin's former command leaned against walls and trees, or lay on the ground. The burned-out wrecks of an M1, a Bradley, and an American vehicle with eight wheels clogged the highway. Bloated bodies lay in heaps along with fresh ones. She didn't want to cover her mouth and nose with her sleeve, but the sweet reek of rotting flesh forced her to choke down vomit.

"Get on your feet and move!" she yelled, stomping among them and kicking some. "I said get up!"

Her personal guards stayed close, rifles at the ready. She could feel their hatred even though they were pledged to defend her to the death. But no threats had any effect. Muhdin's worn-out troops stared at her, some with open contempt. She'd known this moment would come, and had thought long and hard about what she would do when faced with it.

She drew her Beretta M9, the pistol her father had given her when he'd taught her to shoot. Pulling back the slide chambered a round, and she'd hoped the loud metallic *chunk* would get their attention. But it didn't, and that left her with only one choice. Picking out a particularly big man, one with a heavy beard and who didn't bother to hide his disdain for her, she stood by his feet as he lay propped against a tree.

"Get up and fight," she said.

"Don't touch me, bitch." He bared his teeth at her and growled like a dog. The others laughed.

So here it was at last, the moment she'd always known was coming. In a society where women were considered a necessary evil, not to be treated as the equal of the men, having a female army commander sooner or later had to have led to trouble. If she didn't stop it now, once and for all, then she would never have another chance.

"I'm a general in the Sword of the New Prophet," she said in her most threatening tone. "Speaking to me in that way is punishable by death."

"You don't scare me, woman. Maybe those dogs in Ayyub Regiment take orders from a bleeder, but I don't. Get out of here, you unclean—" He never finished, because she raised the Beretta and shot him in the forehead. Brains and blood spattered the men propped up next to him on the tree. The dead man slumped to one side.

Her bodyguards immediately lowered their rifles to shooting position, turning this way and that in search of threats. The others of Muhdin's men scowled at her, and she knew they'd rip her to pieces if they could.

"What about the rest of you? Do you want to risk the Americans sending you to paradise, or do you prefer that I send you to hell?"

One by one they got to their feet, making sure their expressions showed how much they hated her. Nor were her guards exempt. Curling their lips, they filed past muttering "Khinzir." *Pig.* But Gollins had no intention of letting them get away with it. She had intended on making a coordinated attack on the Americans, but now she changed her plan. Muhdin's men could go in first, and alone. Let the Americans use up their ammunition on them. Then she would commit her own regiments.

Johnny Rainwater tried to breathe through his nose but something clogged his nostrils. Lifting his face from the dirt at the bottom of the ridge, he tried blowing it out, to no avail. Whatever it was, it was caked in there. Using his fingers, he dug out chunks of dried blood mixed with dust.

Every part of his body ached, and his head hurt the worst. Rolling on his back, he looked at the sky, and realized that his left eye wouldn't open. More crusted blood had glued it shut. He scraped it until the eye could open again.

What the hell happened?

"I might kill that bloody bitch for what she did to Omar," a voice said from behind a line of creosote bushes. The crunching of boots, combined with flashes of white between the branches, brought memories rushing back and he remembered what had happened. He'd been shooting it out with the Sevens atop the ridge, then something hit the side of his head and... and... he remembered the world spinning, and then nothing more.

Rifle fire echoed down the valley. Running feet beyond the bushes faded, and Rainwater realized they were running north toward The True. The True! Where was everybody? Had they been driven back into the last refuge? Shadows now covered that side of the ridge, so he had to crawl around for a minute to find a rifle with ammunition left in the magazine. It was an AK-47, and the magazine looked full. He blew dust away from the bolt and staggered toward the shooting to help his people.

Inside The True, Shangri-La

Time was something the defenders of The True didn't have. With Johnny Rainwater and Abigail Deak both missing, and the people debating who should lead the defense, Captain Sully declared he was in charge. His tone left no room for argument, even if they had been so inclined. They weren't. Most of the survivors were the old and the very young.

Sully felt like a 10th century English lord defending his castle against Viking invaders when he ordered the dismounted Marine infantry onto the parapets to augment the Shangri-La defenders. He then arranged the LAV-25s into an evenly spaced semi-circular second line of defense to counterattack or lay fire down on any breakthroughs. The specialized LAVs, such as the LAV-ATs with TOW missile launchers, and the mortar vehicles, he stationed by the two gates. Most of the TOW missiles had been used up. Although not designed for use against soft targets, they'd taken a heavy toll on the Sevens by targeting trees, boulders, and other hard targets near the attacking infantry. Each launcher was given two missiles. Machine gun and 25mm ammunition from 3rd Platoon had been shared with those who were out, so all of them had equal amounts.

All of that took time. Sully rushed around, positioning troops and barking orders. He knew that if the Sevens attacked right away, there was little chance of The True holding out. But as the minutes ticked off with no assaults, and he'd done everything he could to prepare, he let everyone grab something to eat and went up to the battlements to eat his MRE with Lieutenant Hakala.

"What're they doing, Onni? Waiting for dark?" he said. The shadows of the coming night already covered part of The True.

"Beats me. It's like the British on D-Day. They had a chance to take Caen without heavy casualties, but waited too long and paid for it in blood."

Sully sat up straight. "I wasn't aware that you studied history."

Hakala shrugged. "It's not really my thing, but we ran out of things to read during my second tour in the sandbox, then somebody had this book about the Brits on D-Day. When I finished it, there still wasn't anything new to read, so I read it again."

"I hope that's why they're not coming now."

"I don't follow."

"Maybe they've got some plan I haven't thought about. Maybe they're coming after dark... that would be smart."

"We've got NVGs."

"But the IPs don't."

"True, I hadn't thought about that."

"We're not used to—"

Without warning, rifle fire raked the battlements, spraying Sully and Hakala with rock chips and dust and... blood? A young girl crouching beside them had exposed too much of her head, and multiple rounds cut her down. The two Marine officers crawled to the ladder and rejoined their LAVs. The final battle had started.

#

Chapter 52

Mercy is reserved for your brother. Unbelievers cannot be your brother.
The Revelations of Nabi Husem Allah, Chapter 8, Verses 6–7

Shangri-La, AKA Jemez Springs, New Mexico
1834 hours, May 5

"Still no answer, General," the radio operator said. Tracy Gollins stopped pacing, blinked several times, and drew her sidearm. The radioman quaked as she aimed the pistol at his head, and it took all of her self-discipline to re-holster the weapon. With disgust, she noted a spreading stain below the waist of his robe.

Daylight was running out fast. Why the fuck wasn't her father answering?

Earlier, she had ordered the four mu'azzins from General Muhdin's regiments, the men who called the faithful to prayer seven times a day instead of the five times of mainstream Islam, to stand by. The men had asked her if she'd assembled them to call the men to prayer before battle, but Gollins shook her head. She didn't give two shits about any of that crap.

"No, call them to attack."

"But, General..."

She pointed the pistol at the speaker. "Do it now."

"I do not know those words in Arabic, General."

"Muhajamat alkafaar," she said. "That's how you say it. Now, either you do it, or I'll put a bullet in your brains and find others who will. Which is it?"

The four terrified men exchanged glances, bowed, and spread out. They began their cries at a low volume, but it gradually rose as they became used to the unfamiliar words. Gollins nodded, satisfied. Her eyes widened with excitement. Let the bloodshed begin!

"Safety Real, this is Nickleback One, we are engaged with what appears to be an enemy rifle platoon blocking the highway. Am deploying to deal with it, request mortar support. Over."

"Nickleback One, permission granted to coordinate mortar support. You are authorized to use TOWs if you deem target value high enough. Do you copy?"

"Roger that, Safety Real, I— shit!"

Dense trees lined a bend in the road, preventing Captain April Jones from assessing the situation personally, and five explosions punctuated a sudden fusillade of rifle, machine gun, and chain gun fire. Within two seconds after the fifth blast, all firing stopped. Then, a few seconds later and before the echoes from the explosions had stopped, a flurry of single shots once again broke the stillness.

"Nickleback One, what's going on up there?"

"Stand by, Safety Real. I have MOS investigating now."

Jones was the fidgety type. It wasn't in her DNA to calmly wait for recon results, but instead to plunge into the unknown personally, and she'd found that to be the hardest transition from platoon to company commander. But she had to do something, so she tapped her foot inside the cupola. And even though that drove her own crew nuts, they would just have to live with it. At least she didn't smoke... not yet, anyway.

"Safety Real, I... it's bad."

"On my way."

The LAV-25 edged past the rest of the column with its left wheels crunching gravel on the shoulder. Jones positioned herself only behind 1st Platoon, so her vehicle pulled up next to Tomas while the smell of gunpowder still hung in the air. Behind sunglasses, it was hard to know for certain, but Jones felt something had shaken her E.O.

"What happened here, Lieutenant?" She said it with a little more authority than called for, knowing it would snap Tomas back into the present.

"It was another makeshift field hospital, Captain. Some guards took cover behind that pile of rocks over there, joined by some walking wounded. Small arms only, no RPGs that we could see. I wondered why they stayed bunched up instead of scattering through the woods, maybe try and flank us, but... I had it wrong. They weren't trying to kill *us*, they were trying to kill their own wounded. All the guards were doing was delaying us. When I heard the first gunshots back in the clearing, and then grenades, I figured it out. I ordered a TOW used against those rocks, but it was too late. One guy shot each of the badly wounded in the forehead, then put the gun in his own mouth. He had a stethoscope around his neck."

"No survivors?"

Tomas shook her head. "My fault, Captain. I should have seen it coming."

"Do you have some psychic ability to predict the actions of unbalanced terrorists, Lieutenant? Because if you do, that should be in your OMPF."

"Negative, ma'am."

"Then let it go. Our job right now isn't to save their lives; it's to end them. Yes, we could have used the intel, but we know where we're headed and speed is of the essence. Get it?"

"Sorry, ma'am. I do."

"Don't be sorry, Marquita, you're one helluva fine Marine. Just get moving."

"Kill, Captain."

"Kill."

The noise inside The True was so loud that even thinking was hard. Over the reports of hundreds of automatic weapons all firing at the same time, an explosion shook the gate doors facing southeast, followed by a second and then a third. Captain Sully was climbing into the back of his LAV-C2 when a high-pitched scream from behind made him stop. He turned his head. An older woman ran toward the body of a boy who had rolled off the battlement. A spreading puddle of blood under the boy's head showed Sully there was nothing he or anyone else could do to help.

He had just gotten inside the LAV when a huge explosion rattled the hull. "What was that?"

"The north gate, Captain," said the driver. "Gotta be a tank round."

Another blast blew the heavy doors open, smashing a jagged hole in one of them. Ten seconds later, a third shell completely destroyed them. More rifles added to the cacophony as the shooters on the east and north battlements opened fire, and thousands more Sevens returned it.

"They're coming through!"

The shattered gate doors hung askew, partially blocking the view beyond. Then the nose of an RPG rocket launcher stuck through a hole in the right side door, and the fight for the gate was on.

Four LAV-25s concentrated their fire there, with the 25mm Bushmaster rounds turning the remnants of the doors into lethal splinters. Shells ripped into the bodies of the first Sevens through the breech. Four chain guns and four machine guns sent hundreds of rounds into and through the smashed gate. Men's bodies jumped, vibrated, and staggered in explosions of blood and body parts.

Within half a minute, human flesh clogged the opening against the second wave of Sevens. Cannon shells and bullets tore through the heaps of dead, splashing gore in all directions. From somewhere out of sight, a rocket flashed through the gap between the ruined doors, and it struck the ground under Onside Three, the LAV-25 directly opposite the gate. Sully, manning the pindle-mounted M240 on his command vehicle, saw the crew bailing out.

Return fire from the Sevens died away, and Sully ordered cease fire. He keyed the mike to call for an ammo check, but the doors of the other gate blew inward in a massive explosion, followed seconds later by the front of an Abrams tank ramming through them.

Keeping his head down, Johnny Rainwater inched toward the edge of the trees that faced the cleared area around The True. Blood soaked the left side of the white robe he'd taken off a dead Seven, so he kept as close to the slope of the ridge as he could. None of the other Sevens paid him any attention, but Rainwater's face reflected his Native American ancestry. If any of them got a good look, it would be time to die. Rainwater had watched the women and children burn to death, and he would not let them take him prisoner.

Thousands of men shot at the walls of the refuge, covering hundreds more who ran toward the battlements. Some fell as they ran, but there was so much covering fire that the defenders couldn't respond with enough to hold them back. They had no ladders and he wondered how they would climb the sheer nine-foot-high walls. Then he saw.

At ten or twelve places, two men got down on all fours next to each other. A third man climbed onto one of them and cupped his hands for a fourth, who stepped onto the other one. Once the fourth man's foot was in the cupped hands, he was boosted up to grab the top edge of the wall. Once that man was up, he leaned down to help the next, and the next, and the next. The defenders shot many of them, but as Rainwater watched, they got onto the wall in four places, maybe more.

He had to do something.

Without wasting another second, he took off at a dead run for the nearest group of Sevens aiding their fellows onto the wall. Because he was dressed in the white robe of soldiers in the Sword of the New Prophet, his friends on the walls thought he was just another Seven. A few bullets hit the dirt around him, but none hit him. Hurdling dead bodies, he arrived at the wall gulping air. Without waiting, he stepped onto a man's back, into a pair of linked hands, and grabbed the wrist of a Seven leaning over to help. In seconds, he was atop the wall and unslung his rifle.

The man kneeling on top of the wall was already helping another Seven climb up. Rainwater put the barrel of his AK-47 against the back of the man's head and pulled the trigger. He toppled over and the others looked up, as the enraged Rainwater set his rifle to automatic fire and emptied the magazine into them at point blank range.

When it ran out, he picked up the rifle of the one who had been on top of the wall, and shot the nearest Sevens. He then started running along the battlement, killing Sevens and telling the defenders to get down and get into the caves. If they were surprised to see their leader back in the fight, dressed in a white enemy robe, none said so. Instead, they obeyed instantly.

Rainwater had gone through three rifles when he finally climbed down a ladder himself. Grabbing extra magazines off a few dead Sevens who had fallen inside the wall, he covered his people at they streamed toward the caves. And then the east gate blew in.

"Badass One, this is T-Bolt, do you copy? Over."

"Copy, T-Bolt, this is Badass One. Over."

"I am crossing into New Mexico air space, approaching your position on course zero-eight-eight, speed three-five-zero. Request new target data, over."

"T-Bolt, our new position is north of Albuquerque, moving toward Jemez Springs area. We are not in contact with enemy, repeat, *not* in enemy contact. We can hear gunfire and possible RPG or tank main battery fire. Advise you seek visual targets there. Also be advised there is a second Marine recon company somewhere north or northwest of the area in question, over."

"Roger that, Badass One. Bring the lightning. T-Bolt out."

HEI ammunition among the LAV-25s for the Bushmasters was virtually gone, but not the M791 armor-piercing rounds. Those they still had plenty of. So when the Abrams smashed into the gate and stuck its nose through, like a great white shark trying to get into a shark cage, the five LAV-25s that could bear opened fire. In response, the 105mm main gun fired at the closest LAV-25, and the subsequent blast blew that vehicle's turret straight up into the air.

Even at point blank range, the 25mm rounds couldn't penetrate the tank's steeply sloped front armor. But they could destroy the treads, gun mantlet, barrel of the main gun, and other vulnerable spots. Moreover, being inside a tank when dozens of cannon rounds were hitting it must have unnerved the crew, because after thirty seconds of such punishment it backed out of the shattered gate. Just before it disappeared, though, the LAV-AT finally had a chance to deploy its main weapon, a TOW missile. As the missile streaked through the ruined gate doors, the flash of a detonation outside the walls indicated a hit on something, but none of the Marines could see on what.

Sully ordered the company back against the ridge, with the LAVs again screening for the defenders and dismounted Marines. This put them all within 100 feet of a cave entrance. They would fight in place until the ammo was gone and then abandon their vehicles for the final defense inside the caves. Even as they pulled back and people ran past them on all sides, hundreds of white-robed Sevens poured through the now undefended gates.

Captain April Jones waved back the company's LAV-R, the specialized battlefield recovery vehicle with a boom and winch, keeping a close eye on the sharp dropoff on the highway's shoulder. With its steel cables tied to one end of a tree that blocked the road, the LAV-R needed to back up far enough to get out of the way before activating the winch.

Jones directed the clearing effort because of the danger that the cable might snap. If it did, the released tension might cause a whipsaw effect that could decapitate someone, and she didn't want to endanger any of her Marines. The LAV-R wasn't designed to move so much dead weight, it was meant to tow vehicles with wheels that could still turn, and the steel cable wasn't tested for moving trees. It hadn't snapped yet and this was the third roadblock they'd had to clear, but just because it hadn't broken yet didn't mean that it wouldn't.

She glanced up as another explosion rumbled through the forest. While the clearing effort was underway, other Marines scouted the road ahead, or moved large branches off the highway.

"Are we clear yet?" she yelled to Lieutenant Tomas, who was across the highway.

"Two more feet."

"Take it slow," Jones said to the LAV-R's commander. The bole of the huge pine tree inched across the pavement with a scraping squeal. Jones kept her eye on the cable, as if by concentrating hard enough she could read how close it was to snapping.

"That's good!" Tomas called out.

After waving her hands to signal releasing the tension on the cable, Jones trotted to the middle of the highway. "Let's go!" she said, using her arms to guide the column past the roadblock. "Move out, Marines, let's go."

Over the high-pitched whine of the Detroit Diesel turbocharged engines, the crunch of rubber tires on pavement, and Marines yelling over the din, Jones heard something she'd never expected to hear again... the unmistakable sound of a jet aircraft. Somebody else heard it, too, because the commander of a passing LAV pointed upward. Jones followed his finger and saw the familiar squared-off wings and tail planes, cigar-shaped body, and twin fuselage-mounted engine pods of an A-10 Warthog.

The walls of the infidels' little fortress had been totally cleared of defenders, so Tracy Gollins had no qualms about exposing herself by standing on Highway 4 near the main gate. Surrounded by messenger runners and her staff, she could now safely watch the moment of victory as her army crowded around the smashed gate to enter the inner compound. Their enthusiasm stemmed from a combination of hatred for the infidels, desire to plunder, and fear of retribution by the emir, or more specifically her as as the emir's representative. She hadn't yet radioed him about their victory because she wanted it finished first, but given her cousin Sati's failure and her success, Gollins could visualize herself becoming the third most powerful figure in the Caliphate.

A murmur went through those around her, each man tapping the one beside him and pointing up at the sky. Gollins noticed and shaded her eyes. Was that an eagle gliding on the wind currents? *Surely that must be a good sign,* she thought. But it didn't fly like a bird, not exactly, and what were those rounds things around its sides?

After he'd flown over the long column of vehicles that belonged to Badass Real, Highway 4 was like an arrow leading Captain Babb to his target. He could follow the course of the battle simply by the wreckage and dead bodies scattered for at least three miles south of the road. It was horrifying. Babb had never seen so many corpses in one place before.

The timing couldn't have worked out better if they'd planned it. The mechanized infantry would be in contact with the enemy in less than twenty minutes, and with any luck they would find the Sevens reeling from Babb's attack. The captain had only heard about the Caliphate after waking up a few days before, but from everything he'd heard, they rivaled ISIS in their brutality. He'd killed a lot of ISIS fighters in Syria and Iraq, and killing more was his *raison d'etre* and for going into Cold Sleep in the first place.

Columns of smoke rose here and there, but straight ahead, due north, was what appeared to be a new fire. Throttling back in anticipation of an attack run, he dropped to 1,000 feet for a shallow dive. Thirty seconds later, he saw an amorphous mob of white crowding the highway around what appeared to be a walled compound of some sort. The situation was unclear, except he already knew that his enemy wore white or gray robes, and there had to be thousands of men dressed that way all crowded around some sort of entrance. And in the midst of that teeming mass... Was that a tank? It was.

Never in his life had he heard of such a target, much less seen one. The biggest group he'd ever targeted before had been a couple dozen men. He'd been briefed that they had Stingers, so he couldn't use the first pass to inspect his target; it had to be an attack run. And he intended to hurt those people very badly.

The GAU-8 had been reloaded with 1,100 rounds of a factory-loaded combat mix of 30mm armor-piercing incendiaries, APIs, and HEIs, at a ratio of four to one. The ground would set off the API rounds. The gun's 3,900 rounds per minute rate of fire meant that it only had about 17 seconds before running out. But every second meant 65 cannon shells flying down range, smothering whatever he aimed at with a deadly rain of steel, and if he'd ever found a target worth smothering, this was it.

Flying at only 250 knots, he closed the range at 422 feet per second. At the relatively close range of 1,800 yards, Babb pushed the red trigger button on the joystick. The peculiar buzzing noise of the Gatling-style gun went on for four seconds, a stream of empty shell casings falling in the Warthog's wake. A huge cloud of dust partially hid the mass of men from the hundreds of cannon shells exploding among them. Babb corrected a slide to the left and fired again, this time for five seconds. Then, three seconds later, he released half the bomb load into the same area.

It all happened so fast that he didn't notice any details, only flashing images. Flying over the target, he pushed the throttle all the way forward and held his breath, waiting for the missile warnings to sound. None did.

#

Chapter 53

"Today's forecast calls for brrrrrrrrrrrt, followed by fuckloads of brrrrrrrrrrt."
Anonymous

Shangri-La, AKA Jemez Springs, New Mexico
1900 hours

One second Tracy Gollins smiled as her army pushed into the infidels' fortress; the next, the highway exploded in geysers of dirt and asphalt. At least forty men had surrounded her, pretending to serve a function to avoid having to fight, and they'd acted as a barrier. Shrapnel and red-hot fragments of road surface cut down a dozen men standing between her and the blasts. Reflexes took over and she ran, along with her entourage, for the safety of the trees.

Over the screams of her men, Gollins heard a roar and looked up. Only twice in her life had she seen an airplane in the sky, and never one with a mouth filled with sharp teeth painted on the nose. But she *had* seen the same type of airplane on the ground before. Snippets of memory flashed through her mind — somewhere in Texas, when she'd been a kid, she'd seen one like it at an old American Air Force Base. That one had been stripped and wrecked, but her father had explained it was some sort of attack plane and that had stuck with her.

"Stingers!" she screamed. "Bring up the Stingers! Where are the Stingers?"

She watched the aircraft bank to its left, turning around to attack again. She kept yelling for somebody to find the shoulder-fired surface-to-air missiles, but when she looked around, there was nobody there. She saw all her staff, bodyguards, and hangers-on running away.

Inside The True, there was no time for proper radio procedure as the line of LAVs hammered away at the invading Sevens.

"On the wall to your left!"

"RPG on the right."

"How many of the fuckers are there?"

"Anybody else lovin' this?"

"There, there, get him!"

The dismounted infantry took up position behind the vehicles to cover the crews once they abandoned them. Machine gun and cannon fire cut down the invaders in explosions of gore, like watermelons lined up on a fence.

Captain Sully manned the pindle-mounted M240 on his command and control LAV-C2, not to be a hero, but to keep eyes on the fighting. In such close quarters combat, he also released another Marine to join the dismounted infantry, increasing the covering fire when it came time to bail out.

He wore heat-shield mitts to facilitate changing hot barrels. The mental stopwatch in his brain clicked to the point where it was time to swap out, but the ammo belt ran out two rounds later, and there was no more. Time to go.

Whang, whang... bullets hit the LAV and Sully felt a tearing burn on the outside of his left upper arm. A ragged rip in his uniform immediately turned red with his blood. Dropping to the LAV's interior, he flexed the fingers of his left hand, relieved to see they still functioned. The bleeding didn't seem too bad, so he decided not to bandage it until after he was in the cave. Turning to exit through the vehicle's back door, he heard something outside, and it took a second for his mind to translate that sound as a string of explosions. It reminded him of a pack of firecrackers all going off at once, except bigger.

He stood up in the hatch again. An eerie silence had fallen over the enclosure of The True as both Marines and Sevens stared at smoke boiling up from beyond the walls. But Sully heard something familiar, something he'd never expected to hear again — jet engines. Banking left in the northern sky was the unmistakable shape of a Warthog.

The carnage was beyond Tracy Gollins' comprehension. Gray and white smoke rose from the M1 Abrams. Even with her vision obscured, she could see a dozen holes in its hull. All around it lay heaps of color, mostly white and red, all that remained of hundreds of her men. Survivors ran out the gates and scattered in every direction, thousands of men running for their lives.

After a few seconds, her wits returned. Picking up a rifle, she moved into a clear space on the asphalt and began trying to rally her men. "Stop and fight, you cowards! Allah is watching! Death holds no fear for a warrior of Allah!"

She reached out and tried to stop the panicked men who ran past her, but it was useless. The few she managed to grab shook free. Finally, she lowered the rifle.

"Either the Americans kill you or I do!" she yelled, aiming at a man running right at her.

Two men on her left stopped and raised their own rifles, pointing them at her. Gollins saw it and turned toward them, but she was too slow. Both men fired and she felt her body pushed backward. Others saw what was happening and joined in. Gollins felt no pain, only terror. Her brain realized this was her moment of death. She fell, unable to move, her eyes locked on the blue sky overhead. Before she died, the American aircraft passed overhead across her line of vision. Then the barrel of a rifle appeared inches from her head.

She wanted to be angry but instead felt only fear. She tried to beg but no words came out. She wanted to keep living but there was a muzzle flash, and then there was nothing.

"Badass Six, this is Apache Red Six, enemy contact three miles north of Canon. There must be thousands of 'em, over."

"Apache Red Six, can you push through, over?"

"Badass Six, enemy is avoiding contact. This looks like a rout, over."

"Roger that."

"Apache Red Six out."

Major Ahmadi thought about what to do next, and then pointed at the radio operator. "Try to raise Kicker Real again."

They'd been trying to get through to the Marines all day, so far with no luck. The operator tried four times before shaking her head to indicate no luck. But before Sully could say anything else, she held up a finger, meaning *wait*. "It's Kicker One, Major."

"Kicker One, this is Badass Six. Can you give a sitrep, over?"

"We are inside a walled compound with all of the IPs and all functioning vehicles. The Sevens broke in and we were about to be overrun… did you see an A-10, over?"

"Roger that, Kicker One. Call sign is T-Bolt, monitoring tac four. Status of Kicker Real, over?"

"Gotta buy that bus driver a drink. Kicker Real is good to go. He's checking on damage to the company, over."

"We have Sevens moving south and avoiding contact, Kicker One. Can you advise their status, over?"

"Badass Six, they overdosed on hot lead and are now a goat rodeo."

Ahmadi shook his head and smiled… Marines. "Roger that, Kicker One. Estimate we are ten mikes from your position. See you soon, Badass Six out."

Captain April Jones heard Bushmasters firing on the highway ahead, followed by M240s, and was about to call Nickleback One for a report when the radio crackled to life in her headphones.

"Nickleback One for Safety Real, over."

"Safety Real here, over."

"Multiple enemies on my front, number unknown but there's a lot. RPGs seen and armor heard, over."

"Nickleback One, are you under attack?"

"Affirmative, Safety Real, we are taking return fire. Burps are moving through the heavy country south of the highway, others over the ridge on the west. Estimate enemy numbers in the hundreds, over."

"Copy that, Nickleback One, am moving to support your flanks. Am releasing mortars to you again. Safety Real out."

The broken nature of the terrain, interspersed with stands of mature ponderosa pine, blue spruce, and aspen trees limiting paths and sight lines in the forest, also limited Jones' support options, particularly with vehicles designed for speed, not close-range fighting against infantry. With 1st Platoon out front on the highway, she deployed 2nd Platoon on the left and 3rd Platoon on the right, with the rest of the company two abreast on the highway. It was an unwieldy formation, but in the confined spaces there was nothing else to be done.

Following a huge explosion, Jones saw gouts of flame through the trees ahead but had no time to decide if a friendly or enemy vehicle had gone up. Bullets *whanged* off the hull of her LAV-C2 near her right hand and she dropped lower in the hatch. Reaching down, she retrieved her own M16 and brought the butt into her shoulder. Blood pounded in her ears as she forced herself to look for targets instead of slipping into the relative safety of the hull. Despite what Marine Corps Commandant General Michael Neller might have later said, Jones had joined the Corps when 'every Marine was a rifleman,' and riflemen didn't hide when somebody shot at them — they shot back. If it was good enough for Chesty Puller, it was good enough for her.

As a Marine Recon Company commander, Jones had been offered one of the few M27 Infantry Automatic Rifles available at Overtime, but turned it down in favor of the M4A1 she'd used in Iraq and Afghanistan. The M4's shorter barrel was easier to maneuver in an LAV, compared to the M16A4 most of the infantry carried. Now, as more fire buzzed around her, she lined up on a white-robed man with a thick red beard, and put two rounds into his sternum.

Something burned her upper left arm but adrenaline stifled the pain as she sought out the shooter. Forward of her, the gunner opened fire with the pindle-mounted M240 machine gun. Jones watched the rounds chew up the bole of an aspen with some Sevens hiding behind it. One spun away and she shot another. From that point forward, she lost situational awareness in a blizzard of gun and cannon fire that went on continuously for nearly five minutes.

Act and react was all any of them could do, as hundreds of Sevens filtered through the woods flanking the highway. Most ran, first north until they found the line of LAV-25s blocking their path, and then to either west or east, depending on which side of the road they were on. Explosions, rocket trails, screams, gunning engines, and the scents of fire, hot oil, and blood overwhelmed her senses.

And then it was over. A few shots rang out here and there, moans came from all around, and something burned in the forest. Straight ahead...

"Nickleback One, sitrep!" Jones said into her helmet mike, louder than she'd intended. "Nickleback One, this is Safety Real, what is your situation?"

"Safety Real, this is Nickleback Two. Enemy Bradley hit Nickleback One with a TOW; enemy was destroyed by return fire. We are attempting rescue of Nickleback One's crew. Over."

"Nickleback Two, what is the status of enemies in your area? Over."

"Enemy withdrawing in disorder in all directions, Safety Real. No current incoming fire. Do we pursue, over?"

"Negative. Take over 1st Platoon, Nickleback Two. The company will follow once back into march column. Detail a squad to assist corpsman with Nickleback One. Get Oscar Mike toward Jemez Springs ASAP, and keep me advised. Safety Real out."

Jones pushed back her helmet to let air cool her sweaty hair. She took a deep breath and exhaled, as she always had after a firefight.

"Hey, Captain," her gunner said. He pointed at her left arm. "You need the medical kit?"

"Huh?" Jones looked where he pointed, only then realizing that blood soaked her sleeve. "Oh, yeah... I guess I do."

Straight ahead, the road opened up, empty and brilliant in the sunlight. Jones wondered if the fighting would soon be over.

She had no way of knowing it already was.

Interstate 25, south of Albuquerque, New Mexico

Abdul-Qudoos Fadil el Mofty sat unmoving in the back seat of his 1976 Mercedes 240D. Arms crossed, he stared at a spot on the floor, glaring. Twilight left the countryside indistinct as they sped past. He had forbidden the use of headlights until they had gone at least an hour south of Albuquerque, so the entire column moved at half the usual speed. A partition separated him and the old man from the driver, so el Mofty didn't have to keep up the façade of being the emir.

"What will you do now?" said the old man sitting beside him.

"I'm thinking about killing people who ask stupid questions."

"If you want me to advise you, I have to know what you're thinking."

"If I want you to advise me, I'll ask you."

When the convoy of 83 vehicles first pulled out from his headquarters in Albuquerque, El Mofty had feared an air attack and posted men with their remaining five Stingers around his car. After half an hour with no air strike, he breathed easier about his chances for making it to Texas. He had no intention of returning to New Khorasan, aka Tucson, since that city couldn't be held if the Americans wanted it. In Texas, however, they wouldn't find things so easy.

"How many men do you think they wound up with?" he finally asked.

"You mean Overtime? My answer hasn't changed… I don't know. I didn't even know for sure that it was a real thing until we moved into Arizona last year. But I'll say this much — it's a bigger force than Tom Steeple originally planned for."

"Are you sure he kept you in the loop?"

The old man shook his head. "No. In fact, I assumed all along that he was lying to me."

"So they could have ten thousand men."

"Or more."

"Do you think they'll move into Texas?"

"Not right away," the old man said. "Eventually, yes, but first they'll have to repair the roads and bridges, maybe get a railway going, establish supply dumps… it will take a while. What I would advise you to do is get ready to defend Texas. Build a new army, dig tank traps around critical places… bleed them for every foot of ground. They only have so many combat troops."

"At the moment, we have none."

"Survivors will return, new leaders will emerge, you can rebuild the army."

"That's assuming that my brother, our beloved New Prophet, doesn't have me shot."

"Yeah," the old man said. He couldn't argue with that gloomy possibility. "Assuming that."

#

Chapter 54

If we live, we live for the Lord; and if we die, we die for the Lord. So, whether we live or die, we belong to the Lord.
Romans, 14:8

Operation Overtime
0912 hours, May 8

For the past few nights, all had seemed right with the world. Or, if not right exactly, at least better. Morgan would be fine physically, although the mental effect from the loss of Christopher Michael, the name they'd given the baby, might not be so easily overcome. The bullet had struck her side at an oblique angle and missed her internal organs. And whatever Friedenthall had given Janine and Cynthia to help them sleep had worked. With Janine by his side and Cynthia lightly snoring in the other bedroom, Angriff slept better than he had since coming out of Long Sleep. Maybe it had something to do with all the physical exertion over the previous two weeks, heaped onto all the stress, worry, and guilt, but when he woke that morning, the effects of fatigue seemed to have evaporated, and his energy level was much improved. Even the coffee that J.C. brought tasted great.

Sitting behind his desk, he ran a cigar under his nose and drew in a deep breath, reveling in the scent of the unlit tobacco. Closing his eyes, he savored the warmth of the morning sun pouring through the gigantic window in the mountainside. The sense of loss from so many dead members of the brigade ate at him in a way that nothing had before. Losing people in battle was always traumatic, but everyone understood that was a very real risk when you made the military your career choice. What made this different was that Angriff blamed himself. But for a moment, a sweet, blessed moment, he forgot all that and enjoyed the fragrance of the cigar.

"I can leave again if you want to smoke that," said a voice from the doorway. "But I'm not going back to Sierra, even if you ask nicely."

Angriff raised an eyebrow at the sight of Norm Fleming against the door frame, arms folded and smirking.

"It's about time you got back from vacation."

"There is no doubt that Sierra is definitely a garden spot. I highly recommend you give it a try. There's another supply run leaving this afternoon."

"I'll take your word for it."

"I brought you back a souvenir."

"Yeah? What is it?"

"I'll give you a hint — it barks a lot."

A grin crossed Angriff's face and softened into a warm smile. "Kona. Janine's going to fall hard for that dog. Thanks, that might be just what she needs."

"Oh?"

"Something's wrong with her and Cynthia both, I think it's some kind of virus they can't shake. I asked them to stay inside as much as they could, just in case it's contagious."

"What does Doctor Friedenthall say?"

"He's not sure, but he says if it's a virus, it's not like anything he's ever seen. They're doing blood work and took a bunch of tests. We should know soon."

"Want me to leave?" Fleming pointed at the cigar.

"Naw, Janine doesn't like the way they make me smell, and I need to ration them anyway. Want to hear a joke, Norm? It's got Marines in it, but it's still funny."

Fleming laughed before Angriff even started telling the story. "Sure, Nick, go ahead. I think we could both use a laugh." He shut the door and sat in one of the chairs facing Angriff's desk.

"Okay, so a sailor and a Marine were in a bar, drinking beer and arguing which was the better service. Ten minutes into the argument the Marine said, 'We have Iwo Jima!' The sailor then said, 'Yeah, but we have the Battle of Midway!' The Marine then said, 'That wasn't just the Navy. A lot of Marines fought and died in that battle.' The sailor conceded that the Navy could not have won the battle without the help of the Marines, and desperately blurted out, 'The Navy invented sex!' To which the Marine answered, 'Maybe you did, but Marines introduced it to women!'"

Fleming smiled.

"Have I told you that one before?" Angriff said.

"A few times."

"Sorry."

"It's all right. It's just good to hear you talk again."

"I could read the phone book if you want me to."

"It's not that good to hear you talk."

"I'm glad you're back, Norm. I'm glad you're safe."

"Jokes aside, Nick, you don't look so good."

"I think I know how General Lee felt after Pickett's Charge, or maybe Grant after the last assault at Cold Harbor. So much blood... so much unnecessary death, all because of one man's hubris. In this case, mine. This was all my fault, every damned bit of it."

Sergeant Schiller knocked on the door, almost like he'd been listening. "Sir, Colonel Friedenthall would like to see you, Mrs. Angriff, and Cynthia in his office. He says it's urgent."

The sadness vanished from his face, replaced by a frown of concern. "Tell him we'll be right there."

Once the Angriffs had settled into the three chairs facing his desk, Colonel Friedenthall withdrew a thick file folder from a locked drawer and laid it in front of him. Angriff knew right away the doctor was stalling.

"I appreciate you coming so quickly," he said, looking down at the folder and not at his patients.

"What's this about, Doctor?" Angriff usually called him by his rank, but clearly something had Friedenthall upset and he hoped calling him doctor might calm him down a bit.

Friedenthall rubbed his eyes with the tips of his fingers. "I'm not sure how to tell all of you this," he said.

"Doctor, the only way to tell it is to tell it."

Friedenthall inhaled and clasped his hands on the desk. "Mrs. Angriff, Cynthia, you both have cancer. Tests show it has metastasized and is spreading very fast. I'm so very sorry."

"Cancer?" Janine Angriff said. It came out sounding like *can-suh*. "I see." She blinked, obviously trying to process the diagnosis. She wrapped an arm around Cynthia, who sat stupefied.

"Are you sure, Doctor?" Nick Angriff said, realizing as he said it how absurd it sounded, yet not regretting saying it. He also realized that the stunned tone in his voice probably sounded just like the spouse of every person whose loved one had just been told they have cancer, and he didn't care about that, either.

"I'm afraid the tests are conclusive, General Angriff. There's no mistake. God help me, I wish there was. We triple-checked everything."

Still maintaining her calm, Janine Angriff did what she always did; she gathered facts. "May I ask what kind of cancer we have?"

"That's the strange part, Mrs. Angriff. We don't know. To my knowledge, nothing like this has ever been found before. I consulted every oncology book and periodical I could find — and we have almost everything ever written in digital form — and came up empty. There's nothing similar in the databases, either. By the way it acts, how fast it spreads, we know it's *some* form of cancer, but what kind, we just can't say. It appears to be something brand new, some genetic mutation of some sort."

Nick Angriff looked up as one word cut through the fog and bored into his brain. "Did you say genetic?"

"Yes, sir. But many cancers have genetic mutation components, so that doesn't necessarily mean anything. We have classified it as a leukemia variant, but the truth is that's just for our own purposes at this point. Otherwise we have no idea. We do know it's a form of blood cancer."

Angriff's mind had clicked into high gear. He rubbed the bridge of his nose and stared at the corner of Friedenthall's desk.

"Nick?" Janine said.

He shook his head, as if waking from a trance. "If I forced you to guess, Doctor, would you say this could be a deliberate genetic manipulation?"

"Deliberate?"

"Yes, deliberate."

"I'm not sure I understand what you mean."

"I'm not sure what I mean, either. I don't know all the medical terms, but could this be a manmade form of cancer, created on purpose?"

"Nick," his wife said, "what do you mean, on purpose?"

"I mean just that, Nini." He patted her hand. "A new cancer that would be resistant to current treatments, call it... call it *weaponized*, like the Wuhan coronavirus I read about in the run-up to the Collapse. That's the flu virus the Chinese were trying to genetically manipulate, but it accidentally got out of the lab, right, Doctor?"

"I was already in Long Sleep when that happened, General, just like you. But I did read about it in the medical journals we have stored in the database. They all denied that it escaped from a Chinese lab."

"I have access to highly classified material from back then, but that doesn't matter now. Could a new form of cancer be *designed*?"

"I don't know why anybody would want to, but I suppose you could manipulate cancer cells that way," Friedenthall said. "But you'd have to be a world-class microbiologist or geneticist to create something like this."

"How about a world-class molecular biologist whose specialty was genetic manipulation?"

"If anyone could, I suppose it could be someone like that... Is there anyone in particular that you're thinking of?"

"Karl Hasso Ullrich."

"Ullrich? Oh, my," Friedenthall said. "Yes, I feel certain he could design something like this, if anybody could. I heard him speak once, in Zurich. He was a brilliant man, a true genius. Yes, I think Ullrich could have done this, although I can't imagine why he *would*. But if you don't mind my asking, how do you know about him, General?"

"I'm afraid that's classified, Doctor." Angriff's face shifted into the scowl he wore when battle reports came into headquarters.

"What's the prognosis and treatment plan?" Janine said. Although her voice sounded wooden, she plowed through the problem like she had always done. After the initial shock wore off, she wanted to make plans to move forward and put it behind her.

"We're fully stocked with the best cancer treatments in existence before the Collapse..."

"But," Angriff said.

"But I don't hold much hope for their efficacy against this particular variant of the disease, and the side effects would be terrible. I can offer palliative care to ease any pain you may have."

"There has to be *some* hope," Cynthia said, speaking for the first time. The quaver in her voice betrayed her fear, as did the tears pooling in her blue eyes.

His eyes met Angriff's, as if the two men could communicate telepathically, and they locked their gazes across the desk. "There is one course of action that might buy time to find a treatment plan."

The gravity in his face brought an image into Angriff's mind. "Long Sleep. Going cold again."

Friedenthall nodded. "Yes, General."

1702 hours

The wind was up on the mountaintop, as it sometimes was. The women's hair rippled like the manes of running horses, even Morgan's, whose hair was cut short to accommodate her combat helmet. She sat motionless as light from the waning sun glittered off her wheelchair. Green Ghost, more and more being called Nick, Jr., by the family, stood with arms crossed and took his cue from the women. Joe Randall was there, too, trying not to be noticed. This was not the type of situation in which he excelled.

Down the slope a large field of solar panels sucked up bright sunlight like a vacuum, storing the energy in huge batteries. Months before, Operation Overtime had switched over to solar power instead of the hydro-generators deep underground, to avoid undue wear on those irreplaceable machines. Solar panels they had in abundance, and backup batteries, too, but not hydro-electric generators. Those were one and done.

Nick, Sr., stood to one side of the loose circle, with his arm around his much smaller wife. "This is not goodbye," he said. "We *will* be reunited, I promise you that."

The first one to cry stunned them all; Nikki dropped to one knee, sobbing with great heaves. "No! It's not fair!" The last word was a scream.

Her brother moved to comfort her, but Janine stopped him with an upraised hand. She squatted beside her distraught stepdaughter and cradled her head, stroking her hair and whispering, "Sssshhh... it's going to be all right, honey, you wait and see." Nikki hugged her back. They stayed that way for most of a minute.

"Daddy," Cynthia said, "tell me the truth. Will I ever see you again?"

"Yes, sweetheart, you will. I make that promise to you. I'm going to find the cure and when you wake up again, we're going to all live the life we were meant to live. I swear by all that's holy, I will make that happen."

They went on like that for a while, knowing that while they said goodbye, below them the medical staff was readying two CHILSS to receive Janine and Cynthia. Only Green Ghost noticed when Nikki slipped away, but he let her go, assuming the scene was too much for her.

He was wrong.

#

Chapter 55

"I'm not your enemy... I'm your executioner."
Attributed to Lupus est, vigilante in Rome, circa 310 a.d.

Operation Overtime
1908 hours, May 8

Nikki pushed her face flat against the bars of the cell door. The guards knew her and let her do it; both were a little scared of her, and liked watching her ass, and she knew it. Tom Steeple didn't hear her, so she watched him for almost five minutes before he finally noticed her.

"I don't get many visitors," he said. The left side of his face was swollen and purple. "To what do I owe the honor of being visited by such a lovely young lady? Unless, of course, you're my executioner, in which case I suppose I know why you're here."

She waited five seconds to answer, as she'd been taught. "If they die," she said, "I'm coming back to cut you into a thousand little pieces, and I'm going to take a long time to do it."

"You have me at a disadvantage. If who dies?"

"I'm going to start with your toes, and then your fingers, your ears, your tongue, and anything else sticking out of your body. I'm going to carve you into a heap of bloody flesh but you won't be dead, no, I'm not going to kill you. I want you to suffer like no man has ever suffered before."

Nikki saw Steeple's head move the slightest bit and knew he was inspecting her. His eyes traced the outlines of her blonde hair, then shifted to her high cheekbones and wound up staring directly into her eyes. People had often described them as cold blue, and Nick said they were just like their father's. "You must be that psychotic young woman I've heard about, Green Ghost's sister... Nipple, right?. I've heard a lot about you."

"I used to be Nipple, just like you used to be a general, but I'm not her any more. But she's still inside me... I'm fighting to keep her there. And I'm dead-ass serious, mister. For your sake, you'd better hope she never comes out again."

Even as she said it, though, she knew it was a lie. She was who she was, and there was never a doubt who was going to win the inner struggle.

Operation Overtime
0622 hours, May 9

Nothing in Operation Overtime's incredible engineering surpassed the CHILSS chamber, where the entire brigade had spent the past fifty years or more. Most of the thousands of CHILSS necessary to accommodate them had been converted to hydroponic uses, as intended by their original design. Angriff had shaken his head at the genius needed to design such machines. On the few occasions when he'd visited the vast chamber, the fresh smell of lush greenery had infused him with a feeling of being back home in Virginia, walking barefoot on a lawn of thick spring grass. Unlike so much of the base, this area was reserved for growing new life. Now it seemed metaphorical.

The arrangement hadn't changed. Fifteen separate levels filled an area larger in square footage than ten football fields. Factoring in those levels meant the work area equaled 150 football fields, a space so enormous that he couldn't see it all from one spot. The flooring was steel mesh to save weight, with titanium support poles lined up in regular rows from the floor to the ceiling far overhead. Regularly spaced powered mesh elevators hefted heavy loads up and down, while stairways also provided access from floor to floor. Conduits clung to each support column, containing power and water systems.

Five people stood beside an open CHILSS on the ground floor — Colonel Friedenthall, two technicians, and Nick and

Janine Angriff. Cynthia Angriff had already gone back into Long Sleep in the CHILSS beside her mother's. The girl had tried not to cry, knowing how much it would upset her mother, but in the end they had all three broken down. Now Janine Angriff clung to her husband, until Friedenthall gently prodded them.

"I'm very sorry, General, Janine, but the drug I gave to help your coughing is going to wear off pretty soon, and that will greatly increase the danger of the Long Sleep procedure. We need to get you under before that happens."

She nodded. "I understand." Taking in a raspy breath, she gazed up at her husband. "Don't forget me, Nick? Promise me that."

Tears rolled down his cheeks, which he didn't bother wiping away. "Never could I forget you, Nini. We'll see each again, mark my words, and in *this* life."

She smiled, as she had the day they'd met. To his eye, her cheeks were full and pink, not sunken and sallow with disease, and her cornflower blue eyes clear instead of bloodshot.

The technicians had provided a small step ladder to help her climb into the CHILSS. With resolution, she turned and climbed in. Blowing a kiss to her husband, she nodded for them to seal the chamber.

#

Chapter 56

"I have never yet done a man to death by torture, but by God, sir, you tempt me!"
Robert E. Howard, "Red Shadows"

Operation Overtime
0731 hours, May 9

Nick Angriff paused before the cell door. He could feel the blood pulsing at his temples. Water from his eyes ran down his cheeks as rage narrowed them. His right fist clenched and unclenched spasmodically. "Open it," he said to the guard. "Then stand down. No matter what you hear, stay out of it. Even gunshots. Got that?"

The guard swallowed. "Aye, sir."

"And if somehow General Steeple walks back out that door instead of me, shoot to kill. That's an order."

"A... aye, sir."

It took several seconds to compose himself enough that he didn't simply go in shooting.

When he stepped inside, Tom Steeple didn't bother to rise from his cot. He lay with his left arm shielding his eyes from the ever-present glare of the overhead light. The slightest movement allowed a quick peek at his newest visitor.

That infuriated Angriff even more. "Stand up, you son of a bitch."

"Another Angriff, what a surprise," Steeple said. "Eventually I'll be visited by the whole family. Come to hit me again?"

Steeple had mastered the art of diversion and Angriff knew it, so he tried to stay focused on why he'd come. "You know my temper, so you'd better stand up. I'm not going to hit you, but I might kill you, and nothing means more to you than your own precious life," Angriff said. "You're the ultimate narcissist, Tom, so I'm going to give you the chance to save your life, right here, right now. One chance."

"You like to threaten unarmed people, don't you? I guess it runs in the family."

Angriff blinked. Steeple's previous comment about meeting his whole family finally registered in his consciousness. "Was Green Ghost here?" He now regretted mentioning his son to Steeple back in the Crystal Palace.

"If *he'd* been here, I'd probably be dead right now. His sister, however, is a different story. You know, your oldest daughter? The one with the daddy issues?"

"You're playing a dangerous game, Tom."

"I don't think so, *Nick*." Steeple finally sat up and swung his legs over the side of his bunk. "You came here ready to kill me, and dead is dead no matter how it happens. But you can only kill me once, and you won't do that until you get the information you came for. What's fascinating to me is that you didn't ask how I knew about Nipple. Or should I say Nikki?"

Angriff *had* planned to ask that, but in a different way. Alarms had gone off in his head as soon as he'd heard Steeple mention Nipple and Nikki... how could he know such things in the brig? Had *he* mentioned them? Angriff couldn't remember... maybe he had.

But he had intended to trap Steeple into telling him what he wanted to know, not be directly confronted with it. He'd forgotten how good Steeple was at this sort of game. Just as Angriff had no equal on the battlefield, Tom Steeple was unparalleled at circular conversations. But Angriff learned fast. Instead of exploding, as he wanted to do and Steeple no doubt expected, he nodded. "Thanks, that tells me who it must be. Now I know who the mole is."

Steeple squinted. "You're bluffing."

"You think you're so clever, Tom, yet you keep underestimating me. I knew Bettison wasn't your only contact inside Overtime, and sooner or later I expected the others to expose themselves. So I've laid traps here and there along the way, like the Navy did at Midway in 1942. Remember? Intelligence needed to know Yamamoto's target, so they signaled that Midway was out of fresh water. When the Japanese repeated the message, they knew Midway was his target. I did the same thing and there were only two people around when I said that about Nipple and me, so it has to be one of those two."

They locked eyes. Steeple tried to read Angriff for signs of deception, but unlike when they were in the unmarked airplane back in Switzerland, this time he couldn't read anything. "I still think you're bluffing."

"And I still don't care. I came here for answers. If I don't get them, I'll kill you right here and now and not think twice about it. I don't care about who you were, about court-martials or procedures. Those times are over, at least in your case. As far as I'm concerned you're the greatest enemy that Overtime has, which makes your death a necessity. So you'll either tell me what I want to know, or I swear before God I'll beat you to death with my own hands."

"*I'm* Overtime's greatest enemy? You ignorant, presumptuous bastard! If it wasn't for me, there wouldn't *be* an Operation Overtime! The Seventh Cavalry wouldn't exist if I hadn't created it! Look around you; everything inside this mountain is here because of *me*. Not you, not Norm Fleming or any politician, it's here because of me and only me. I'm the one who listened to Roger Deeson when he was thrown out of every other office in the Pentagon. I'm the one who had the vision when this mountain was still solid rock. I gave my entire life to building this place, I found every dollar needed to construct it, I requisitioned every nut, bolt, and bullet, and I personally oversaw every man and woman on its rolls. I did whatever it took to build this place, including things that horrified me, and do you know why I did it?

"Because I loved my country more than I loved myself, that's why. America was a remarkable idea that can't be allowed to die. I saw the computer projections and I believed them, and I took action based on those beliefs. And now, eight decades after I started, my creation is the only thing that stands between my beloved United States and the dustbin of history. If you think I'm not proud of that, if you think I haven't been willing to die to save my country, then you're as dense as everyone said you were."

Angriff paused long enough for Steeple to stop breathing hard from his tirade. "How long have you been practicing that speech?"

"Fuck you, Angriff. If you came here to kill me, then get it over with."

"You would do anything to get this place built, wouldn't you, including murder?"

"You want honesty? Fine. The answer is yes, I would."

"Congratulations, you've distracted me again, Tom, so let's get to why I'm here. I told you I'd give you a chance to save your miserable life, and I think you've been expecting this moment. It's not enough that you manipulated me and slaughtered two dozen people with that so-called terrorist attack at Lake Tahoe, or let me think my daughter died in Syria; you had to keep Janine and Cynthia in Long Sleep just in case I got out of line. Two aces up your sleeve, right? Except we rescued them and screwed everything up.

"But that didn't worry you, and I've been wondering why. The whole time you've been in here, you treated it more like you were on vacation than in a cell deep underground. I figured you had more aces to play, and now I know what one of them is. So let's cut to the chase. Janine and Cynthia have an aggressive form of cancer the doctors have never seen before. They think it's genetically engineered. That means there could be an off switch that stops it cold, and I think you know what that is. So tell me now and I let you keep breathing."

"Cancer? I am so sorry to hear that, Nick. But what makes you think I know anything about it?"

Angriff's face folded into the same scowl that once graced the covers of magazines and newspapers. He withdrew a Desert Eagle, slid back the bolt, and chambered a round with a loud *snick* before pointing it at Steeple's forehead. "Last chance, Tom."

Steeple's attitude didn't change. He appeared unfazed by imminent death. "Let's hypothetically say I could help you. What's in it for me?"

"I won't kill you."

"You think being in this cage again isn't a form of death? If that's all you've got, then shoot me now and end my misery."

"Don't tempt me."

"Go ahead, pull the trigger. I'll kneel if it makes it easier."

"Tell me what you know and maybe we'll work something out."

"God Almighty, Angriff, that's insulting. Just how stupid do you think I am?"

The huge pistol trembled in Angriff's hand as he suppressed the urge to start shooting. He lowered the gun but didn't re-holster it.

"That's more like it. Assuming I can help you, and your lovely bride and daughter, I want my command back."

"You mean Operation Comeback?"

"No, Comeback was part of Operation Overtime. They were intended to complement each other, two parts of one whole. I didn't tell you because you didn't need to know. I mean that I want command of the whole shooting match... no pun intended."

"Let me get this straight. You want to command both Comeback and Overtime? And, by extension, outrank me again? After everything you've just pulled?"

"Yes."

"I guess you're right, Tom. I should just shoot you now." He raised the pistol, took aim, and placed his finger on the trigger.

"Who are you kidding? Shoot me and your wife and daughter are dead."

"You mean *dead again*, don't you?" Angriff's finger squeezed the trigger ever so slowly.

Steeple straightened his back and smoothed his filthy uniform. Then he took a step forward, as if daring Angriff to shoot. "Fire away, then! But don't dare tell me you've never caused collateral damage."

The muzzle of the huge pistol didn't waver from between Steeple's eyes until Angriff pulled it back and pointed it at the ceiling. His finger rested on the side of the trigger guard. "That's what my family is to you, collateral damage?"

"Yes."

"And using them to blackmail me doesn't bother you?"

"Bother? Yes. Stop? No."

Angriff squinted. "You are one sick man to do that to a brother officer."

"How is this any different from you ordering a strike on a town with women and children because the enemy is using them for human shields? You might accomplish your mission, but at the cost of innocent lives. Still, you'd do it because you had to. How many times have you sent troops into battle knowing someone's mother or father, son or daughter, won't be coming back? But you did it anyway, because you had to. We killed sixty thousand Frenchmen bombing the occupying

Germans during World War Two, and have you ever heard the French bitch about it? I had a mission to complete and your family stood in the way of me completing it, a mission few have ever had to face before... saving our country. So I did what you'd have done. I did what I had to. But I didn't kill them like you've done a hundred times in your career. I brought them here, to you, and I can cure their cancer, too. But only if you do what I say."

"You know they're not the same thing."

"And you know they are."

"What happened to you, Tom? Were you always like this?"

"You mean patriotic? Yes, I've always loved my country."

"I meant a heartless narcissist." Angriff holstered his pistol and turned to leave.

"Walk out that door and your wife and daughter die. Are you really willing to sacrifice their lives to keep me out of command?"

Angriff stopped in mid-turn. "Yes, I am... let that sink in. But fortunately I won't have to. We've put them back into Long Sleep to stop the progression of the disease."

"That doesn't cure them."

"No, it doesn't. But it does keep you in here, where you belong. And someday we may yet discover a cure. At least I'll have that hope to hang onto."

When Steeple didn't answer, Angriff turned to the door and raised his fist to knock, since there was no inside handle.

"There's so much you don't know and it's all headed straight for you."

Angriff paused, fist still raised, but didn't turn around. "That's at least the third time you've said something like that. Is it the only chip you've got left?"

"It's been true every time, and it's true now."

"So tell me."

"What's in it for me?"

"Make me an offer I'll accept."

"I command Comeback as your deputy commander."

Without his realizing it, Angriff's upper lip curled. He turned halfway back around. "First, tell me something I don't know. Then we'll talk."

Steeple scratched his bottom lip, thinking. "All right, you want proof of my goodwill? I'll tell you how to save your family's lives and maybe that will do it. There's a hidden chamber behind a wall in a warehouse on the western side. Sub-Floor Five, I think. Behind it you'll find—"

"—we'll find ten CHILSS containing world-renowned molecular biologist Karl Hasso Ullrich and his team. He's the man who designed the cancer that's eating my wife and daughter up from the inside out."

Tom Steeple was known as a man who could never be caught unawares, a man who could not be shocked. But for the very first time, Angriff saw him stunned into silence. Then he narrowed his eyes. "If you found Ullrich, then why come to me? You'd be furious at what I did to your family, but you're scared, and yet you already have the cure. That means something went wrong."

It was Angriff's turn to study Steeple. The wan lighting hid much of his face, making it difficult to read slight nuances. Did he really not know? "Ullrich and his team were dead when we found them. Their CHILSS had been smashed open, and then the killer, or killers, ransacked the room. Whatever else was in there was gone."

This second shock left Steeple slack-jawed and silent. He fell onto his cot like he'd been cold-cocked, but that only lasted a few seconds before he rose and began to pace. Angriff eyed him to make sure he didn't come within striking range. "How long have they been dead?" he finally asked.

"A long time."

"Shit. Damn, damn, damn. Yes, Ullrich was my last ace in the hole in case you refused to get with the program. He designed the cancer, although he was unaware of my intentions for it, and he simultaneously created a cure. The cancer cells have a built-in flaw that lets them be completely eradicated, so the patient can never have a relapse. But the serum was kept in the chamber with Ullrich, along with the formula and all his notes. If those are missing..."

"If those are missing, my wife and daughter are going to die."

Steeple nodded.

"And it's entirely your fault," Angriff said, again fighting the urge to empty his pistols into the man.

Steeple rubbed his eyes. "Unless... unless *they* want to blackmail you."

That made Angriff pause, but only for a moment. "Since I take it you have no idea who *they* may be, I need to go see to my family."

"What about me?"

"I intend to forget you're down here."

"Transport to anywhere I name."

"What?"

"Despite your family's situation, you're still going to get run over by something you'll never see coming. I'll give you this much for free. It's officially called Operation Hail Mary, but those who funded it call it Project Evolution."

"You mean Rosos."

"That's right. I'll tell you everything I know in exchange for a rifle, ammo, all the water I can carry, a week's rations, and transport to a place of my choosing."

"You'd make up anything to get out of here."

"I've never once lied to you, Nick. Not once. My talent lies in twisting words, and answering specific questions with evasive answers. I'm a classic counter-puncher, but when it comes to facts I'm a straightforward, stick-to-the-template sort. I cannot just create all of this in my mind."

"No deal."

"I'll throw in the weapons depot."

"Now you *are* making things up."

"Am I? Overtime has a bunch of fixed-wing pilots, right? You probably haven't even thawed them yet. I forget the number, but they're all qualified for single-seat fighters. Don't try to deny it, either, because everything in this mountain is here because of me. And I'm sure you've wondered why we put them here if they didn't have any planes to fly. You probably also know that Comeback has two dozen A-10s, but what you don't know is that those are just the tip of the iceberg. The Air Force wanted into Overtime in a big way, so there are more aircraft at the weapons depot, along with every piece of surplus and prototype equipment I could beg, borrow, or steal. The planes are F-22s and more A-10s, both put out of a job when the F-35 came on line in big numbers. There's a fleet more Humvees, Bradleys, even some joint light tactical vehicles, plus spare parts, ammo, the works. Let me go, and you get all that, too."

"You'll supply me like you supplied our enemies with Stingers?" For the second time that day, Angriff shocked his former superior.

"It's obvious that you think I know what you're referencing, but I don't."

"Benghazi."

For at least the third time that day, Steeple blanched. "I completely underestimated you."

"So did Ansar al-Sharia, Alois Steyer, and the Secretary of State. You signed off on the Zombies taking out Steyer in Egypt, and you must have also approved of leaving them to die in the middle of the Red Sea."

Steeple opened his mouth but Angriff cut him off.

"What you didn't expect was me putting all the pieces together and saving them anyway. You got sloppy, Tom, which is what happens when paper-pushers try to plan tactical operations. And just so you know, I'm also aware of the four cases of Stingers being shipped to the Caliphate."

"*What?*"

"Nice try."

"I truly have no idea what you're talking about."

"If I believe that, then yet another turncoat with their own agenda has infiltrated your grandiose creation, so which is it, Tom? Are you a traitor, or just sloppy?"

Steeple had no reply. After a short pause, Angriff started to walk out.

He turned one last time. "Sooner or later, Tom, God's gonna cut you down. And when He does, I hope I'm there to see it."

Then he walked out.

#

Chapter 57

Caesar extended mercy to his enemies and they killed him.
Quintus Varis

The Crystal Palace, Operation Overtime
0900 hours, May 9

"I hate to say it, but he's got a point," Green Ghost said, leaning against the opaque electro-glass near the door. "Those planes are a game changer, if they're real."

Hands clasped behind his back, unlit cigar in his jaw, Angriff stood in his favorite spot in the Crystal Palace and stared out at the desert.

"Your father knows that," Norm Fleming said from his seat on the couch. "He's torn. The General Angriff half wants to make the deal, but the Nick the husband and father part wants to kill him."

"Does my opinion count?" Green Ghost said. "On the family side of it, I mean."

Angriff glanced over his shoulder. "Janine has claimed you as her own son, and Cynthia's your sister. Hell, yes, your opinion counts."

"Agree to his terms. Verify everything he tells you before you let him go. If he won't agree to that, then the deal's off, but he will."

"How can you be so sure?"

Norm Fleming interrupted. "I agree with Nick, Jr. Tom Steeple *always* has a backup plan. Always. The man is walking redundancy. He'll hem and haw, but he'll agree. He's got another play out there somewhere."

Green Ghost waited to ensure Fleming had finished before continuing. "Take an inventory of the weapons depot, check out this Hail Mary thing, verify every detail of whatever he tells you. If it all checks out, then keep your word and let him go."

"I can't believe you two. Am I the only one who remembers what's been going on the past few weeks? Steeple has caused this brigade an immense amount of pain and death. Norm, you're right about him having a backup plan, which is what makes him so dangerous. If we release him, we're going to have to deal with him again, sooner or later, and probably sooner. Who knows where he'll go once we turn him loose?"

"I'll know," Green Ghost said. "Just because you agree to release him doesn't mean you won't have him tracked. By me. Once you find out where he wants to go, have a Comanche drop me off before he gets there."

"Son, I've lost a grandson, and effectively lost my wife and youngest daughter. My oldest daughter appears to have regressed mentally after losing the first man she ever loved, and Morgan is recovering from her second major wound in less than a year. And now you want me to send you on a solo mission into enemy territory? I can't do it."

"It's a good plan, Nick," Fleming said.

"Is it? It feels half-assed to me, desperate... it's also a lie, and nothing good ever comes from a lie. Tom Steeple is the ultimate liar and I can't think of one good thing he's ever done. Even Overtime was built on the bodies of the innocent."

"So was Rome, but don't think of it as a lie. Think of it as a *ruse de guerre.*"

"That's what I hate about you, Norm, you always know just what to say."

"It's a curse."

Angriff tilted his head back and rubbed his eyes. "You really think it's my best option?"

"I would *prefer* telling you to hang him, but you pay me to be honest."

"I'm paying you?"

"Figuratively."

"Fine, go ahead and do it. But Nick, by God you'd better not get yourself killed. I don't think I could stand that now."

"You've got my word. But first you need to give me twelve hours. I have something I have to do first."

"We've got to verify everything Steeple tells us, and that will take a few days anyway. Go do whatever you've got to do."

Trauma Center, Operation Overtime
1453 hours, May 9

Sara Snowtiger didn't know what day it was, or what time, or even if she was alive. There had been the blackness of the void, and then there wasn't. There had been nothing and now there was something.

From high above, she saw Dennis Tompkins asleep in a chair next to a hospital bed, where a woman lay in an apparent coma. It was her. Tubes connected to plastic bags filled with liquid ran into her arms and another tube went down her throat, while machines beeped all around the bed.

Why had her spirit left her body? Was she dying? She knew she'd been shot, but everything after that was blank. There had to be a reason that her consciousness had returned, but what was it?

The face of Govind materialized in her sight. His mouth worked and he spoke words. She didn't hear them using her ears, but instead they rang in her mind, or her spirit, whatever her detached consciousness was.

"Ohoyo," he said. "You live!"

For some reason, seeing him sparked a memory of Govind stating his belief that Sara and Lara were the physical incarnations of Child of Water and Slayer of Monsters, the twin daughters of Changing Woman, who was more or less the Sun, and represented eternal life and youth. She had never before considered that he could be right, but now she did not doubt that her sister had called her back to the world of the living one last time.

"The Ghost comes to you," she told him without speaking, as if he stood before her. "He will ask your help. Your destiny lies with him."

"I cannot see you, Ohoyo. I hear your words as I always have, but your face is hidden to me."

"Find the Ghost, Govind. Aid him. I know not the ending this path will lead to. I can only see the journey. Farewell, my friend."

Green Ghost took his personalized Humvee and headed across the desert to the spot where the beeping had occurred when they'd brought in Idaho Jack. He had no idea what might be in the stash left for Task Force Zombie decades before, and that was the whole point: he had no idea what he might find there. And if this stash was the same thing as Tom Steeple's weapons depot, then locating it would save Nick, Sr. from having to release the man in exchange for the information.

The trip out took four hours, longer than he remembered from going the other way with Idaho Jack in the back seat. It was well after dark when the beeping started again. He'd brought night-vision goggles, but preferred navigating by starlight whenever possible, and soon the beeping increased as he sped toward the tall rock formation at the end of a ridge. Everything was as he remembered it, except for the tall man standing by the cliff face and the rotting bodies scattered across the desert.

"Aren't you the one called Govind, chief of his tribe?" Climbing out of the Humvee, Green Ghost walked toward the tall Apache with hand outstretched. The Humvee's hot engine ticked in the cool night, but the beeping had stopped.

"And you would be the one they call Ghost."

"Green Ghost."

"It is an unusual name for an *indaa*. A white man."

"I've heard much about you."

"And I about you."

"How so?"

"The land observes all. The desert knows you."

"People I know call *you* the Ghost of the Desert."

Govind smiled, although Green Ghost could barely see it in the wan moonlight. "The desert knows many spirits."

"How did you know I was coming?"

"If I told you that, you would not believe me. But I know *why* you have come. You seek that which is in the cave."

"Do I? I came because a signal told me to, without knowing what was here or where it was."

"It is what you would call a... what is the word in English? Cash?"

Green Ghost thought a moment. "Do you mean *cache*, as in many?"

"Maybe that is the wrong word, cache. There is a cave in the cliffside. Back into the hill, deep in the darkness, there is this... cache you seek, but I cannot allow you to climb the rocks."

"Why not?"

"The cave is sacred to my people as the resting place of Ohoyo, the one named Sara Snowtiger. It has been cleansed of evil spirits as we await her remains."

"So what do we do now? I don't want to fight you."

"Or I you."

Scratching the stubble on his cheek, Green Ghost tried to think of a way not to fight the man he'd waited so long to meet. "I make you this proposal, then," he said after a minute or so. "You go up and bring down things a man might carry in a foot pursuit over the desert. I have guns and knives and ammunition. Bring anything small, whether you recognize it or not. Are you allowed to do this much?"

"I am," Govind said. "But I can bring you all of it."

It was that small? Not the weapons depot, then, or a cache, but something else. Could there be more than one? "That works, too. And I haven't eaten yet, but I scrounged some firewood on the way here and so may cook something. Would you eat with me when you come back?"

"I would be honored. What are you eating?"

"I don't know. I haven't caught it yet."

#

Chapter 58

> *"I am always ready to learn, although I do not always like being taught."*
> Sir Winston S. Churchill

Near Sara Snowtiger's Cave, Central Arizona
1457 hours, May 10

Govind retrieved the package easily enough and Green Ghost recognized a leather-sided collapsible case like those they had often used during operations. It was constructed to fold flat, and then fold over twice to form a small, square package. This one was full. The first items were two quarterback sleeves. One had small tactical maps of Arizona, Texas, New Mexico, and Colorado, printed two maps to each side. The operator could then reverse it for whichever area he needed. A folded up 10X magnifying glass slipped into a pocket on the sleeve. The second one had two pens with a specially-developed oil-based ink that stayed liquid virtually forever.

Next were three skull caps to keep sweat out of his eyes while he wore a helmet, and a black fanny pack. "I can use these," he said, holding them up and explaining their use to Govind. The next item was heavier but something virtually unseen in the postwar world — a brand new Dewalt Sawzall. Two Timex watches were in a small cloth pouch.

There were two guns, a Heckler & Koch UMP9 submachine gun with three of its distinctly curved magazines, and something he was very happy to see, a brand new Glock 19 with three 15-round magazines and fitted with an Apex tactical trigger, Grey Ghost precision slide, and Streamlight TLR-4 light and laser. The last items were a pair of satellite phones and four medium-range handheld radios.

"You are expecting to fight an army?" Govind said.

"If I have to."

"I try not to let my enemies get that close."

"I mean to kill this man, Govind. If that means I have to fight my way through an army to do it, I will. But one way or another, he is going to die."

"The world has many such men in these days. It has always been so, but they seem more numerous when you are the one living through it."

"Who do you consider the worst?"

"The one who serves evil... he has many names. The Navajo call him *Chindi*. Apache sometimes call him *Ndeen Lligai*, the liar. You know him as the devil. He is the false god who lives to the south and tortures all who do not swear allegiance to him."

"You mean the Caliph, the leader of the Sevens?"

"Yes, the Sevens are demons in human flesh."

"I'm not arguing with you, but why do you hate them so much?" Green Ghost peeled the skin off the roasted hind leg of a spiny lizard, and tore at the flesh like eating a chicken drumstick. The taste was smoky and rancid, but he'd long ago taught himself to eat nearly anything that wasn't poisonous.

"Many years ago," Govind said, "when the man who calls himself Caliph first came to Arizona, my kinsmen to the south were the first to meet them. In the beginning everyone smiled, and their leader pretended to be our friend. He was charming and persuasive. My father's brother liked him and trusted him, and brought him north to meet us. I was a little boy, but even then I did not like his look. He had a dishonest face. I told my father this but he laughed and said the years would bring wisdom, but first I must live those years.

"The Caliph suggested we have a feast to celebrate our new friendship, at a campsite they had laid out. He begged us to bring our wives and children. My uncle agreed, being completely taken in by the deception. But despite his desire to befriend the newcomers, my father was no fool. The meeting place had one entrance and high ridges on three sides. He sent his own men over the mountain to approach the canyon from the other side, and there they found men of the Caliph waiting with guns. They stood ready to ambush my people and kill us all.

"Without his men shooting at us from above, we were able to fight our way out of the trap. We killed many of them, but lost too many of our own in the fight. My mother fell that day with a bullet in her head. From that day forward, we have known the Sevens cannot be trusted and have killed them when we can. The place of our sorrow is translated as Trap Gulch."

"If I pursue him into the Caliphate, I'll let you know."

"This man you seek, he is a friend of theirs?"

"I honestly don't know, but he knows all about them, so if he does head into their territory, then it would be safe to say he's on their side."

"Your people have the helicopters that kill from the sky, yes? Why did you not send them to help Dennis Tompkins and our beloved Ohoyo?"

"My father General Angriff ordered them to do that, but this man I speak of, Tom Steeple, canceled it. He would not let them help those trapped in the cave."

"So he is evil also?"

"Like you wouldn't believe. He's hurt my family a lot, and if he hooks up with the Sevens, he could do it to yours, too. To everybody."

"Then I will come with you, if you would have me."

"I won't know where I'm going until we take off. We're flying, you see."

"Can you bring me a message with your destination? I will bring horses, and I *will* find you. We will track this man together."

"That's very generous of you."

"Whether we like it or not, the Sevens are coming into our lands again. That means my people are now part of this war. If we find this man—"

"*When* we find him."

The firelight cast deep shadows over Govind's face, accentuating his straight nose and high cheekbones. "*When* we find him, what do we do with him?"

Instead of answering right away, Green Ghost handed Govind one of the radios and showed him how to use it. Once satisfied the Apache chief could send and receive messages, he said, "I will only call on you to help if he's going to the Sevens. But in that case, when we find him, we kill him."

#

Part Eight

Home Game

Chapter 59

> *Tears come from the heart, and not from the brain.*
> *Leonardo da Vinci*

The desert west of Albuquerque, New Mexico
1326 hours, May 11

Tank Girl banked south at Nick Angriff's request. From 500 feet, he read the sprawling battlefield like a textbook, instantly recognizing the moves made by each side. The primary combat zone stretched seven miles long and two miles wide. None of the wrecked vehicles still burned and American salvage teams had already towed friendly vehicles to a central clearing on the outskirts of Albuquerque, where repair crews could decide whether to fix them or scrap them for parts.

With Norm Fleming back at Overtime, and Green Ghost reunited with all of the Zombies, back from Phoenix with an incredible story to tell, there was zero chance of a repeat of Tom Steeple's escape. And so he'd come east to inspect where his troops had fought, praise them in the field for their bravery, and pray at the memorial service for the fallen citizens of Shangri-La. Earlier that morning, he had toured the little community, where signs of battle remained everywhere even after almost a week's cleanup effort. He'd personally awarded the Silver Star to Captain Sully, his EO Lieutenant Hakala, and Captain April Jones, along with many other decorations. To Shangri-La's leader Johnny Rainwater, he awarded the Medal of Freedom, and the same award posthumously to the Chief of the Jemez Pueblos, Abigail Deak.

The speaker in his helmet crackled from the intercom. "General Angriff, General Fleming is on the radio for you, I'll patch it through," said his son-in-law, Captain Joe Randall. Randall glanced backward over his shoulder into the cargo bay and Angriff gave him the thumb's up sign.

"Nick?"

"I'm here, Norm."

"Steeple wasn't lying. The recon team found the depot, right where he said it was. They sent a preliminary video, and it's impressive."

"Do we have an inventory yet?"

"Not yet. That will probably take a few days."

"Assemble the staff, and alert my son that I'm going to want Steeple brought to my office. We're heading home."

"Got it, out."

"Let's go home, boys," he said over the intercom.

The Crystal Palace, Operation Overtime
1700 hours, May 11

Angriff chambered a round into one of the Desert Eagles and laid the big pistol on his desk, with the barrel pointed toward Tom Steeple. The disgraced general wore handcuffs and ankle chains, and his daily shower routine had been reduced to once a week, so he stank of body odor and sweat. Likewise, he wore a baggy one-piece coverall instead of his uniform. Everyone in the room knew the purpose of such degradation was to render the fastidious Steeple as uncomfortable as humanly possible, and, much as he tried to hide it, they could all see it had worked. Steeple was clearly miserable.

But not yet a spent force.

Norm Fleming and Rip Kordibowski sat on the leather couch and stared holes through Steeple's back. Colonel Walling parked his wheelchair to the right of the doorway, while Green Ghost leaned against the wall behind Angriff's desk, arms crossed, his eyes never leaving Steeple. Khin Saw had left for Sierra already, Dennis Tompkins was inconsolable after the loss of Sara Snowtiger, and Major General Schiller was in command at Comeback. That left Lt. Colonel Desiree Santorio to sit in the chair beside Steeple, and she appeared decidedly uncomfortable being there.

Angriff never took his eyes off Steeple. He stuck a half-smoked cigar butt in his jaw, knowing the smell bothered the disgraced general. Despite his discomfort and fatigue, Steeple tried to match Angriff's stare.

"General Fleming, have we investigated the prisoner's claims of equipment and weapons dumps in Arizona and Nevada?"

"We have, sir, and while we do not have a detailed inventory yet, it would appear that in substance the information given was accurate."

Despite the deep lines etched into his face from lack of sleep, Steeple managed a wry smile. He still hadn't broken his gaze away from Angriff's. It was a private contest between the two men, something the others could observe but not participate in, but the outcome was never in doubt. Angriff let all of the hurt and loss that he laid at Steeple's feet be reflected in his eyes, while Steeple only had his pride in return. At length, Steeple turned away.

"Colonel Kordibowski, do you have the questions you would like answered ready to ask the prisoner?"

"I do, General Angriff."

"You may proceed."

Kordibowski cleared his throat. "What can the prisoner tell us about the organization known as the Caliphate of the New Prophet?"

That took Steeple by surprise. "You don't want to start with Operation Hail Mary?" He addressed the question to Angriff, who maintained a stone face.

"Will the prisoner answer the question?" Kordibowski said.

"The Caliphate was not a military operation. That initiative was the brainchild of the CIA, with the secret involvement of the NSA, starting late in 2009, or maybe early 2010... I cannot remember now. A cup of tea would help my memory."

Green Ghost took a squeezer of water off Angriff's desk and tossed it to Steeple without comment.

He took a long pull. "It is most generous of you fine people to allow the condemned a last cup of water."

"Please finish answering the question."

"Before I do that, I think I need to hear reassurance you are going to release me according to my terms, if I supply you with the information that you require of me."

"I've given you my word," Angriff said in a deep, slow tone.

Steeple held up one hand in a placating gesture. "I understand that, Nick, but you cannot blame me for verifying that our agreement is still in place."

Instead of answering, Angriff's eyes narrowed even more.

Steeple drew in a deep, theatrical breath. "What do I know about the Sevens? Quite a bit and nothing. I can tell how it began, but after I went cold... you know as much as I do. The Caliphate began as a way to attract the most radical Islamists to a new sect that promised violence against the West. This would allow Homeland Security to keep tabs on them, investigate their ties to other terror groups, and arrest them whenever they chose. From what I understand, they considered ways to manipulate existing terror organizations, but those were too globally entrenched. And there was always the problem of opposition imams and sects arguing theology. To my mind, the solution was ridiculous and likely to do more harm than good.

"But nobody from the CIA asked me, although I did have a source inside the program. Instead of using the Koran to try and turn up the radicalization of people who were already radicalized, they wrote a new book, *The Prayers of the New Prophet*, or some such. They could have changed the title later. The idea was based on the success of *The Protocols of the Elders of Zion*, the supposed dossier about Jewish plans to rule the world. Allah was displeased that his followers had not yet installed worldwide Sharia Law, so he sent a new prophet with a new set of marching orders."

Kordibowski shook his head. "The Koran states that Mohammad was Allah's last prophet."

"I said it was a ridiculous idea, but that part worked in the CIA's favor. Only the most radical would follow a new prophet. He would attract the worst of the worst terrorists, who felt their own organizations were not doing enough to destroy the West. The most important component of the whole operation was picking the right man to be the prophet. They wanted an American if possible—"

"Why?"

"I was not privy to such information. There are few people on the planet more secretive than higher-ups in the CIA when it comes to an active operation. I only know that they chose two brothers who were in the Texas state prison system, for fraud and deception, to pose as the prophet and his brother. In exchange, they would be given pardons and put into the

Witness Protection Program. They launched the program in Houston because it had more mosques per capita than any other state in the union, and from everything I heard it was an instant hit. The brothers' cover story was that they were both Christian ministers, until Allah appeared to the New Prophet one day and ordered him to write a new book, I forget the title, expressing Allah's displeasure with how things were turning out on Earth. Speaking through his New Prophet, Allah also said that his people were not pious enough and now needed to pray seven times a day instead of only five.

"As I said, the whole charade worked better than the CIA dreamed it would. Before long, the New Prophet had more than five thousand men showing up for prayers. And remember, these were men who wanted *action*, not just words. Then they, the CIA, realized the operation had gotten out of hand. To arrest that many dangerous men would require the use of troops, large numbers of them, which could only come from the Army or the Army National Guard. I was a special advisor to the president then, and an NSA consultant, which is how I learned about it. An entire brigade would be used, including armor, heavy weapons, and air support. The mosque was on a hundred acres west of the main city, so collateral damage would be minimal. The date was set for May 7... 2025." Steeple waited to see a reaction in Angriff's face, or Green Ghost's, and when he didn't see one, he looked at Santorio beside him, and then at Walling. "Surely one of you recognizes the implications of that date."

Fleming answered him. "It was three weeks after the nuke went off in the New Madrid Fault, triggering the sequence of events that led to the Collapse."

This time Steeple couldn't hide his own surprise. He tried, but fatigue made it seem like too much effort. "How did you know that a nuclear device was involved? That was never released to the public, or disseminated through Army channels. Only a handful of people knew about that."

"I told them," Green Ghost said. "First Squad from Task Force Zombie missed them by five minutes at an airport in southern Arkansas. We were airborne when it went off."

"Who authorized you to operate inside our national borders?"

Angriff spoke for the first time. If hate had a vocal component, he used it. "You're not asking the questions here."

"Finish telling us about the Caliphate," Fleming said.

Steeple drank some more water. "The breakdown of order played right into their hands. Reliable news became spotty right away, all over the country, but the last word from Texas before I went cold was of the prophet's men battling the police in the streets."

He drank more water and waited for someone to at least acknowledge that he'd answered the question well. No one did.

Fleming went on like he was reading the minutes from the last meeting of the neighborhood book club. "Tell us about Operation Hail Mary."

Steeple told the story in a straight-ahead tone, almost monotone, imbuing it with none of his usual linguistic nuances.

In the years leading up to the Collapse, the world's super-rich had spent insane amounts of money building luxurious doomsday bunkers, designed and built by many of the same architects and engineers who'd worked on Operations Overtime and Comeback. The site of by far the biggest complex was in North Dakota, using the abandoned Stanley R. Mickelson Safeguard Program bunker complex as a starting point. Located near the tiny settlement of Nekoma, North Dakota, the base was best known for its pyramidal radar building, but also housed numerous missile silos and underground support facilities, all built to withstand anything from an earthquake to a nuclear warhead. Since the Safeguard Program had been a U.S. Army initiative to protect U.S. Air Force missile silos, Steeple had jurisdiction to allow its use by an outsider.

Because of those outsiders' financial support for the various Army operations, Steeple had also agreed to let them recruit selected foreign military personnel for Long Sleep. That was intended to give them protection in a post-Collapse environment. He'd expected some Russians or Chinese special ops types, and there were some of those. But mostly the wealthy had brought in mercenaries, lots of Germans, South Africans, and Americans. They'd bought surplus weaponry, mostly American but some foreign, and Steeple had signed off on increasingly worrisome weapons systems and quantities. In a matter-of-fact voice, he explained that he'd had no other choice.

"Their money came in at a time when federal funding had temporarily dried up, so I more or less approved anything they asked of me. I did what I had to do, to keep Overtime and Comeback on track."

As the community building around Hail Mary grew larger, a leader had begun to emerge — Györgi Rosos, Sr. Rosos had recruited new members from among the ultra-wealthy, based on their political belief in a sort of hybrid plutocratic communist state. The workers would own the means of production, but since the masses would, of necessity, spend their lives working, they would need a government of well-educated men to allocate the goods they produced.

"That sounds a lot like everyday communism," Fleming interjected.

"More like Stalinism in its execution, but the difference was that the ruling class would take a percentage of what the workers produced, in return for their benevolent leadership. For example, men like General Claringdon are true believers. As Stalin himself put it, they're useful idiots. Rosos would use men like him, but the instant his usefulness came to an end, he would be eliminated."

"Claringdon isn't a general. He's been reduced in rank back to major," Colonel Walling said, also in a matter-of-fact tone. Then he realized he'd spoken out and apologized.

Steeple shrugged. "Useful idiots never succeed in the long run."

Continuing, he explained that Rosos had constructed an underground runway system using the same firm that built the Air Force Annex at Operation Comeback, and all of the luxury bunkers connected to it for mutual use. Topside, the collected billionaires had built a settlement that included homes and farms, both to grow food and to raise livestock, including horses. Schools were supplied with a carefully written curriculum and several thousand textbooks, since only books would be useful if the power grid went down. The actual lessons taught were basic math and English skills, and a heavy dose of history that downplayed the role of capitalism and democratic republicanism, and substituted plutocrats in place of men like George Washington. Collectivism was glorified, and both Marx and Lenin lauded as geniuses who recognized the role of the rich in guiding the common man. Religion of any sort was cast as superstition designed to dupe the masses, even as Rosos and his sons became the new Trinity in the Christian mode.

"That explains why the horsemen you call Rednecks are such fanatics," Steeple commented. "They have had it drilled into them since birth that the Rosos family are gods, and all of the other plutocrats are their angels."

"How many of these horsemen does he have?"

Steeple shrugged. "I do not know that. Thousands, I would think."

"May I ask a question?" Colonel Santorio said.

"Certainly," Fleming replied.

"Didn't Rosos gain his wealth through capitalism?"

"You're overthinking this, Colonel," Steeple said. "Remember that Rosos is the man who founded and funded *Antikapilista, Antikap*. Yes, he made a fortune through capitalism, but do not make the mistake of ascribing morals to him, or shame of any sort. He is utterly amoral and his youngest son, Károly, is even more so. Györgi Junior has no scruples either, but he tends to be lazy. He is not driven to rule others like his father and brother."

"Before we finish, can I ask one favor?" Steeple said, rushing to finish before anyone could stop him. "What's to become of Colonel Mwangi? She only did what I told her to do."

Everyone looked at Fleming, knowing that she had been his cousin. His wide face remained impassive, even though Steeple couldn't easily turn around to face him. "Amy is dead," he said, his deep baritone dropping half an octave. "It seems she was hiding under an M270 when it took a direct hit."

"Oh." For the first time since the meeting had started, Steeple's face showed genuine emotion. "That's a shame. She was a fine officer."

"She was," Fleming said. "One of the best, until she met you."

Steeple shook his head, as if denying whatever charge was being thrown at him. "I think it's important for us all to remember that I did everything I did to make this place a reality. None of it was for me."

"So the end justifies the means?" said Fleming, voice finally betraying that he was barely able to restrain his anger.

"Sometimes, yes, if your intentions are good. And if that sounds brutal, it's because it is."

But Angriff wasn't having it. "There's a vast difference between what you intended and what you did. The road to Hell is paved with good intentions, but none of that matters when the fire licks at your flesh."

"Are there any more depots out there?" Green Ghost said.

"Not of which I am aware." The instant he said the words, Angriff knew Steeple was lying. But even though he pressed him, Steeple continued to refuse knowing about any more.

The meeting lasted another twenty minutes, after which One-Eye and Wingnut dragged Steeple back to his cell, taking pains not to show him any respect. Instead of taking an emvee, they walked, forcing Steeple to shuffle along with his ankles chained together. Every person they passed glared at their former commander. Halfway there a third Zombie joined the group... Nikki Bauer. Just before they threw Steeple back into his cell, she whispered in his ear, "I hope I get to cut your spine, if you have one, and then leave you in the desert for whatever's hungry."

#

Chapter 60

"I always like walking in the rain, so no one can see me crying."
Charlie Chaplin

The Crystal Palace, Operation Overtime
1829 hours, May 11

Elbows propped on his desk, Angriff rubbed his face before clasping his hands together. "Did he tell the truth?"

Neither Fleming nor Angriff wanted to speak up first, knowing their opinions might influence the others to agree, even if they privately disagreed. The tableau of silence held for an uncomfortable twenty seconds.

Finally Green Ghost said, "I watched him the whole time, never took my eyes off. I think he held back details on some things, but overall he spilled his guts. I don't think any of it was BS."

Angriff had cocked his head to listen, and now turned back to the others. "Rip?"

"I've got to agree with Green Ghost. I'm good at reading audible deceptions and for the most part I didn't hear any."

Walling and Santorio quickly agreed, which Angriff put down to their relative insecurity in being part of his brain trust. "Norm?"

"I'm with them, Nick. For once in his life, I think Tom Steeple told the unvarnished truth. Not all of it perhaps, but what he did say was not only true, but extremely helpful. In my opinion, he fulfilled his part of the bargain. So where does that leave us?"

"By us, you mean me. This would have been so much easier had he lied."

"I will gladly change my opinion, if that helps," Fleming said, trying to relieve Angriff's burden of decision with humor.

Angriff managed a smile. "I wish you could. So what do I do now? That's not a rhetorical question, either. I genuinely don't know. On the one hand, I gave him my solemn word that if he answered our questions about the Sevens and about Rosos truthfully, and gave us the locations of the weapons and aircraft storage sites, I would have him transported to anywhere within our capabilities. But the other side of the equation is whether he's too dangerous for me to honor that pledge, and the evidence all surely points to a *yes* answer. What are your thoughts?"

Of all the people in the room, it surprised Angriff when Desiree Santorio spoke up first. "Sir, before waking up at Overtime, I had only heard of you by reputation. Everyone I met who had served under you said that you were a strict disciplinarian, but exceedingly fair and honest. I don't know him at all, but General Steeple appears to be a very dangerous and conniving man—"

"You have no idea *how* dangerous and conniving," Angriff said.

"I'm sure that's true, sir, and so as far as Overtime is concerned, I think you should keep him confined. But I worry about the effect that will have on you."

"On me? I could hang him using piano wire and not think twice about it."

"Pardon my saying so, General, but I doubt that. What I meant was that to go back on your word seems like a denial of everything you've ever stood for, and meaning no offense to anyone else in the room, if there is one indispensable person at Overtime, it's you."

Angriff looked out the window to avoid answering. When Fleming spoke up, he turned to listen.

"Desiree is right, Nick," Fleming said, "deception in battle is one thing, but breaking a solemn vow is something entirely different."

After digesting that for a few seconds, he glanced at Green Ghost. "What about you?"

"Give the word and I'll replace his brain with lead. It won't bother me one little bit. But I'm afraid I have to agree with the others."

After a few more minutes of discussion, Angriff held up a hand. "So I'm the only one who thinks I should renege on my promise. It goes against every instinct I've got to let such a threat loose again in the world, but when my entire staff think I'm wrong, only a fool would ignore that."

"The ways of the future are hidden to us," Fleming said. "I believe that Steeple may yet have a hand to play in all of this, for good or ill."

That actually brought a slight smile from Angriff. "When you start paraphrasing Tolkien to me, I know that I've lost."

Green Ghost lingered after the others had left. "Am I cleared to follow?"

"I hate the idea."

"If you didn't know I was your son, would you clear it? We both know you would. Look, I've got the team back together, I'll be with six of the most dangerous people on Earth, and everything will work out fine."

"Does that include Nikki?"

"No. I said the most dangerous, not the craziest."

That actually made his father chuckle. "All right, Task Force Zombie is cleared to follow Tom Steeple using whatever means and assets you feel necessary. Find him, and try to ascertain whatever intel you can from anyone he meets or anywhere he goes. Once you feel that he has no further intelligence value, I order you to kill him."

"You don't need to make that an order."

"I know."

1035 hours, May 12

After the family gathering atop the mountain, Morgan had been returned to the trauma center as a precautionary move. Green Ghost spent the morning at her bedside, replacing Joe Randall, who was busy helping Rossi and her ground crew service *Tank Girl* after his return from Sierra Army Depot and their return from Creech Air Force Base. When Morgan nodded off, he slipped out.

The trauma center and the regular hospital four levels above it were both full of battle casualties brought in from Prescott, Sierra, and New Mexico, giving him a complete picture of the devastation wrought by Tom Steeple. Not that he'd needed additional motivation to punish Steeple, but if he had, the torn bodies of the Americans who had fought to protect the innocent would have given it to him. While at the trauma center he stopped in to visit with Dennis Tompkins, but the old general didn't want to talk. Green Ghost could tell from his demeanor that he didn't much care about anything right at that moment.

The hallway leading back to the main corridor passed the ICU waiting room, where among the crowd he saw a lone figure seated cross-legged in a chair, staring straight ahead with glassy eyes. She wore the uniform of a Marine first sergeant, with the caramel skin and high cheekbones of a Native American. He recognized her right away, as would anybody in the 7th Cavalry — Medal of Honor winner Lara Snowtiger.

None of the others in the room sat near her. On a whim he entered, and when several people stood to attention he waved them to relax. Then he sat next to her. Up close, he could tell that she hadn't bathed in days, and the hollowness of her cheeks meant she probably hadn't slept, either.

"You lost somebody," he said.

The only thing that moved was her lips. "Yes, sir, I lost my twin sister and... and a fellow Marine I was close with."

"That's tough, First Sergeant, really tough. So why are you sitting in here? Is there somebody else you're waiting for word on?"

"No, sir."

"Then why?"

"Because I don't know what else to do, sir."

He had a sudden thought. "We're going hunting... wanna join us?"

"Hunting, sir? I don't think so, but thank you anyway."

"We're not hunting dinner, Snowtiger." He dropped his voice. "We're hunting Tom Steeple."

She blinked several times. "Count me in, sir."

1829 hours, May 12

Adder's eyes fluttered open. He squinted from the room's bright LED lighting, but when he tried raising his right hand to shield his face, it wouldn't move. While he blinked, it took him a few seconds to realize he was strapped to the bed. He finally focused on the two men standing on the other side, near the steel railing at the bed's foot.

"How long have I been out?" he said.

"Why?" Joe Randall said in response, his arms folded.

"Who the fuck are you?"

"He's your judge and jury," said Green Ghost. "He decides what happens to you."

"Yeah? Who appointed him to that job?"

"I did."

"You? Who the fuck appointed you, then? That dead blowhard general you worshipped so much?"

"You mean the one who's back in charge of Overtime?"

Adder started to respond, but even drug-addled and weak as he was, he could tell that Green Ghost wasn't kidding. "So Saint Nick lives, huh? Well, that's too bad."

"Not for you. He's the only reason my sister didn't get hold of you."

"Your sister, yeah? Send her down here. I'd like to fuck her."

"That's one of Joe's options, to let Nipple have you. Only I don't think you'd like the result."

"Well, then, what does big bad Captain Joe have to say about little old Adder?"

"Why did you shoot my wife? Why did you kill my son?"

"I didn't know about your kid, but if I kept any more fucking Angriffs from entering this world, then I'm happy about it. There's too fucking many already."

Randall stood quiet for a few seconds, rubbing his chin. There was a light in his eyes that Green Ghost hadn't seen before, the light of a killer. He imagined it was how Randall looked during a strafing run.

"Strap him to a gurney," Randall finally said.

Green Ghost had no idea what Randall had in mind, but called for orderlies and a gurney. By the look on his brother-in-law's face, Randall was not planning to show mercy

The top of the mountain had the housing terminus for the elevator shaft, a large building capable of holding the industrial-sized elevator which was mainly used for hauling up whatever was needed to maintain Overtime's solar array. The panels themselves lined one part of the slope where the downward angle was only about twenty degrees. A flat concrete area allowed for the easy transport of heavy items. Beside that gentle slope, however, was a sheer drop of more than three thousand feet.

The two hospital orderlies wheeled the gurney with Adder strapped to it off the elevator and to the spot Randall indicated. Both were women. Neither said anything, as if sensing what was coming.

Five people stood on the landing — Green Ghost, Nikki, Nick Angriff, then Morgan and Joe Randall. Morgan leaned on her husband for support. All stared at Adder without speaking. The air held a chill, as it always did up so high. Angriff loved bringing his family to this spot for private conversations, but he doubted he could ever do that again. Not after the last two occasions, both of which represented so much pain and loss. It would only remind him of what once was, and what could have been.

"Is this supposed to scare me?" Adder said, raising his voice to be heard over the rushing wind. "I've gone through a lot worse than this."

"This isn't about you," Randall said. "I don't care how you feel about it. This is about what will let me sleep at night."

"Yeah? Well, I hope you never sleep again, you little prick."

Nikki took a step forward, but Green Ghost grabbed her arm. "We agreed."

"Let her go, Ghost. I shot her man, I killed him, and I enjoyed doing it. I wish I could do it again. But if you kill me now, you'll never learn who else was involved with springing Steeple out of jail, and I know you want to know *that*. So stop all this bullshit and let's go back inside, where it's warm."

"We know who did it," Angriff said. "You've got nothing to bargain with."

"Naw. If you knew, I'd be dead already."

Angriff met Randall's eyes and nodded once. Joe Randall pushed the gurney toward the sheer cliff.

Adder laughed, but then as the empty void came closer, he stopped laughing and started to scream. "It was a guy named McComb!"

"I told you we already knew that," said Angriff.

Randall shoved the gurney again, hard, and it fell off the edge and into the abyss. Adder's screams could be heard until he struck a rocky outcropping two thousand feet below, bounced off, separated from the gurney, and rolled over the rocks to the ground. Whatever was left came to rest close by the base of the mountain.

"Leave him there," Angriff said. "Let the buzzards and coyotes have him."

"Did you really know about McComb?" Green Ghost said.

"I do now."

0813 hours, May 13

Steeple supervised the loading of the Bell UH-1Y Venom with everything he'd asked for, fitting everything into the supply container personally. The only thing he didn't yet have was ammo, which he was promised would be handed over by one of the guards after they'd landed. The only thing he overloaded on was water. He planned to drink as much as possible before setting off.

Angriff watched with arms folded. The glare he kept fixed on Steeple ensured that any personnel in that part of the hangar deck gave him a wide berth.

"I'm ready," Steeple said.

"The pilot needs a heading," Angriff said.

"I'll give it to him once we're airborne."

"No, you'll give it to me now. I'm not putting my people in harm's way and I'm not going to make a snap decision."

The pilot, a stout young woman with close-cropped hair, came around the Venom's nose and stopped when she saw the two generals arguing. Steeple glanced her way, then back, stalling. He pursed his lips. "This wasn't our agreement," he said at length.

Angriff didn't move and didn't speak.

"Fine. Course one-three-five to maximum range."

"You're heading for the Sevens?" Angriff didn't bother hiding his disgust.

"My business is my business."

Angriff turned to the pilot. "You only have to go as far as you feel safe. I'm going to have a Comanche ahead of you to clear your flight path. You'll get their call sign once you're airborne, and for purposes of this mission, that pilot is in command. Clear?"

"Aye, sir."

"Good. And let me repeat, the safety of you and your aircraft comes before completion of the mission."

Once she and her co-pilot were in the cockpit, the two guards climbed up, leaving Angriff and Steeple alone.

"I want you to know that nothing I ever did was personal," Steeple said. "My only consideration was completing Overtime. I still consider you the finest battlefield commander I've ever known."

"You can tell yourself whatever you want, but attacking my family felt very personal to me. Killing my grandson felt very personal to me, as did injecting my wife and little girl with cancer..."

Steeple started to answer but Angriff cut him off.

"You'd best get out of my sight before I lose control and blow your head off, because right now that's a real possibility."

Steeple considered saying more, but Angriff's face and ears had turned dark red, and he thought better of it. The pilot started the engine so further conversation was impossible. When the turbine first engaged, it sounded like a faint tornado siren, gradually becoming the familiar high-pitched whine. Once the rotors began turning, Angriff stepped back, his eyes never leaving Steeple. The hangar doors slid open and within half a minute the Venom had cleared the mountain into the bright morning sunshine.

Joe Randall patted Bunny Carlos on the shoulder and pointed to the rear with his thumb, indicating he was going into the cargo bay. Space in the cockpit was tight, with the shared console between the two seats, but there was just enough room to step over it and squeeze through a doorway in the bulkhead. Once in the bay, he sat next to Green Ghost. The only way they could hear each other was to put their mouth to the other's ear.

"Heading is one-three–five. We're going into Sevens territory."

Green Ghost shrugged. "No surprise there. Any idea what's down there?"

"Only as far as last year's battlefield," Randall said. "And you've seen that ground, same as I have."

Green Ghost handed him a slip of paper. "I need you to go here first. It's a little out of the way..."

Randall opened the paper and read the numbers written there. He did the mental calculations quickly. "A *little* out of the way?"

"Govind is waiting to hear from me, but we only need to get within radio range, so I can tell him where to meet us with the horses."

With the visor open on his flight helmet, Green Ghost could see most of Randall's face, including his smile.

"Playin' the player," Randall said, shouting to be heard. "I like it. Hey, one more thing... you went cold later than anybody else in the brigade, so I was wondering if you'd ever heard of someone named Judge Isaiah."

Green Ghost shook his head. "No, I can't..." But then his mind caught up with his mouth. "Where did you hear those names?"

"Names? You mean like two people? I thought it was just one."

"It might be, but the commander of Task Force Zombie's Third Squad was named Judge, and his second was named Isaiah. We called them the Bible Boys, although they had some women in the squad, too. One named Ruth. Where did you hear it?"

"At Groom Lake. They recently got a call from this Judge Isaiah to shut down the base to outsiders, and the only thing they know is that it came from East Tennessee."

"Son of a bitch," Green Ghost said. His team had nothing else to do except watch their conversation and read their faces, so he laughed as if they were telling jokes. "Don't say anything to the others yet. Let me do it after this op."

Randall smiled and nodded. After Randall squeezed back into the cockpit, Green Ghost talked over the mission instructions with Wingnut, third in command after Vapor. He did nothing to betray his excitement at the chance that two more Zombies had somehow survived.

It was strange for Green Ghost to hear Wingnut speak a full sentence, which was more words than he could remember Wingnut ever saying in all the years they'd served together.

"It makes sense that Steeple wants to connect with the Sevens, G.G. But there's a play here we don't know anything about. I can feel it."

"Steeple always has a play that nobody knows about. But it doesn't matter. We're going to kill him, all the same."

#

Chapter 60

They are not dead who live in the hearts they leave behind.
Tuscarora

Sara Snowtiger's cave, Central Arizona
1103 hours, May 13

    Govind stood at the entrance to Snowtiger's cave and blinked back tears. In his heart, he knew there was nothing more to be gained from coming here, yet he couldn't stop himself. After decades of protecting Ohoyo against all dangers, the numerous blood pools and splatters were a reminder that the gentlest spirit he had ever encountered had died a violent death that he didn't prevent. Bits of metal and blasted rock covered what was left of the ledge, but his mind fought the reality of it all. It seemed impossible that his tribe's beloved Ohoyo would never be coming back.
    "Only my physical body is gone," said the voice of Sara Snowtiger in his head. "I am part of this place now, because your people have accepted me as a *gaan*. Come here when you wish to speak with me, Govind. Perform the ritual dance and I will come to you."
    Govind glanced around as if he expected Snowtiger to be standing beside him. Was his mind tricking him? "Are you dead, Ohoyo?"
    "Death is not the end, my friend, but I no longer need my flesh. I am become something more."
    The mental image of her smiling face came unbidden into his mind.

"Am I dreaming this?" he said.

"What are dreams but another way of speaking? But he comes now, Govind, the one called Ghost. You are expecting him."

Govind cocked his head at the characteristic *whump-whump-whump* of a helicopter. "Should I be afraid?" he said.

"Afraid of what? This man is your friend. Do you not trust him?"

"I do, but I worry about what we will face, and whether I will return to lead my people."

"I cannot see that far ahead now, Govind. My sight has passed to another. But do not be afraid. Your path is your path, to whatever end it leads. It is enough to know that you do what you must."

"I find your words comforting, Ohoyo, as I always have."

"And I am glad for that, as I always was. Go now. Walk the way appointed to you."

She was gone. He didn't know how he knew that, but he did.

A minute later, in his mind's eye, he saw a huge helicopter hovering twenty feet from the cave entrance. Govind clearly saw the image of a large-chested blonde woman sitting astride a rocket, under writing that said *Tank Girl*. Green Ghost waved, and then leaned out of the cargo bay, pointing at the radio in his left hand. In his right was something metallic... a long-bladed knife that he threw toward the cave mouth. Govind let it land rather than trying to catch it and found blood on the blade. When he looked up, the helicopter was flying away. With a nod and a wave, he acknowledged understanding the message.

Green Ghost waved back. The helicopter banked away south and disappeared. Govind descended the cliff and gathered the horses.

The Crystal Palace, Operation Overtime
1306 hours, May 13

In addition to the Air Force Annex at Comeback, and aside from its combat pilots still in Long Sleep, Operation Overtime had a small Air Force contingent, limited to two batteries of M167 Vulcan Air Defense Systems, VADS. These were towed, short-range guns rendered surplus when replaced in the mid and late 90s by more modern systems. The brigade's Army contingent fielded up-to-date Patriot missile batteries.

The commander of Overtime's Air Force contingent was Captain Dalton Walker, who now stood at rigid attention in the Crystal Palace.

"At ease, Captain," Angriff said. "How are you enjoying life in our brave new world?"

"Truth be told, sir, I don't feel like I'm contributing very much."

"I'm glad to hear you say that. I want you to put on your best uniform, all your fruit salad, shine your boots, and get ready to represent this brigade to a United States Air Force unit."

"Air Force, General? Do you mean Creech?"

"Not Creech or Comeback."

"There are more?"

"Looks that way. Pick one man or woman to take with you on a flight to Groom Lake."

"Wha... you mean Area 51, sir? May I ask what my orders are?"

"You are to open lines of communication with the base command staff, and to that end I'm sending two communications specialists with you so we can be in contact. Furthermore, you are to ascertain the base's current strength, level of training, and combat capabilities. This will all be preliminary, as I'll be sending a follow-up team within a day or two, but I need to know what they have right now. Can you perform this duty, Major?"

"Yes, sir, without a doubt I'm you're man."

"Good. For this mission you're elevated to acting lieutenant colonel, so make sure your insignia is updated. I'm going to be honest with you, Walker. I would normally send General Fleming on this mission, or even go myself, but after the events of recent weeks I don't want either one of us to leave Prime. So I'm counting on you to pave the way. Oh, and be aware... they arrested the last two of our people who showed up there."

#

Chapter 61

"Wake up and die, asshole."
Nipple

As a construction foreman, Norris McComb rated a small private room down the hallway from the four-person shared suites of his team. McComb had left strict instructions not to be disturbed once he'd entered his room, and none of his people had ever violated that edict. So when someone shook him awake, he swatted at the hand without opening his eyes. "Get the fuck out of here!"

Something hard and cold pressed against his forehead.

Opening his eyes, he discovered the lights on and the barrel of a very large pistol between his eyes. "Are you out of your mind?" he said, until he woke up enough to recognize the face of the man holding the pistol.

Nick Angriff could see that McComb recognized him by the hate that overcame his face. "Because of you, a lot of good men and women are dead now," he said. "Because of you, my grandson is dead. I'll give you until three to explain why I shouldn't blow your brains out right here and now."

"You'd never get it, you fossil. You're too wrapped up in yourself and your flag to ever understand."

"One."

"The freedom you talk about is an illusion, it's the opposite of the truth, but you and your other so-called patriots are too stupid to know it! All you care about is bullying those weaker than you."

"Two."

But Norris' voice began to get shaky, as if it were finally sinking in that Nick Angriff might just be serious. "You're not the kind of man to shoot somebody in cold blood."

"Three."

#

Epilogue

> "The Navy has both a tradition and a future — and we look with pride and confidence in both directions."
> Admiral George Anderson, CNO

Juneau, Alaska
1720 hours

The bald eagle circling overhead swept lower as Kodiak Kate picked her way through the lower slope of Mount Juneau. The forest thinned as she approached the terminus of a road on the outskirts of the city.

Nestling against the shore of the Gastineau Channel, Juneau never failed to make Kate feel like she'd made it home. In the shadow of Mount Juneau, the turquoise water of the Channel separated the two parts of the city, one on the eastern mainland side and the other on Douglas Island to the west. The bridge connecting them had long since fallen into the water, destroyed by an earthquake. Ferries now plied the crossing instead.

Kate had never lived in Juneau, yet the friendliness of the inhabitants, even in such hard times, always made her feel welcome. It didn't hurt that she usually brought items she'd scraped further south, items the people of Juneau always wanted. This time what she brought was news, her most valuable commodity.

Emerging from the dense forest, she urged her big Quarter horse, Cinnabar, onto the two-lane paved road that would bring her into the city. In the gathering darkness, she spotted the ruined houses that marked the edge of Alaska's capital city.

Cinnabar had taken about ten paces when a voice called out from a stand of hemlocks. "Stand where you are, unless you want to get shot full of holes!"

Kate pulled the reins and Cinnabar stopped.

"Who are you, and what're you doing in these parts?"

Kate snorted, loud enough to be heard across the road. "Alfred Boxley, how many six-foot-tall black women you know that got orange hair?"

The voice in the trees dropped an octave. "Kodiak Kate?"

"Damn, Alfred, I know I'm big as a grizzly bear, but have you ever heard one talk? Who the hell else would it be?"

The man emerged holding a Tikka T3x rifle, chambered for a .308 round and finished in matte black. She knew the rifle well, since it had been Kate who'd scraped it from a burned-out house down in Washington State, northwest of Seattle.

Boxley grinned and did a little dance, circling on the pavement. He wasn't a young man, being past thirty, and as his daddy said, it wouldn't have been a bad thing if he'd had as many brains as God gave a squirrel, but Kate liked him. And while Alfred might be simple-minded, there wasn't anything wrong with his aim. She'd seen him take out a goose on the wing at three hundred yards.

"You gotta stay out here on watch?" she said.

"I do. Been wolves prowling close ever since winter, and somebody's gotta keep an eye out."

"Is Captain Darby still in town?"

"Last I heard."

"I've gotta find him quick, Alfred, but you listen to me... don't go getting yourself eaten up by wolves, you hear me?"

Even in the dim lighting, she could see Alfred smile. "I promise, Kate."

The four marble columns of the old Alaska State Capitol still supported the portico at the head of the steps that led inside. Homemade light bulbs powered by solar panels gave a dim illumination inside the main entrance, while a brighter glow came from an open doorway further down the hall. The old blue carpeting had been ripped up since the previous summer, so Kate's steel-reinforced boots clopped on bare concrete as she crossed the spacious lobby. Wooden benches still lined the hallway beyond.

As she approached the illuminated room, a young woman stuck her head into the hallway to see who was coming. When she saw Kate, her face brightened. "Kodiak Kate is back!" she yelled into the room. "Kate's here!"

A dozen or so people crowded around her after she'd entered, hugging her, patting her shoulder, and all talking at once. Kate had arrived during a meeting of the Juneau Council, a loose form of government that fitted the small population of independent-minded Alaskans living in Juneau. Most were from indigenous Indian tribes, such as the Tlingit, Haida, and Tsimshian. Their nominal leader was Captain Olivia Darby, USN, the venerable officer stranded in Juneau after the Naval Battle of Los Angeles. The old woman's deeply wrinkled face cracked in a smile when she saw Kate.

The life of a scraper meant long days and nights spent in wild, often hostile territory. Food was always a concern, so when Kate was half pushed, half led to a chair at one end of the L-shaped tables, the pile of salt herring, potatoes, and musk ox stew, with a generous portion of bannock to sop up the gravy, was most welcome. Nor did she resist their hospitality; Kate was a large woman, and much of her bulk was muscle, not fat. She needed to eat a lot more calories than the average person, and so gobbled the food with gusto, washing it down with a local version of the ubiquitous 'tea' drunk everywhere she'd visited.

The gathering let Kate eat for a few minutes, restraining their bursting enthusiasm as long as they could, but eventually Captain Darby herself leaned forward. "Winter was hard up here. Was it any better down south?"

"Wrrph..." Kate mumbled through a mouthful of bannock. Washing the bread down with a gulp of tea, she finished chewing before answering. "Wet," she said, "very, very wet. It rained a lot in the forests and mountains. Not much snow, though."

"Not here," Darby said, "we had more than twelve feet of snow here in the city, more on the mountaintops. And it was cold as an admiral's stare. Worst winter in a long time."

Kate chewed and nodded. She hadn't realized how hungry she was. "Yeah," was all she could manage in response, hoping to delay the inevitable onslaught of questions that would start once she'd revealed her news.

Darby didn't read her body language, though, and asked the question Kate had hoped to put off answering. "So what news do you bring us from the south?"

Kate inhaled and blew it out like a kiss. "Well, Captain, I think you're going to have to send a boat to Dutch Harbor this summer."

"Oh? Why's that?"

"Because America is back."

"Are you saying... that it's time to wake up Commander Kennedy and his squadron? Because I always felt better when there were A6Es armed and ready to go."

"That's what I'm saying," Kate said. "I think it is, and I can't wait to meet this man I've heard so much about."

"If we're going to face enemies, nobody likes putting a five-hundred-pounder on target than Kennedy."

The End

If you enjoyed Standing with Righteous Rage, I would appreciate it if you'd help others enjoy it, too!

Recommend it! Please help other readers find this book by recommending it to family, friends, readers' groups, libraries, and discussion boards.

Review it! *The best way to support an author is to leave a review. Please take a minute to review Standing with Righteous Rage on Amazon or Goodreads!*

Thank you again and happy reading!

About the Author

He's the world's oldest teenager. Reading, writing, and rock & roll make for an awesome life. The occasional beach doesn't hurt, either.

Bill grew up in West Tennessee, riding his bike on narrow rural roads lined with wild blackberry bushes, in the days before urban sprawl. He spent those long rides dreaming of new worlds of adventure. Childhood for him was one interesting activity after another, from front yard football to naval miniatures, but from the very beginning reading was the central pillar of his life.

Any and all military history books fascinated him, beginning before age eight. By his teenage years, he had discovered J.R.R. Tolkien and Robert E. Howard, Robert Heinlein and Fritz Leiber. Teachers ripped comic books out of his hands during Spanish and accounting classes. Oops!

College found him searching for his favorite rock groups, smuggling beer into his dorm room, and growing his hair long. He read a book a day back then, sometimes two, and always SFF. He even went to class sometimes.

After college, he turned to writing history and nonfiction and was published a number of times, including in *World War Two* magazine.

In September of 2014, he wrote the first pages of what would become *Standing The Final Watch* and its direct sequel, *Standing In The Storm*, plus the fill-in work *The Ghost of Voodoo Village*. That was followed in 2017 by the launch of a brand new fantasy series **Sharp Steel and High Adventure**, starting with the novella *Two Moons Waning*. Who says you can't teach an old dog new tricks? And if you like his work, a whole slew of new books are on the schedule for 2019 and 2020.

Bill is an Active (voting) member of the Science Fiction & Fantasy Writers of America, the Society For Military History, and the Alliance of Independent Authors. He writes exclusive stories for those on his mailing list at his website, www.thelastbrigade.com.

OTHER WORKS BY WILLIAM ALAN WEBB

The Last Brigade
Standing The Final Watch
The Ghost of Voodoo Village: Short Story and Bonus Chapters for Standing The Final Watch
Standing In The Storm
Standing At The Edge
Standing Before Hell's Gate
Standing In Righteous Rage
Standing Among The Tombstones (coming in 2020)
The Hairy Man, A Story in the World of The last Brigade
The Moles of Vienna, A Story in the World of The Last Brigade
The River of Walking Spirits, A Story in the World of The Last Brigade (coming in 2020)
Nalusa Malaya, A Story in the World of The Last Brigade (coming in 2020)
In At The Start, A Story in the World of The Last Brigade (coming in 2020)

Task Force Zombie
The Nameless
Out For Blood (coming in 2020)
Not Enough Bullets (coming in 2020)

The Time Wars
Jurassic Jail
Cretaceous Kill (with J. Gunnar Grey, coming in 2020)
Dark Time (coming in 2021)
Tail Gunner Joe, A Story in the World of The Time Wars

Sharp Steel & High Adventure
Two Moons Waning
The Queen of Death and Darkness
A Night at the Quay
Sharp Steel (Collecting volumes 1–3)
The Demon in the Jewel
Island of Bones (coming in 2020)
Beyond the Dead River (coming in 2020)
The Dragons of Anthar (coming in 2020)

Hit World
Kill Me When You Can
Shoot First (with Larry Hoy)
Kill Me If You Will (coming in 2020)
Double Down (coming in 2020)

The Four Horseman Universe
High Mountain Hunters (coming in 2020)
Roland the Headless Mecha Driver, A Story in the Four Horsemen Universe (coming in 2020)
Shadows in the Key of Fear (coming in 2020)

Cthulu Universe
The Granite Man (coming in 2020)

The Germany Rising series
Ghosts of the Coast (coming in 2020)

Independent Stories
Grinning Soul (with Thomas Lyon Russell)
The Sting of Fate
Drumsticks Along the Mohawk (coming in 2020)
Winter Storm (coming in 2020)
Shooting the Lights Out (coming in 2020)
Bigfoot Goes to Hollywood (coming in 2020)

Non-Fiction
Killing Hitler's Reich, The Battle for Austria, 1945
Killing Hitler's Reich, The Battle for Velikiye-Luki, 1942-1943 (coming in 2020)

Killing Hitler's Reich, The Battle for Hungary, 1945 (coming in 2021)

The Last Attack: 6th SS Panzer Army and the Defense of Hungary and Austria, 1945

The Combat History of SS-Kampfgruppe Division Böhmen und Mähren (coming in 2021)

The Combat History of 37. SS-Kavallerie Division Lützow (coming in 2021)

Unsuck Your Book: 8 Months From First Draft to the Promised Land, Revised Edition

Unsuck Your Writing Career: What I've Learned So Far (coming in 2020)

Also from
Dingbat Publishing

*Memphis, Tennessee
1878*

Why do some people not understand that the very act of doing nothing is sometimes every bit as important as actually taking an action? Thus, when Fannie Lester decided to ignore the two men in a rowboat on the night of August 1, 1878, who's to say how many thousands of lives might have been saved, fortunes retained, millions of dollars in commerce not lost, and orphans not created, if only she had acted to sound the alarm? Then again, the tragedy might well have happened no matter what Fannie did.

All of Memphis was on edge, what with yellow fever being reported in July, first in New Orleans, then in Vicksburg. The city had prohibited the docking of any steamboats traveling up the Mississippi River from the south, hoping and praying they could avoid the disease spreading to Memphis this year. They certainly had previous experience, as the city had endured recent epidemics of yellow-jack in 1867 and 1873.

Many old-timers were talking about how the wet weather of a mild spring, and the hellishly hot, humid summer they were enduring, were strong predictors of yet another fever year. For the last month, the newspapers had been full of stories about the latest outbreak of the fever in the Caribbean, as well as downriver, and every Memphis citizen was fully aware that the big island immediately below their city had already been designated as a quarantine stop for steamboats traveling upstream. Other quarantine stations were established fifteen miles east of the city on the Memphis and Charleston Rail Line at Germantown, as well as six miles to the south on the Mississippi and Tennessee Railroad at White Haven.

Some of the more sanctimonious citizens blamed the earlier epidemic of 1873 on God's wrath, due to the shameful local celebration of Mardi-Gras. But that pagan custom had been abolished in Memphis well before the summer of 1878, so those who were quick to blame idolatrous and evil living for bringing forth the bacterial and viral vengeance of the Almighty were at a loss to find someone or something to blame.

However, on this night, Fannie was preoccupied with her own troubles. She was worried she might be pregnant — let alone suspicious that her man-friend, Willis Abbott, had taken off back to Mississippi when she'd told him why she was upset. Apparently his devotion was short-lived when he discovered there might be dues to be paid.

Fannie had visualized Abbott as her knight in shining armor, come to rescue her from life as a chambermaid at the Peabody Hotel. He was armed with a believable story that he was in town to see a couple of cotton merchants in order to pre-sell his cotton, which he predicted to be "the biggest crop in Tunica County." In Fannie's mind, he not only had money to spend, but a future to offer.

When she thought about improving her poor prospects, it wasn't in terms of wearing beautiful dresses and living in a fine house. She just wanted to have enough money to stop walking everywhere she went. She coveted nothing so much as riding in a buggy wherever she needed to go. The daily trek from her rooming house on Chickasaw Street to the Peabody on Union Street, some fourteen blocks distant, involved wading through muddy and manure-filled streets, which often remained that way for a good week after a significant rain. Her shoes, battered and bedraggled as they always were, had been pulled off her feet by the mud on more than one occasion.

Worse, there was the aspect of dealing with all the vulgar comments and catcalls from the lowlife miscreants who seemed to inhabit half the street corners along those many blocks. An attractive female who had to walk during the early evening was apparently assumed to be a woman of the town, no matter how much she tried to carry herself like a lady. When the weather was extremely bad, she had spent her hard-earned cash a few times to ride the horse trolley, but that indulgent expense consumed a fourth of her daily income.

Now with Abbott's cowardly retreat, her dream of escaping her job and her poverty, let alone all the walking, was not going to happen. So she stood at the foot of Union Street, contemplating for at least the tenth time whether or not she should commit the most grievous of sins, thus making it impossible to even be buried in the Catholic cemetery. However, depression blinded her to the future, and she continued to gaze out at the roiling current of the Mississippi, considering if she should just simply wade out into the river and allow herself to be swept away.

Perhaps it was understandable that she did not raise the cry for a constable when the small boat appeared out of the fog and gloom. The only light was but a glow from the sparse street lamps up on the bluff. The black man rowing the boat was wearing bib overalls without a shirt. His arms and torso were covered with a sheen of beef tallow mixed with ground-up marigold petals, presumably in an effort to repel the clouds of mosquitoes hovering in the quiet water near the shoreline. The rippling muscles in the boatman's arms and shoulders were testimony that he was well practiced in maneuvering his small craft through the whirlpools and unexpected surges of current, which were everywhere in the powerful river; but the object of suspicion for even a casual observer was the young white man slumped in the front seat, his head held tightly in both hands.

When the boat ground to a halt on the rounded stones of the landing, the boatman hurried forward to assist his passenger as the man struggled to climb over the side and gain his footing. Despite the temperature being close to ninety degrees just after nine o'clock in the evening, the man gathered his jacket tightly around his hunched shoulders and slowly began to make his way up the riverbank to the town.

With his back turned to her, Fannie found herself staring at the black man's right shoulder blade. Although she couldn't be certain, it appeared that the raised scar on his back was actually in the form of letters. What in the world could have caused such an injury?

Oblivious to her attention, and assured that his two-legged cargo was headed to his destination, the man rowing the boat, John Johnson, quickly shoved his craft back into the river and hopped aboard. He shot Fannie something more than a curious glance, hoping she would stay silent long enough for him to disappear into the gloom of the river as he headed back downstream. The last thing he needed was for some skinny white woman to holler for a constable. He knew without a doubt he wouldn't fare well if a policeman answered her call. However, the prospect of earning three dollars simply to row a man four miles had been too tempting to worry about the law and their quarantine.

Fannie watched the boat's arrival and departure, but was so caught up in the drama of her own life that she probably couldn't have given anyone an accurate description of the man — except for the hellish scar — ten minutes after the rowboat had headed back to the south. Finally making her decision, she made her way across the cobblestones to the river, hitched her hem-frayed dress up to her calves, and stepped to the edge of the water. She paused briefly, considering whether or not to leave her hat on the riverbank. However, it possessed a considerable droop, having lost its shape as well as two of its three feathers, so she decided it was no particular loss for the hat to remain on her head.

She couldn't help but reflect on her pap, who was rumored to have fallen in the river somewhere along the Memphis riverbank, and how his loss had been so devastating to her, as it had occurred on the same day as her mam's burial. As a result, in Fannie's case, there was no one left now to mourn her passing.

For the first time that evening, she became conscious of the overwhelming putrid smell of the river, as it was the depository of well over a million privies all the way from Minnesota to where she stood, some thousand miles downstream.

Additionally, Memphis' own vile sewer ditch discharged into the river only three hundred yards upstream of where she stood. Fannie was repulsed by the slimy foulness floating on the surface and changed her mind, suddenly and irrevocably deciding she had no desire to meet her Maker at the pearly gates while covered with a sheen of all that nastiness.

Perhaps it was her condition which made her squeamish, or maybe the realization of what she had almost done, but nevertheless her stomach heaved and she lost what little supper she had eaten. Finally raising her head, she turned her back on the river and began the long walk to her rooming house in the Pinch District. For the first time that evening, she was conscious of the irritating mosquitoes which were engulfing her ankles, and swished her dress at the pesky creatures as she retreated back to her life.

William Warren continued his shuffling journey up the embankment, finally reaching Front Street at the top of the river bluff. His headache at this point was almost unbearable, and despite the fierce August humidity, he was shaking with a chill. He had left his ship, which was tied up to the south on President's Island, just after sundown, after finally convincing the fisherman, John Johnson, to row him ashore for an exorbitant price so he might find a doctor.

Warren was quickly coming to the realization that he was not able to wander around seeking medical help much longer, so he began looking for a business that might still be open. Maybe they could direct him to a physician. Besides, his dizziness was only getting worse, and he had to find a place to sit down.

Thankfully, he spied a couple of gas lanterns which illuminated the ground floor of a building across the street, and weakly found his way to the door. The place appeared to be empty, save the proprietor. The woman who greeted him had a big smile on her face, which almost immediately disappeared as she assessed her new customer.

Kate Bionda was a full-figured Italian woman of some thirty-five years of age who, along with her husband, ran the fruit stand and snack-house. Mr. Bionda had manned the store all day long, but once Kate was able to get her daughters in bed, he went upstairs to the living quarters and Kate took his place downstairs in case they had any more customers. They were hard-working, but business had not been good at all since the city had imposed its quarantine.

Their specialty was fried fish, along with whatever other meats might be available. As was the case with most businesses along the waterfront, the slops and refuse from the shop were sometimes thrown out in the street, but most often down the side of the bluff toward the river. In daytime or night, the rats and dogs usually took full advantage of the opportunity.

The Biondas' business location made it very understandable that dockworkers, as well as crewmen from steamboats and flatboats, visited the eating establishment at all hours, so it wasn't surprising her customer showed up well after the supper hour. She immediately noticed the shellback turtle tattoo on his right forearm (which indicated he had sailed across the equator at some point in his nautical career); but her attention was drawn to his pasty gray skin color, his blood-filled eyes, and the lank hair which was plastered against his forehead with sweat. "When's the last time you had a decent meal, mister?"

His response was slow, and so weak she had to strain to understand him. "I cain't hardly keep nothin' on my stomach, miss. I didn't hardly feel like eatin' a-tall the last few days."

She reached over and tentatively placed the palm of her hand on his forehead. "You're hot as the devil's outhouse! Have you seen a doctor?"

"No, miss. I need one bad. Where might I find one?"

"Old Doc Henderson stays just a couple blocks away at the Gayoso House Hotel. I'd imagine he'd see you tonight."

Warren pushed himself to his feet, but the dizziness grabbed hold of him and he collapsed back into the chair.

"Looks like you're in no shape to go anywhere. Why don't I send my cook up the street to fetch the doctor? You just stay put."

Dr. Thomas Henderson appeared in about fifteen minutes. He was completely bald, bigger about the waist than he was in the shoulders, and visibly in his cups, having already consumed a bit more than one dose of whiskey that evening. After taking his patient's temperature, as well as some rudimentary poking and prodding, the doc looked suspiciously at his new patient. "Just where did you say you came from, young man?"

"I come off the *Golden Crown* from downriver."

The physician cut his eyes sideways. "Whereabouts downriver?"

"New Orleans."

"Damn, son!" The doc backed up halfway across the room. "We've got to get you in the hospital!"

Noting the alarm in his voice, Kate grabbed the physician's arm. "Just what are you takin' on about, Doc?"

He turned his back on Warren and looked her in the eye. "Did you have the yellow fever back during any of the recent outbreaks?"

"The fever?" Kate looked as though she was about to run out of her own café. "No, sir. I was sure enough lucky not to catch it."

"Then you best pray I'm wrong."

"What difference does it make if I had it or not?"

"Most of us believe if you had the yellow-jack before, you've got a resistance to catching it again."

Kate pointed at Warren and said in a hushed voice, "Oh, my Lord — my family is just upstairs. I suppose I've got my own self in trouble. He's been in here a good half hour, and I been waitin' on him hand an' foot. But what about my family?"

"I'll get him out of here and in the city hospital. Probably get him started on Simmons Liver Regulator, but it looks like it might be too late for him. You'll have to air your place out, then scrub everything down with some lime or carbolic acid as an antiseptic and fumigator."

She began to cry. "But my girls upstairs — and my husband, too. What should they do?"

"Hard to say. But they need to stay completely away from anywhere this fellow has been."

"Shouldn't I start takin' that Liver Regulation myself?"

"Wouldn't hurt. It cleanses the stomach and the bowels, and gets rid of all the dangerous humors."

"Where can I get some?"

"Now, honey, you get on up to Robinson's Drug Store on Second Street. And don't you be telling anyone what I think we've got here. Sure don't want to start a panic."

#

Thanks for reading! Dingbat Publishing strives to bring you quality entertainment that doesn't take itself too seriously. I mean honestly, with a name like that, our books have to be good or we're going to be laughed at. Or maybe both.

If you enjoyed this book, the best thing you can do is buy a million more copies and give them to all your friends... erm, leave a review on the readers' website of your preference. All authors love feedback and we take reviews from readers like you seriously.

Oh, and c'mon over to our website:
www.DingbatPublishing.ninja

Who knows what other books you'll find there?

Cheers,

Gunnar Grey,
publisher, author, and Chief Dingbat

δ

Printed in Great Britain
by Amazon